Coming Home

created, written & illustrated by
CHRIS GIARRUSSO

web design, book design & color assists by
DAVE GIARRUSSO

edited by
BRANWYN BIGGLESTONE

www.chrisGcomics.com

IMAGE COMICS, INC.
Robert Kirkman - chief operating officer
Erik Larsen - chief financial officer
Todd McFarlane - president
Marc Silvestri - chief executive officer
Jim Valentino - vice-president
Eric Stephenson - publisher
Ron Richards - director of business development
Jennifer de Guzman - pr & marketing director
Branwyn Bigglestone - accounts manager
Emily Miller - accounting assistant
Jamie Parreno - marketing assistant
Jenna Savage - administrative assistant
Kevin Yuen - digital rights coordinator
Jonathan Chan - production manager
Drew Gill - art director
Tyler Shainline - print manager
Monica Garcia - production artist
Vincent Kukua - production artist
Jana Cook - production artist
www.imagecomics.com

For International Rights contact - foreignlicensing@imagecomics.com

G-MAN, VOL 3: COMING HOME. First Printing.
Published by Image Comics, Inc. Office of publication: 2001 Center Street, 6th Floor, Berkeley, CA 94704.
Copyright © 2013 Chris Giarrusso. All rights reserved.
Originally published in single issue digital form as G-MAN: COMING HOME #1-5.
G-MAN™ (including all prominent characters featured herein), its logo and all character likenesses are trademarks of Chris Giarrusso, unless otherwise noted. Image Comics® and its logos are registered trademarks of Image Comics, Inc. No part of this publication may be reproduced or transmitted, in any form or by any means (except for short excerpts for review purposes) without the express written permission of Image Comics, Inc. All names, characters, events and locales in this publication are entirely fictional. Any resemblance to actual persons (living or dead), events or places, without satiric intent, is coincidental.

PRINTED IN CANADA.

ISBN: 978-1-60706-571-5

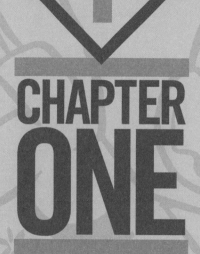

1

CHAPTER ONE

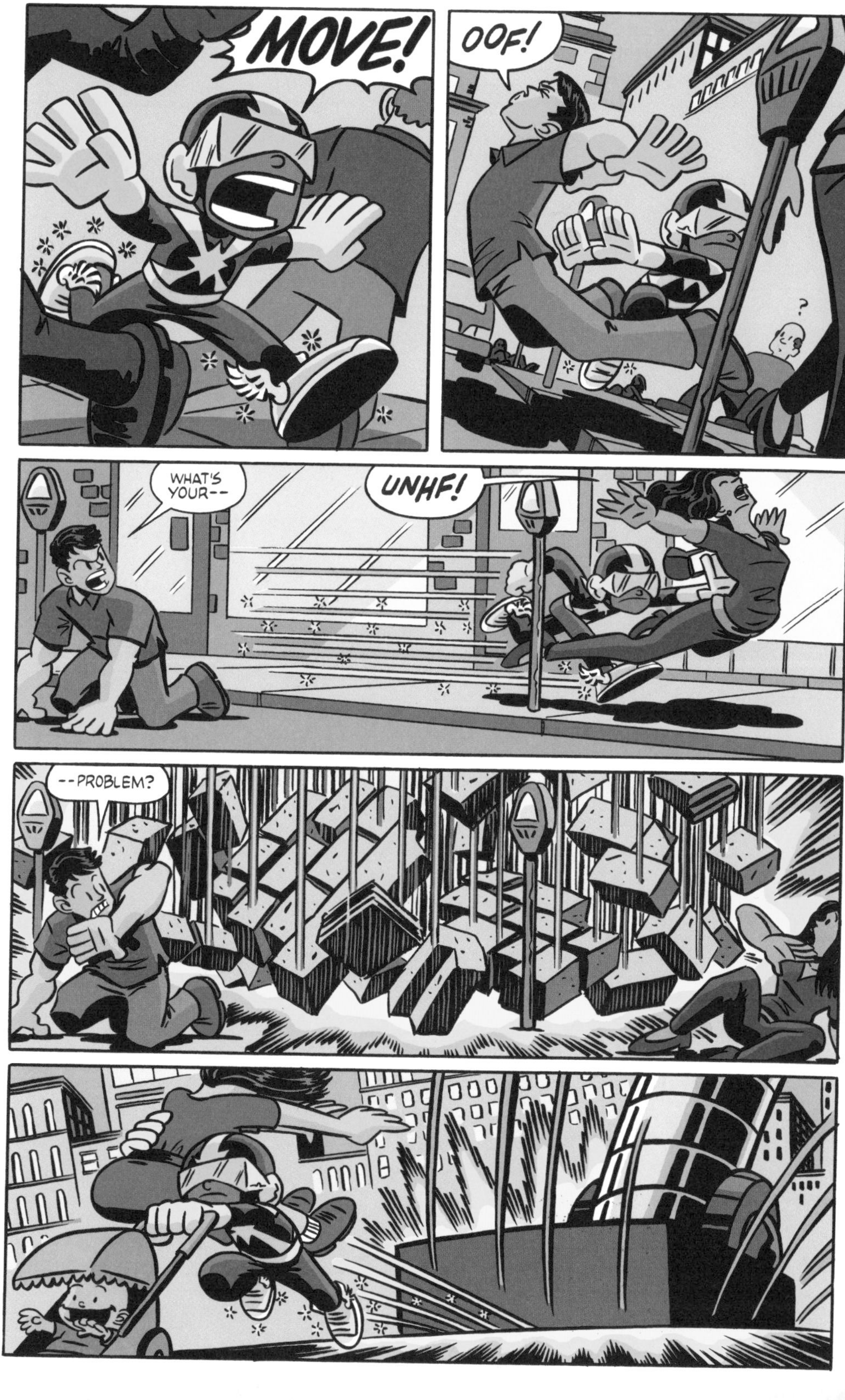
MOVE!
OOF!
?
WHAT'S YOUR--
UNHF!
--PROBLEM?

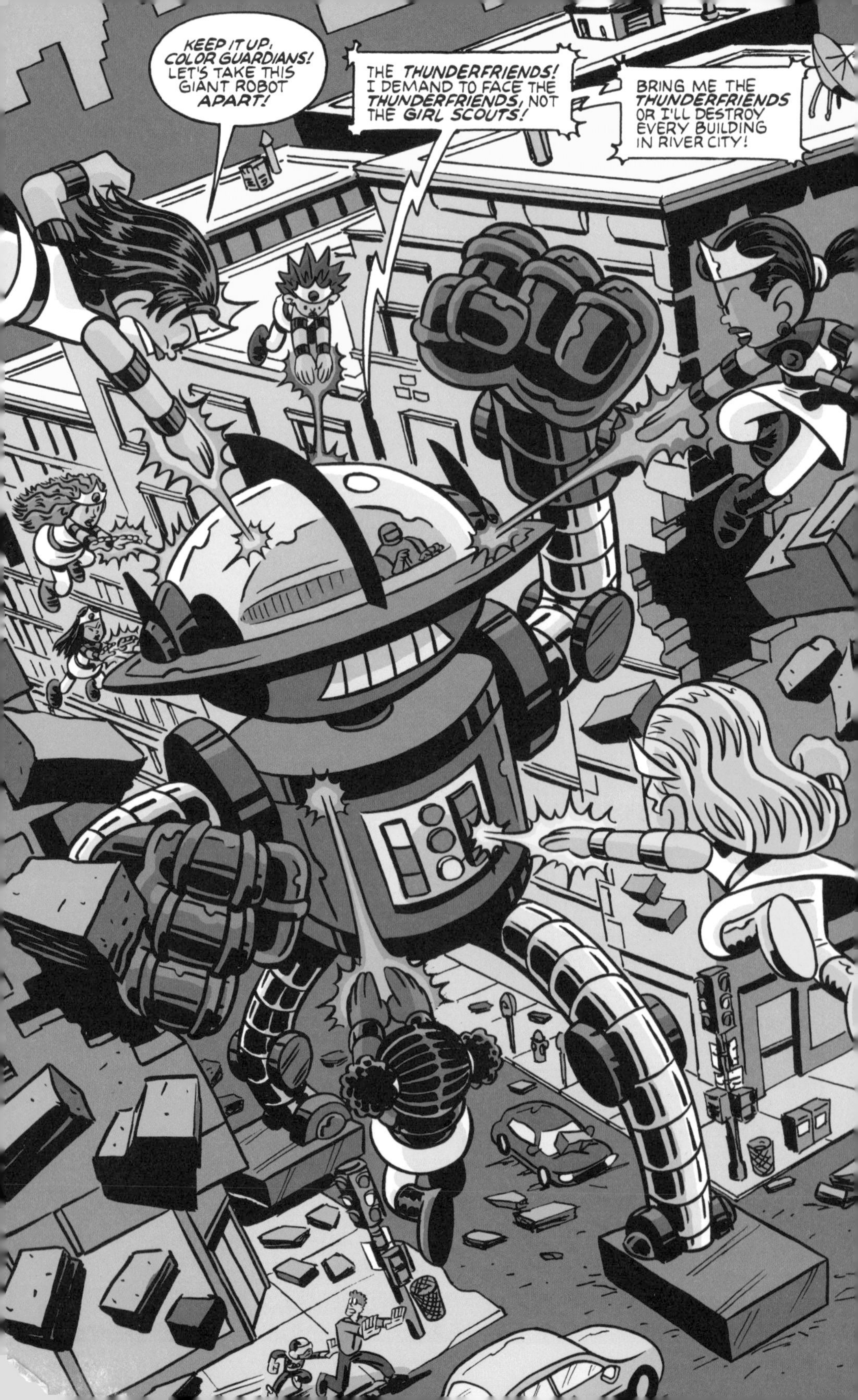
KEEP IT UP, COLOR GUARDIANS! LET'S TAKE THIS GIANT ROBOT APART!
THE THUNDERFRIENDS! I DEMAND TO FACE THE THUNDERFRIENDS, NOT THE GIRL SCOUTS!
BRING ME THE THUNDERFRIENDS OR I'LL DESTROY EVERY BUILDING IN RIVER CITY!

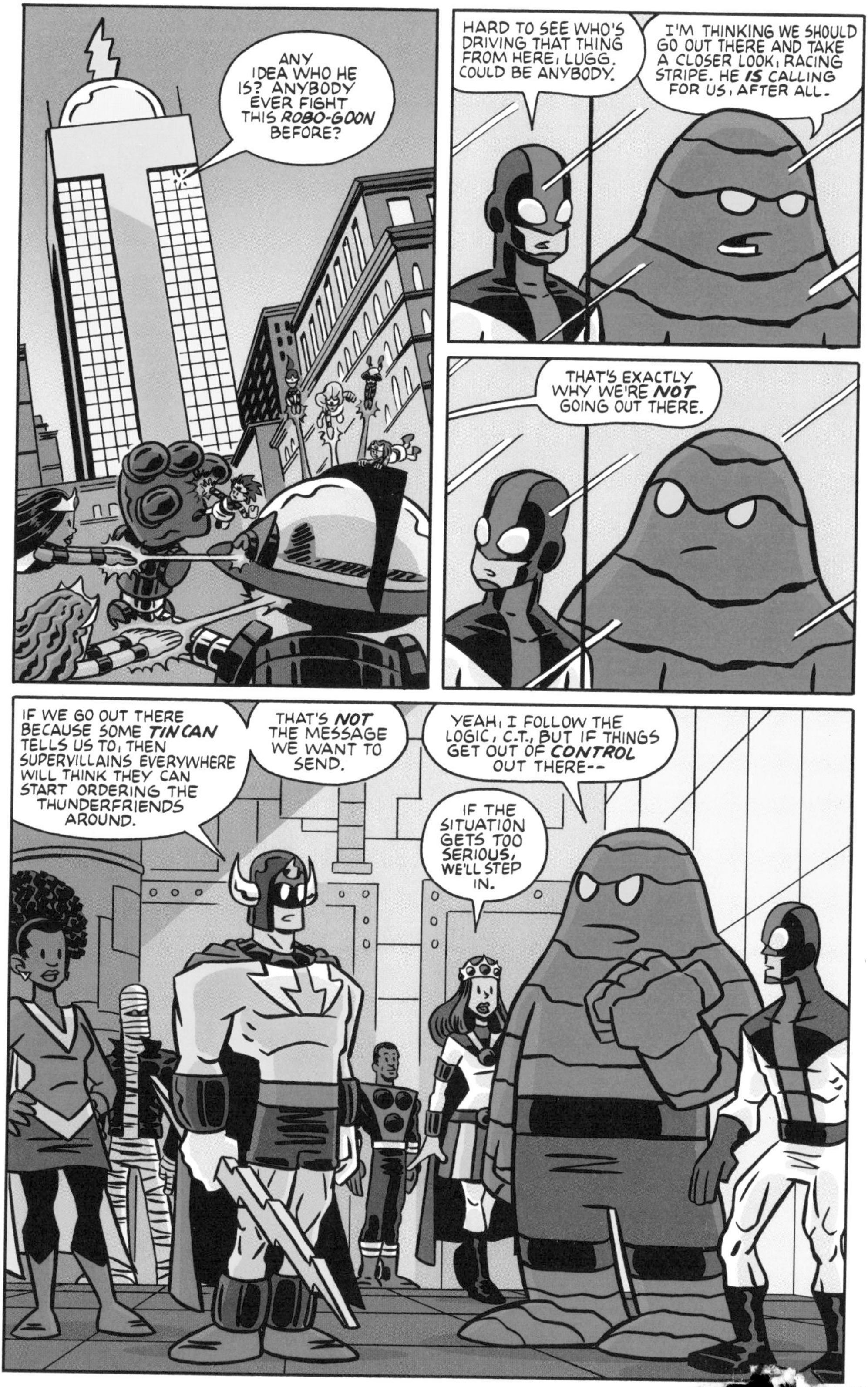
ANY IDEA WHO HE IS? ANYBODY EVER FIGHT THIS ROBO-GOON BEFORE?
HARD TO SEE WHO'S DRIVING THAT THING FROM HERE, LUGG. COULD BE ANYBODY.
I'M THINKING WE SHOULD GO OUT THERE AND TAKE A CLOSER LOOK, RACING STRIPE. HE IS CALLING FOR US, AFTER ALL.
THAT'S EXACTLY WHY WE'RE NOT GOING OUT THERE.
IF WE GO OUT THERE BECAUSE SOME TIN CAN TELLS US TO, THEN SUPERVILLAINS EVERYWHERE WILL THINK THEY CAN START ORDERING THE THUNDERFRIENDS AROUND.
THAT'S NOT THE MESSAGE WE WANT TO SEND.
YEAH, I FOLLOW THE LOGIC, C.T., BUT IF THINGS GET OUT OF CONTROL OUT THERE--
IF THE SITUATION GETS TOO SERIOUS, WE'LL STEP IN.

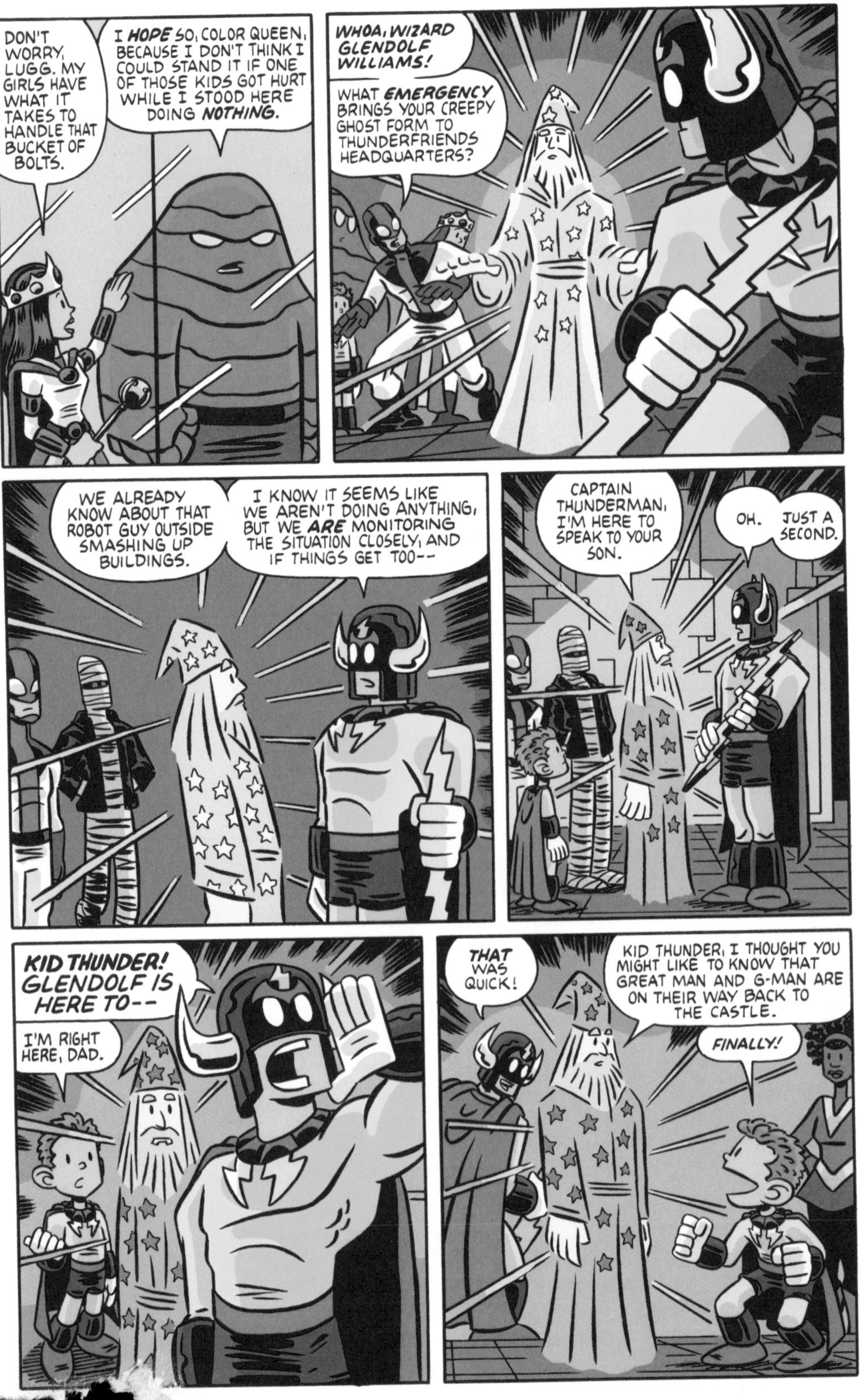
DON'T WORRY, LUGG. MY GIRLS HAVE WHAT IT TAKES TO HANDLE THAT BUCKET OF BOLTS.
I **HOPE** SO, COLOR QUEEN, BECAUSE I DON'T THINK I COULD STAND IT IF ONE OF THOSE KIDS GOT HURT WHILE I STOOD HERE DOING **NOTHING**.
WHOA, WIZARD GLENDOLF WILLIAMS!
WHAT **EMERGENCY** BRINGS YOUR CREEPY GHOST FORM TO THUNDERFRIENDS HEADQUARTERS?
WE ALREADY KNOW ABOUT THAT ROBOT GUY OUTSIDE SMASHING UP BUILDINGS.
I KNOW IT SEEMS LIKE WE AREN'T DOING ANYTHING, BUT WE **ARE** MONITORING THE SITUATION CLOSELY, AND IF THINGS GET TOO--
CAPTAIN THUNDERMAN, I'M HERE TO SPEAK TO YOUR SON.
OH. JUST A SECOND.
KID THUNDER! GLENDOLF IS HERE TO--
I'M RIGHT HERE, DAD.
THAT WAS QUICK!
KID THUNDER, I THOUGHT YOU MIGHT LIKE TO KNOW THAT GREAT MAN AND G-MAN ARE ON THEIR WAY BACK TO THE CASTLE.
FINALLY!

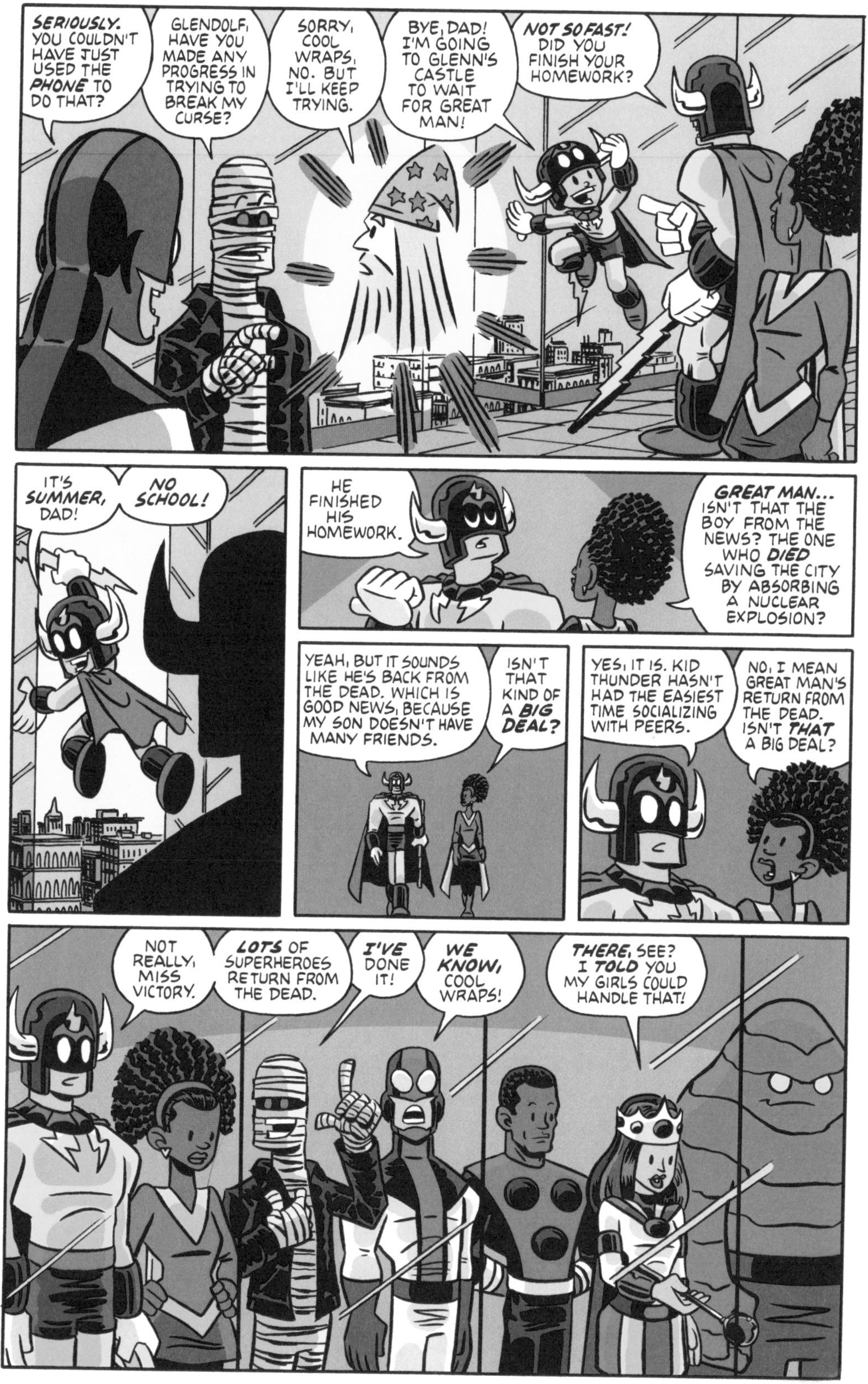
SERIOUSLY. YOU COULDN'T HAVE JUST USED THE PHONE TO DO THAT?
GLENDOLF, HAVE YOU MADE ANY PROGRESS IN TRYING TO BREAK MY CURSE?
SORRY, COOL WRAPS, NO. BUT I'LL KEEP TRYING.
BYE, DAD! I'M GOING TO GLENN'S CASTLE TO WAIT FOR GREAT MAN!
NOT SO FAST! DID YOU FINISH YOUR HOMEWORK?
IT'S SUMMER, DAD!
NO SCHOOL!
HE FINISHED HIS HOMEWORK.
GREAT MAN... ISN'T THAT THE BOY FROM THE NEWS? THE ONE WHO DIED SAVING THE CITY BY ABSORBING A NUCLEAR EXPLOSION?
YEAH, BUT IT SOUNDS LIKE HE'S BACK FROM THE DEAD. WHICH IS GOOD NEWS, BECAUSE MY SON DOESN'T HAVE MANY FRIENDS.
ISN'T THAT KIND OF A BIG DEAL?
YES, IT IS. KID THUNDER HASN'T HAD THE EASIEST TIME SOCIALIZING WITH PEERS.
NO, I MEAN GREAT MAN'S RETURN FROM THE DEAD. ISN'T THAT A BIG DEAL?
NOT REALLY, MISS VICTORY.
LOTS OF SUPERHEROES RETURN FROM THE DEAD.
I'VE DONE IT!
WE KNOW, COOL WRAPS!
THERE, SEE? I TOLD YOU MY GIRLS COULD HANDLE THAT!

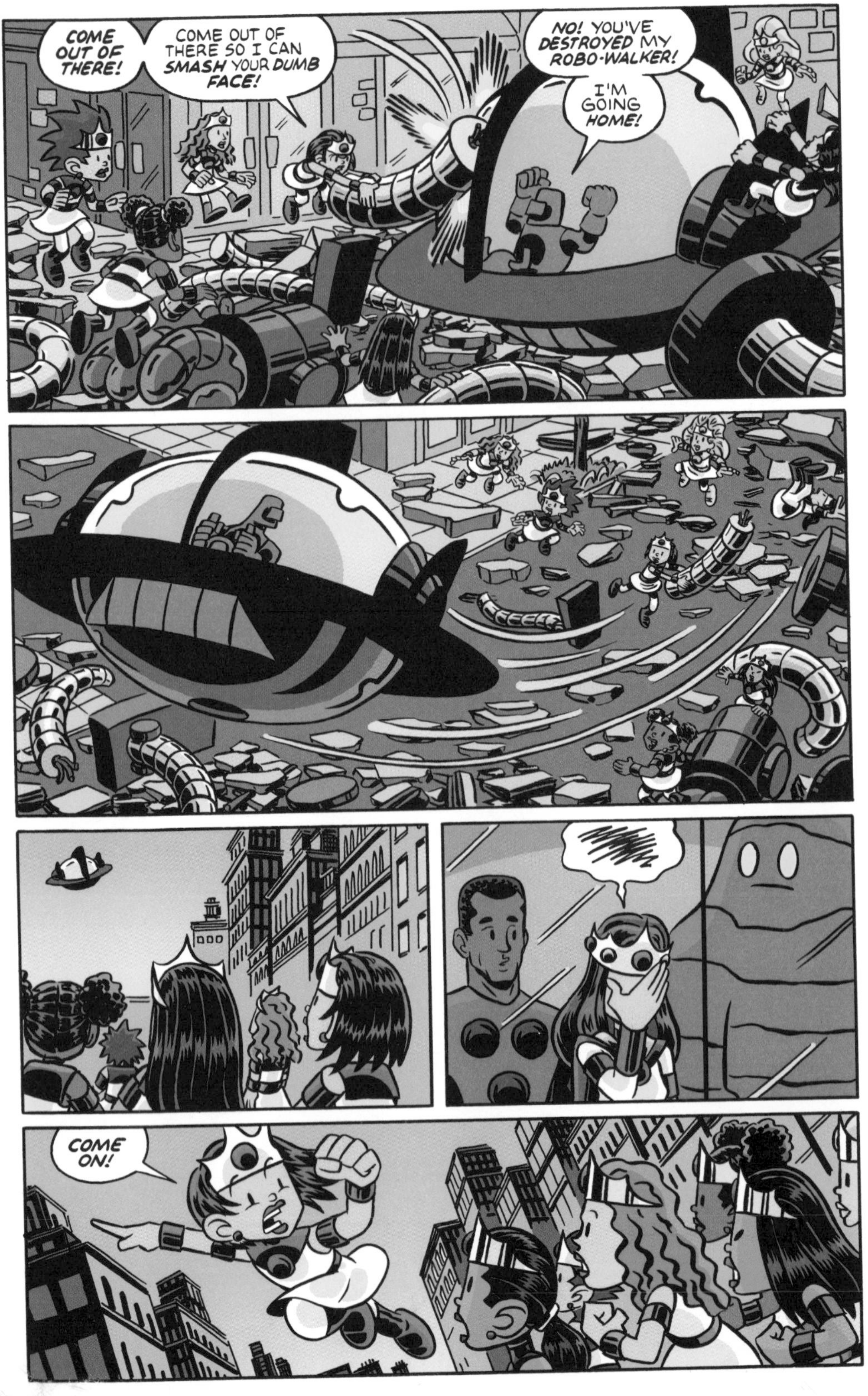
COME OUT OF THERE!
COME OUT OF THERE SO I CAN SMASH YOUR DUMB FACE!
NO! YOU'VE DESTROYED MY ROBO-WALKER!
I'M GOING HOME!
COME ON!

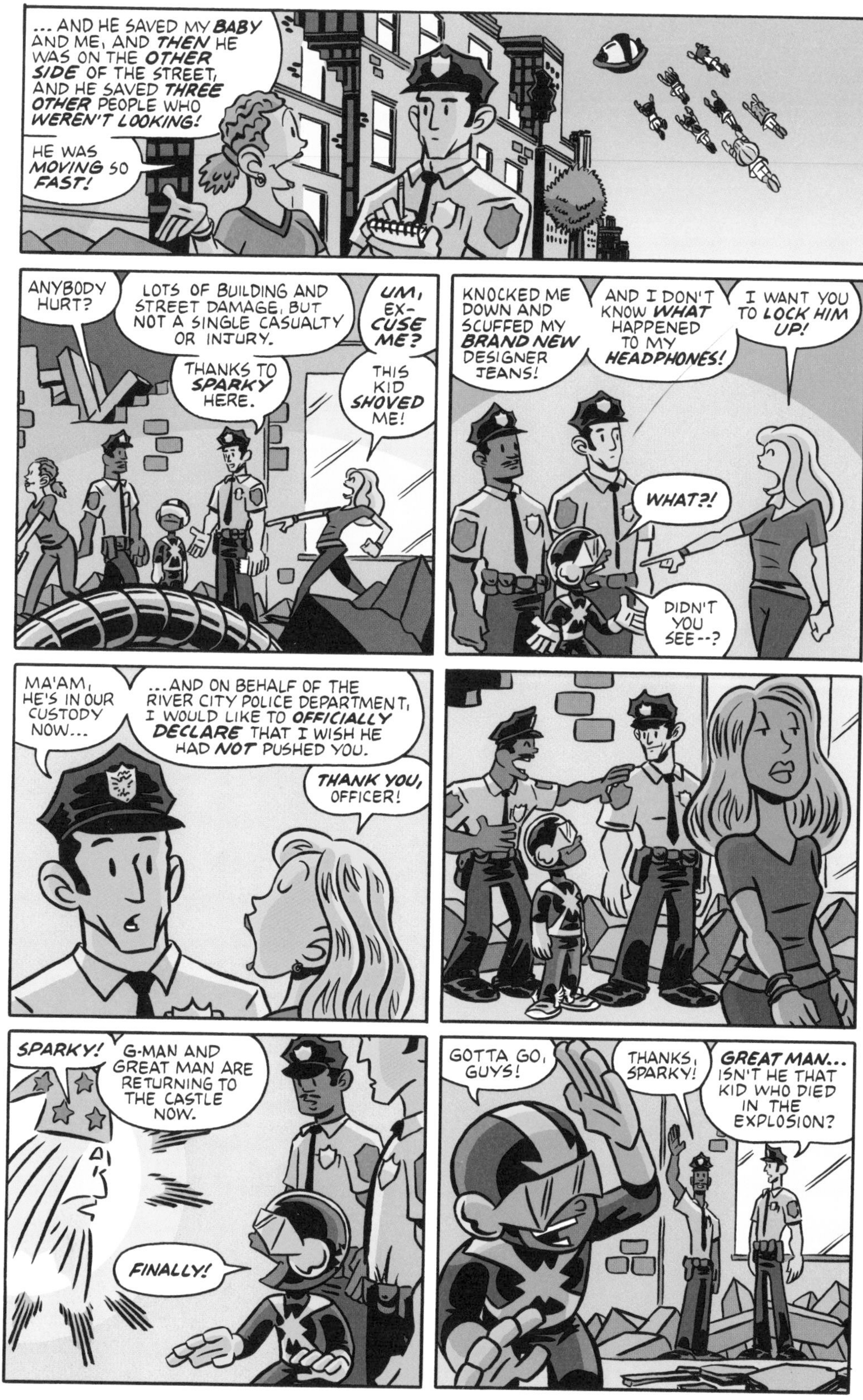

...AND HE SAVED MY BABY AND ME, AND THEN HE WAS ON THE OTHER SIDE OF THE STREET, AND HE SAVED THREE OTHER PEOPLE WHO WEREN'T LOOKING!
HE WAS MOVING SO FAST!
ANYBODY HURT?
LOTS OF BUILDING AND STREET DAMAGE, BUT NOT A SINGLE CASUALTY OR INJURY.
THANKS TO SPARKY HERE.
UM, EX-CUSE ME?
THIS KID SHOVED ME!
KNOCKED ME DOWN AND SCUFFED MY BRAND NEW DESIGNER JEANS!
AND I DON'T KNOW WHAT HAPPENED TO MY HEADPHONES!
I WANT YOU TO LOCK HIM UP!
WHAT?!
DIDN'T YOU SEE--?
MA'AM, HE'S IN OUR CUSTODY NOW...
...AND ON BEHALF OF THE RIVER CITY POLICE DEPARTMENT, I WOULD LIKE TO OFFICIALLY DECLARE THAT I WISH HE HAD NOT PUSHED YOU.
THANK YOU, OFFICER!
SPARKY!
G-MAN AND GREAT MAN ARE RETURNING TO THE CASTLE NOW.
FINALLY!
GOTTA GO, GUYS!
THANKS, SPARKY!
GREAT MAN... ISN'T HE THAT KID WHO DIED IN THE EXPLOSION?

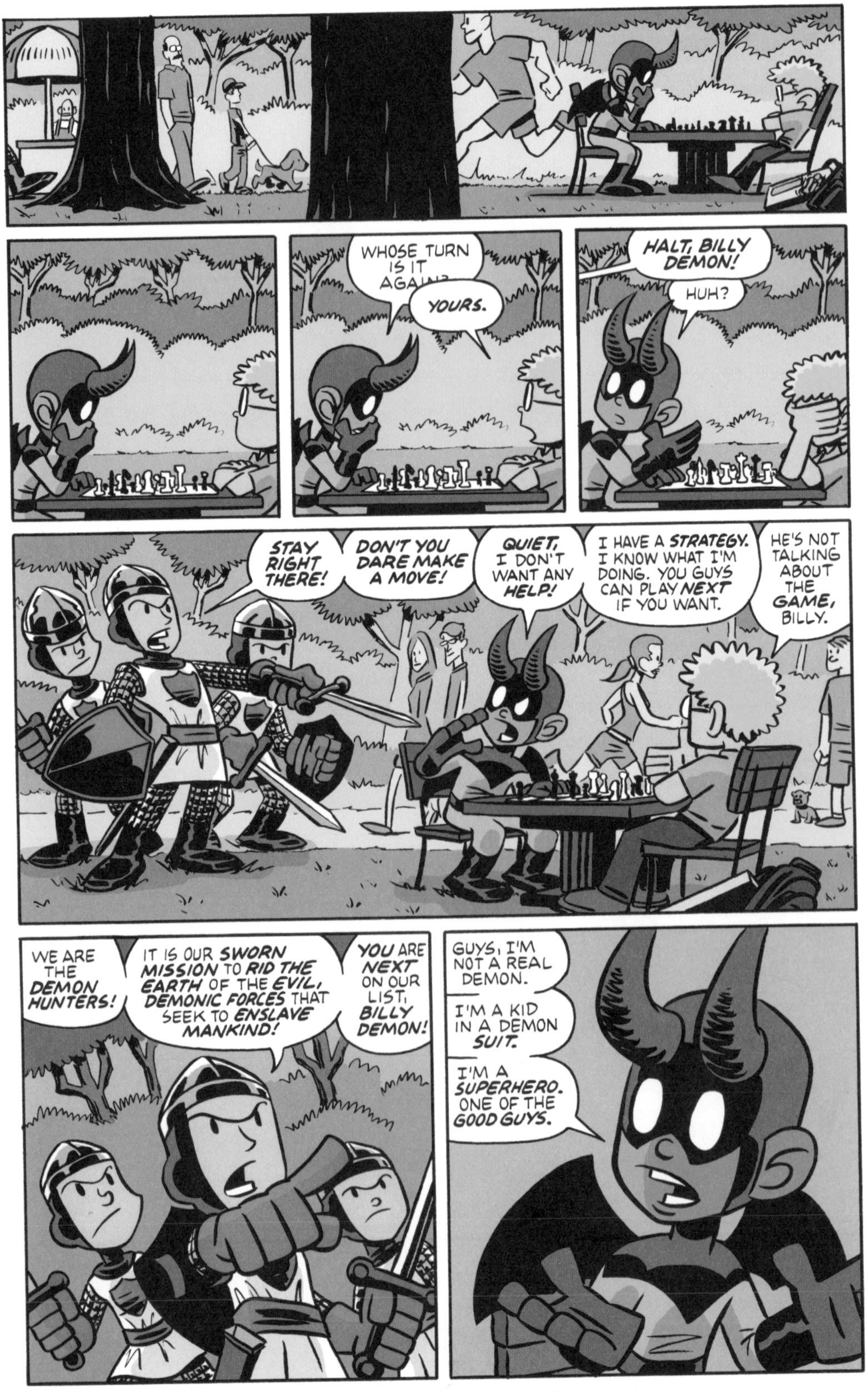
WHOSE TURN IS IT AGAIN?
YOURS.
HALT, BILLY DEMON!
HUH?
STAY RIGHT THERE!
DON'T YOU DARE MAKE A MOVE!
QUIET, I DON'T WANT ANY HELP!
I HAVE A STRATEGY. I KNOW WHAT I'M DOING. YOU GUYS CAN PLAY NEXT IF YOU WANT.
HE'S NOT TALKING ABOUT THE GAME, BILLY.
WE ARE THE DEMON HUNTERS!
IT IS OUR SWORN MISSION TO RID THE EARTH OF THE EVIL, DEMONIC FORCES THAT SEEK TO ENSLAVE MANKIND!
YOU ARE NEXT ON OUR LIST, BILLY DEMON!
GUYS, I'M NOT A REAL DEMON.
I'M A KID IN A DEMON SUIT.
I'M A SUPERHERO. ONE OF THE GOOD GUYS.

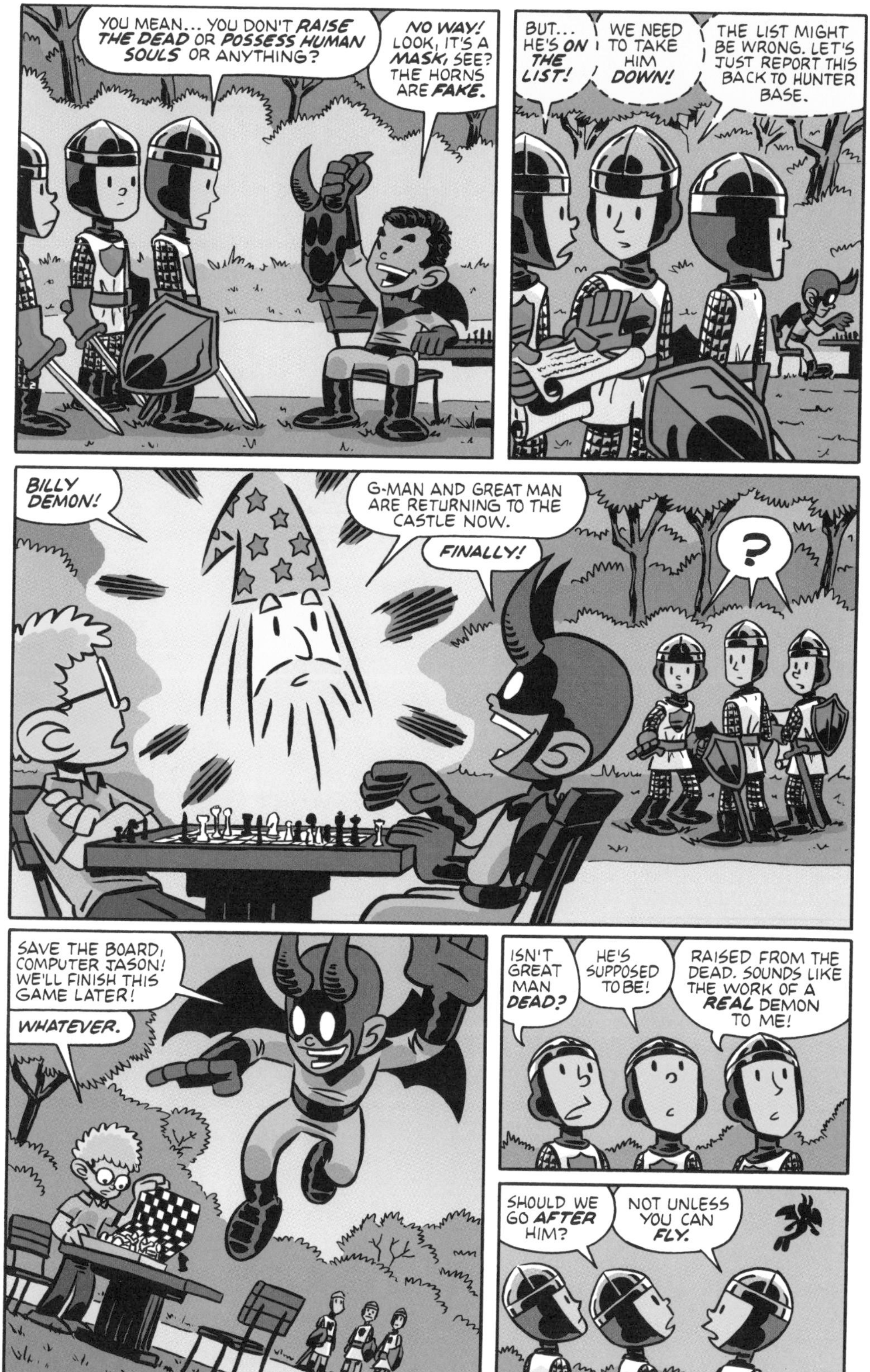

YOU MEAN... YOU DON'T RAISE THE DEAD OR POSSESS HUMAN SOULS OR ANYTHING?
NO WAY! LOOK, IT'S A MASK, SEE? THE HORNS ARE FAKE.
BUT... HE'S ON THE LIST!
WE NEED TO TAKE HIM DOWN!
THE LIST MIGHT BE WRONG. LET'S JUST REPORT THIS BACK TO HUNTER BASE.
BILLY DEMON!
G-MAN AND GREAT MAN ARE RETURNING TO THE CASTLE NOW.
FINALLY!
?
SAVE THE BOARD, COMPUTER JASON! WE'LL FINISH THIS GAME LATER!
WHATEVER.
ISN'T GREAT MAN DEAD?
HE'S SUPPOSED TO BE!
RAISED FROM THE DEAD. SOUNDS LIKE THE WORK OF A REAL DEMON TO ME!
SHOULD WE GO AFTER HIM?
NOT UNLESS YOU CAN FLY.

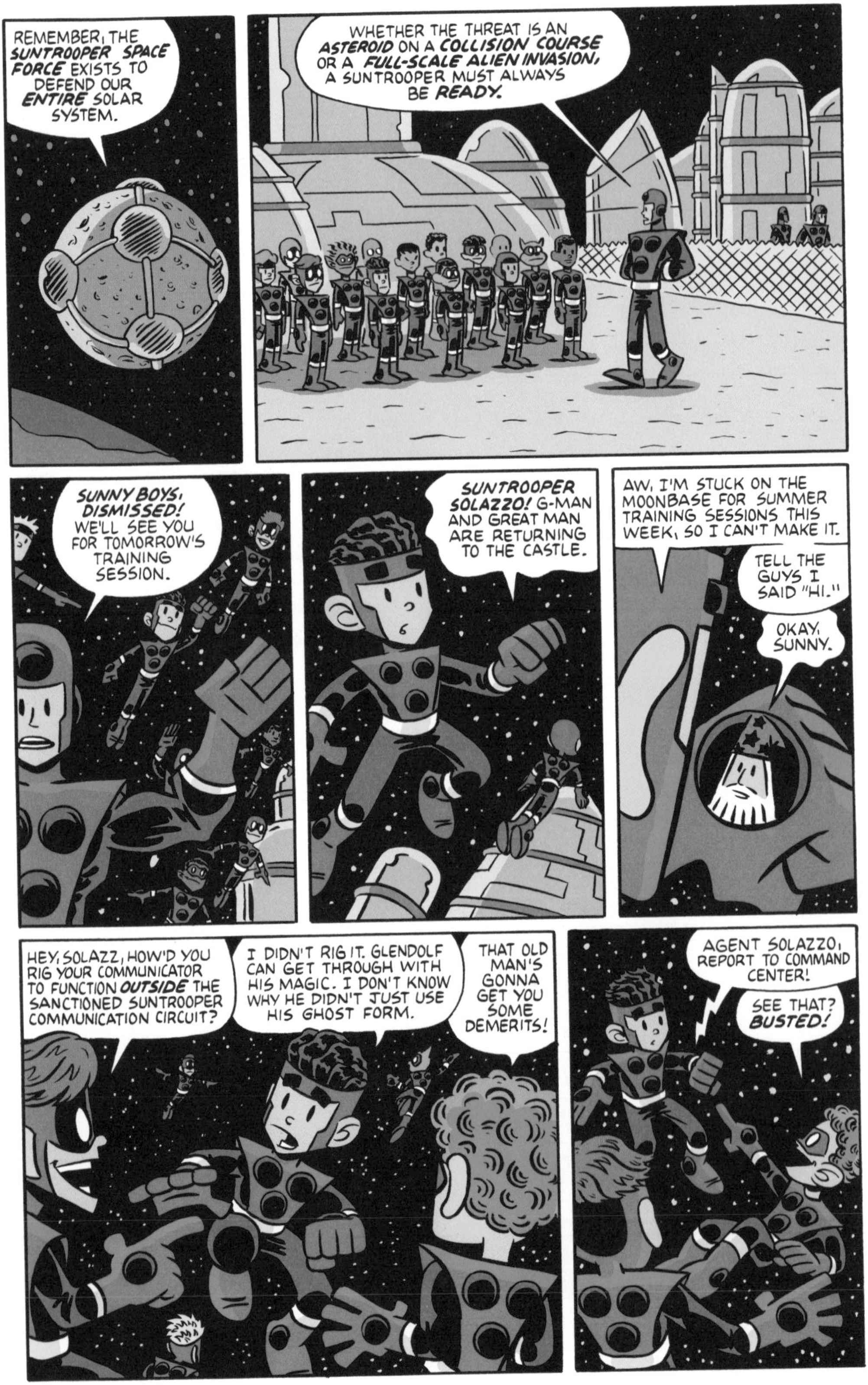
REMEMBER, THE SUNTROOPER SPACE FORCE EXISTS TO DEFEND OUR ENTIRE SOLAR SYSTEM.
WHETHER THE THREAT IS AN ASTEROID ON A COLLISION COURSE OR A FULL-SCALE ALIEN INVASION, A SUNTROOPER MUST ALWAYS BE READY.
SUNNY BOYS, DISMISSED! WE'LL SEE YOU FOR TOMORROW'S TRAINING SESSION.
SUNTROOPER SOLAZZO! G-MAN AND GREAT MAN ARE RETURNING TO THE CASTLE.
AW, I'M STUCK ON THE MOONBASE FOR SUMMER TRAINING SESSIONS THIS WEEK, SO I CAN'T MAKE IT.
TELL THE GUYS I SAID "HI."
OKAY, SUNNY.
HEY, SOLAZZ, HOW'D YOU RIG YOUR COMMUNICATOR TO FUNCTION OUTSIDE THE SANCTIONED SUNTROOPER COMMUNICATION CIRCUIT?
I DIDN'T RIG IT. GLENDOLF CAN GET THROUGH WITH HIS MAGIC. I DON'T KNOW WHY HE DIDN'T JUST USE HIS GHOST FORM.
THAT OLD MAN'S GONNA GET YOU SOME DEMERITS!
AGENT SOLAZZO, REPORT TO COMMAND CENTER!
SEE THAT? BUSTED!

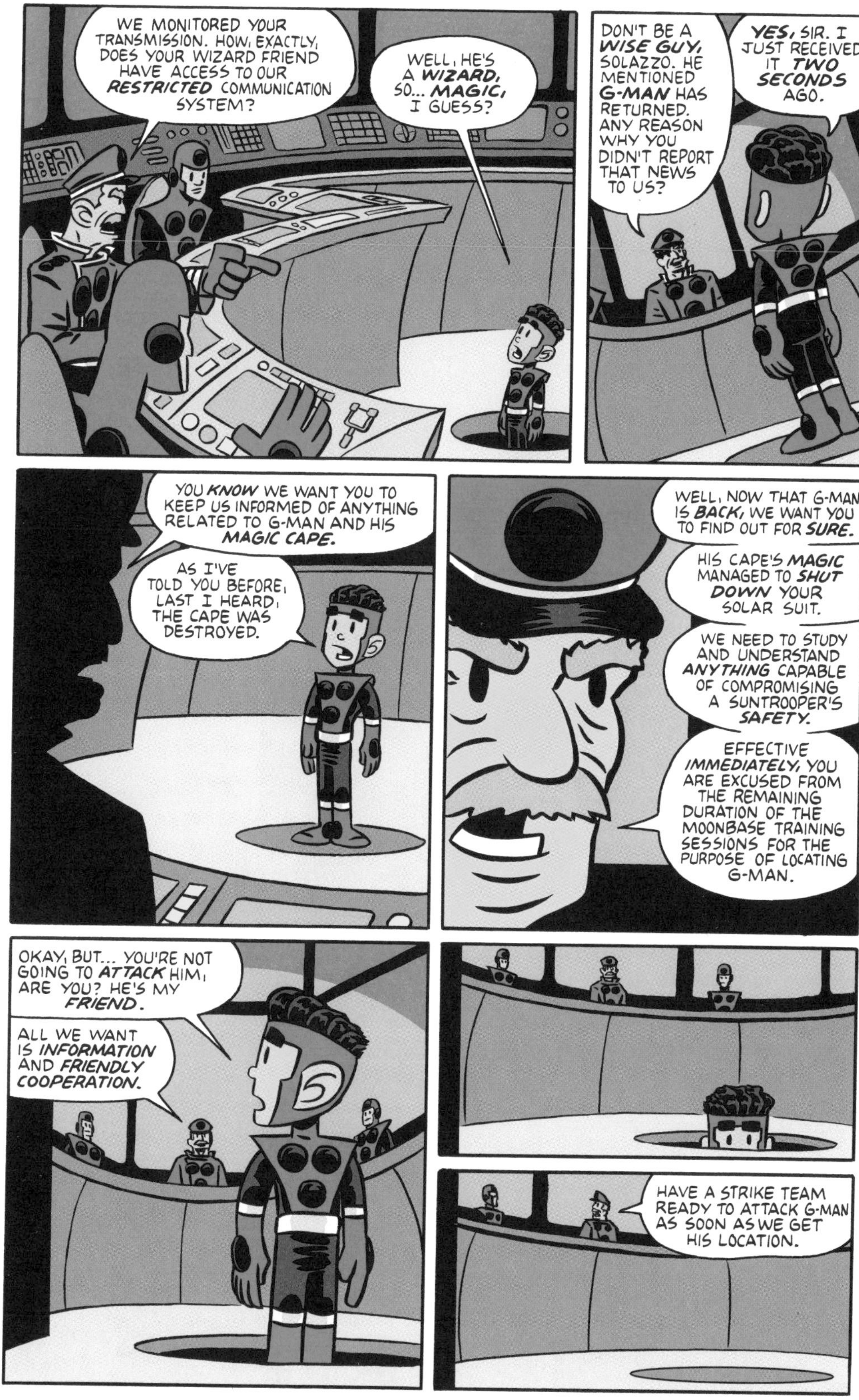
WE MONITORED YOUR TRANSMISSION. HOW, EXACTLY, DOES YOUR WIZARD FRIEND HAVE ACCESS TO OUR RESTRICTED COMMUNICATION SYSTEM?
WELL, HE'S A WIZARD, SO... MAGIC, I GUESS?
DON'T BE A WISE GUY, SOLAZZO. HE MENTIONED G-MAN HAS RETURNED. ANY REASON WHY YOU DIDN'T REPORT THAT NEWS TO US?
YES, SIR. I JUST RECEIVED IT TWO SECONDS AGO.
YOU KNOW WE WANT YOU TO KEEP US INFORMED OF ANYTHING RELATED TO G-MAN AND HIS MAGIC CAPE.
AS I'VE TOLD YOU BEFORE, LAST I HEARD, THE CAPE WAS DESTROYED.
WELL, NOW THAT G-MAN IS BACK, WE WANT YOU TO FIND OUT FOR SURE.
HIS CAPE'S MAGIC MANAGED TO SHUT DOWN YOUR SOLAR SUIT.
WE NEED TO STUDY AND UNDERSTAND ANYTHING CAPABLE OF COMPROMISING A SUNTROOPER'S SAFETY.
EFFECTIVE IMMEDIATELY, YOU ARE EXCUSED FROM THE REMAINING DURATION OF THE MOONBASE TRAINING SESSIONS FOR THE PURPOSE OF LOCATING G-MAN.
OKAY, BUT... YOU'RE NOT GOING TO ATTACK HIM, ARE YOU? HE'S MY FRIEND.
ALL WE WANT IS INFORMATION AND FRIENDLY COOPERATION.
HAVE A STRIKE TEAM READY TO ATTACK G-MAN AS SOON AS WE GET HIS LOCATION.

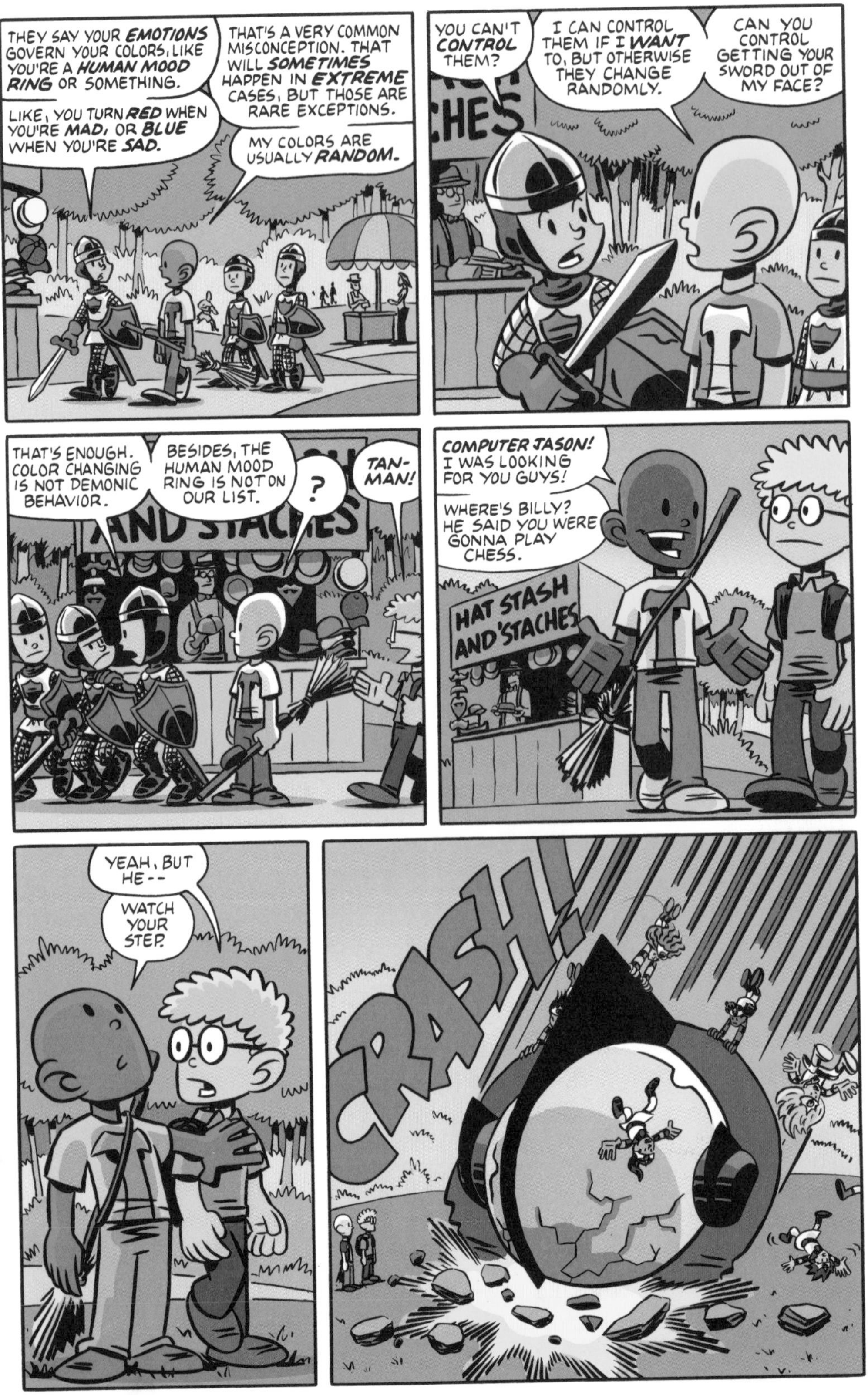
THEY SAY YOUR EMOTIONS GOVERN YOUR COLORS, LIKE YOU'RE A HUMAN MOOD RING OR SOMETHING.
LIKE, YOU TURN RED WHEN YOU'RE MAD, OR BLUE WHEN YOU'RE SAD.
THAT'S A VERY COMMON MISCONCEPTION. THAT WILL SOMETIMES HAPPEN IN EXTREME CASES, BUT THOSE ARE RARE EXCEPTIONS.
MY COLORS ARE USUALLY RANDOM.
YOU CAN'T CONTROL THEM?
I CAN CONTROL THEM IF I WANT TO, BUT OTHERWISE THEY CHANGE RANDOMLY.
CAN YOU CONTROL GETTING YOUR SWORD OUT OF MY FACE?
THAT'S ENOUGH. COLOR CHANGING IS NOT DEMONIC BEHAVIOR.
BESIDES, THE HUMAN MOOD RING IS NOT ON OUR LIST.
?
TAN-MAN!
AND STACHES
COMPUTER JASON! I WAS LOOKING FOR YOU GUYS!
WHERE'S BILLY? HE SAID YOU WERE GONNA PLAY CHESS.
HAT STASH AND 'STACHES
YEAH, BUT HE--
WATCH YOUR STEP.
CRASH!

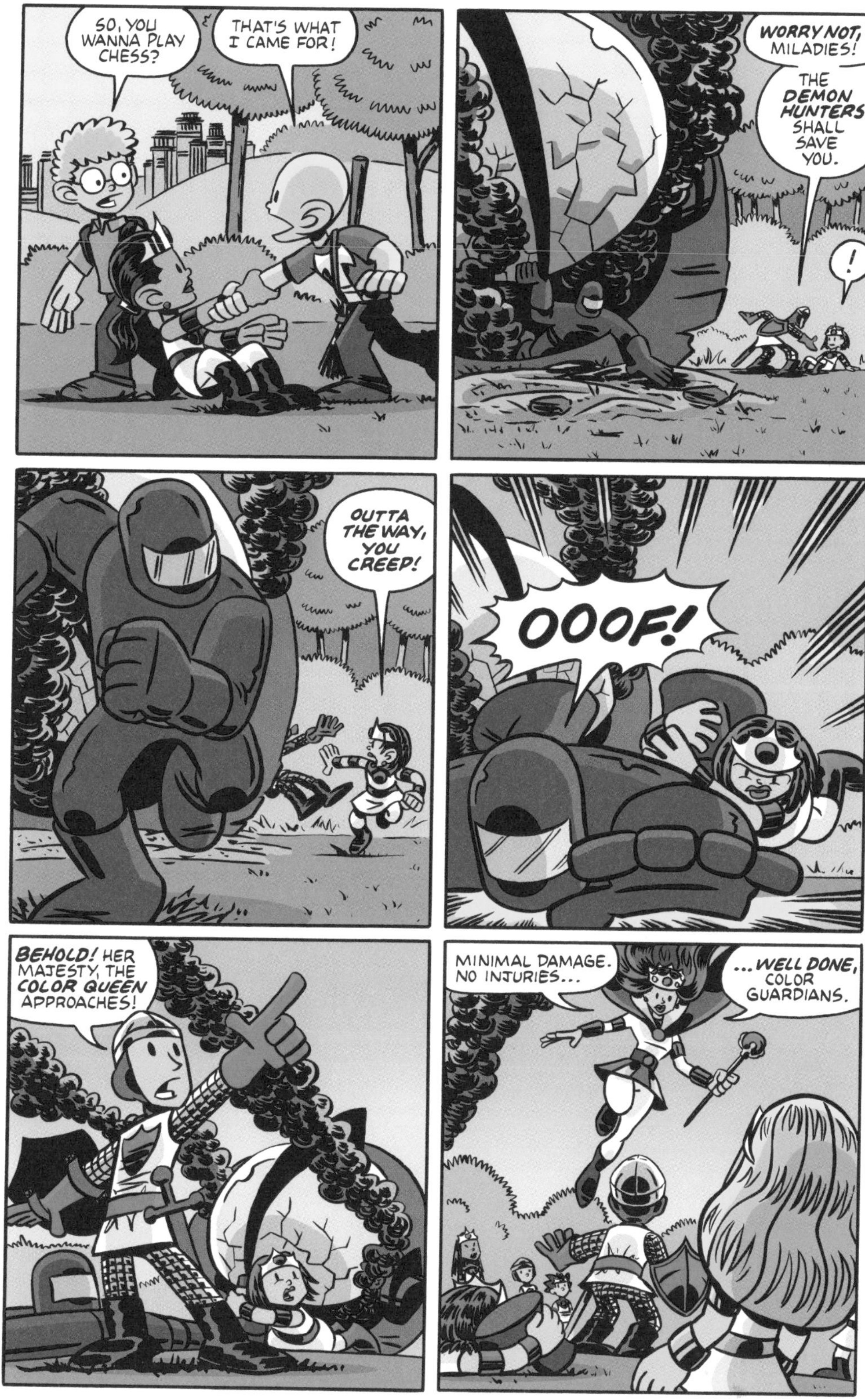
SO, YOU WANNA PLAY CHESS?
THAT'S WHAT I CAME FOR!
WORRY NOT, MILADIES!
THE DEMON HUNTERS SHALL SAVE YOU.
!
OUTTA THE WAY, YOU CREEP!
OOOF!
BEHOLD! HER MAJESTY, THE COLOR QUEEN APPROACHES!
MINIMAL DAMAGE. NO INJURIES...
...WELL DONE, COLOR GUARDIANS.

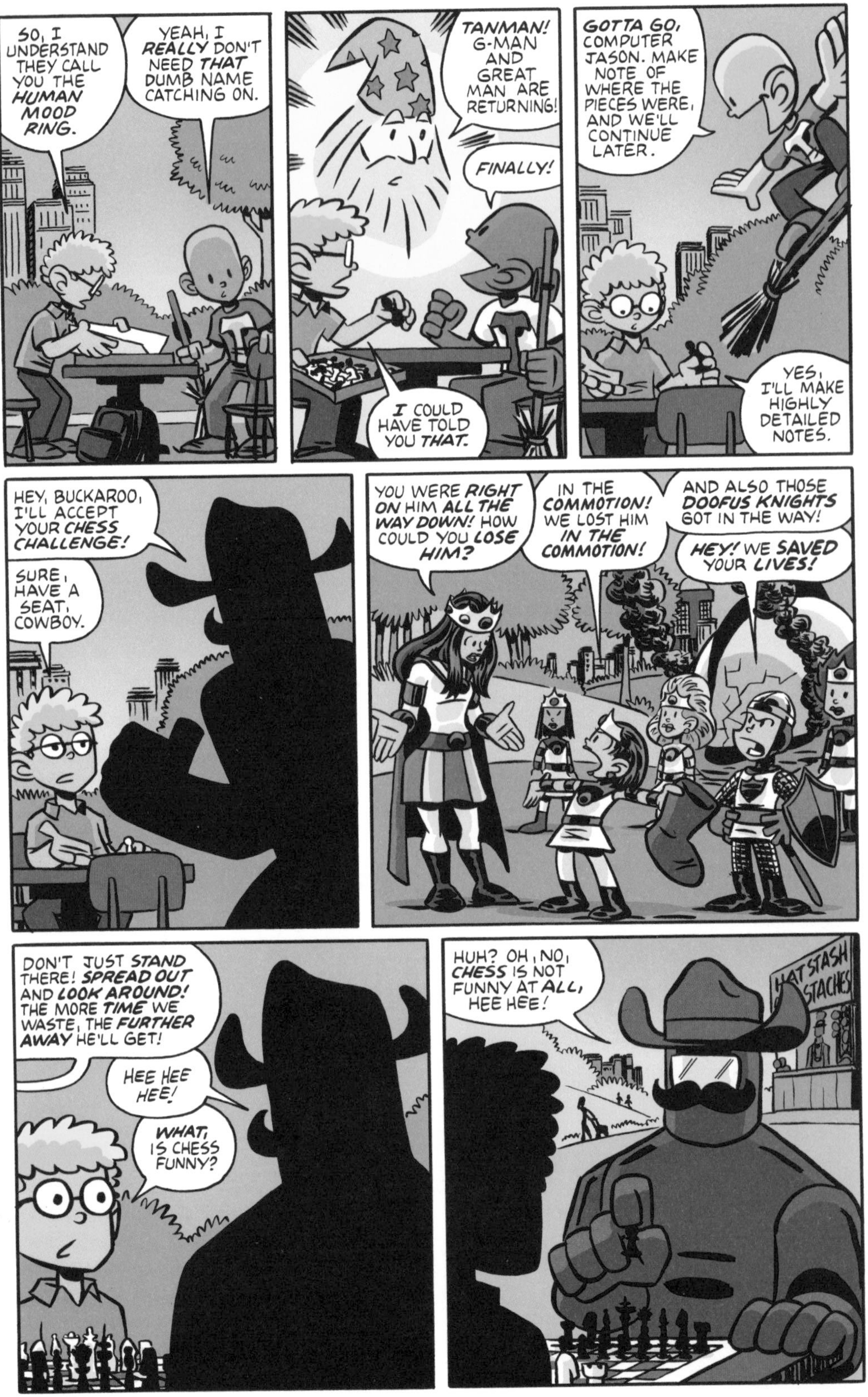
SO, I UNDERSTAND THEY CALL YOU THE HUMAN MOOD RING.
YEAH, I REALLY DON'T NEED THAT DUMB NAME CATCHING ON.
TANMAN! G-MAN AND GREAT MAN ARE RETURNING!
FINALLY!
I COULD HAVE TOLD YOU THAT.
GOTTA GO, COMPUTER JASON. MAKE NOTE OF WHERE THE PIECES WERE, AND WE'LL CONTINUE LATER.
YES, I'LL MAKE HIGHLY DETAILED NOTES.
HEY, BUCKAROO, I'LL ACCEPT YOUR CHESS CHALLENGE!
SURE, HAVE A SEAT, COWBOY.
YOU WERE RIGHT ON HIM ALL THE WAY DOWN! HOW COULD YOU LOSE HIM?
IN THE COMMOTION! WE LOST HIM IN THE COMMOTION!
AND ALSO THOSE DOOFUS KNIGHTS GOT IN THE WAY!
HEY! WE SAVED YOUR LIVES!
DON'T JUST STAND THERE! SPREAD OUT AND LOOK AROUND! THE MORE TIME WE WASTE, THE FURTHER AWAY HE'LL GET!
HEE HEE HEE!
WHAT, IS CHESS FUNNY?
HUH? OH, NO, CHESS IS NOT FUNNY AT ALL, HEE HEE!
HAT STASH
STACHES

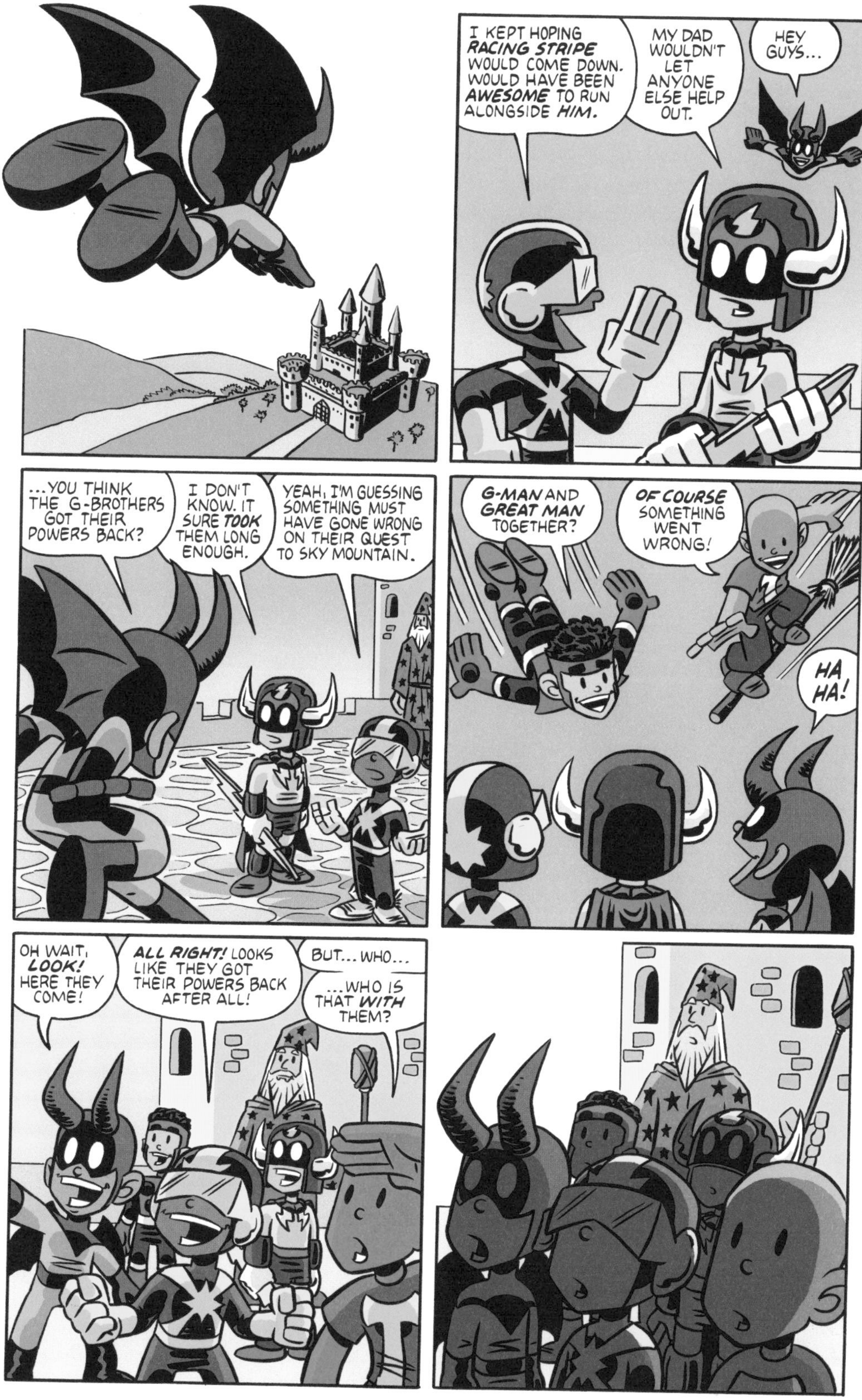
I KEPT HOPING RACING STRIPE WOULD COME DOWN. WOULD HAVE BEEN AWESOME TO RUN ALONGSIDE HIM.
MY DAD WOULDN'T LET ANYONE ELSE HELP OUT.
HEY GUYS...
...YOU THINK THE G-BROTHERS GOT THEIR POWERS BACK?
I DON'T KNOW. IT SURE TOOK THEM LONG ENOUGH.
YEAH, I'M GUESSING SOMETHING MUST HAVE GONE WRONG ON THEIR QUEST TO SKY MOUNTAIN.
G-MAN AND GREAT MAN TOGETHER?
OF COURSE SOMETHING WENT WRONG!
HA HA!
OH WAIT, LOOK! HERE THEY COME!
ALL RIGHT! LOOKS LIKE THEY GOT THEIR POWERS BACK AFTER ALL!
BUT... WHO...
...WHO IS THAT WITH THEM?

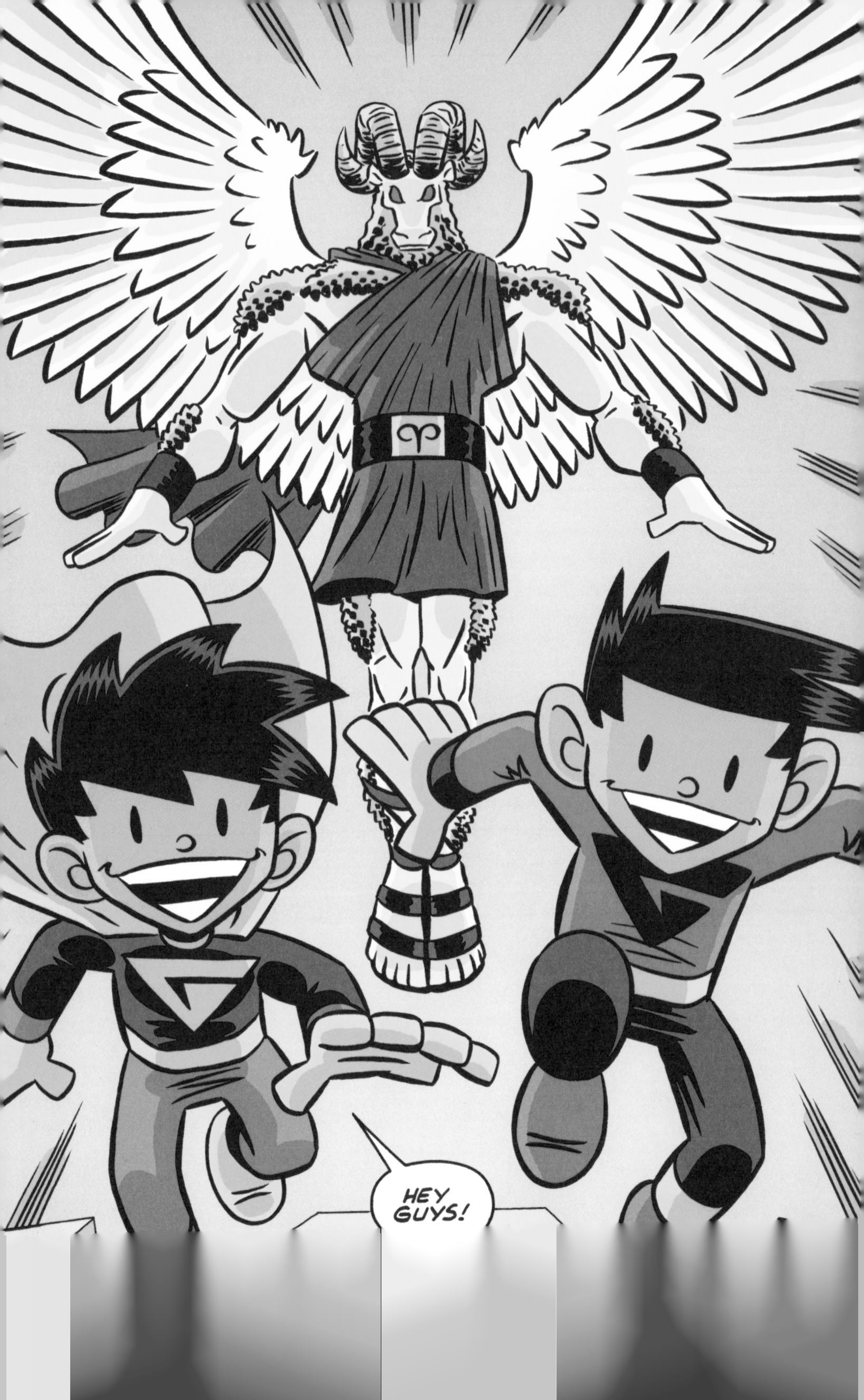
HEY GUYS!

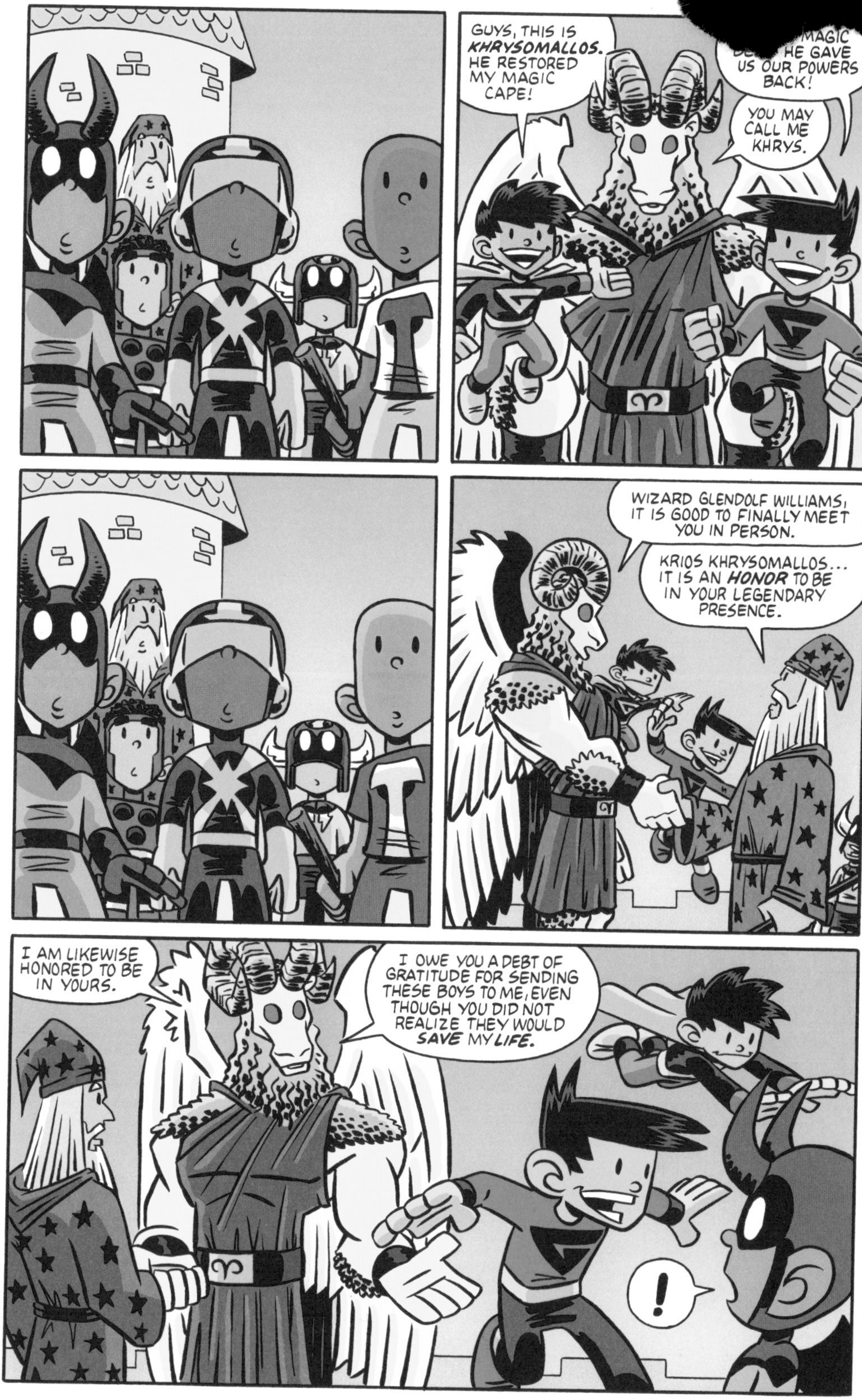
GUYS, THIS IS KHRYSOMALLOS. HE RESTORED MY MAGIC CAPE!
MAGIC … HE GAVE US OUR POWERS BACK!
YOU MAY CALL ME KHRYS.
WIZARD GLENDOLF WILLIAMS, IT IS GOOD TO FINALLY MEET YOU IN PERSON.
KRIOS KHRYSOMALLOS... IT IS AN HONOR TO BE IN YOUR LEGENDARY PRESENCE.
I AM LIKEWISE HONORED TO BE IN YOURS.
I OWE YOU A DEBT OF GRATITUDE FOR SENDING THESE BOYS TO ME, EVEN THOUGH YOU DID NOT REALIZE THEY WOULD SAVE MY LIFE.
!

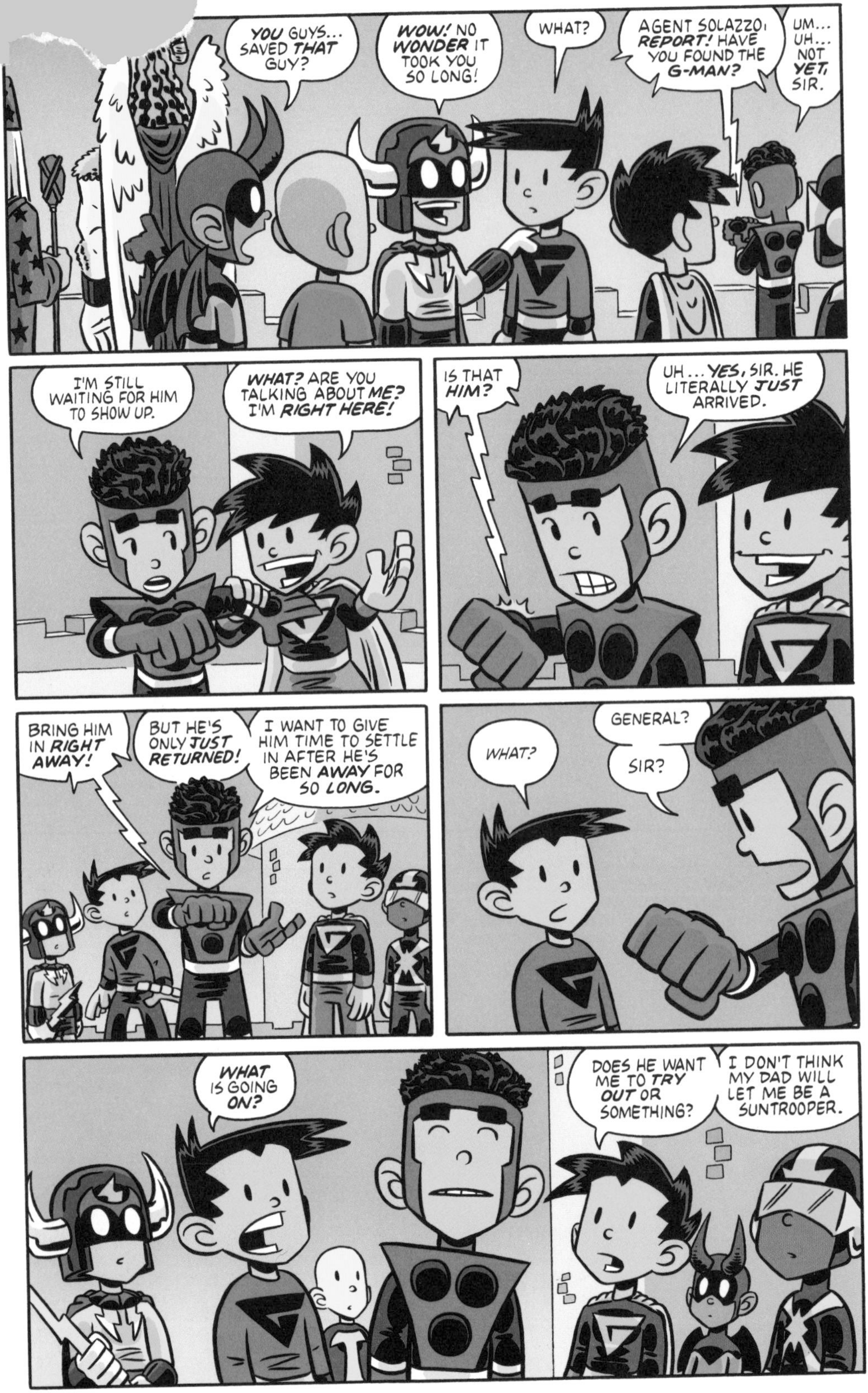
YOU GUYS... SAVED THAT GUY?
WOW! NO WONDER IT TOOK YOU SO LONG!
WHAT?
AGENT SOLAZZO! REPORT! HAVE YOU FOUND THE G-MAN?
UM... UH... NOT YET, SIR.
I'M STILL WAITING FOR HIM TO SHOW UP.
WHAT? ARE YOU TALKING ABOUT ME? I'M RIGHT HERE!
IS THAT HIM?
UH ... YES, SIR. HE LITERALLY JUST ARRIVED.
BRING HIM IN RIGHT AWAY!
BUT HE'S ONLY JUST RETURNED!
I WANT TO GIVE HIM TIME TO SETTLE IN AFTER HE'S BEEN AWAY FOR SO LONG.
WHAT?
GENERAL?
SIR?
WHAT IS GOING ON?
DOES HE WANT ME TO TRY OUT OR SOMETHING?
I DON'T THINK MY DAD WILL LET ME BE A SUNTROOPER.

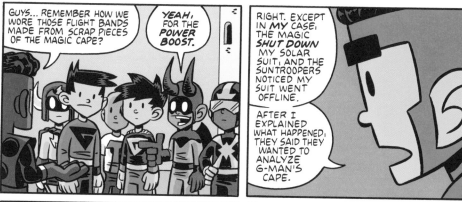

GUYS... REMEMBER HOW WE WORE THOSE FLIGHT BANDS MADE FROM SCRAP PIECES OF THE MAGIC CAPE?

YEAH, FOR THE *POWER BOOST.*

RIGHT. EXCEPT IN *MY* CASE, THE MAGIC *SHUT DOWN* MY SOLAR SUIT, AND THE SUNTROOPERS NOTICED MY SUIT WENT OFFLINE.

AFTER I EXPLAINED WHAT HAPPENED, THEY WANTED TO ANALYZE G-MAN'S CAPE.

BY THEN, THE CAPE AND ALL THE EXTRA PIECES WERE DESTROYED, AND I DIDN'T KNOW EXACTLY *WHERE* G-MAN WAS, OR *WHEN* HE'D EVER BE *BACK.*

WHAT?

ALL SUMMER LONG THEY'VE BEEN ON MY CASE ABOUT BRINGING IN G-MAN ON THE CHANCE THAT HIS CAPE MIGHT BE RESTORED.

WHY DO YOU KEEP TALKING LIKE WE'VE BEEN GONE SO LONG? IT'S BARELY BEEN A DAY!!! WE LEFT HERE THIS MORNING!!!

RIGHT?

GREAT MAN...

... YOU GUYS HAVE BEEN GONE FOR *THREE MONTHS.*

WHAT?

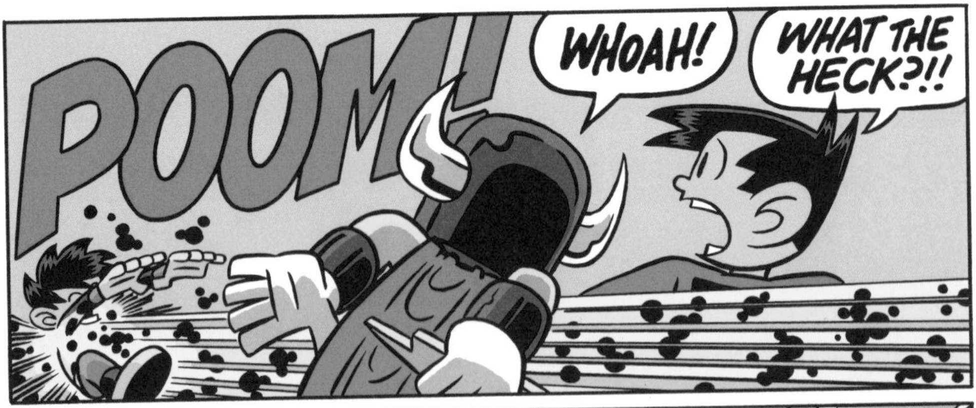
POOM!
WHOAH!
WHAT THE HECK?!!

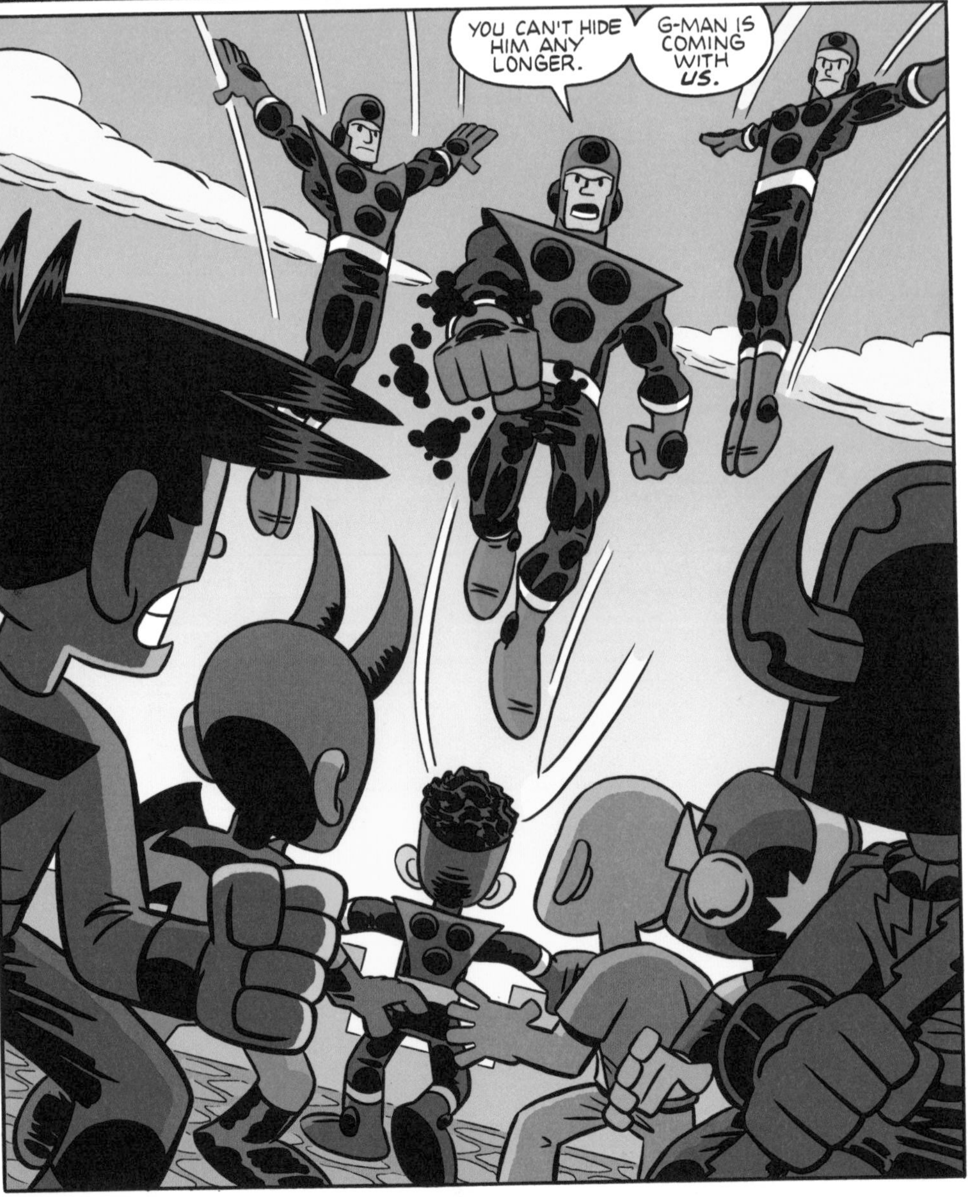
YOU CAN'T HIDE HIM ANY LONGER.
G-MAN IS COMING WITH US.

CHAPTER TWO

WHAT ARE YOU DOING?

UHHNN...

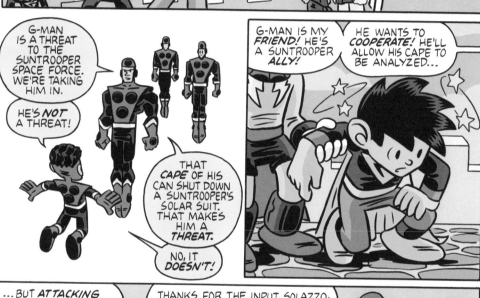

G-MAN IS A THREAT TO THE SUNTROOPER SPACE FORCE. WE'RE TAKING HIM IN.

HE'S *NOT* A THREAT!

THAT *CAPE* OF HIS CAN SHUT DOWN A SUNTROOPER'S SOLAR SUIT. THAT MAKES HIM A *THREAT*.

NO, IT *DOESN'T!*

G-MAN IS MY *FRIEND!* HE'S A SUNTROOPER *ALLY!*

HE WANTS TO *COOPERATE!* HE'LL ALLOW HIS CAPE TO BE ANALYZED...

...BUT *ATTACKING* HIM WILL ONLY MAKE THINGS *WORSE!*

PLEASE JUST LET *ME* HANDLE THIS!

THANKS FOR THE INPUT, SOLAZZO, BUT I DON'T TAKE MY ORDERS FROM A *SUNNY BOY.*

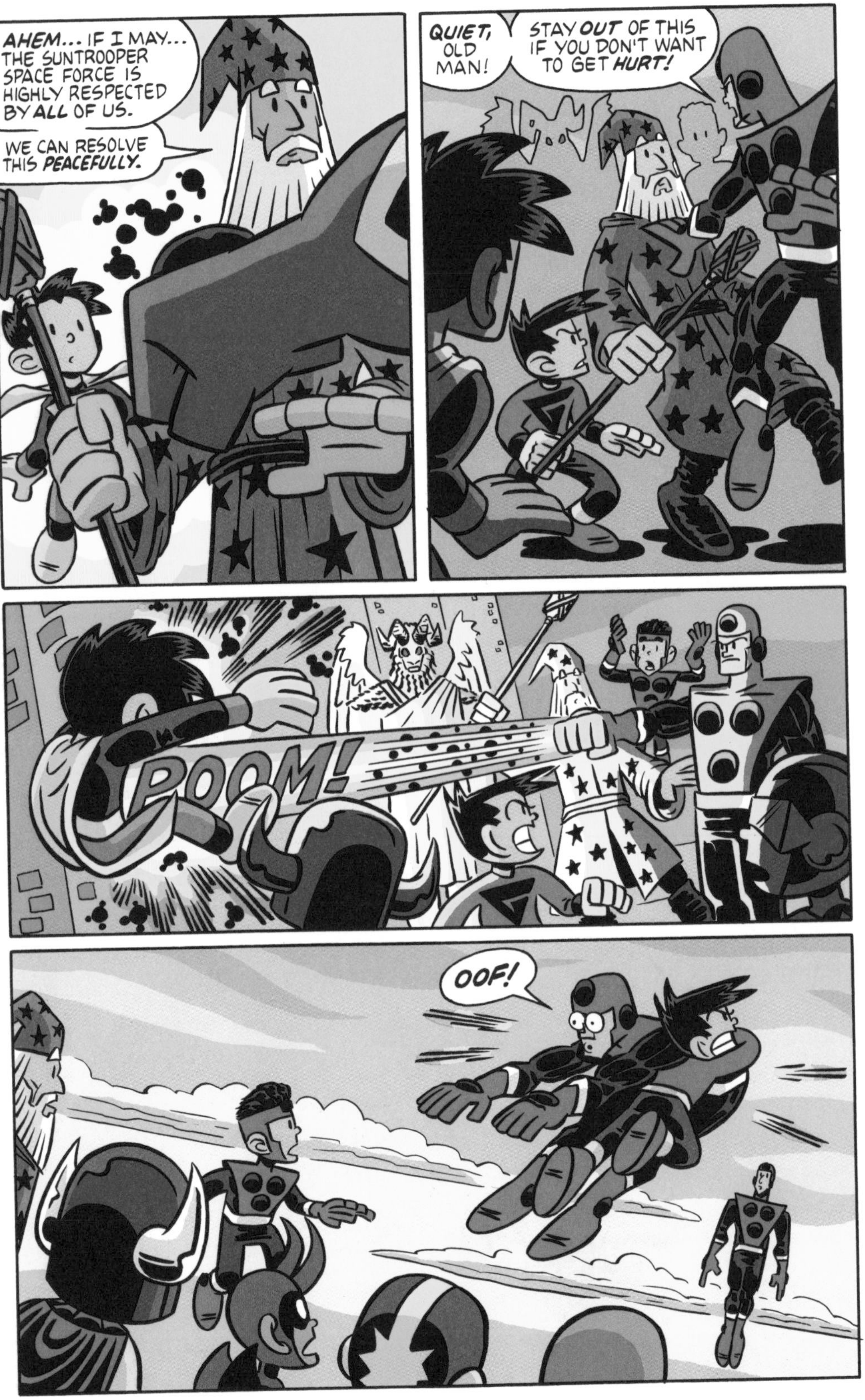
AHEM... IF I MAY... THE SUNTROOPER SPACE FORCE IS HIGHLY RESPECTED BY ALL OF US.
WE CAN RESOLVE THIS PEACEFULLY.
QUIET, OLD MAN!
STAY OUT OF THIS IF YOU DON'T WANT TO GET HURT!
POOM!
OOF!

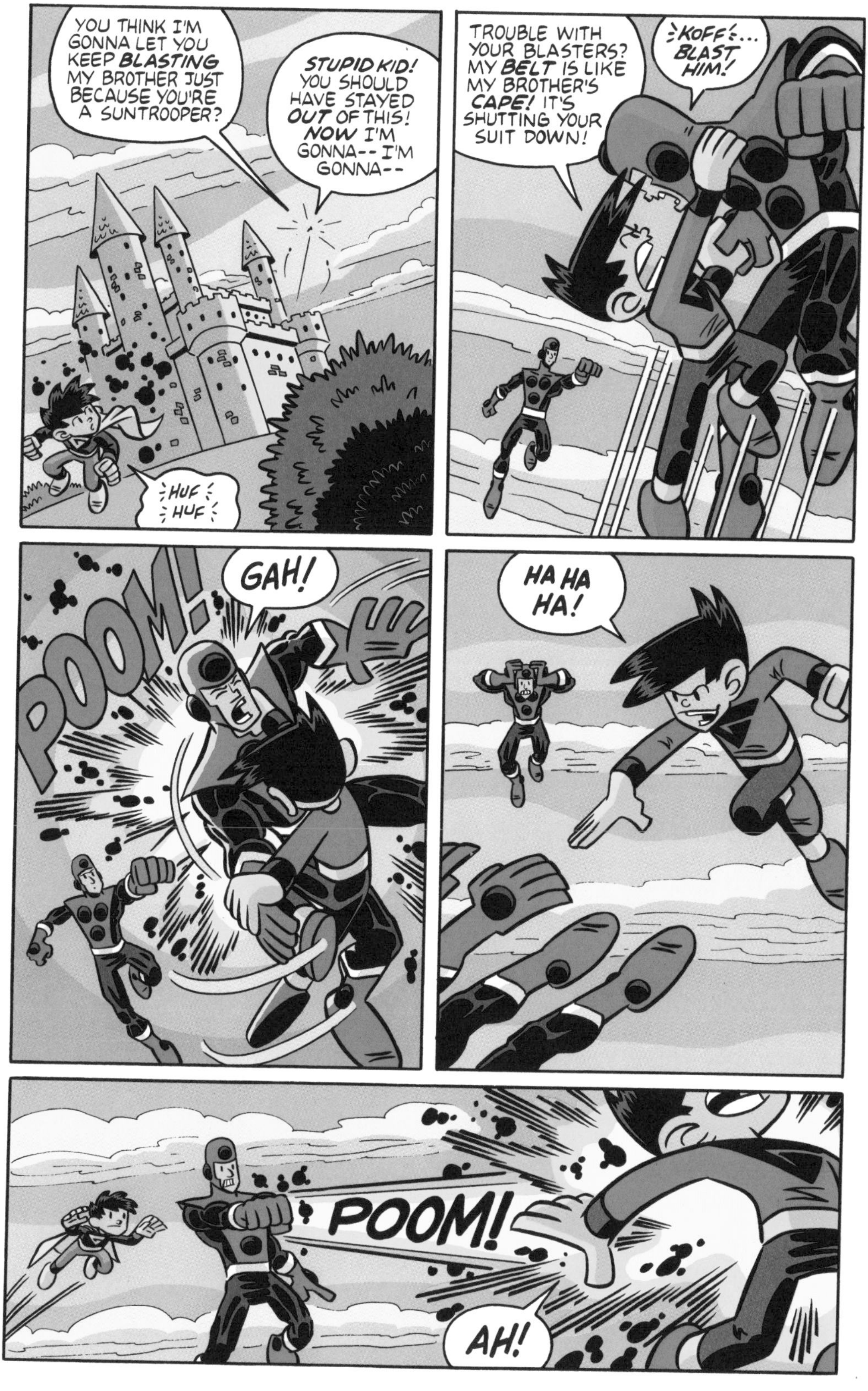
YOU THINK I'M GONNA LET YOU KEEP BLASTING MY BROTHER JUST BECAUSE YOU'RE A SUNTROOPER?
STUPID KID! YOU SHOULD HAVE STAYED OUT OF THIS! NOW I'M GONNA-- I'M GONNA--
HUF HUF
TROUBLE WITH YOUR BLASTERS? MY BELT IS LIKE MY BROTHER'S CAPE! IT'S SHUTTING YOUR SUIT DOWN!
KOFF... BLAST HIM!
POOM!
GAH!
HA HA HA!
POOM!
AH!

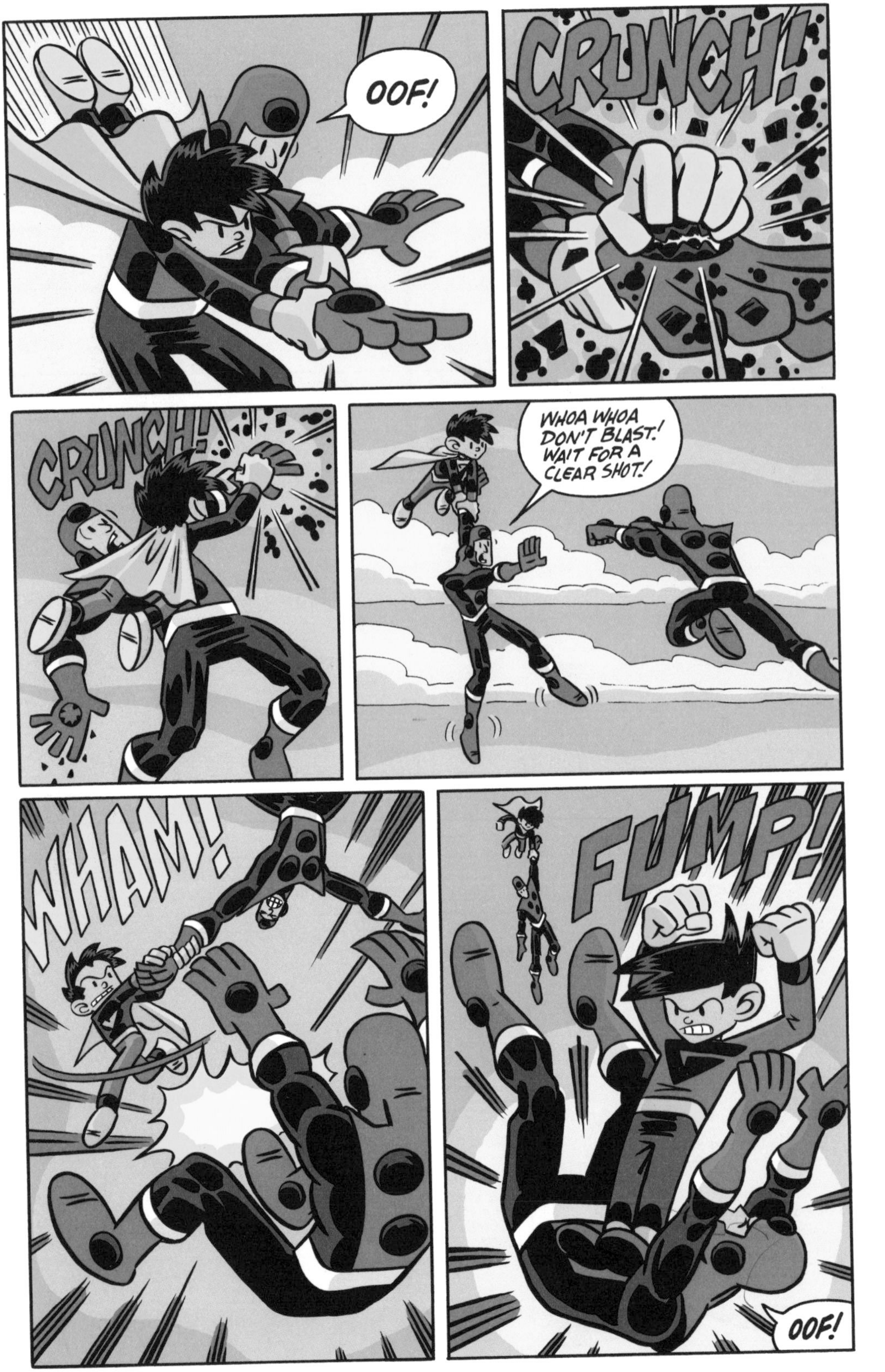
OOF!
CRUNCH!
CRUNCH!
WHOA WHOA DON'T BLAST! WAIT FOR A CLEAR SHOT!
WHAM!
FUMP!
OOF!

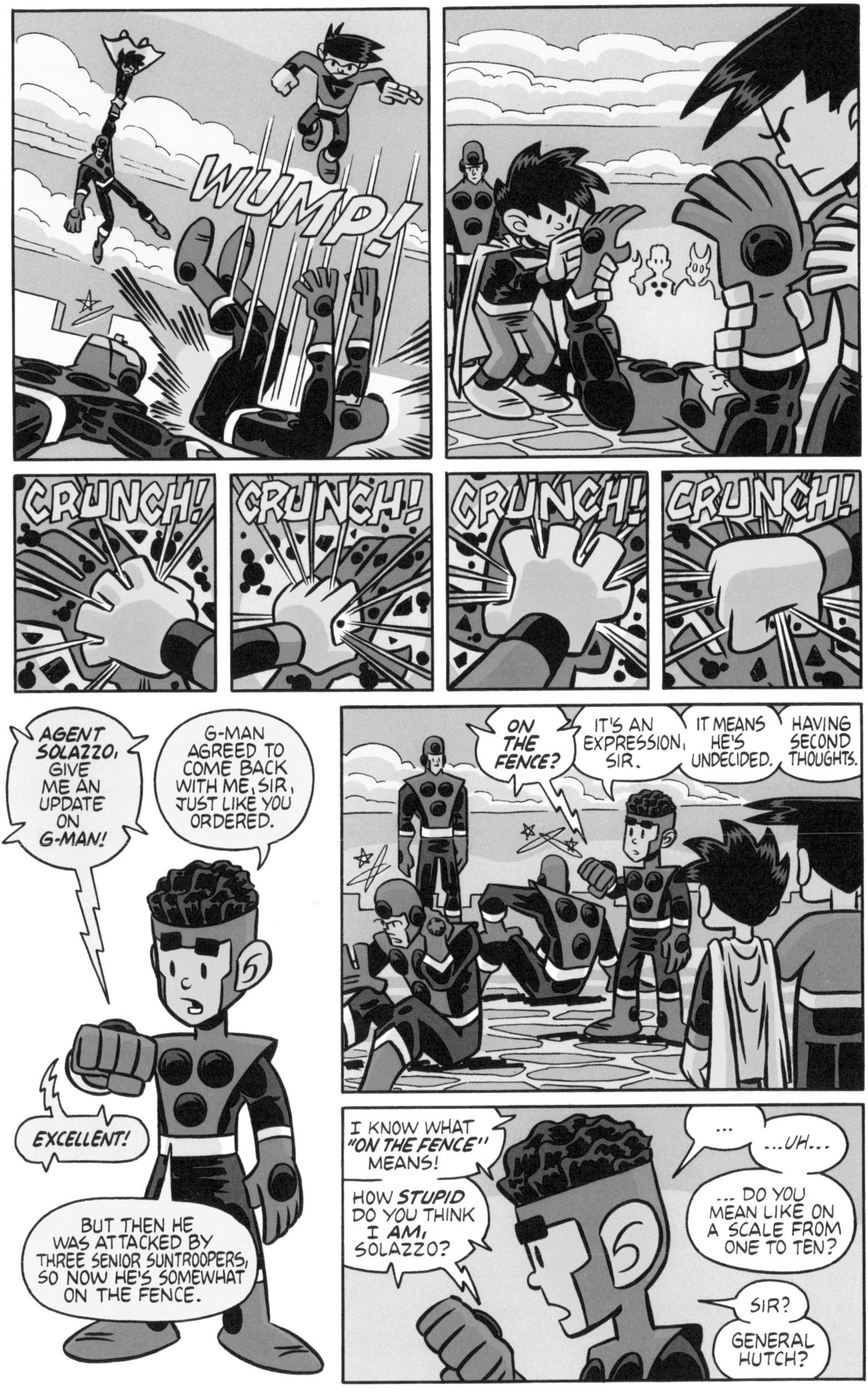
WUMP!
CRUNCH!
CRUNCH!
CRUNCH!
CRUNCH!
AGENT SOLAZZO, GIVE ME AN UPDATE ON G-MAN!
G-MAN AGREED TO COME BACK WITH ME, SIR, JUST LIKE YOU ORDERED.
EXCELLENT!
BUT THEN HE WAS ATTACKED BY THREE SENIOR SUNTROOPERS, SO NOW HE'S SOMEWHAT ON THE FENCE.
ON THE FENCE?
IT'S AN EXPRESSION, SIR.
IT MEANS HE'S UNDECIDED.
HAVING SECOND THOUGHTS.
I KNOW WHAT "ON THE FENCE" MEANS!
HOW STUPID DO YOU THINK I AM, SOLAZZO?
...
...UH...
... DO YOU MEAN LIKE ON A SCALE FROM ONE TO TEN?
SIR?
GENERAL HUTCH?

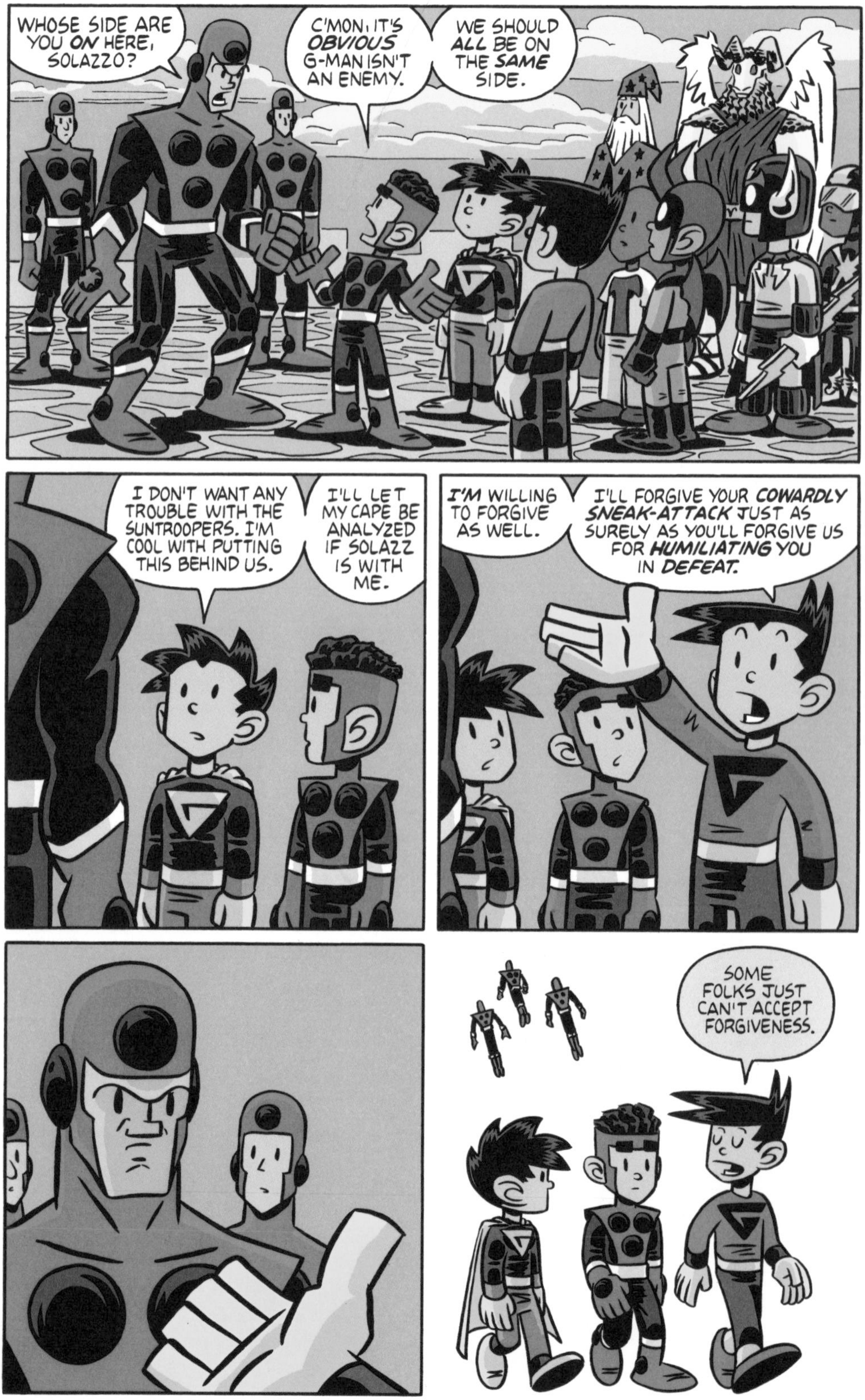
WHOSE SIDE ARE YOU ON HERE, SOLAZZO?
C'MON, IT'S OBVIOUS G-MAN ISN'T AN ENEMY.
WE SHOULD ALL BE ON THE SAME SIDE.
I DON'T WANT ANY TROUBLE WITH THE SUNTROOPERS. I'M COOL WITH PUTTING THIS BEHIND US.
I'LL LET MY CAPE BE ANALYZED IF SOLAZZ IS WITH ME.
I'M WILLING TO FORGIVE AS WELL.
I'LL FORGIVE YOUR COWARDLY SNEAK-ATTACK JUST AS SURELY AS YOU'LL FORGIVE US FOR HUMILIATING YOU IN DEFEAT.
SOME FOLKS JUST CAN'T ACCEPT FORGIVENESS.

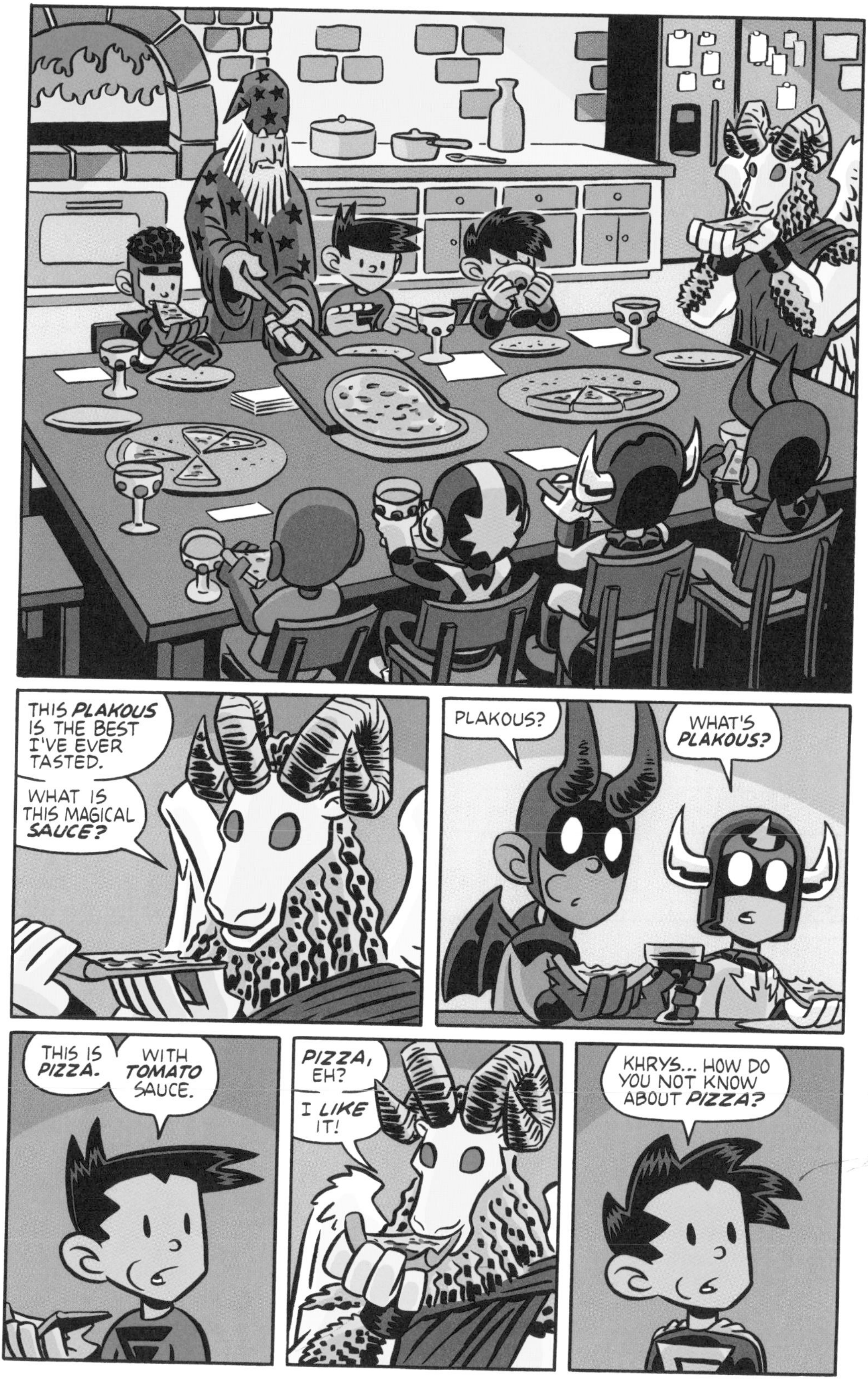
THIS PLAKOUS IS THE BEST I'VE EVER TASTED.
WHAT IS THIS MAGICAL SAUCE?
PLAKOUS?
WHAT'S PLAKOUS?
THIS IS PIZZA.
WITH TOMATO SAUCE.
PIZZA, EH?
I LIKE IT!
KHRYS... HOW DO YOU NOT KNOW ABOUT PIZZA?

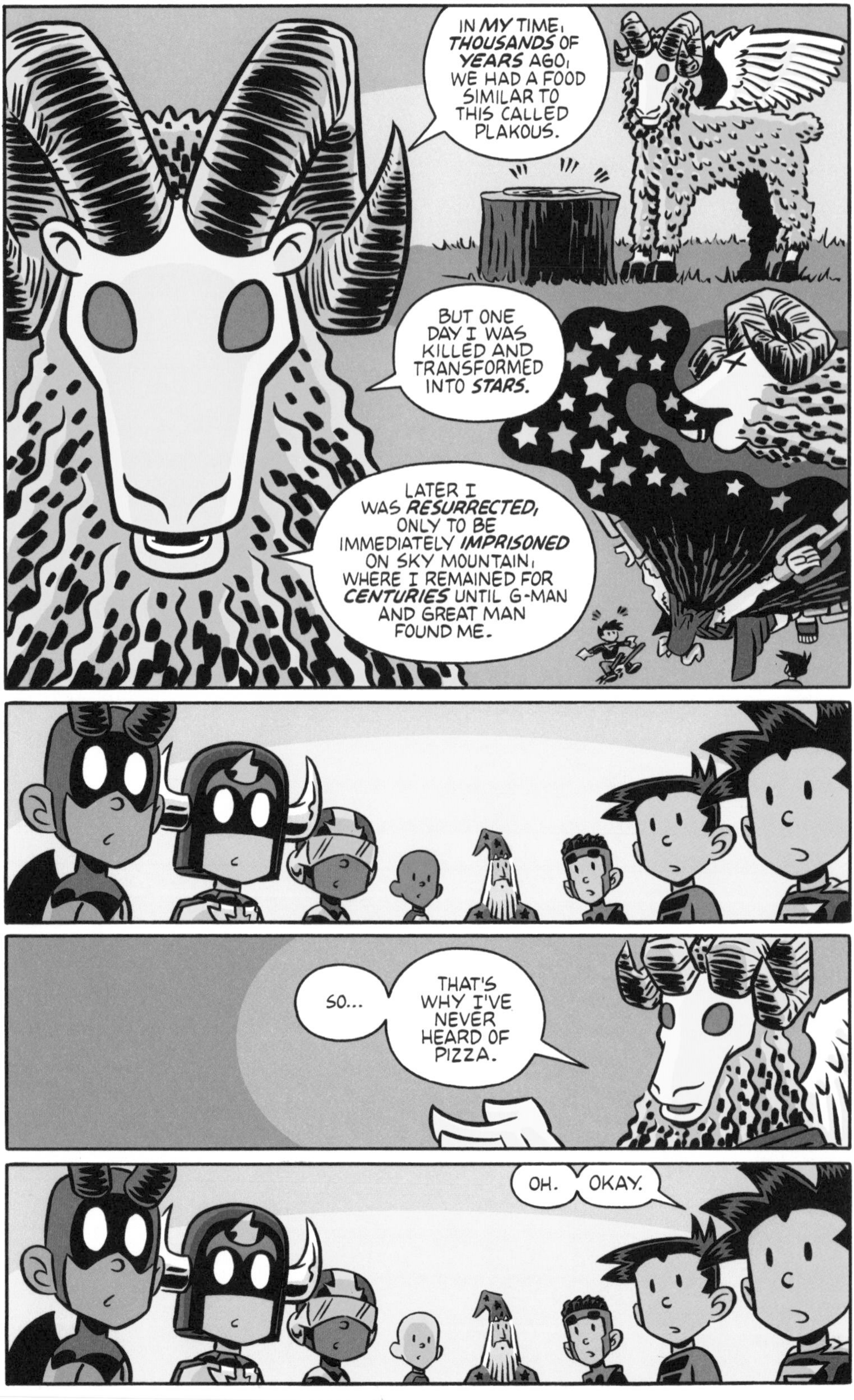
IN MY TIME, THOUSANDS OF YEARS AGO, WE HAD A FOOD SIMILAR TO THIS CALLED PLAKOUS.
BUT ONE DAY I WAS KILLED AND TRANSFORMED INTO STARS.
LATER I WAS RESURRECTED, ONLY TO BE IMMEDIATELY IMPRISONED ON SKY MOUNTAIN, WHERE I REMAINED FOR CENTURIES UNTIL G-MAN AND GREAT MAN FOUND ME.
SO...
THAT'S WHY I'VE NEVER HEARD OF PIZZA.
OH.
OKAY.

WELL, *GLENDOLF'S* PIZZA IS THE *BEST*.

REMEMBER THAT TIME WE ATE LIKE *FIVE* PIZZAS?

REMEMBER THAT TIME GLENN WAS DISQUALIFIED FROM THE PIZZA CONTEST ON SUSPICION OF MAGIC DOUGH?

RE... TIM... ATTAC... AND E... STOOD... WAT...

AW, *C'MON* GREAT MAN, IT WASN'T LIKE *THAT*. EVERYTHING HAPPENED SO *FAST*.

WE'VE ALWAYS BEEN TAUGHT THE SUNTROOPERS ARE AN INVINCIBLE FORCE FOR *GOOD*, WORTHY OF ULTIMATE *RESPECT*. I THINK THAT'S WHY WE ALL HESITATED.

AND *SOLAZZ* WAS TRYING TO TALK SENSE TO THEM. I THOUGHT HE MIGHT SMOOTH IT ALL OUT.

ALSO, IT WAS *OBVIOUS* YOU DIDN'T NEED ANY HELP ONCE THE FIGHTING BEGAN.

I'M SORRY I COULDN'T STOP IT, BUT I'M PRETTY SURE THIS ISN'T OVER.

THEY'RE GOING TO COME AFTER YOU AGAIN.

FINE WITH *US*!

I HOPE THEY BRING THE *ENTIRE SUNTROOPER SPACE FORCE*!

MIKEY AND I WILL SEND THEM RIGHT *BACK* WHERE THEY *CAME FROM*!

YEAH, UH...

I HOPE IT'S JUST THREE GUYS AGAIN.

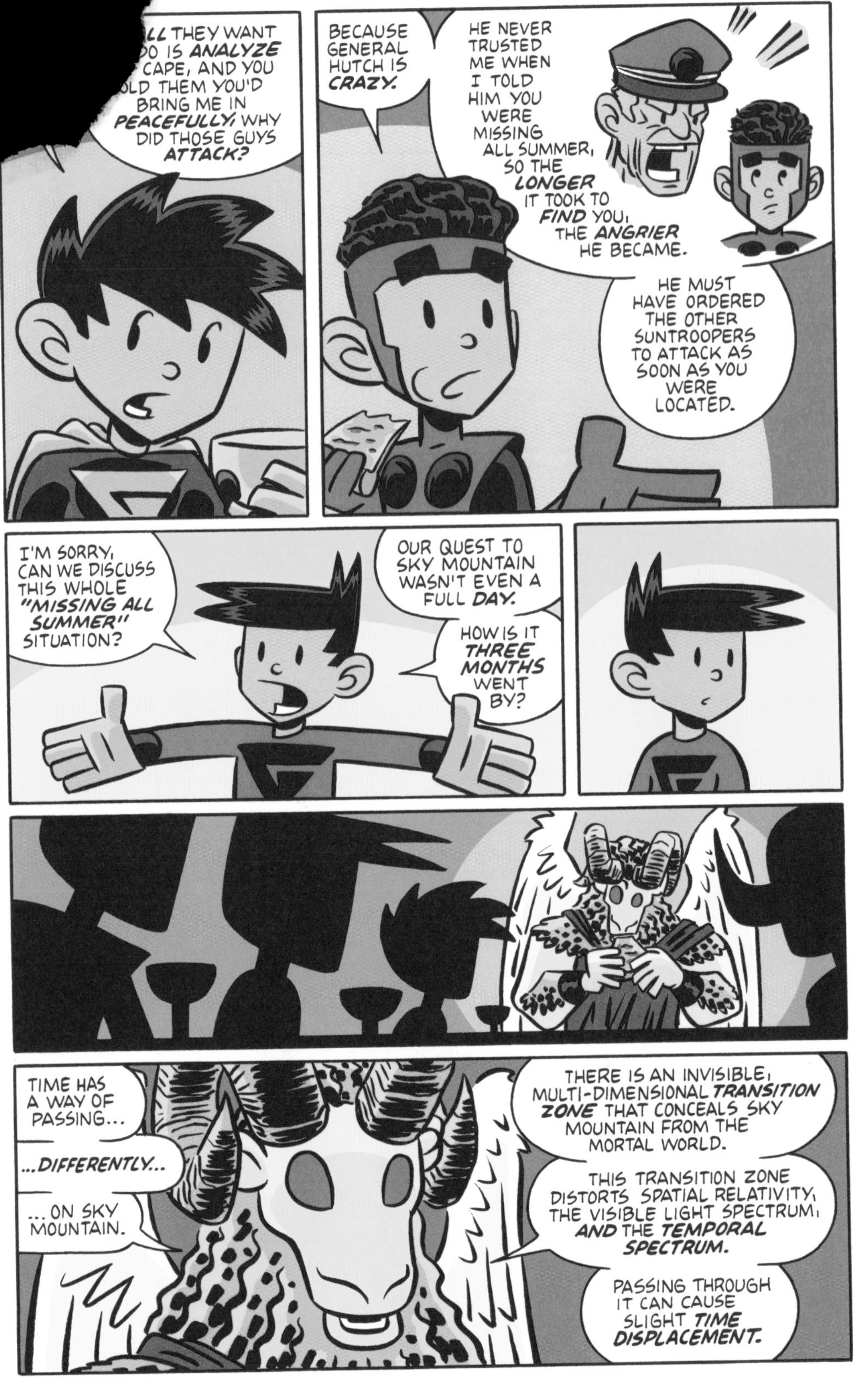
THEY WANT IS ANALYZE CAPE, AND YOU THEM YOU'D BRING ME IN PEACEFULLY, WHY DID THOSE GUYS ATTACK?
BECAUSE GENERAL HUTCH IS CRAZY.
HE NEVER TRUSTED ME WHEN I TOLD HIM YOU WERE MISSING ALL SUMMER, SO THE LONGER IT TOOK TO FIND YOU, THE ANGRIER HE BECAME.
HE MUST HAVE ORDERED THE OTHER SUNTROOPERS TO ATTACK AS SOON AS YOU WERE LOCATED.
I'M SORRY, CAN WE DISCUSS THIS WHOLE "MISSING ALL SUMMER" SITUATION?
OUR QUEST TO SKY MOUNTAIN WASN'T EVEN A FULL DAY.
HOW IS IT THREE MONTHS WENT BY?
TIME HAS A WAY OF PASSING...
...DIFFERENTLY...
...ON SKY MOUNTAIN.
THERE IS AN INVISIBLE, MULTI-DIMENSIONAL TRANSITION ZONE THAT CONCEALS SKY MOUNTAIN FROM THE MORTAL WORLD.
THIS TRANSITION ZONE DISTORTS SPATIAL RELATIVITY, THE VISIBLE LIGHT SPECTRUM, AND THE TEMPORAL SPECTRUM.
PASSING THROUGH IT CAN CAUSE SLIGHT TIME DISPLACEMENT.

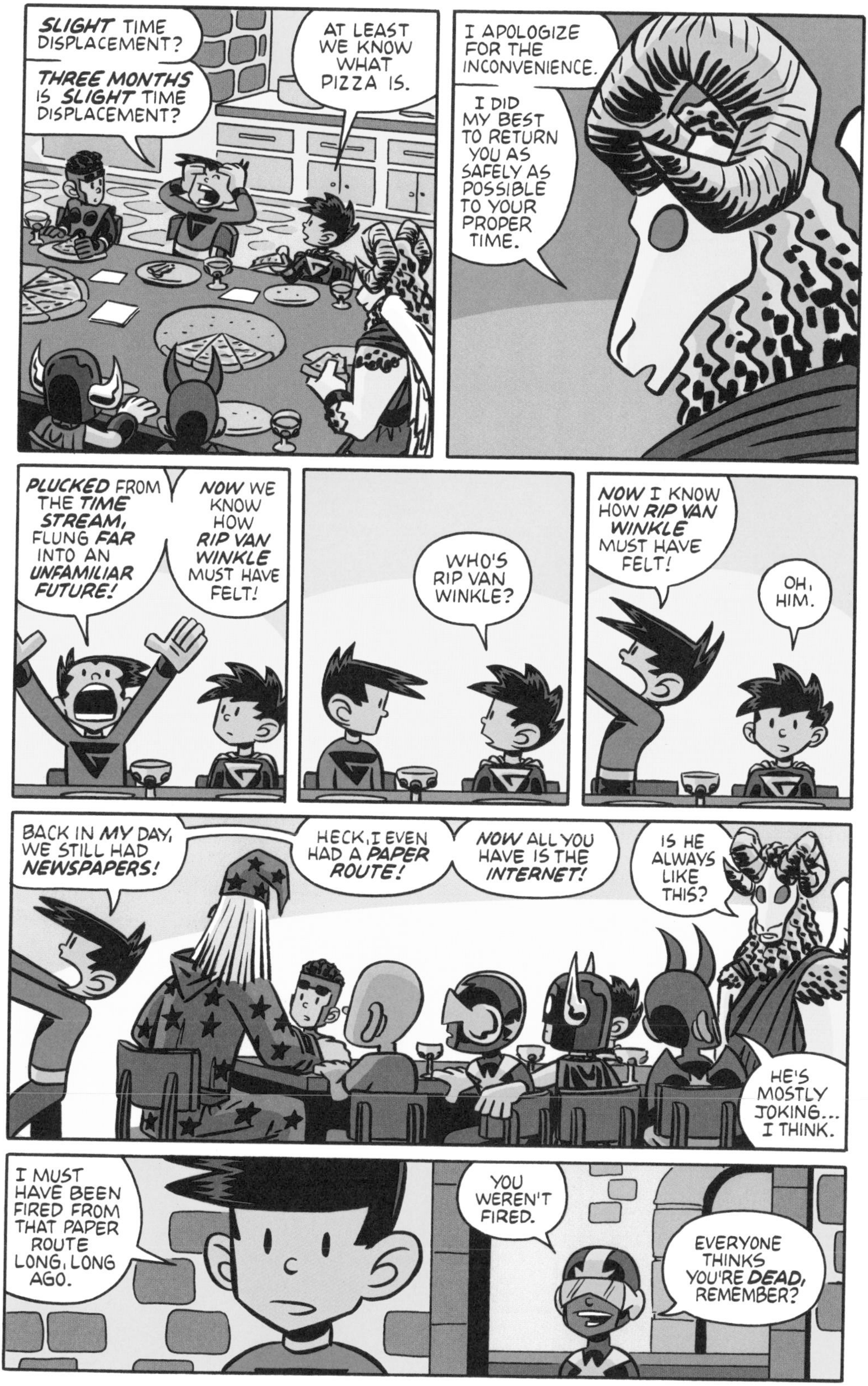
SLIGHT TIME DISPLACEMENT?
THREE MONTHS IS SLIGHT TIME DISPLACEMENT?
AT LEAST WE KNOW WHAT PIZZA IS.
I APOLOGIZE FOR THE INCONVENIENCE.
I DID MY BEST TO RETURN YOU AS SAFELY AS POSSIBLE TO YOUR PROPER TIME.
PLUCKED FROM THE TIME STREAM, FLUNG FAR INTO AN UNFAMILIAR FUTURE!
NOW WE KNOW HOW RIP VAN WINKLE MUST HAVE FELT!
WHO'S RIP VAN WINKLE?
NOW I KNOW HOW RIP VAN WINKLE MUST HAVE FELT!
OH, HIM.
BACK IN MY DAY, WE STILL HAD NEWSPAPERS!
HECK, I EVEN HAD A PAPER ROUTE!
NOW ALL YOU HAVE IS THE INTERNET!
IS HE ALWAYS LIKE THIS?
HE'S MOSTLY JOKING... I THINK.
I MUST HAVE BEEN FIRED FROM THAT PAPER ROUTE LONG, LONG AGO.
YOU WEREN'T FIRED.
EVERYONE THINKS YOU'RE DEAD, REMEMBER?

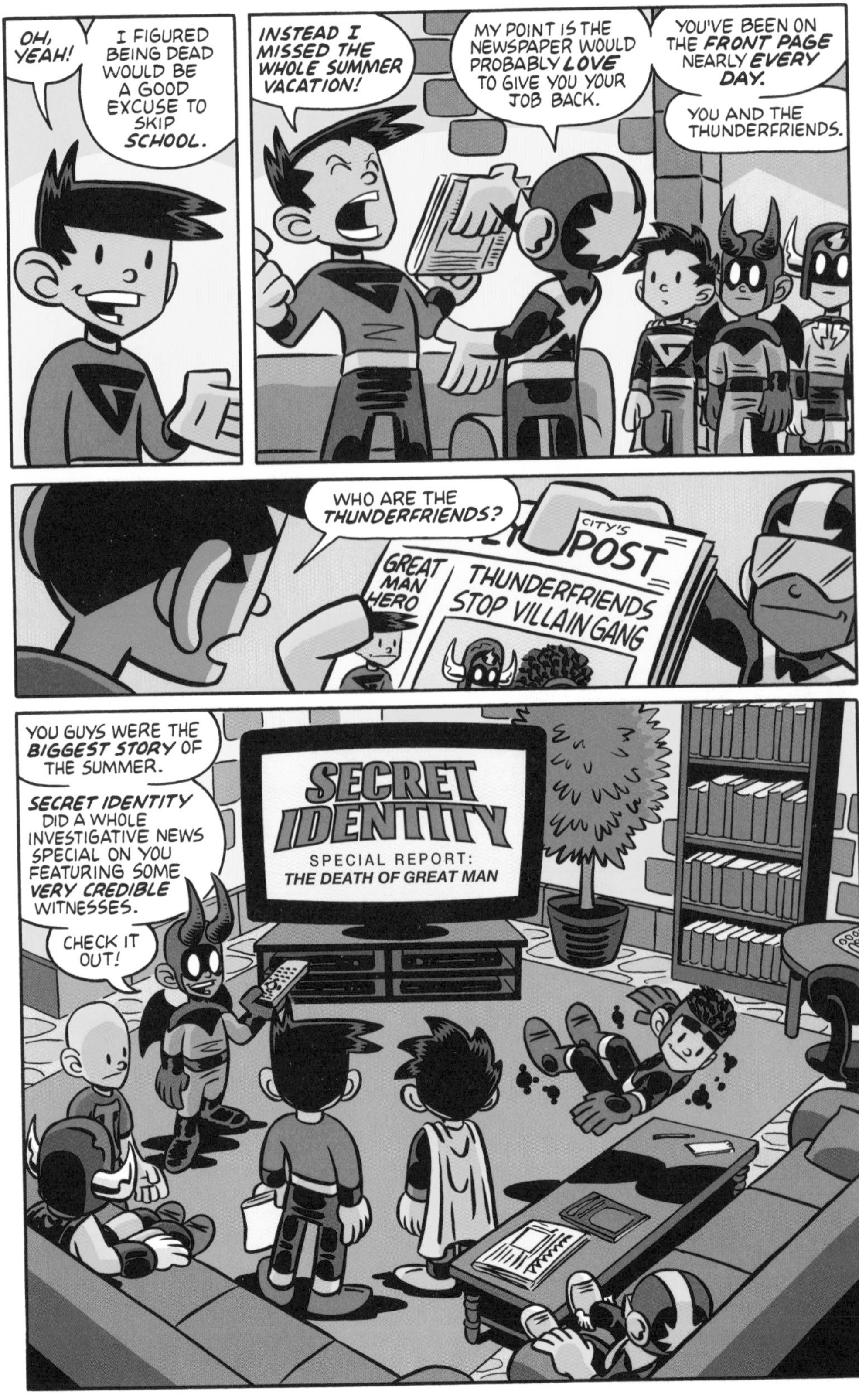
OH, YEAH!
I FIGURED BEING DEAD WOULD BE A GOOD EXCUSE TO SKIP SCHOOL.
INSTEAD I MISSED THE WHOLE SUMMER VACATION!
MY POINT IS THE NEWSPAPER WOULD PROBABLY LOVE TO GIVE YOU YOUR JOB BACK.
YOU'VE BEEN ON THE FRONT PAGE NEARLY EVERY DAY.
YOU AND THE THUNDERFRIENDS.
WHO ARE THE THUNDERFRIENDS?
CITY'S POST
GREAT MAN HERO
THUNDERFRIENDS STOP VILLAIN GANG
YOU GUYS WERE THE BIGGEST STORY OF THE SUMMER.
SECRET IDENTITY DID A WHOLE INVESTIGATIVE NEWS SPECIAL ON YOU FEATURING SOME VERY CREDIBLE WITNESSES.
CHECK IT OUT!
SECRET IDENTITY
SPECIAL REPORT:
THE DEATH OF GREAT MAN

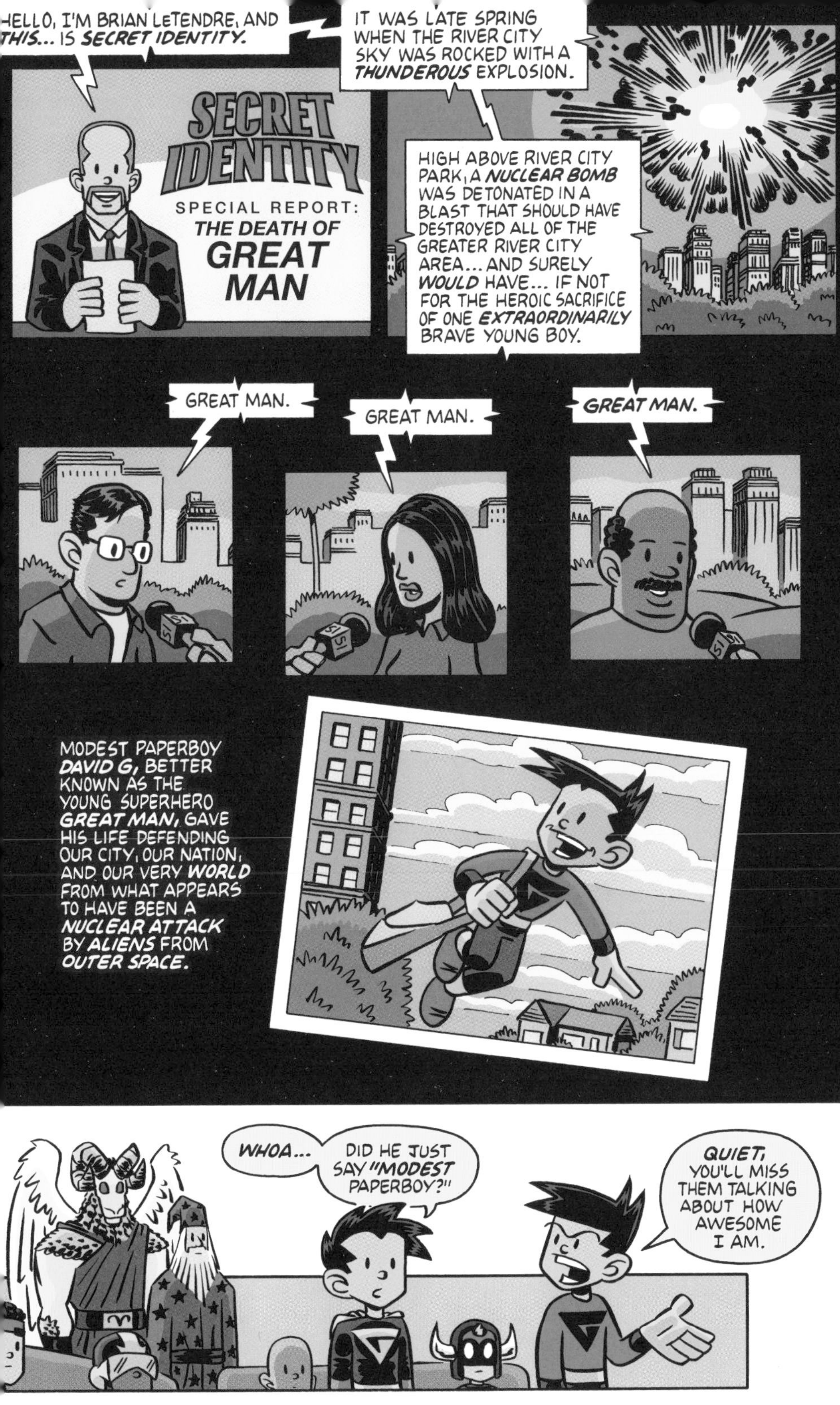
HELLO, I'M BRIAN LETENDRE, AND THIS... IS SECRET IDENTITY.
SECRET IDENTITY
SPECIAL REPORT: THE DEATH OF GREAT MAN
IT WAS LATE SPRING WHEN THE RIVER CITY SKY WAS ROCKED WITH A THUNDEROUS EXPLOSION.
HIGH ABOVE RIVER CITY PARK, A NUCLEAR BOMB WAS DETONATED IN A BLAST THAT SHOULD HAVE DESTROYED ALL OF THE GREATER RIVER CITY AREA... AND SURELY WOULD HAVE... IF NOT FOR THE HEROIC SACRIFICE OF ONE EXTRAORDINARILY BRAVE YOUNG BOY.
GREAT MAN.
GREAT MAN.
GREAT MAN.
MODEST PAPERBOY DAVID G, BETTER KNOWN AS THE YOUNG SUPERHERO GREAT MAN, GAVE HIS LIFE DEFENDING OUR CITY, OUR NATION, AND OUR VERY WORLD FROM WHAT APPEARS TO HAVE BEEN A NUCLEAR ATTACK BY ALIENS FROM OUTER SPACE.
WHOA...
DID HE JUST SAY "MODEST PAPERBOY?"
QUIET, YOU'LL MISS THEM TALKING ABOUT HOW AWESOME I AM.

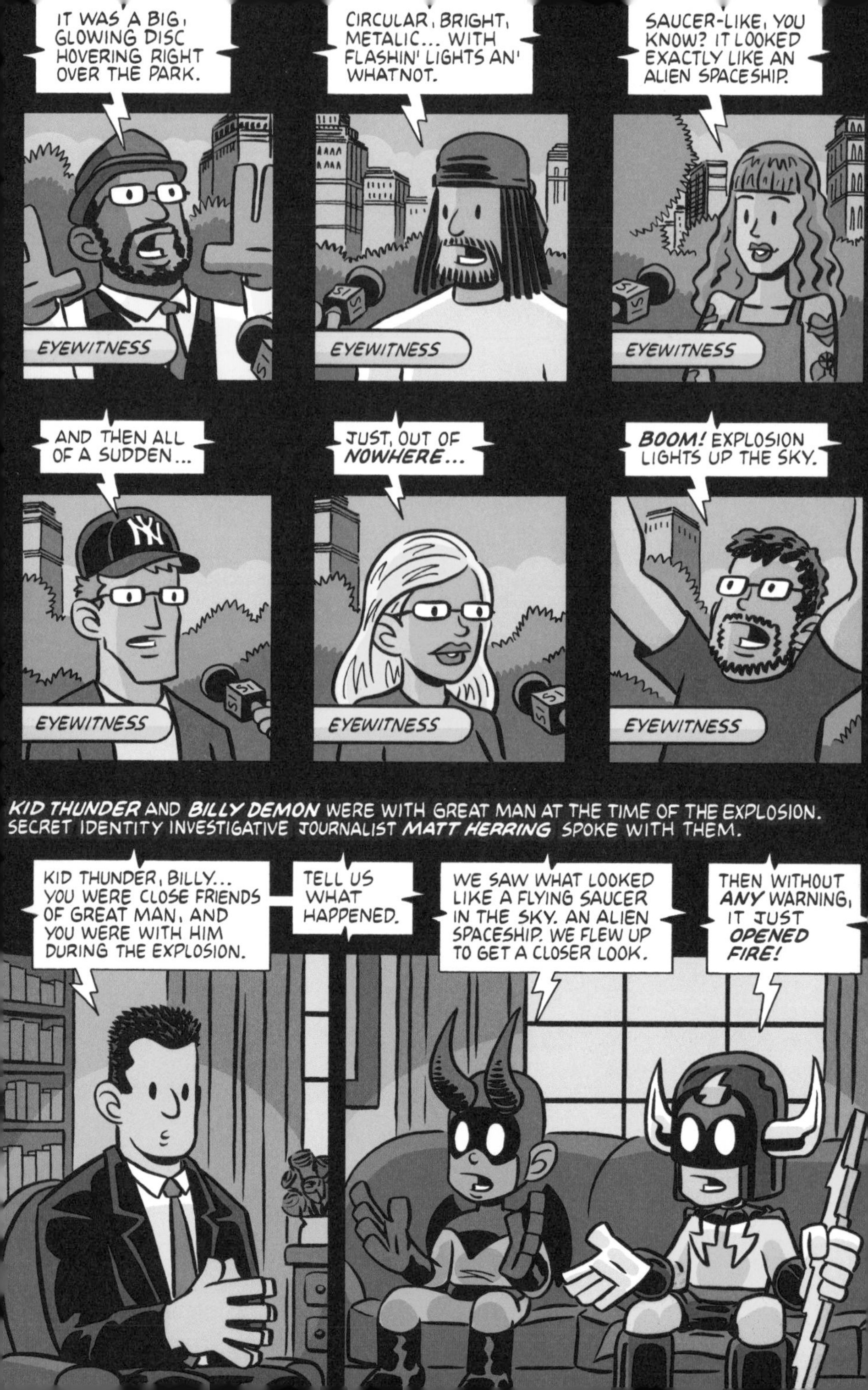
IT WAS A BIG, GLOWING DISC HOVERING RIGHT OVER THE PARK.
EYEWITNESS
CIRCULAR, BRIGHT, METALIC... WITH FLASHIN' LIGHTS AN' WHATNOT.
EYEWITNESS
SAUCER-LIKE, YOU KNOW? IT LOOKED EXACTLY LIKE AN ALIEN SPACESHIP.
EYEWITNESS
AND THEN ALL OF A SUDDEN...
EYEWITNESS
JUST, OUT OF NOWHERE...
EYEWITNESS
BOOM! EXPLOSION LIGHTS UP THE SKY.
EYEWITNESS
KID THUNDER AND BILLY DEMON WERE WITH GREAT MAN AT THE TIME OF THE EXPLOSION. SECRET IDENTITY INVESTIGATIVE JOURNALIST MATT HERRING SPOKE WITH THEM.
KID THUNDER, BILLY... YOU WERE CLOSE FRIENDS OF GREAT MAN, AND YOU WERE WITH HIM DURING THE EXPLOSION.
TELL US WHAT HAPPENED.
WE SAW WHAT LOOKED LIKE A FLYING SAUCER IN THE SKY. AN ALIEN SPACESHIP. WE FLEW UP TO GET A CLOSER LOOK.
THEN WITHOUT ANY WARNING, IT JUST OPENED FIRE!

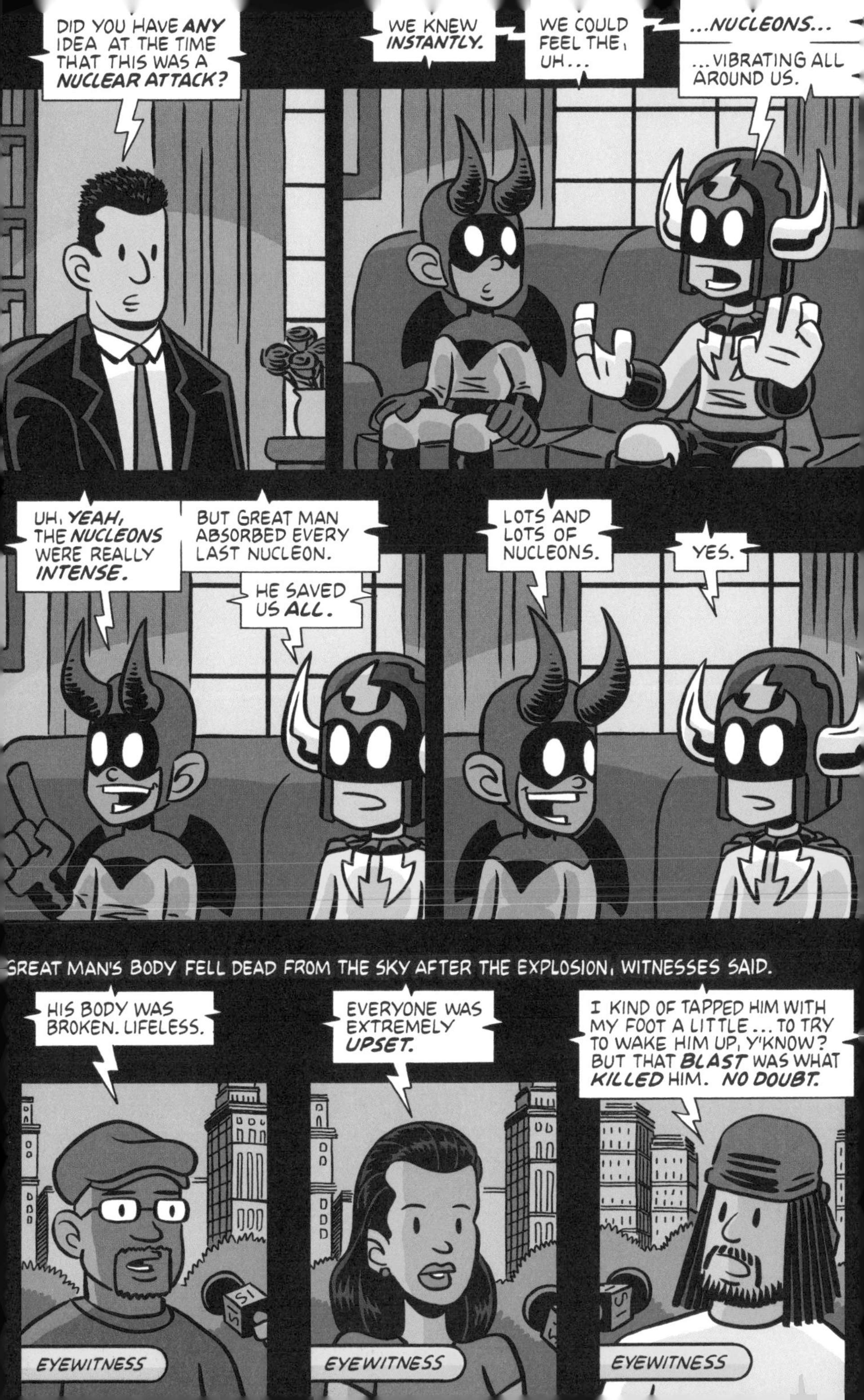
DID YOU HAVE ANY IDEA AT THE TIME THAT THIS WAS A NUCLEAR ATTACK?
WE KNEW INSTANTLY.
WE COULD FEEL THE, UH...
...NUCLEONS...
...VIBRATING ALL AROUND US.
UH, YEAH, THE NUCLEONS WERE REALLY INTENSE.
BUT GREAT MAN ABSORBED EVERY LAST NUCLEON.
HE SAVED US ALL.
LOTS AND LOTS OF NUCLEONS.
YES.
GREAT MAN'S BODY FELL DEAD FROM THE SKY AFTER THE EXPLOSION, WITNESSES SAID.
HIS BODY WAS BROKEN. LIFELESS.
EYEWITNESS
EVERYONE WAS EXTREMELY UPSET.
EYEWITNESS
I KIND OF TAPPED HIM WITH MY FOOT A LITTLE... TO TRY TO WAKE HIM UP, Y'KNOW? BUT THAT BLAST WAS WHAT KILLED HIM. NO DOUBT.
EYEWITNESS

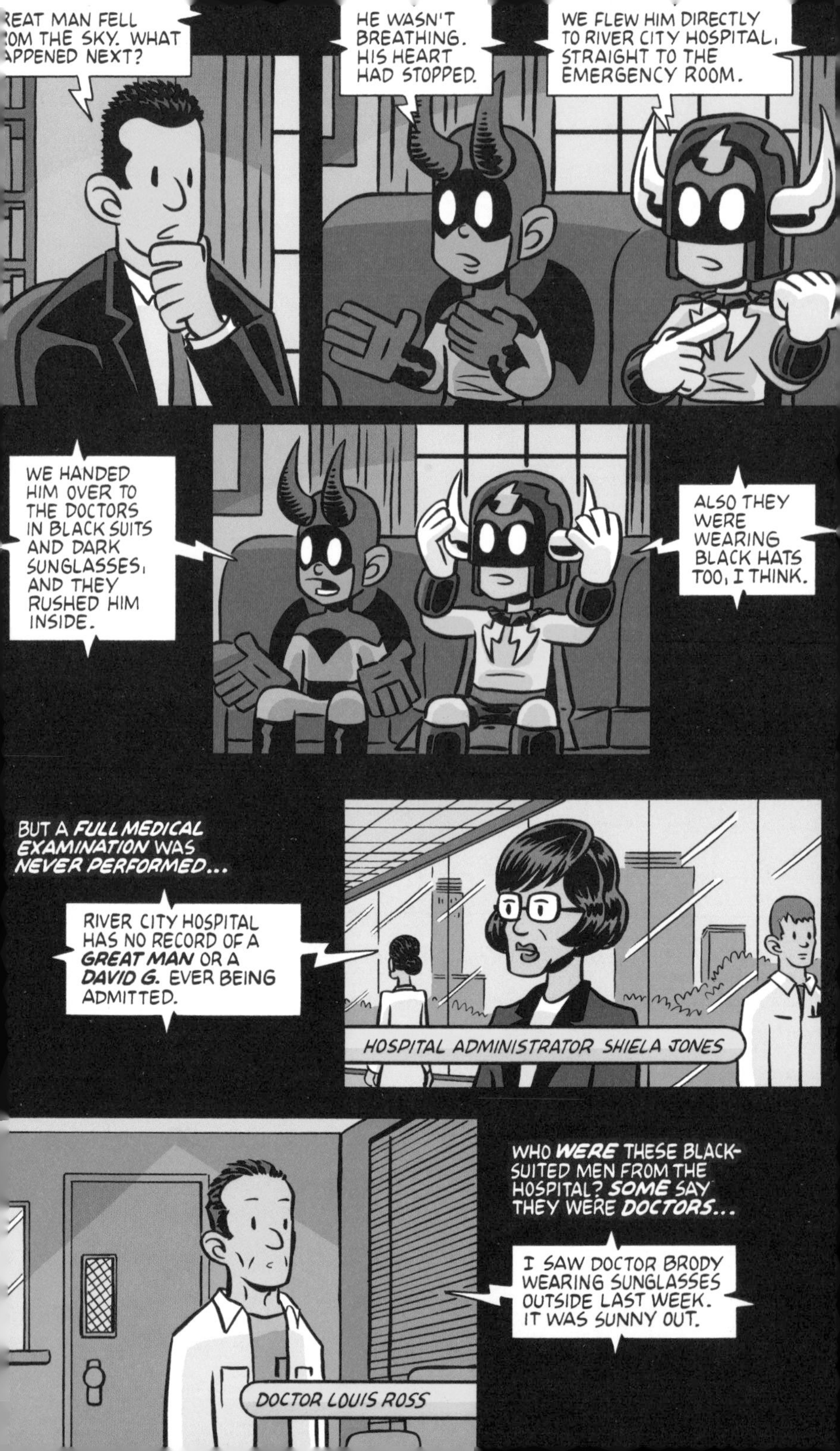

REAT MAN FELL
ROM THE SKY. WHAT
APPENED NEXT?
HE WASN'T BREATHING. HIS HEART HAD STOPPED.
WE FLEW HIM DIRECTLY TO RIVER CITY HOSPITAL, STRAIGHT TO THE EMERGENCY ROOM.
WE HANDED HIM OVER TO THE DOCTORS IN BLACK SUITS AND DARK SUNGLASSES, AND THEY RUSHED HIM INSIDE.
ALSO THEY WERE WEARING BLACK HATS TOO, I THINK.
BUT A FULL MEDICAL EXAMINATION WAS NEVER PERFORMED...
RIVER CITY HOSPITAL HAS NO RECORD OF A GREAT MAN OR A DAVID G. EVER BEING ADMITTED.
HOSPITAL ADMINISTRATOR SHIELA JONES
WHO WERE THESE BLACK-SUITED MEN FROM THE HOSPITAL? SOME SAY THEY WERE DOCTORS...
I SAW DOCTOR BRODY WEARING SUNGLASSES OUTSIDE LAST WEEK. IT WAS SUNNY OUT.
DOCTOR LOUIS ROSS

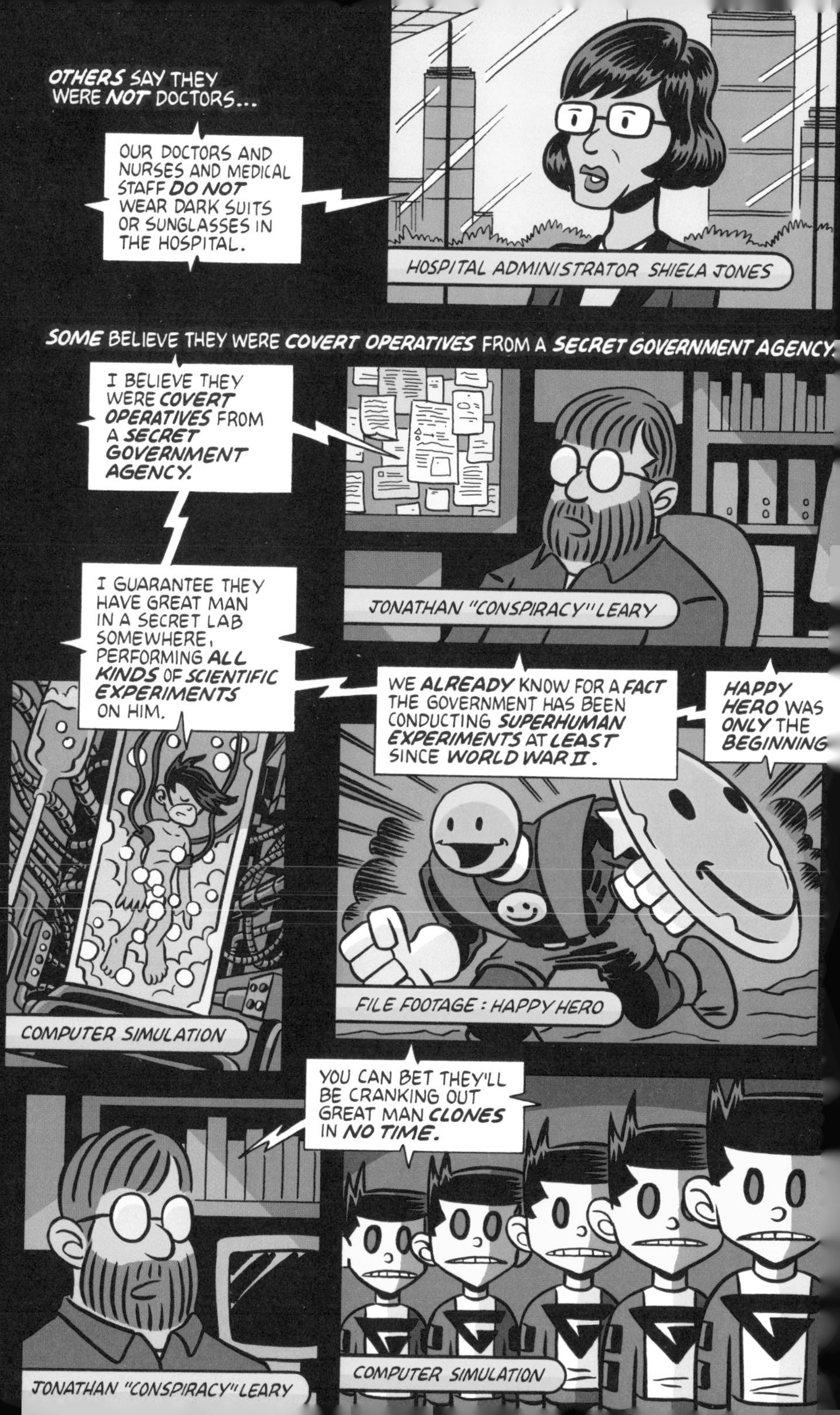
OTHERS SAY THEY WERE NOT DOCTORS...
OUR DOCTORS AND NURSES AND MEDICAL STAFF DO NOT WEAR DARK SUITS OR SUNGLASSES IN THE HOSPITAL.
HOSPITAL ADMINISTRATOR SHIELA JONES
SOME BELIEVE THEY WERE COVERT OPERATIVES FROM A SECRET GOVERNMENT AGENCY.
I BELIEVE THEY WERE COVERT OPERATIVES FROM A SECRET GOVERNMENT AGENCY.
JONATHAN "CONSPIRACY" LEARY
I GUARANTEE THEY HAVE GREAT MAN IN A SECRET LAB SOMEWHERE, PERFORMING ALL KINDS OF SCIENTIFIC EXPERIMENTS ON HIM.
COMPUTER SIMULATION
WE ALREADY KNOW FOR A FACT THE GOVERNMENT HAS BEEN CONDUCTING SUPERHUMAN EXPERIMENTS AT LEAST SINCE WORLD WAR II.
HAPPY HERO WAS ONLY THE BEGINNING
FILE FOOTAGE : HAPPY HERO
YOU CAN BET THEY'LL BE CRANKING OUT GREAT MAN CLONES IN NO TIME.
JONATHAN "CONSPIRACY" LEARY
COMPUTER SIMULATION

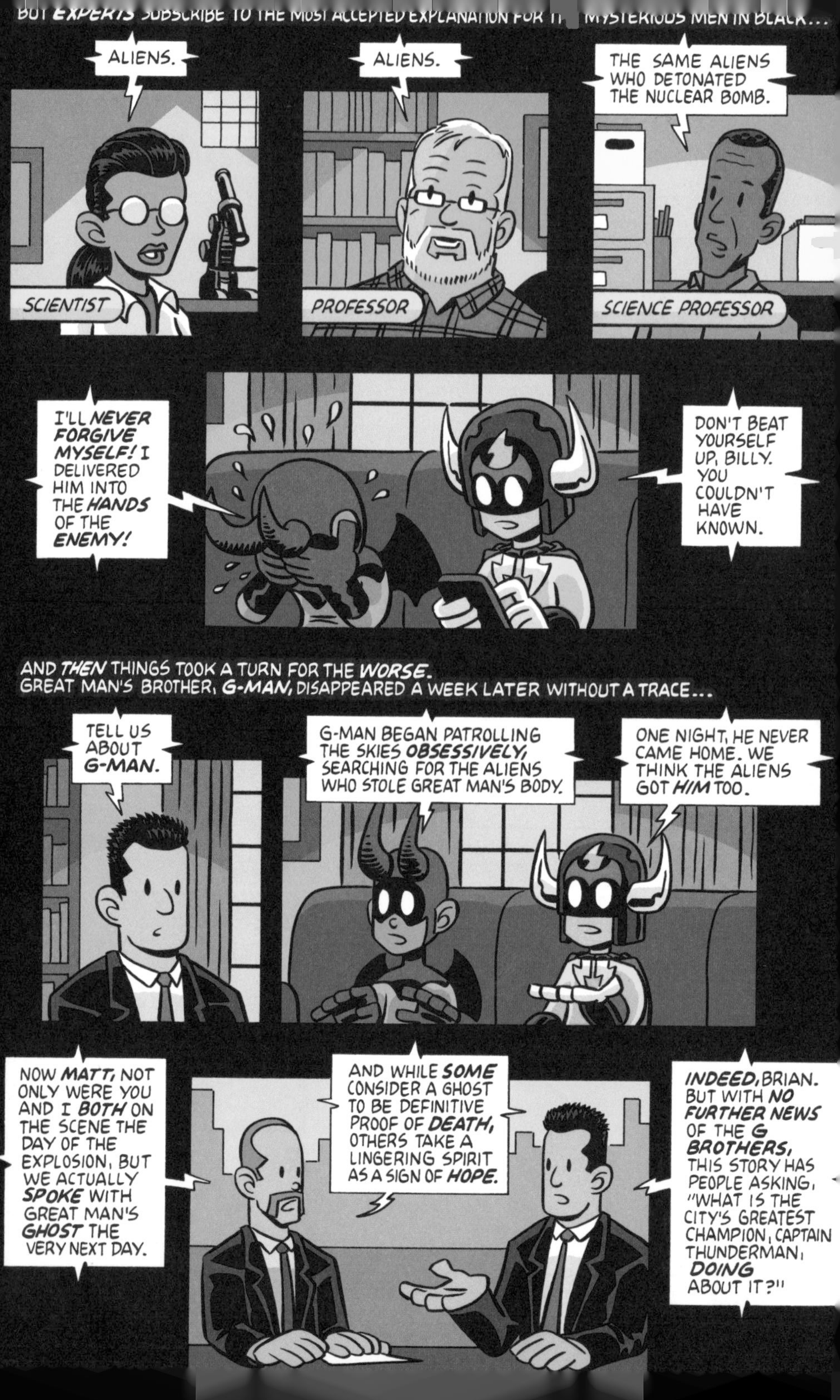
BUT EXPERTS SUBSCRIBE TO THE MOST ACCEPTED EXPLANATION FOR THE MYSTERIOUS MEN IN BLACK...
ALIENS.
SCIENTIST
ALIENS.
PROFESSOR
THE SAME ALIENS WHO DETONATED THE NUCLEAR BOMB.
SCIENCE PROFESSOR
I'LL NEVER FORGIVE MYSELF! I DELIVERED HIM INTO THE HANDS OF THE ENEMY!
DON'T BEAT YOURSELF UP, BILLY. YOU COULDN'T HAVE KNOWN.
AND THEN THINGS TOOK A TURN FOR THE WORSE.
GREAT MAN'S BROTHER, G-MAN, DISAPPEARED A WEEK LATER WITHOUT A TRACE...
TELL US ABOUT G-MAN.
G-MAN BEGAN PATROLLING THE SKIES OBSESSIVELY, SEARCHING FOR THE ALIENS WHO STOLE GREAT MAN'S BODY.
ONE NIGHT, HE NEVER CAME HOME. WE THINK THE ALIENS GOT HIM TOO.
NOW MATT, NOT ONLY WERE YOU AND I BOTH ON THE SCENE THE DAY OF THE EXPLOSION, BUT WE ACTUALLY SPOKE WITH GREAT MAN'S GHOST THE VERY NEXT DAY.
AND WHILE SOME CONSIDER A GHOST TO BE DEFINITIVE PROOF OF DEATH, OTHERS TAKE A LINGERING SPIRIT AS A SIGN OF HOPE.
INDEED, BRIAN. BUT WITH NO FURTHER NEWS OF THE G BROTHERS, THIS STORY HAS PEOPLE ASKING, "WHAT IS THE CITY'S GREATEST CHAMPION, CAPTAIN THUNDERMAN, DOING ABOUT IT?"

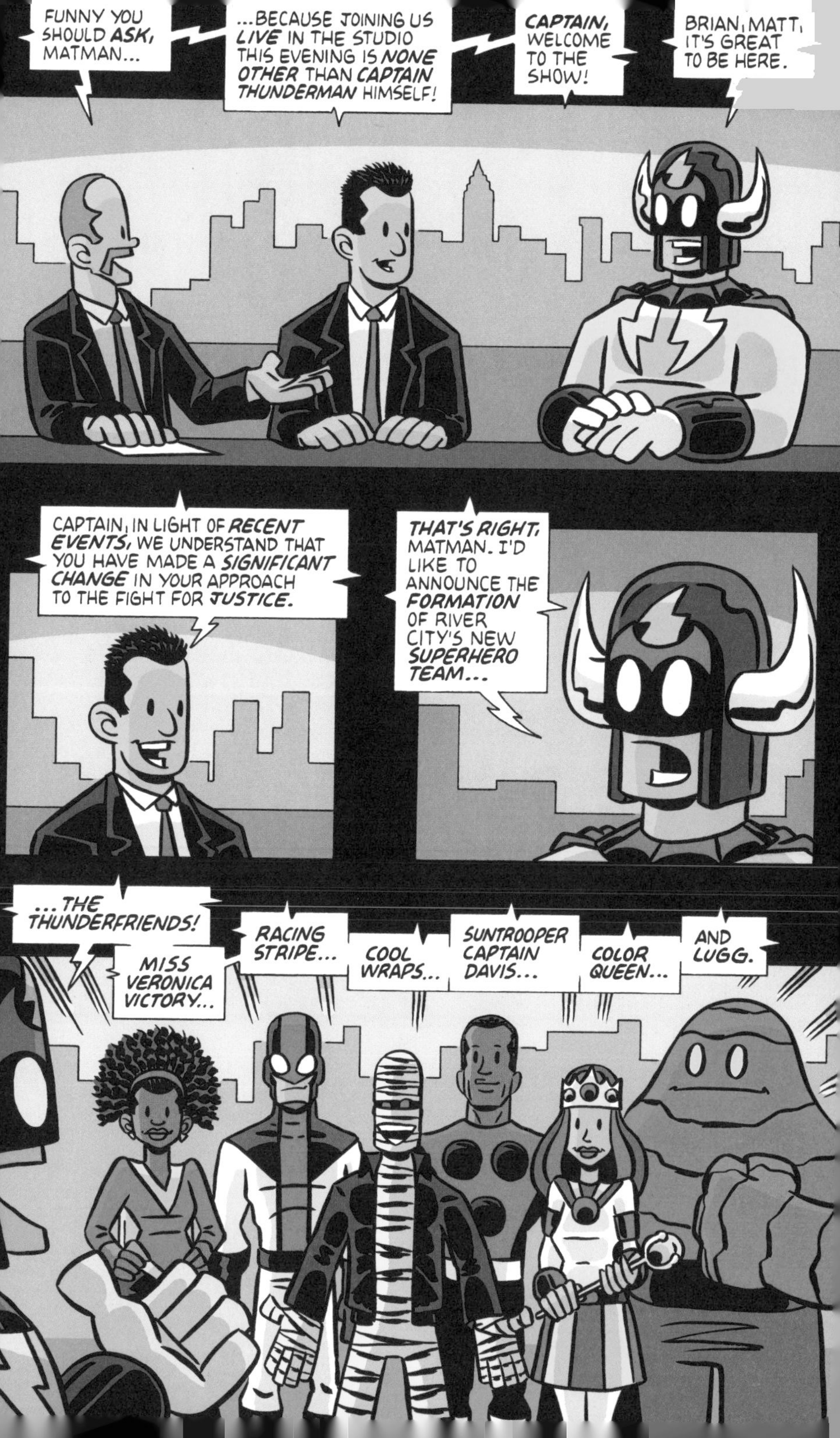
FUNNY YOU SHOULD ASK, MATMAN...
...BECAUSE JOINING US LIVE IN THE STUDIO THIS EVENING IS NONE OTHER THAN CAPTAIN THUNDERMAN HIMSELF!
CAPTAIN, WELCOME TO THE SHOW!
BRIAN, MATT, IT'S GREAT TO BE HERE.
CAPTAIN, IN LIGHT OF RECENT EVENTS, WE UNDERSTAND THAT YOU HAVE MADE A SIGNIFICANT CHANGE IN YOUR APPROACH TO THE FIGHT FOR JUSTICE.
THAT'S RIGHT, MATMAN. I'D LIKE TO ANNOUNCE THE FORMATION OF RIVER CITY'S NEW SUPERHERO TEAM...
...THE THUNDERFRIENDS!
MISS VERONICA VICTORY...
RACING STRIPE...
COOL WRAPS...
SUNTROOPER CAPTAIN DAVIS...
COLOR QUEEN...
AND LUGG.

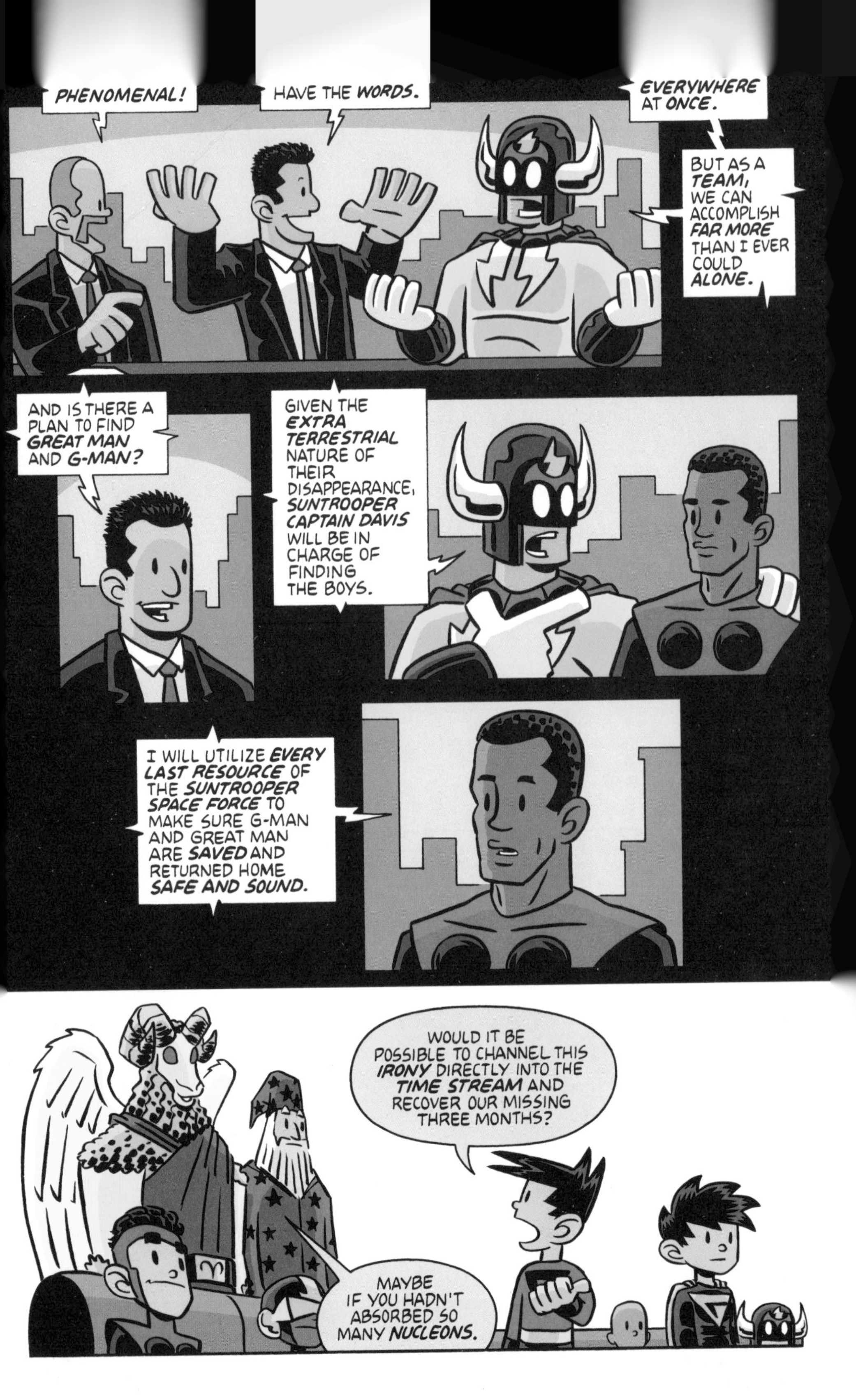
PHENOMENAL!
HAVE THE WORDS.
EVERYWHERE AT ONCE.
BUT AS A TEAM, WE CAN ACCOMPLISH FAR MORE THAN I EVER COULD ALONE.
AND IS THERE A PLAN TO FIND GREAT MAN AND G-MAN?
GIVEN THE EXTRA TERRESTRIAL NATURE OF THEIR DISAPPEARANCE, SUNTROOPER CAPTAIN DAVIS WILL BE IN CHARGE OF FINDING THE BOYS.
I WILL UTILIZE EVERY LAST RESOURCE OF THE SUNTROOPER SPACE FORCE TO MAKE SURE G-MAN AND GREAT MAN ARE SAVED AND RETURNED HOME SAFE AND SOUND.
WOULD IT BE POSSIBLE TO CHANNEL THIS IRONY DIRECTLY INTO THE TIME STREAM AND RECOVER OUR MISSING THREE MONTHS?
MAYBE IF YOU HADN'T ABSORBED SO MANY NUCLEONS.

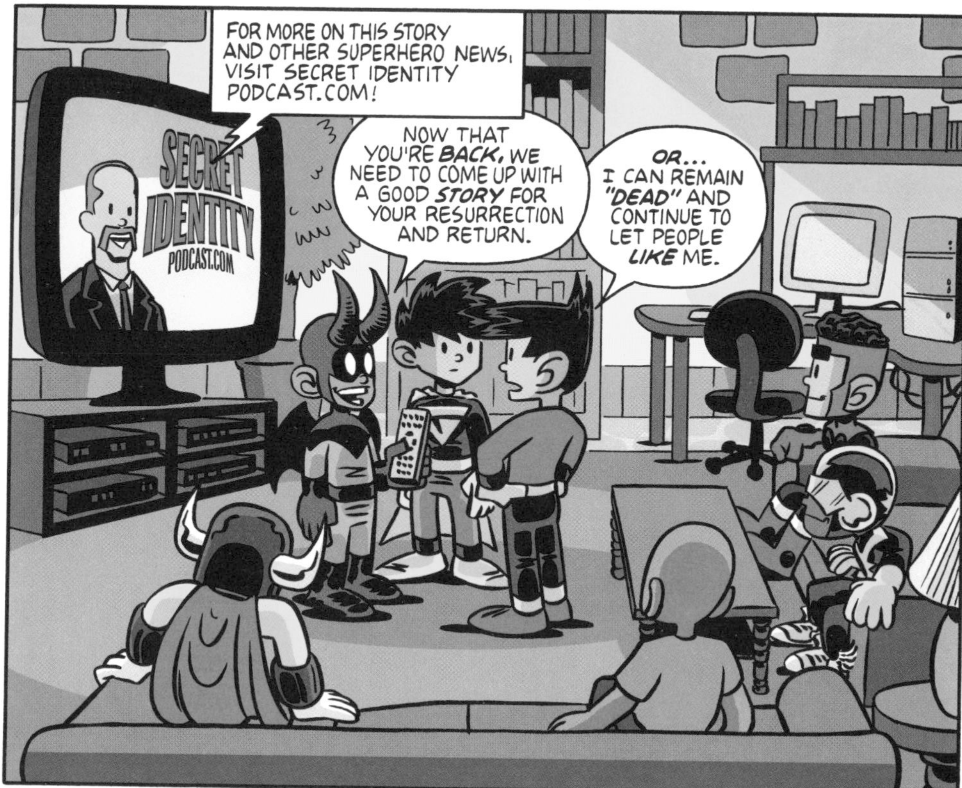
FOR MORE ON THIS STORY AND OTHER SUPERHERO NEWS, VISIT SECRET IDENTITY PODCAST.COM!
SECRET IDENTITY PODCAST.COM
NOW THAT YOU'RE BACK, WE NEED TO COME UP WITH A GOOD STORY FOR YOUR RESURRECTION AND RETURN.
OR... I CAN REMAIN "DEAD" AND CONTINUE TO LET PEOPLE LIKE ME.

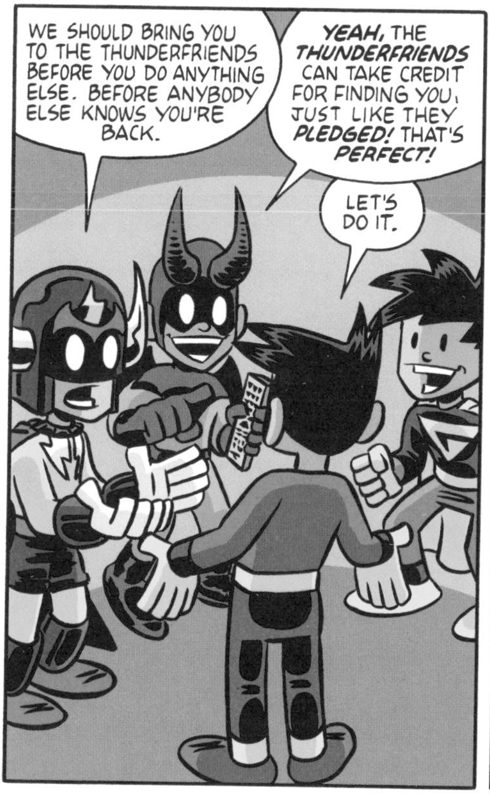
WE SHOULD BRING YOU TO THE THUNDERFRIENDS BEFORE YOU DO ANYTHING ELSE. BEFORE ANYBODY ELSE KNOWS YOU'RE BACK.
YEAH, THE THUNDERFRIENDS CAN TAKE CREDIT FOR FINDING YOU, JUST LIKE THEY PLEDGED! THAT'S PERFECT!
LET'S DO IT.

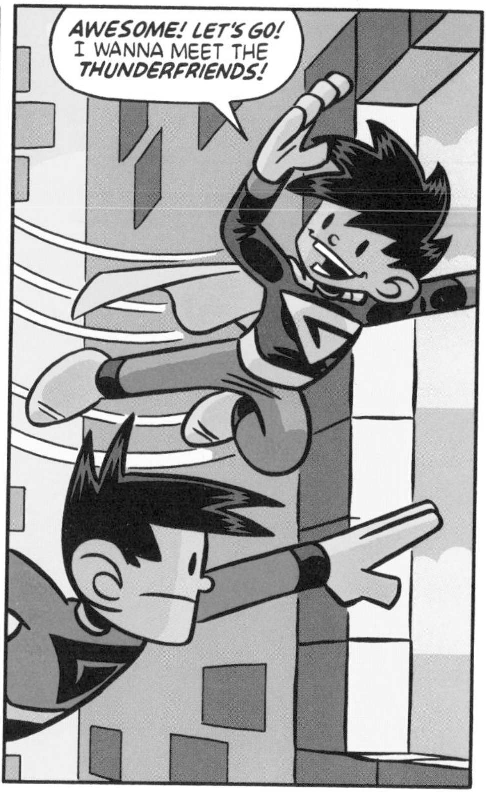
AWESOME! LET'S GO! I WANNA MEET THE THUNDERFRIENDS!

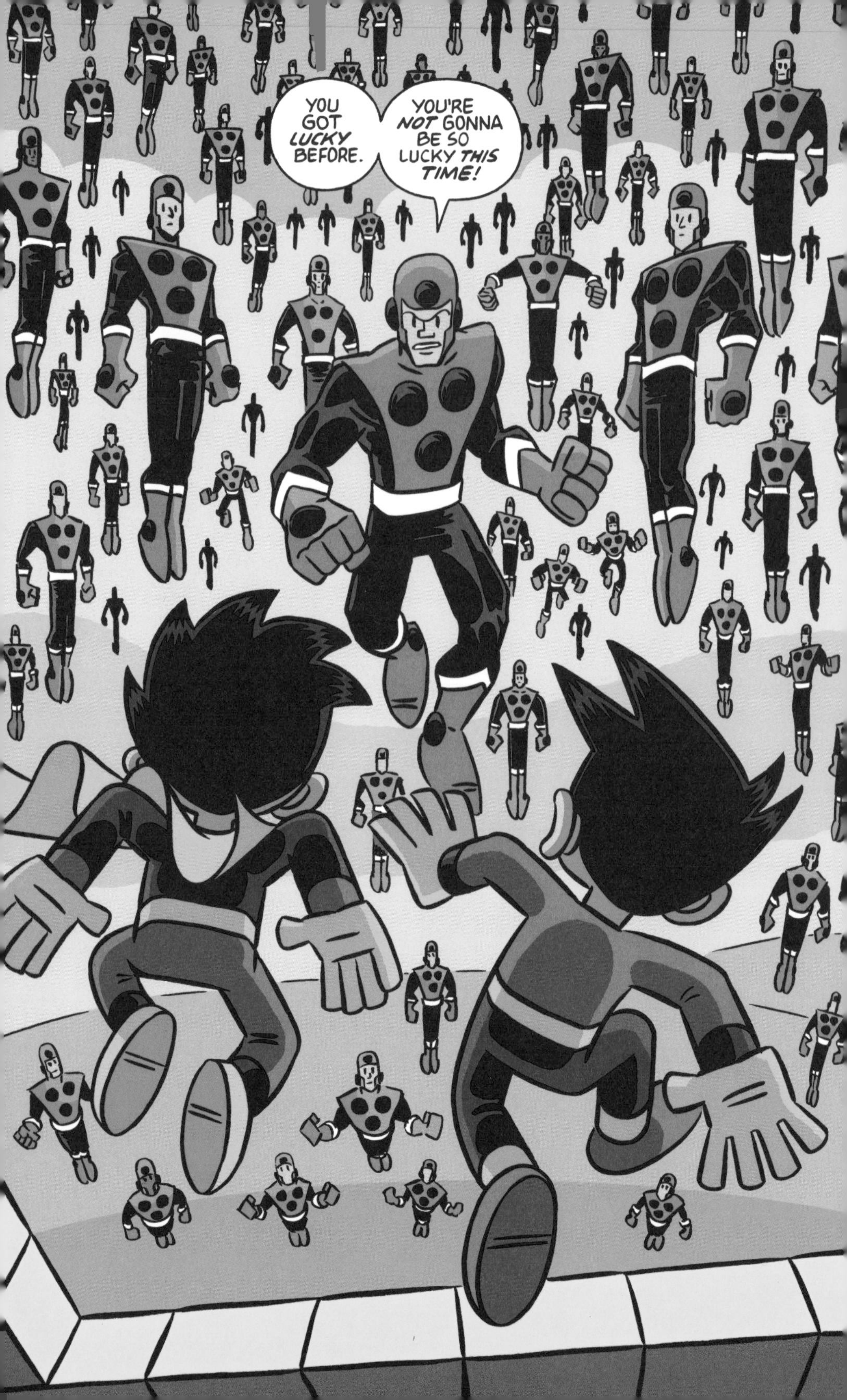
YOU GOT LUCKY BEFORE.
YOU'RE NOT GONNA BE SO LUCKY THIS TIME!

WHAT'S THE MATTER, *WISE GUY?*

YOUR *SMART MOUTH* NOT *WORKING* ALL OF A SUDDEN?

HOW WOULD YOU EVEN TAKE ME AWAY?

. . .

WHAT?

YOUR SUIT WILL SHUT DOWN AS SOON AS YOU *TOUCH* ME.

HOW WOULD YOU EXPECT TO CARRY ME BACK TO YOUR *BASE?*

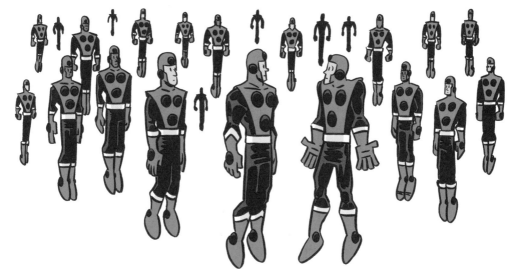

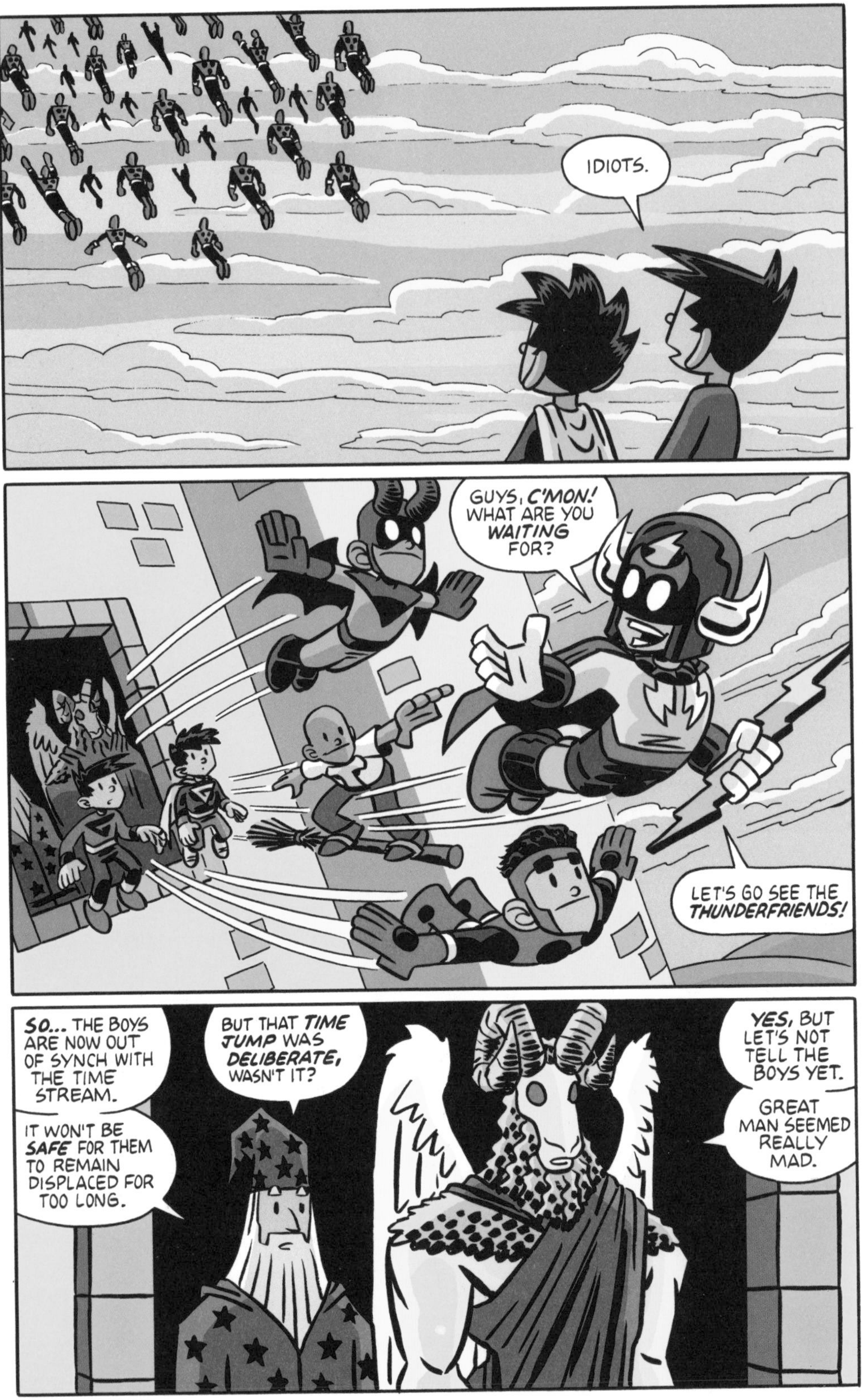
IDIOTS.
GUYS, C'MON! WHAT ARE YOU WAITING FOR?
LET'S GO SEE THE THUNDERFRIENDS!
SO... THE BOYS ARE NOW OUT OF SYNCH WITH THE TIME STREAM.
IT WON'T BE SAFE FOR THEM TO REMAIN DISPLACED FOR TOO LONG.
BUT THAT TIME JUMP WAS DELIBERATE, WASN'T IT?
YES, BUT LET'S NOT TELL THE BOYS YET.
GREAT MAN SEEMED REALLY MAD.

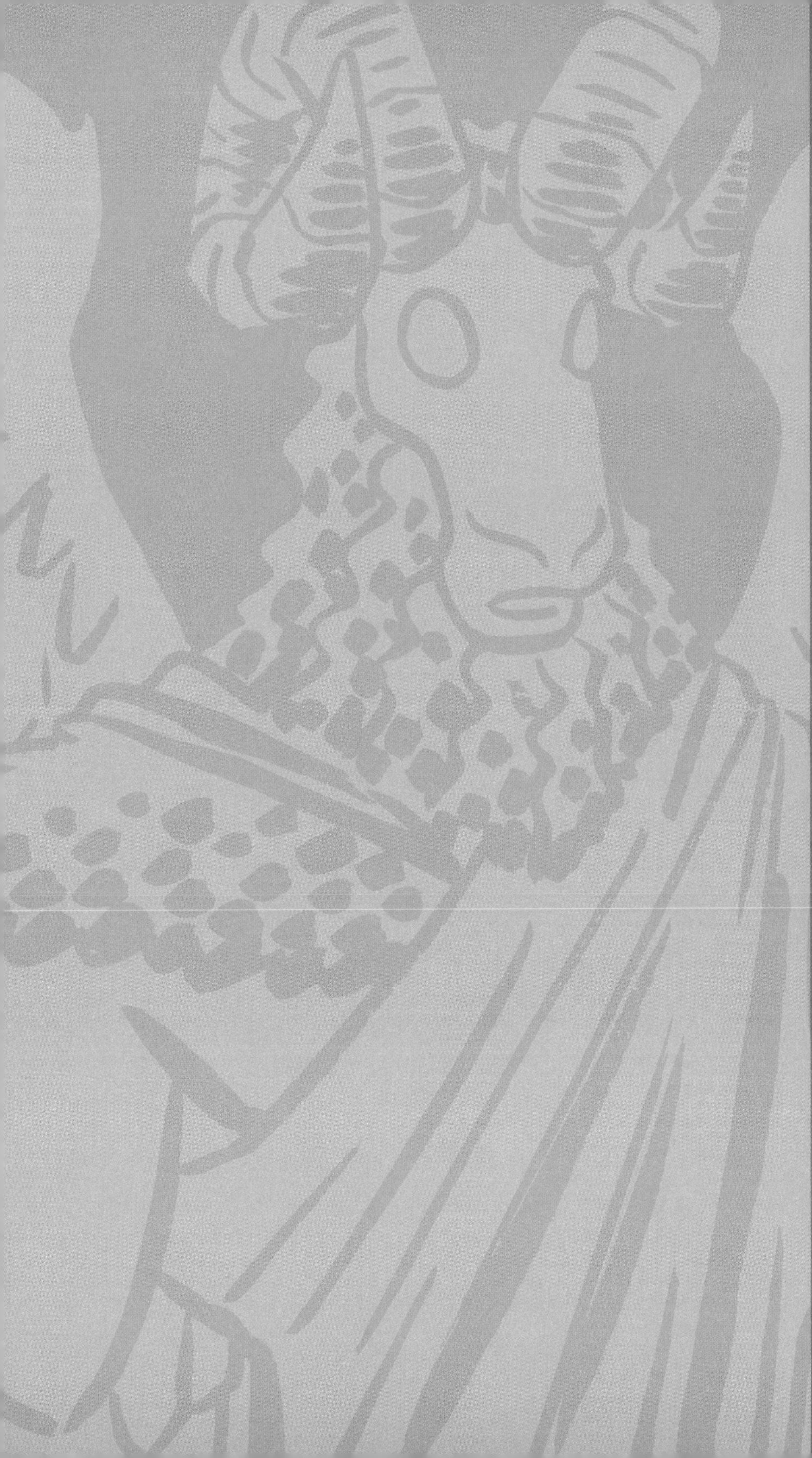

3

CHAPTER THREE

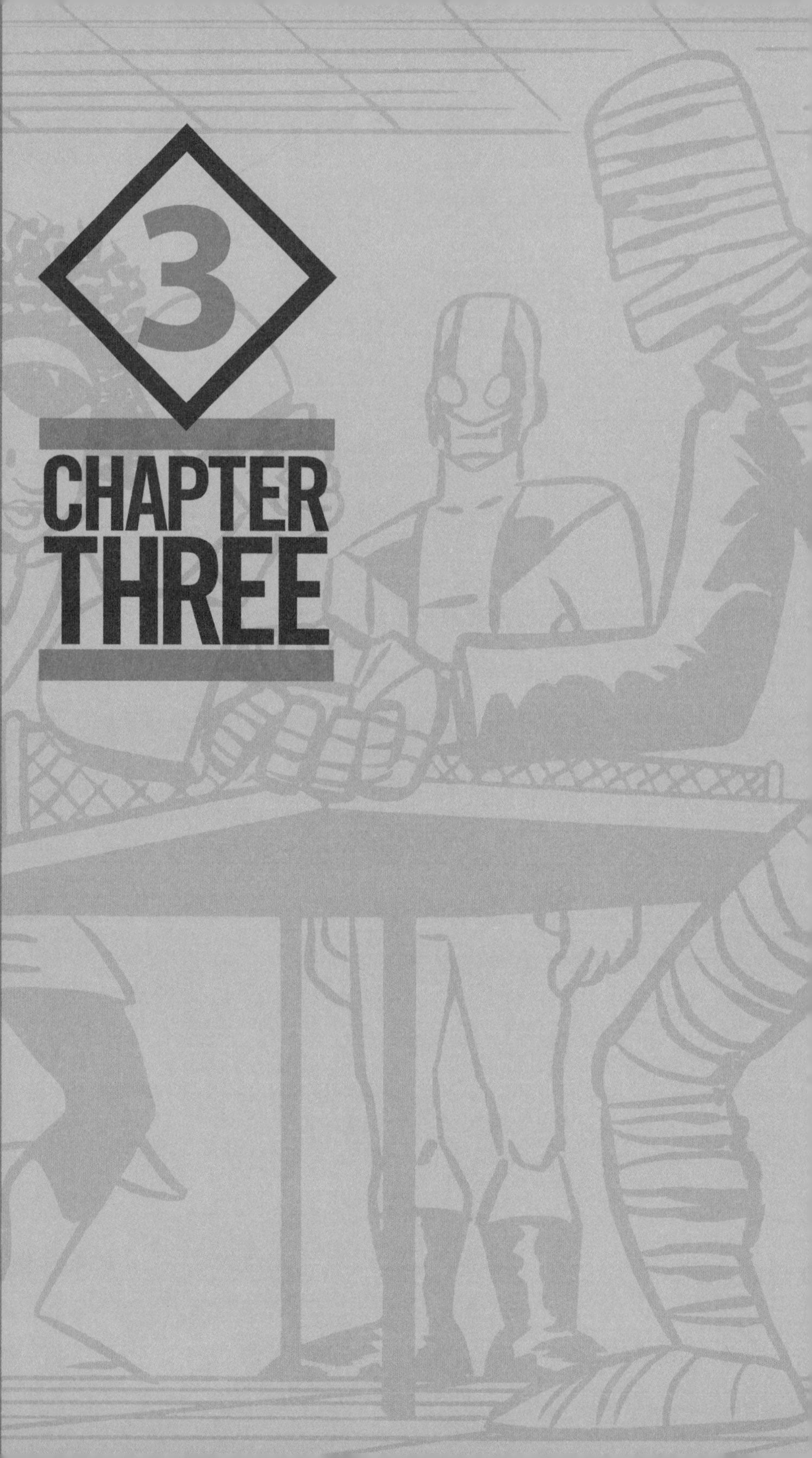

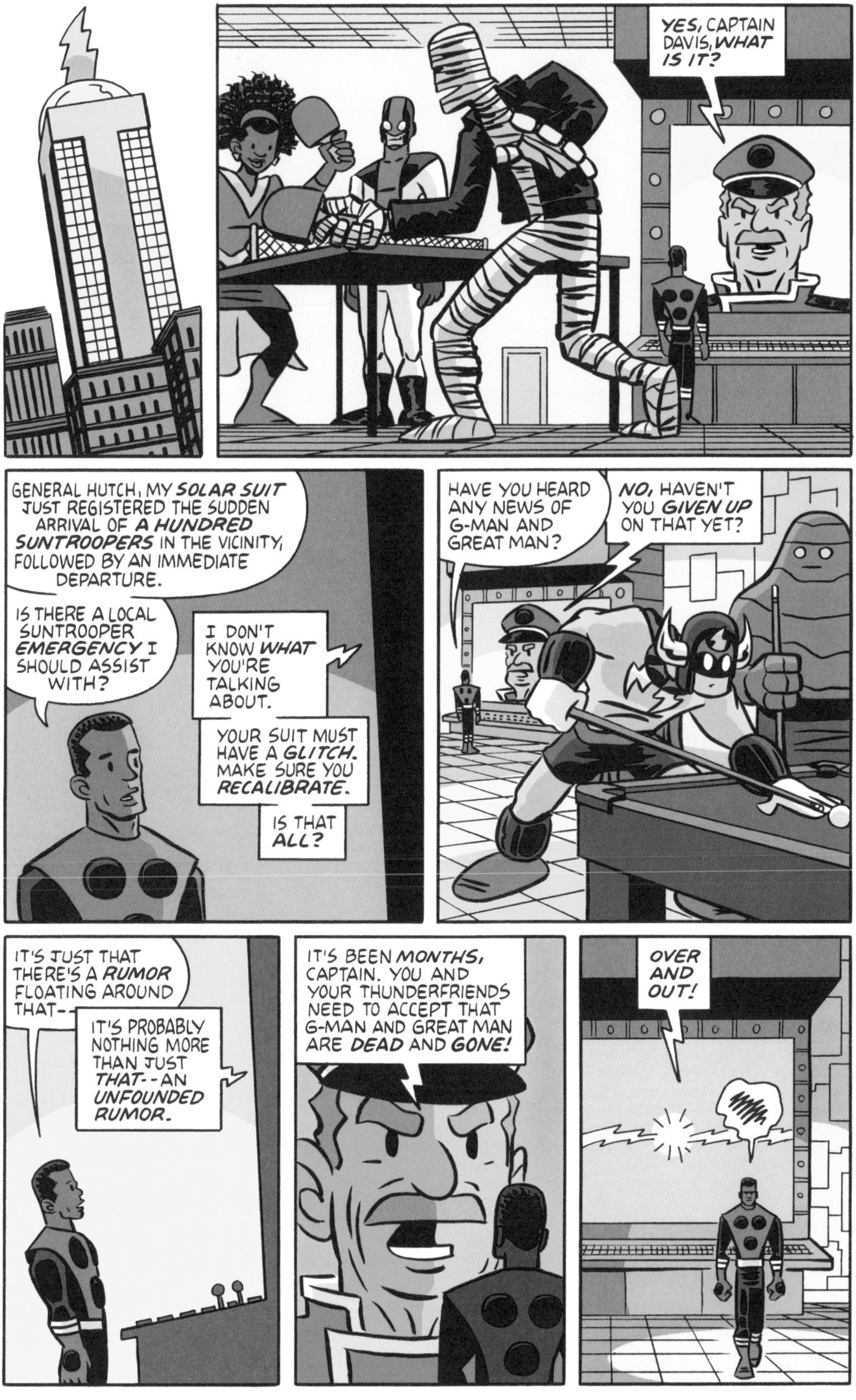
YES, CAPTAIN DAVIS, WHAT IS IT?
GENERAL HUTCH, MY SOLAR SUIT JUST REGISTERED THE SUDDEN ARRIVAL OF A HUNDRED SUNTROOPERS IN THE VICINITY, FOLLOWED BY AN IMMEDIATE DEPARTURE.
IS THERE A LOCAL SUNTROOPER EMERGENCY I SHOULD ASSIST WITH?
I DON'T KNOW WHAT YOU'RE TALKING ABOUT.
YOUR SUIT MUST HAVE A GLITCH. MAKE SURE YOU RECALIBRATE.
IS THAT ALL?
HAVE YOU HEARD ANY NEWS OF G-MAN AND GREAT MAN?
NO, HAVEN'T YOU GIVEN UP ON THAT YET?
IT'S JUST THAT THERE'S A RUMOR FLOATING AROUND THAT--
IT'S PROBABLY NOTHING MORE THAN JUST THAT--AN UNFOUNDED RUMOR.
IT'S BEEN MONTHS, CAPTAIN. YOU AND YOUR THUNDERFRIENDS NEED TO ACCEPT THAT G-MAN AND GREAT MAN ARE DEAD AND GONE!
OVER AND OUT!

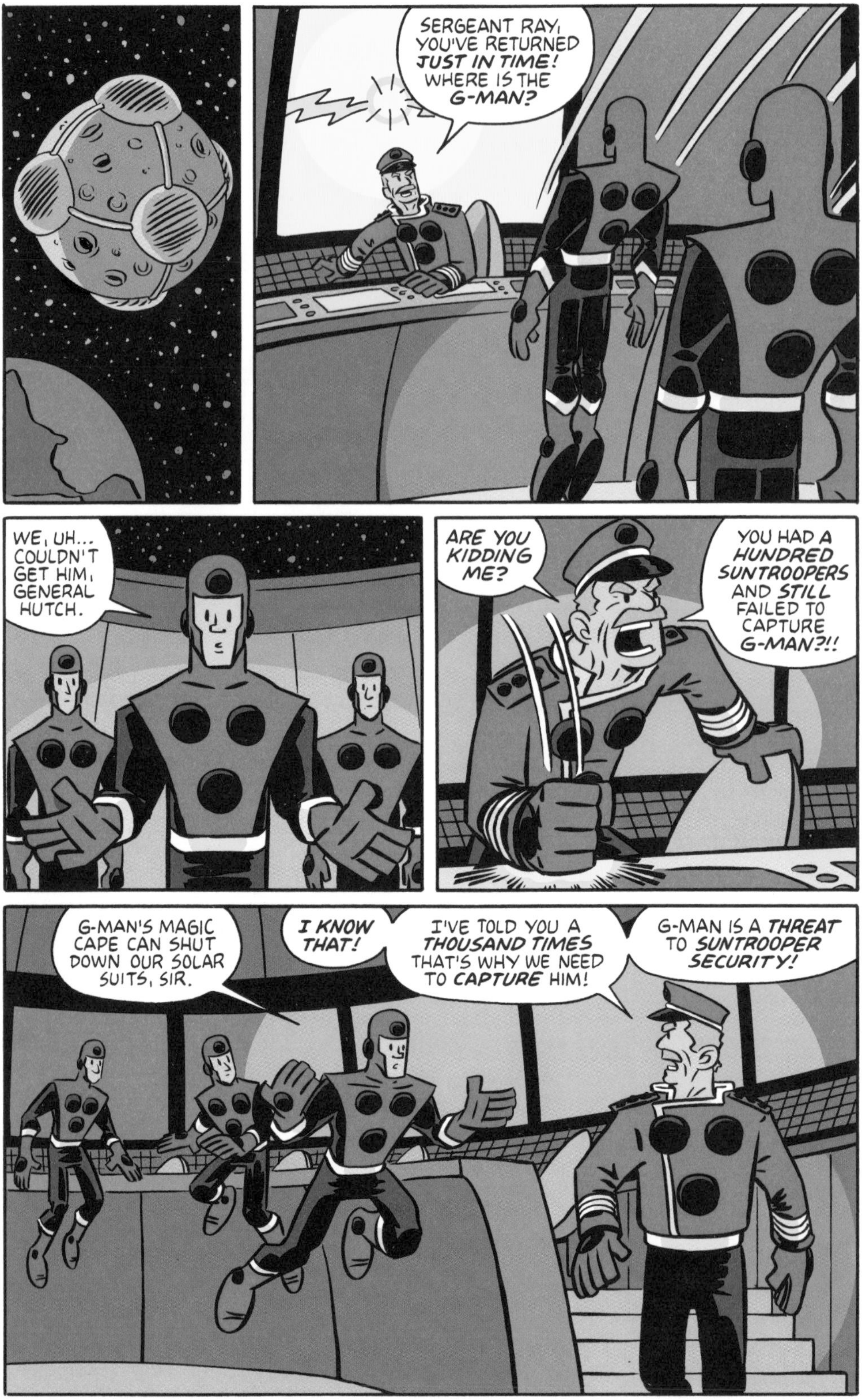
SERGEANT RAY, YOU'VE RETURNED ***JUST IN TIME!*** WHERE IS THE ***G-MAN?***
WE, UH... COULDN'T GET HIM, GENERAL HUTCH.
ARE YOU KIDDING ME?
YOU HAD A ***HUNDRED SUNTROOPERS*** AND ***STILL*** FAILED TO CAPTURE ***G-MAN?!!***
G-MAN'S MAGIC CAPE CAN SHUT DOWN OUR SOLAR SUITS, SIR.
I KNOW THAT!
I'VE TOLD YOU A ***THOUSAND TIMES*** THAT'S WHY WE NEED TO ***CAPTURE*** HIM!
G-MAN IS A ***THREAT*** TO ***SUNTROOPER SECURITY!***

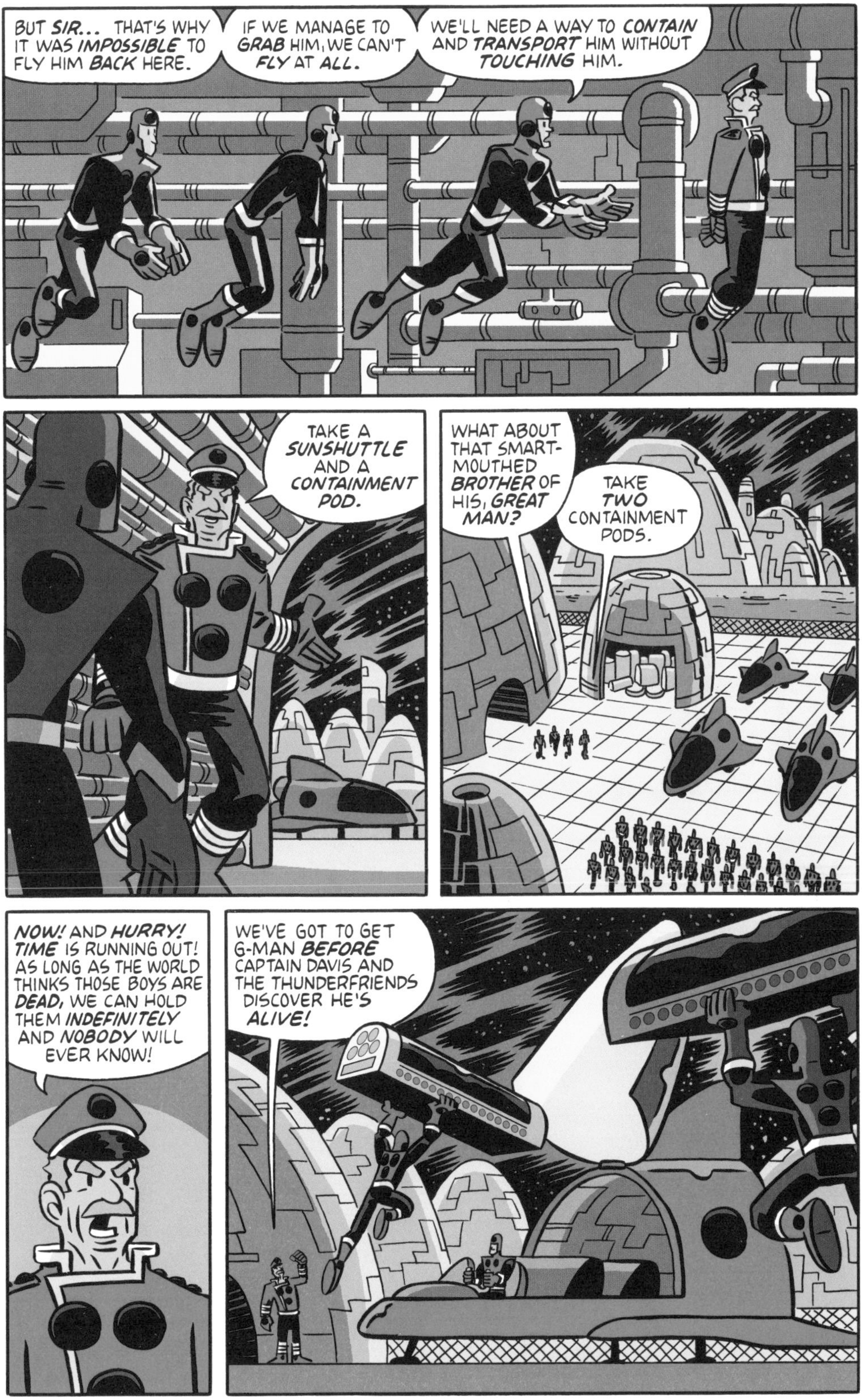
BUT SIR... THAT'S WHY IT WAS IMPOSSIBLE TO FLY HIM BACK HERE.
IF WE MANAGE TO GRAB HIM, WE CAN'T FLY AT ALL.
WE'LL NEED A WAY TO CONTAIN AND TRANSPORT HIM WITHOUT TOUCHING HIM.
TAKE A SUNSHUTTLE AND A CONTAINMENT POD.
WHAT ABOUT THAT SMART-MOUTHED BROTHER OF HIS, GREAT MAN?
TAKE TWO CONTAINMENT PODS.
NOW! AND HURRY! TIME IS RUNNING OUT! AS LONG AS THE WORLD THINKS THOSE BOYS ARE DEAD, WE CAN HOLD THEM INDEFINITELY AND NOBODY WILL EVER KNOW!
WE'VE GOT TO GET G-MAN BEFORE CAPTAIN DAVIS AND THE THUNDERFRIENDS DISCOVER HE'S ALIVE!

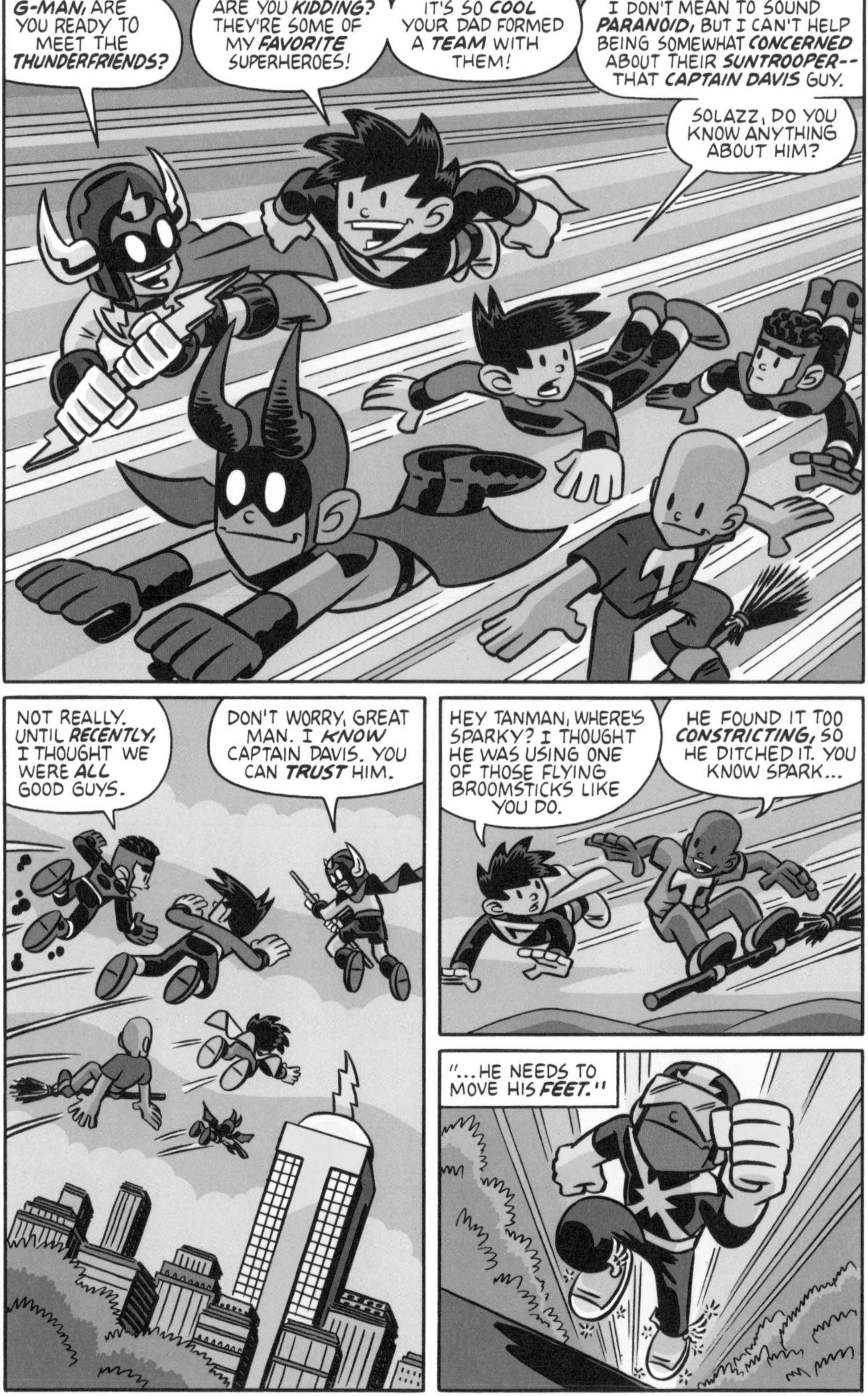
G-MAN, ARE YOU READY TO MEET THE THUNDERFRIENDS?
ARE YOU KIDDING? THEY'RE SOME OF MY FAVORITE SUPERHEROES!
IT'S SO COOL YOUR DAD FORMED A TEAM WITH THEM!
I DON'T MEAN TO SOUND PARANOID, BUT I CAN'T HELP BEING SOMEWHAT CONCERNED ABOUT THEIR SUNTROOPER-- THAT CAPTAIN DAVIS GUY.
SOLAZZ, DO YOU KNOW ANYTHING ABOUT HIM?
NOT REALLY. UNTIL RECENTLY, I THOUGHT WE WERE ALL GOOD GUYS.
DON'T WORRY, GREAT MAN. I KNOW CAPTAIN DAVIS. YOU CAN TRUST HIM.
HEY TANMAN, WHERE'S SPARKY? I THOUGHT HE WAS USING ONE OF THOSE FLYING BROOMSTICKS LIKE YOU DO.
HE FOUND IT TOO CONSTRICTING, SO HE DITCHED IT. YOU KNOW SPARK...
"...HE NEEDS TO MOVE HIS FEET."

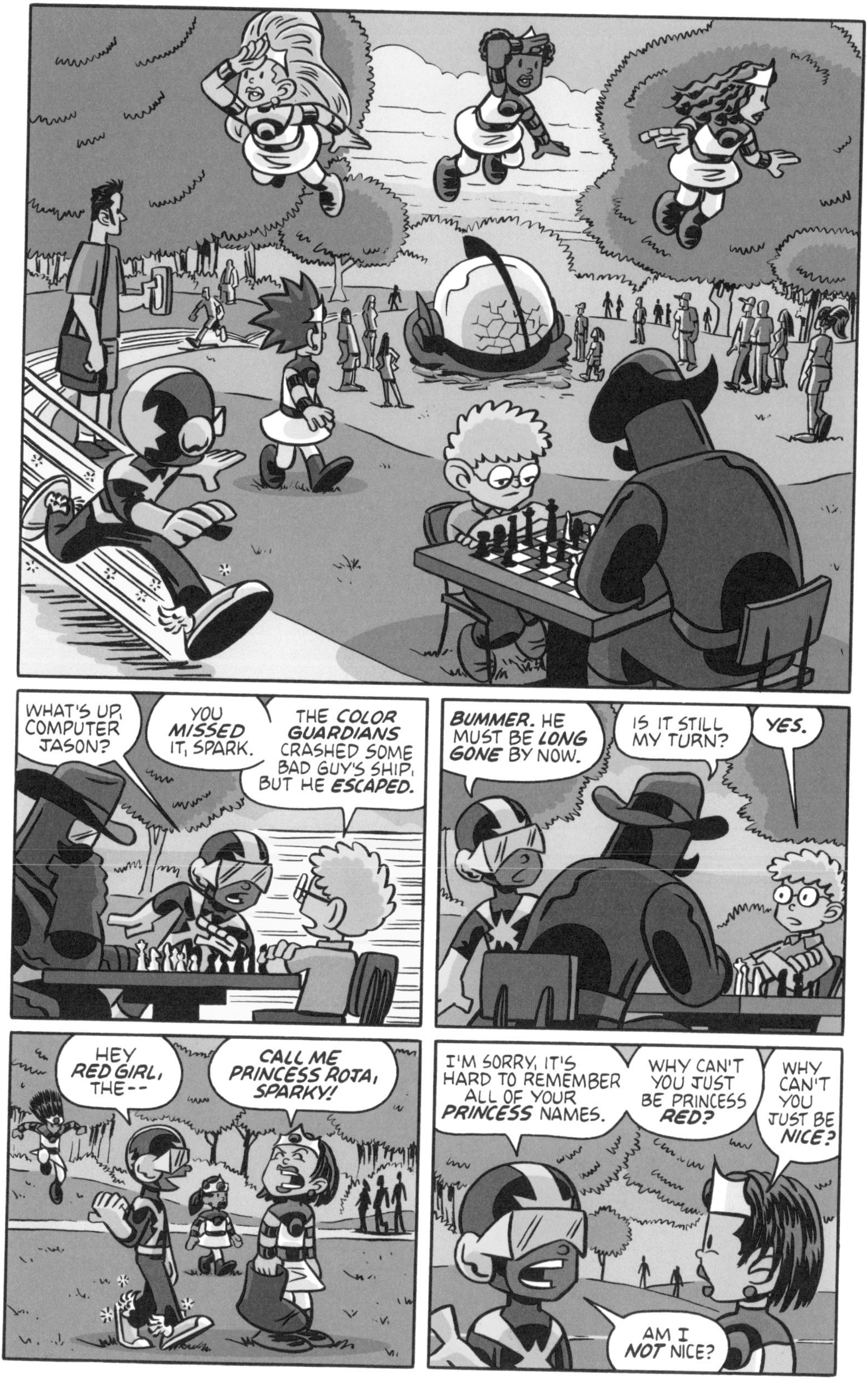
WHAT'S UP, COMPUTER JASON?
YOU MISSED IT, SPARK.
THE COLOR GUARDIANS CRASHED SOME BAD GUY'S SHIP, BUT HE ESCAPED.
BUMMER. HE MUST BE LONG GONE BY NOW.
IS IT STILL MY TURN?
YES.
HEY RED GIRL, THE--
CALL ME PRINCESS ROJA, SPARKY!
I'M SORRY, IT'S HARD TO REMEMBER ALL OF YOUR PRINCESS NAMES.
WHY CAN'T YOU JUST BE PRINCESS RED?
WHY CAN'T YOU JUST BE NICE?
AM I NOT NICE?

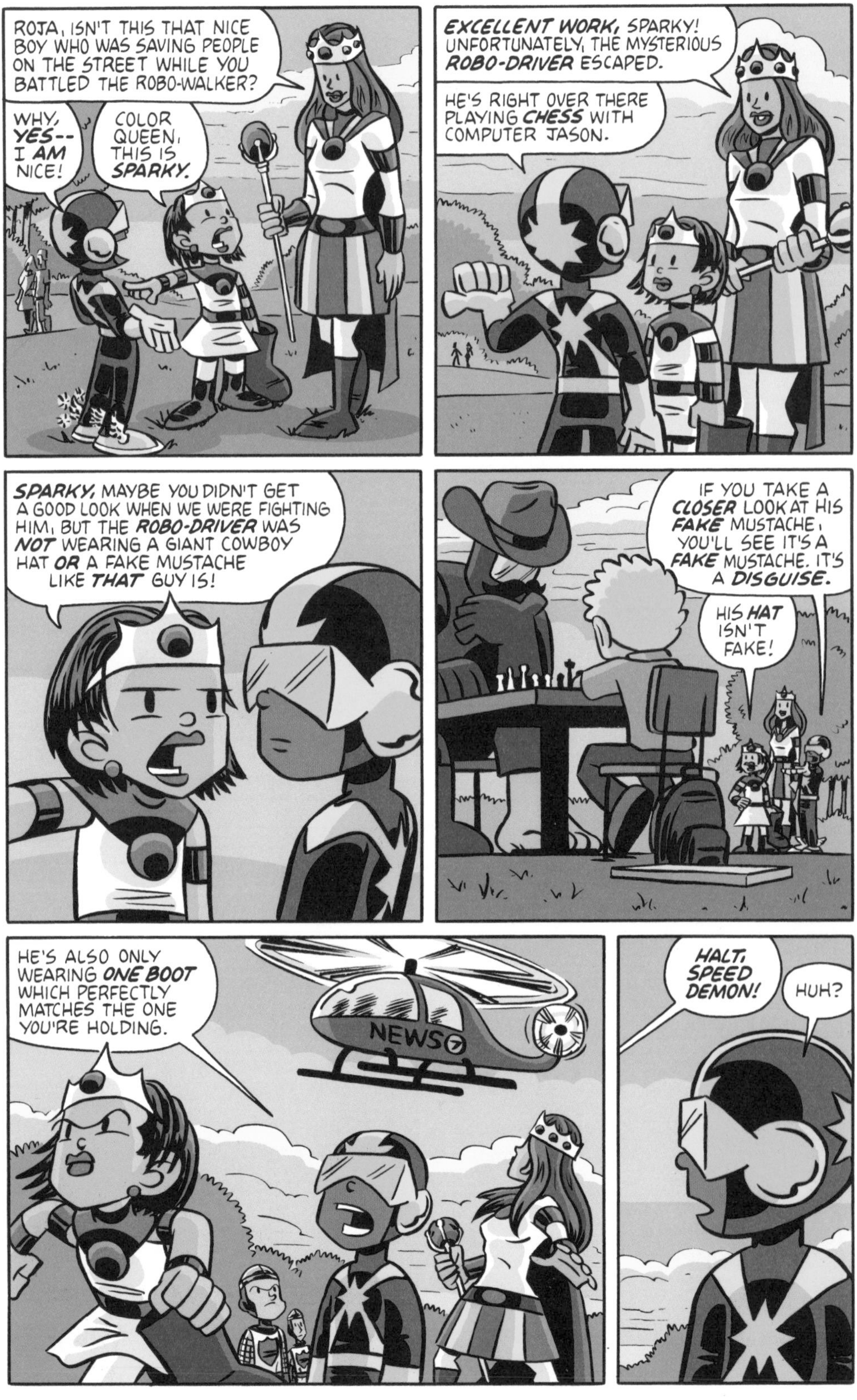
ROJA, ISN'T THIS THAT NICE BOY WHO WAS SAVING PEOPLE ON THE STREET WHILE YOU BATTLED THE ROBO-WALKER?
WHY, YES-- I AM NICE!
COLOR QUEEN, THIS IS SPARKY.
EXCELLENT WORK, SPARKY! UNFORTUNATELY, THE MYSTERIOUS ROBO-DRIVER ESCAPED.
HE'S RIGHT OVER THERE PLAYING CHESS WITH COMPUTER JASON.
SPARKY, MAYBE YOU DIDN'T GET A GOOD LOOK WHEN WE WERE FIGHTING HIM, BUT THE ROBO-DRIVER WAS NOT WEARING A GIANT COWBOY HAT OR A FAKE MUSTACHE LIKE THAT GUY IS!
IF YOU TAKE A CLOSER LOOK AT HIS FAKE MUSTACHE, YOU'LL SEE IT'S A FAKE MUSTACHE. IT'S A DISGUISE.
HIS HAT ISN'T FAKE!
HE'S ALSO ONLY WEARING ONE BOOT WHICH PERFECTLY MATCHES THE ONE YOU'RE HOLDING.
NEWS 7
HALT, SPEED DEMON!
HUH?

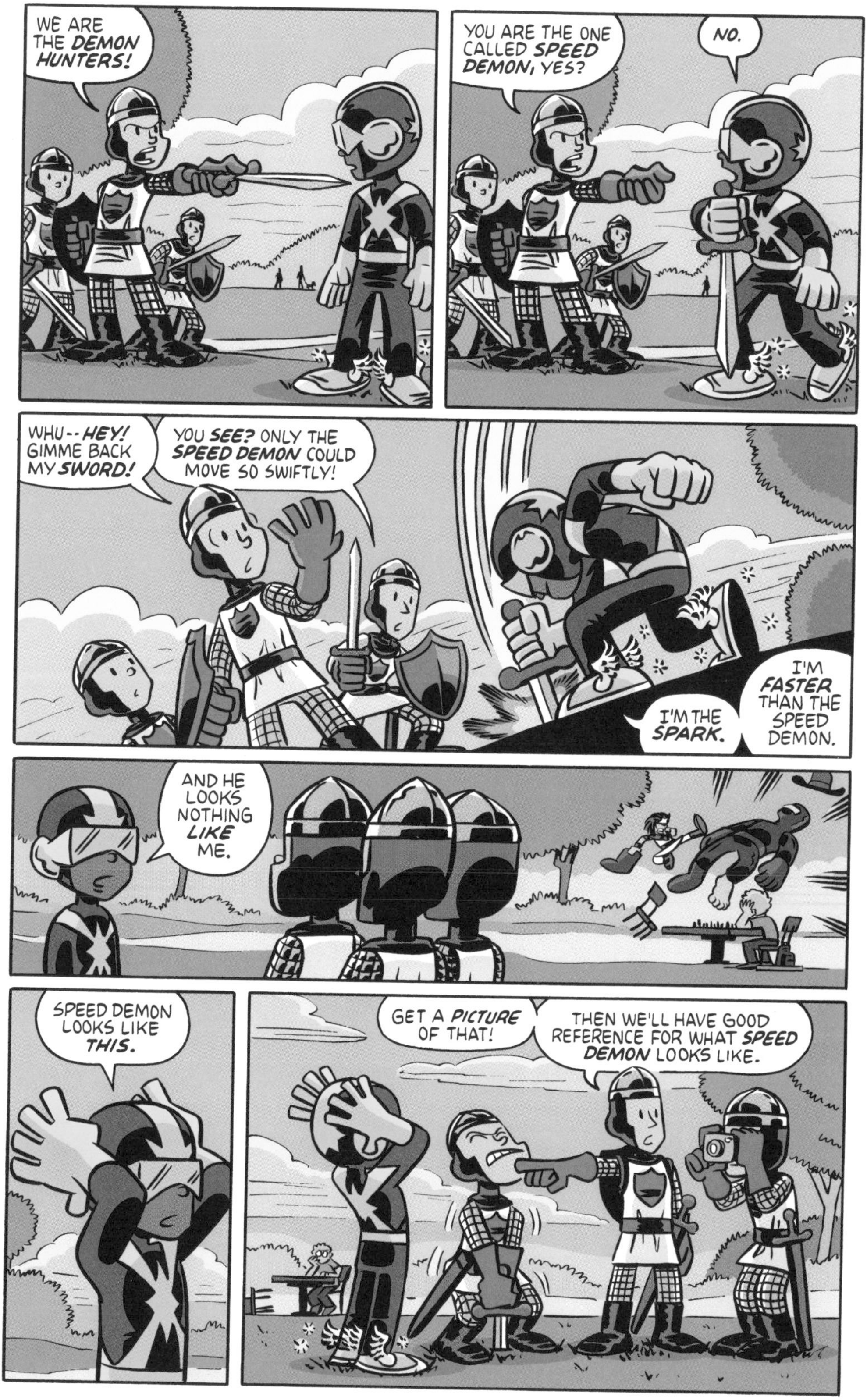
WE ARE THE DEMON HUNTERS!
YOU ARE THE ONE CALLED SPEED DEMON, YES?
NO.
WHU-- HEY! GIMME BACK MY SWORD!
YOU SEE? ONLY THE SPEED DEMON COULD MOVE SO SWIFTLY!
I'M THE SPARK.
I'M FASTER THAN THE SPEED DEMON.
AND HE LOOKS NOTHING LIKE ME.
SPEED DEMON LOOKS LIKE THIS.
GET A PICTURE OF THAT!
THEN WE'LL HAVE GOOD REFERENCE FOR WHAT SPEED DEMON LOOKS LIKE.

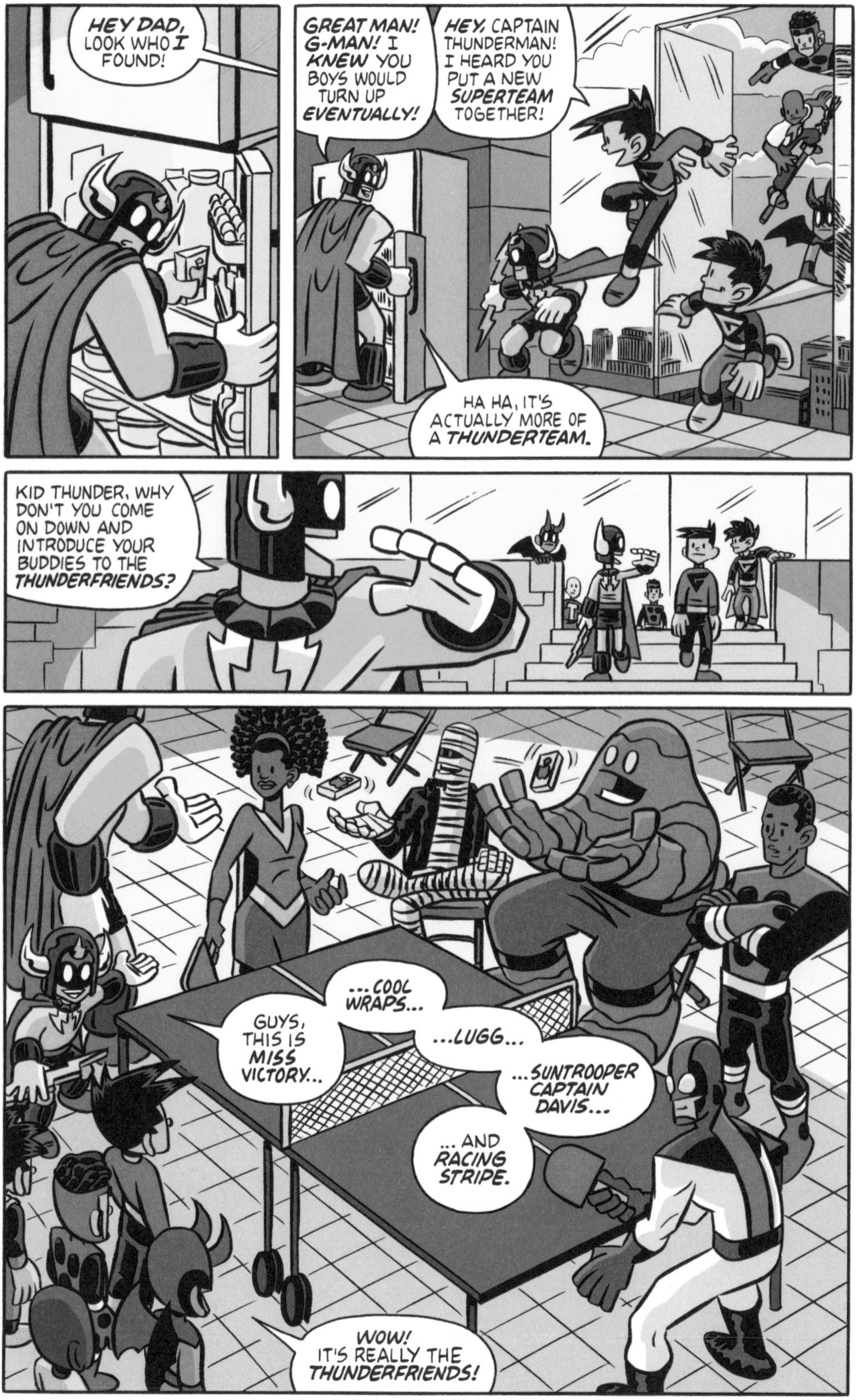
HEY DAD, LOOK WHO I FOUND!
GREAT MAN! G-MAN! I KNEW YOU BOYS WOULD TURN UP EVENTUALLY!
HEY, CAPTAIN THUNDERMAN! I HEARD YOU PUT A NEW SUPERTEAM TOGETHER!
HA HA, IT'S ACTUALLY MORE OF A THUNDERTEAM.
KID THUNDER, WHY DON'T YOU COME ON DOWN AND INTRODUCE YOUR BUDDIES TO THE THUNDERFRIENDS?
GUYS, THIS IS MISS VICTORY...
...COOL WRAPS...
...LUGG...
...SUNTROOPER CAPTAIN DAVIS...
...AND RACING STRIPE.
WOW! IT'S REALLY THE THUNDERFRIENDS!

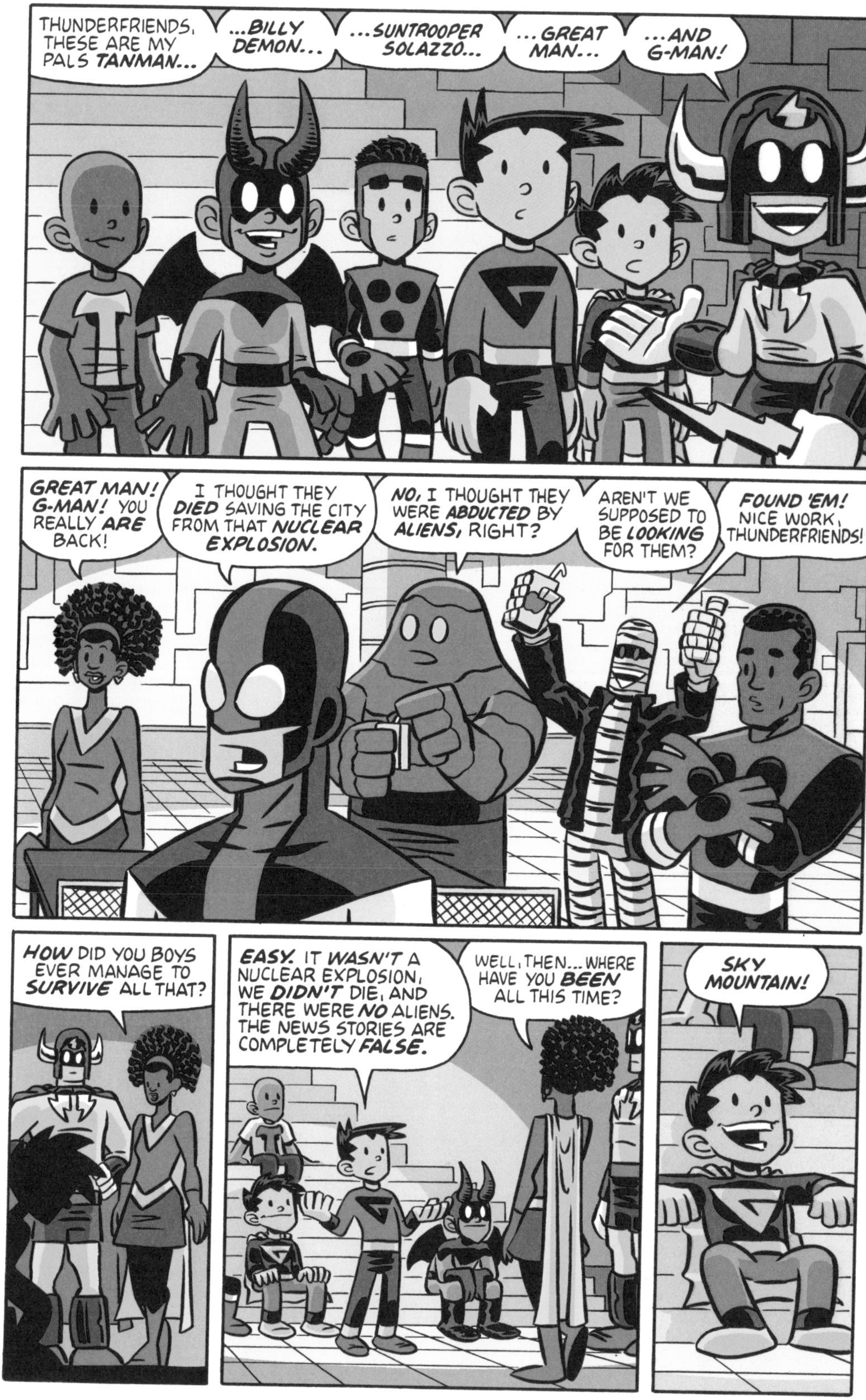
THUNDERFRIENDS, THESE ARE MY PALS TANMAN...
...BILLY DEMON...
...SUNTROOPER SOLAZZO...
...GREAT MAN...
...AND G-MAN!
GREAT MAN! G-MAN! YOU REALLY ARE BACK!
I THOUGHT THEY DIED SAVING THE CITY FROM THAT NUCLEAR EXPLOSION.
NO, I THOUGHT THEY WERE ABDUCTED BY ALIENS, RIGHT?
AREN'T WE SUPPOSED TO BE LOOKING FOR THEM?
FOUND 'EM! NICE WORK, THUNDERFRIENDS!
HOW DID YOU BOYS EVER MANAGE TO SURVIVE ALL THAT?
EASY. IT WASN'T A NUCLEAR EXPLOSION, WE DIDN'T DIE, AND THERE WERE NO ALIENS. THE NEWS STORIES ARE COMPLETELY FALSE.
WELL, THEN... WHERE HAVE YOU BEEN ALL THIS TIME?
SKY MOUNTAIN!

NO **WAY.**

SERIOUSLY?

I **TOLD** YOU GUYS THIS **BEFORE!** YOU NEVER **LISTEN** TO ME!

THAT'S BECAUSE THERE'S **NO SUCH THING** AS **SKY MOUNTAIN.**

ACTUALLY, THERE **IS.**

OKAY, **FINE.** YOU WERE ON THIS **MYTHICAL** SKY MOUNTAIN...

...FOR **THREE MONTHS?**

NOT **REALLY.** WE ONLY SPENT A **DAY** THERE, BUT SOMEHOW WE JUMPED **FORWARD** IN **TIME.**

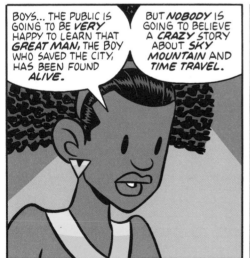

BOYS... THE PUBLIC IS GOING TO BE **VERY** HAPPY TO LEARN THAT **GREAT MAN,** THE BOY WHO SAVED THE CITY, HAS BEEN FOUND **ALIVE.**

BUT **NOBODY** IS GOING TO BELIEVE A **CRAZY** STORY ABOUT **SKY MOUNTAIN** AND **TIME TRAVEL.**

I KNOW. IF WE DON'T GO ALONG WITH THE **FAKE** STORY, EVERYONE WILL THINK WE'RE **LIARS** PERPETRATING A **HOAX.**

WE WERE HOPING YOU GUYS COULD JUST SAY YOU RESCUED US FROM ALIENS.

FOUND 'EM! NICE WORK, THUNDERFRIENDS!

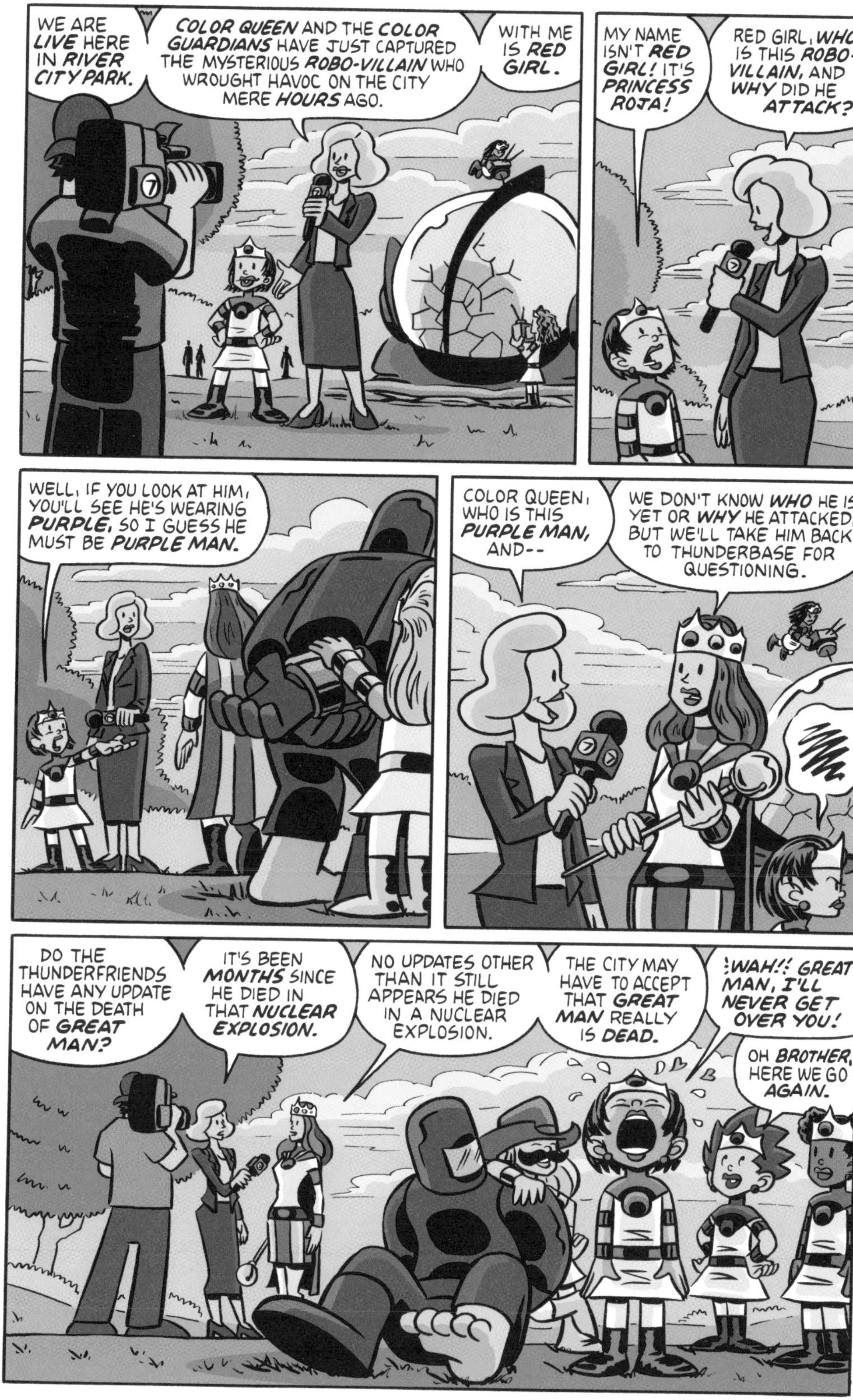
WE ARE LIVE HERE IN RIVER CITY PARK.
COLOR QUEEN AND THE COLOR GUARDIANS HAVE JUST CAPTURED THE MYSTERIOUS ROBO-VILLAIN WHO WROUGHT HAVOC ON THE CITY MERE HOURS AGO.
WITH ME IS RED GIRL.
MY NAME ISN'T RED GIRL! IT'S PRINCESS ROJA!
RED GIRL, WHO IS THIS ROBO-VILLAIN, AND WHY DID HE ATTACK?
WELL, IF YOU LOOK AT HIM, YOU'LL SEE HE'S WEARING PURPLE, SO I GUESS HE MUST BE PURPLE MAN.
COLOR QUEEN, WHO IS THIS PURPLE MAN, AND--
WE DON'T KNOW WHO HE IS YET OR WHY HE ATTACKED, BUT WE'LL TAKE HIM BACK TO THUNDERBASE FOR QUESTIONING.
DO THE THUNDERFRIENDS HAVE ANY UPDATE ON THE DEATH OF GREAT MAN?
IT'S BEEN MONTHS SINCE HE DIED IN THAT NUCLEAR EXPLOSION.
NO UPDATES OTHER THAN IT STILL APPEARS HE DIED IN A NUCLEAR EXPLOSION.
THE CITY MAY HAVE TO ACCEPT THAT GREAT MAN REALLY IS DEAD.
¡WAH!¡ GREAT MAN, I'LL NEVER GET OVER YOU!
OH BROTHER, HERE WE GO AGAIN.

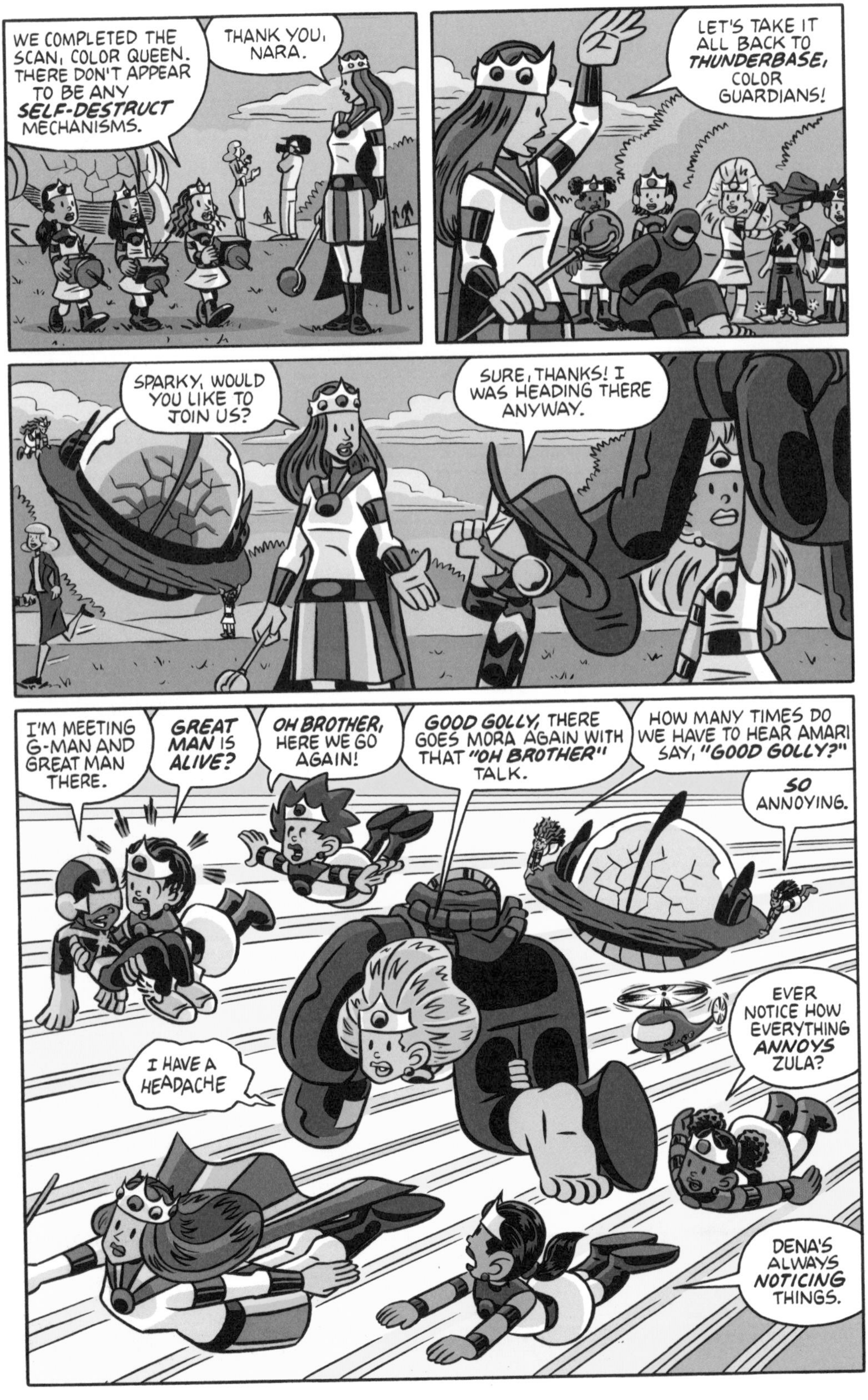
WE COMPLETED THE SCAN, COLOR QUEEN. THERE DON'T APPEAR TO BE ANY SELF-DESTRUCT MECHANISMS.
THANK YOU, NARA.
LET'S TAKE IT ALL BACK TO THUNDERBASE, COLOR GUARDIANS!
SPARKY, WOULD YOU LIKE TO JOIN US?
SURE, THANKS! I WAS HEADING THERE ANYWAY.
I'M MEETING G-MAN AND GREAT MAN THERE.
GREAT MAN IS ALIVE?
OH BROTHER, HERE WE GO AGAIN!
GOOD GOLLY, THERE GOES MORA AGAIN WITH THAT "OH BROTHER" TALK.
HOW MANY TIMES DO WE HAVE TO HEAR AMARI SAY, "GOOD GOLLY?"
SO ANNOYING.
EVER NOTICE HOW EVERYTHING ANNOYS ZULA?
I HAVE A HEADACHE
DENA'S ALWAYS NOTICING THINGS.

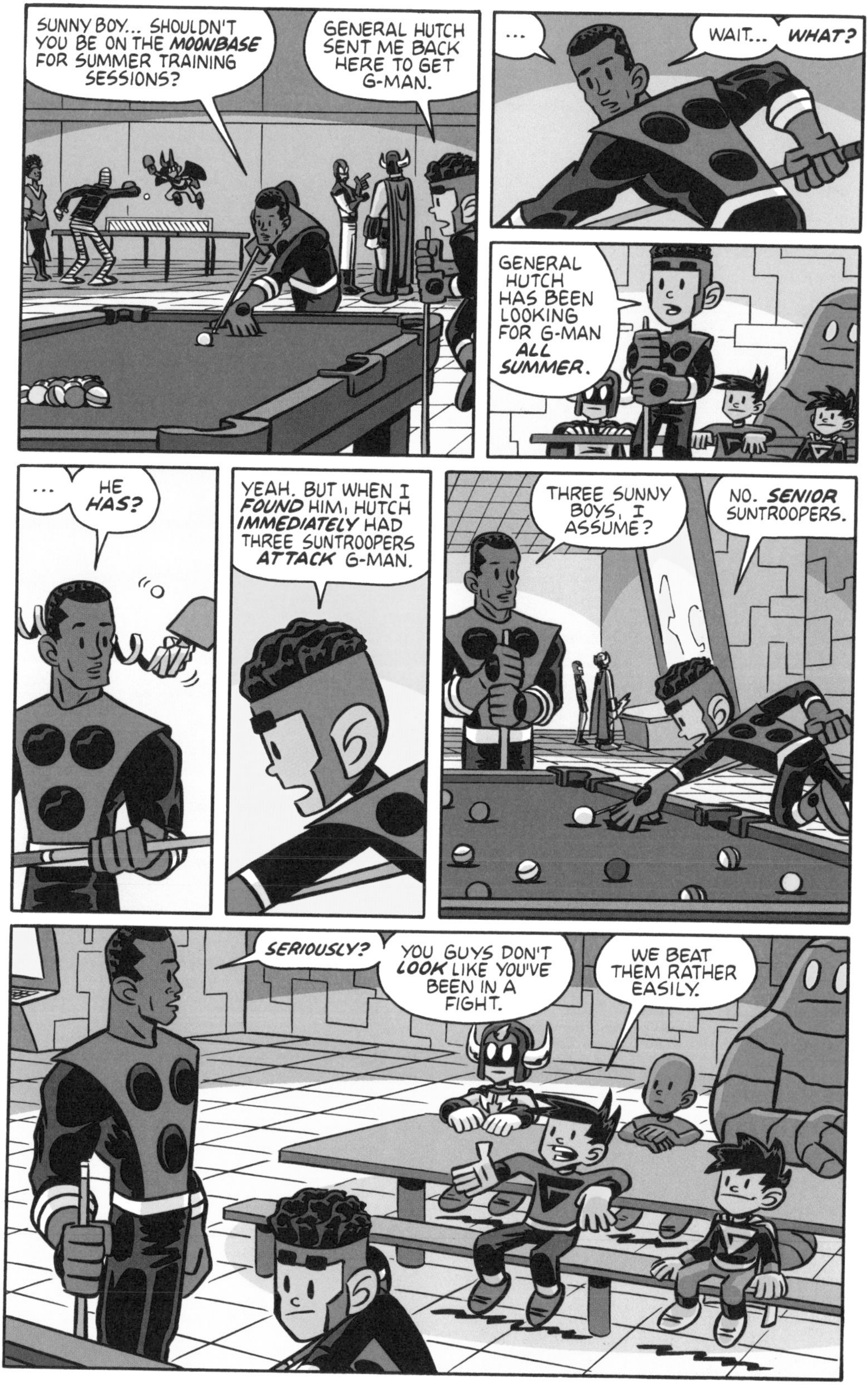
SUNNY BOY... SHOULDN'T YOU BE ON THE MOONBASE FOR SUMMER TRAINING SESSIONS?
GENERAL HUTCH SENT ME BACK HERE TO GET G-MAN.
...
WAIT... WHAT?
GENERAL HUTCH HAS BEEN LOOKING FOR G-MAN ALL SUMMER.
...
HE HAS?
YEAH. BUT WHEN I FOUND HIM, HUTCH IMMEDIATELY HAD THREE SUNTROOPERS ATTACK G-MAN.
THREE SUNNY BOYS, I ASSUME?
NO. SENIOR SUNTROOPERS.
SERIOUSLY?
YOU GUYS DON'T LOOK LIKE YOU'VE BEEN IN A FIGHT.
WE BEAT THEM RATHER EASILY.

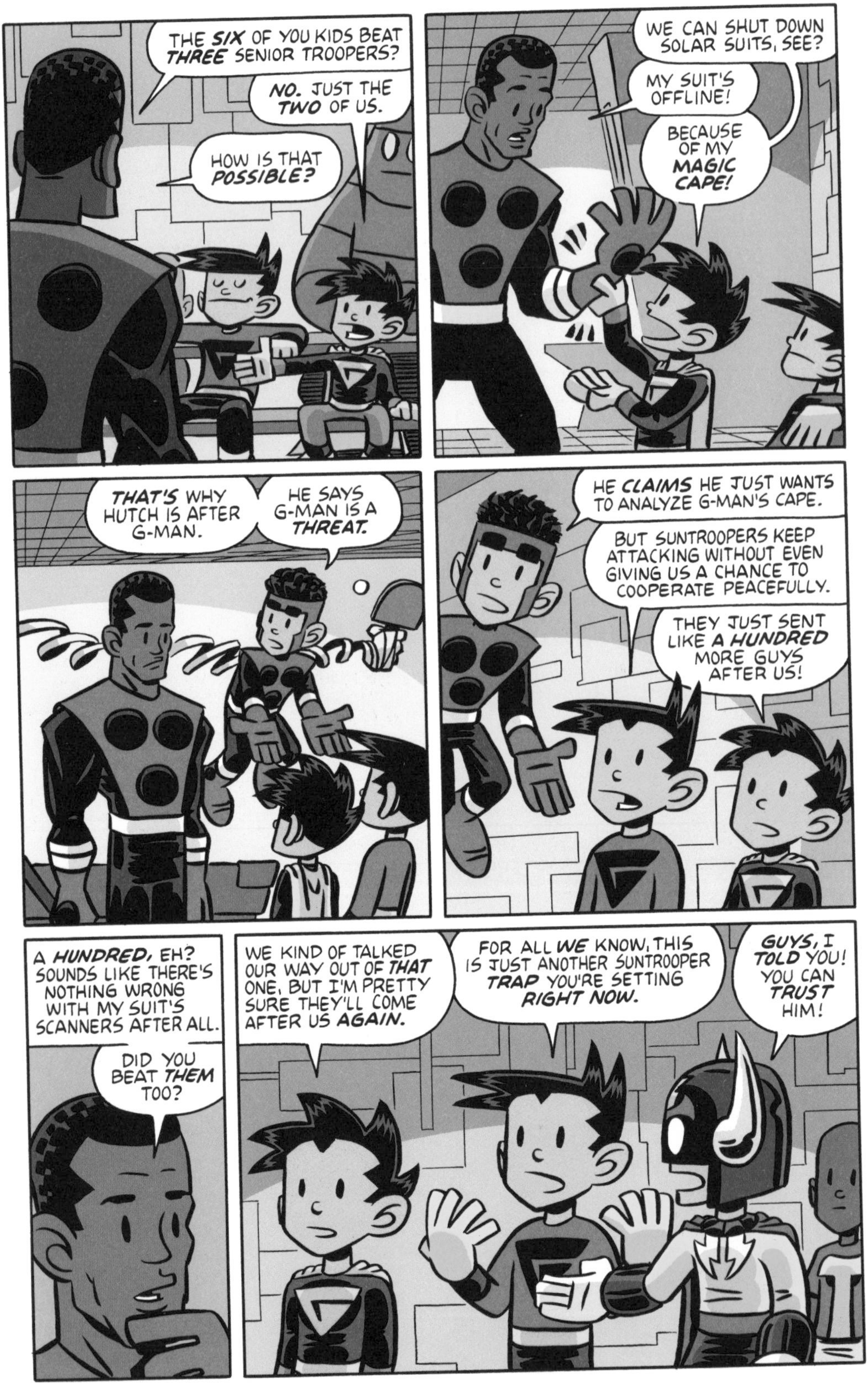

THE SIX OF YOU KIDS BEAT THREE SENIOR TROOPERS?
NO. JUST THE TWO OF US.
HOW IS THAT POSSIBLE?
WE CAN SHUT DOWN SOLAR SUITS, SEE?
MY SUIT'S OFFLINE!
BECAUSE OF MY MAGIC CAPE!
THAT'S WHY HUTCH IS AFTER G-MAN.
HE SAYS G-MAN IS A THREAT.
HE CLAIMS HE JUST WANTS TO ANALYZE G-MAN'S CAPE.
BUT SUNTROOPERS KEEP ATTACKING WITHOUT EVEN GIVING US A CHANCE TO COOPERATE PEACEFULLY.
THEY JUST SENT LIKE A HUNDRED MORE GUYS AFTER US!
A HUNDRED, EH? SOUNDS LIKE THERE'S NOTHING WRONG WITH MY SUIT'S SCANNERS AFTER ALL.
DID YOU BEAT THEM TOO?
WE KIND OF TALKED OUR WAY OUT OF THAT ONE, BUT I'M PRETTY SURE THEY'LL COME AFTER US AGAIN.
FOR ALL WE KNOW, THIS IS JUST ANOTHER SUNTROOPER TRAP YOU'RE SETTING RIGHT NOW.
GUYS, I TOLD YOU! YOU CAN TRUST HIM!

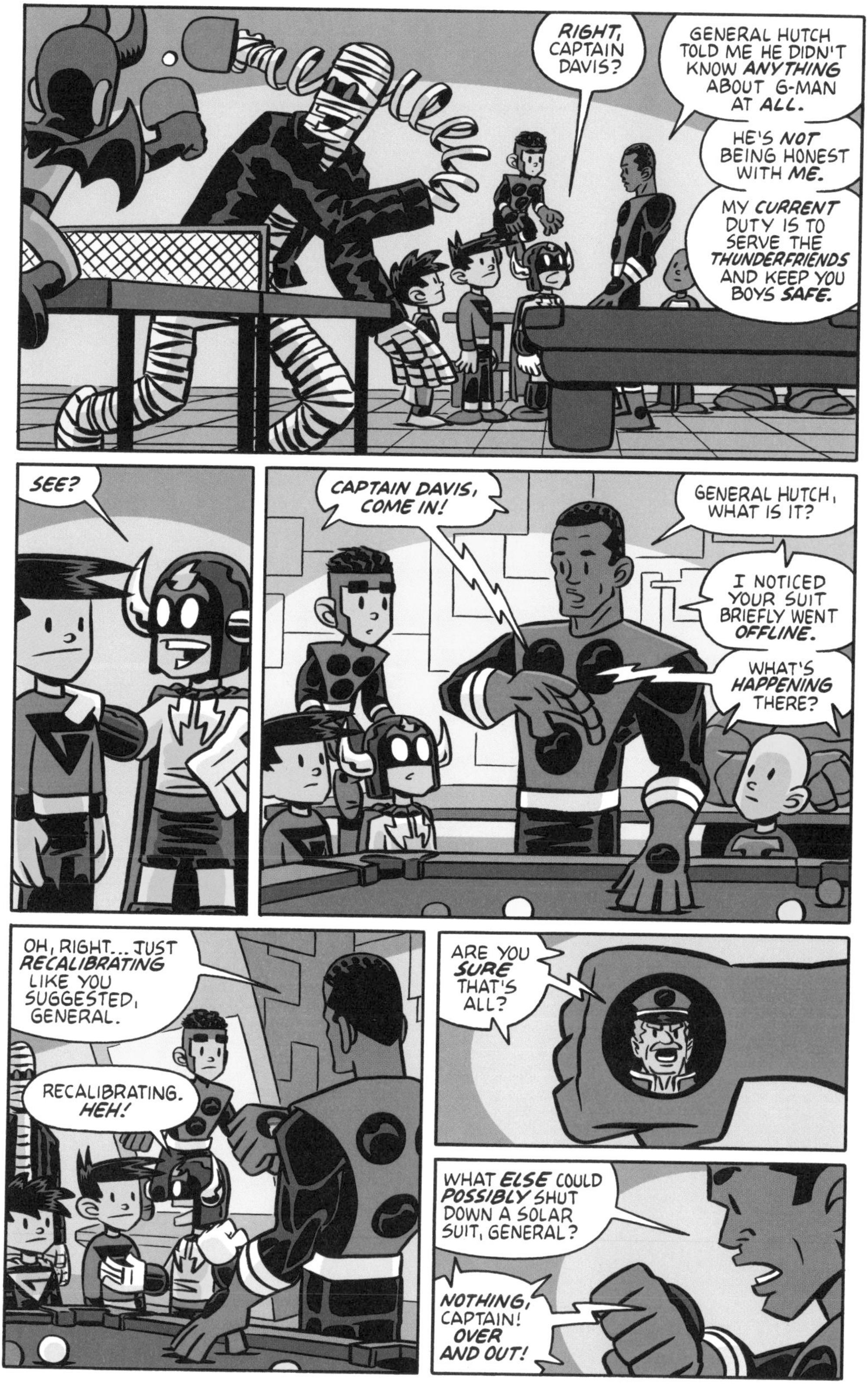
RIGHT, CAPTAIN DAVIS?
GENERAL HUTCH TOLD ME HE DIDN'T KNOW ANYTHING ABOUT G-MAN AT ALL.
HE'S NOT BEING HONEST WITH ME.
MY CURRENT DUTY IS TO SERVE THE THUNDERFRIENDS AND KEEP YOU BOYS SAFE.
SEE?
CAPTAIN DAVIS, COME IN!
GENERAL HUTCH, WHAT IS IT?
I NOTICED YOUR SUIT BRIEFLY WENT OFFLINE.
WHAT'S HAPPENING THERE?
OH, RIGHT... JUST RECALIBRATING LIKE YOU SUGGESTED, GENERAL.
RECALIBRATING. HEH!
ARE YOU SURE THAT'S ALL?
WHAT ELSE COULD POSSIBLY SHUT DOWN A SOLAR SUIT, GENERAL?
NOTHING, CAPTAIN! OVER AND OUT!

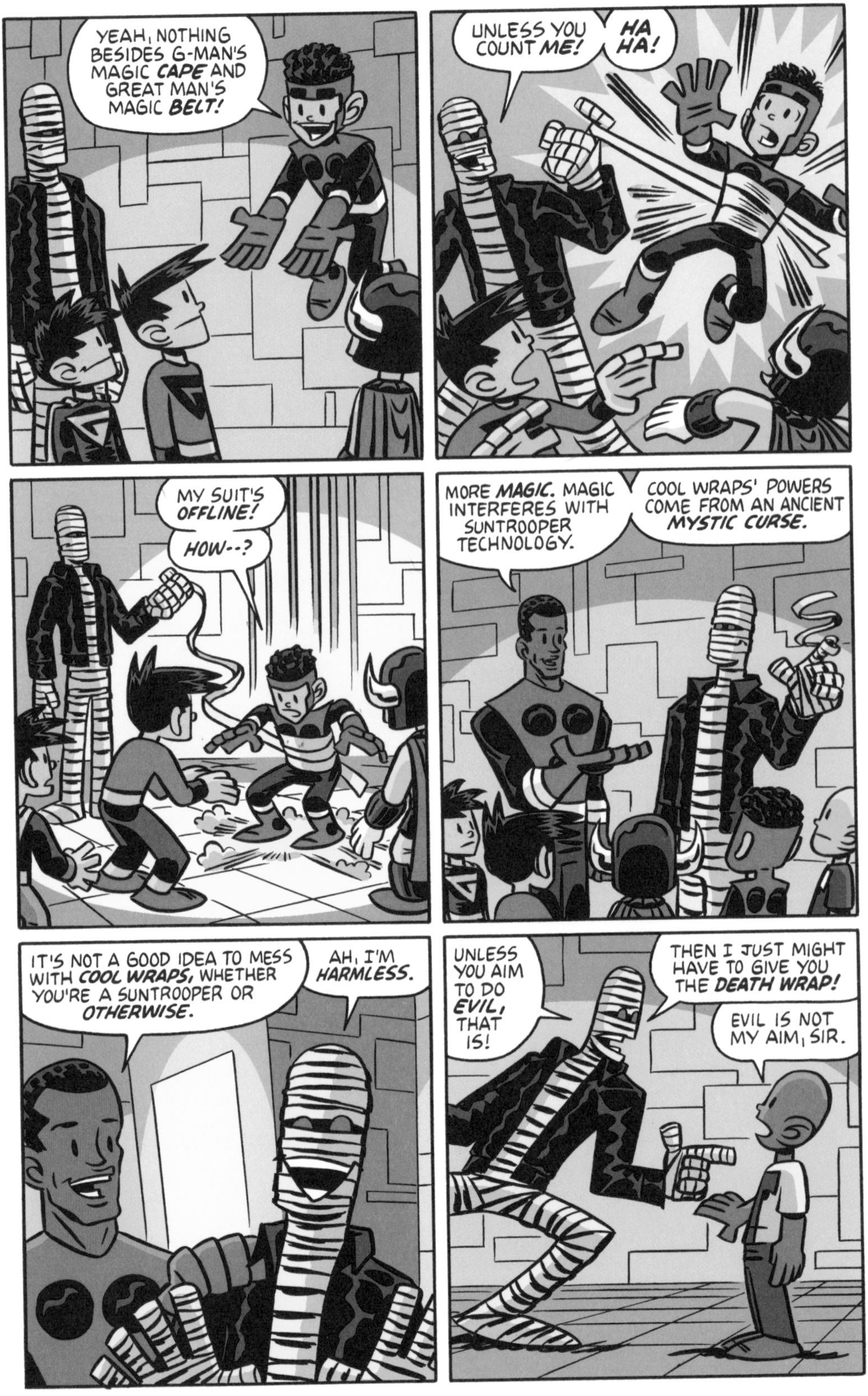
YEAH, NOTHING BESIDES G-MAN'S MAGIC CAPE AND GREAT MAN'S MAGIC BELT!
UNLESS YOU COUNT ME!
HA HA!
MY SUIT'S OFFLINE!
HOW--?
MORE MAGIC. MAGIC INTERFERES WITH SUNTROOPER TECHNOLOGY.
COOL WRAPS' POWERS COME FROM AN ANCIENT MYSTIC CURSE.
IT'S NOT A GOOD IDEA TO MESS WITH COOL WRAPS, WHETHER YOU'RE A SUNTROOPER OR OTHERWISE.
AH, I'M HARMLESS.
UNLESS YOU AIM TO DO EVIL, THAT IS!
THEN I JUST MIGHT HAVE TO GIVE YOU THE DEATH WRAP!
EVIL IS NOT MY AIM, SIR.

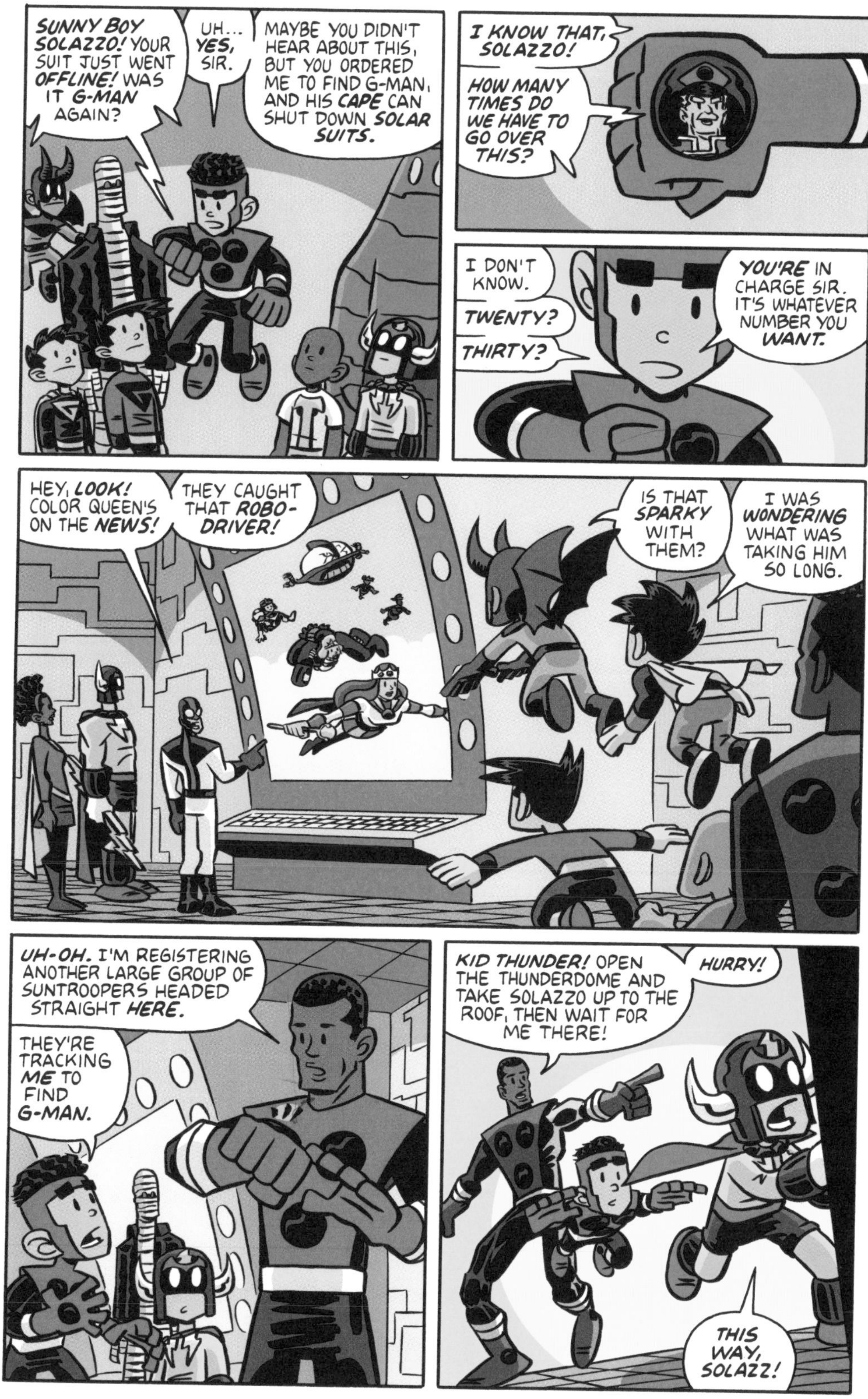
SUNNY BOY SOLAZZO! YOUR SUIT JUST WENT OFFLINE! WAS IT G-MAN AGAIN?
UH... YES, SIR.
MAYBE YOU DIDN'T HEAR ABOUT THIS, BUT YOU ORDERED ME TO FIND G-MAN, AND HIS CAPE CAN SHUT DOWN SOLAR SUITS.
I KNOW THAT, SOLAZZO!
HOW MANY TIMES DO WE HAVE TO GO OVER THIS?
I DON'T KNOW.
TWENTY?
THIRTY?
YOU'RE IN CHARGE SIR. IT'S WHATEVER NUMBER YOU WANT.
HEY, LOOK! COLOR QUEEN'S ON THE NEWS!
THEY CAUGHT THAT ROBO-DRIVER!
IS THAT SPARKY WITH THEM?
I WAS WONDERING WHAT WAS TAKING HIM SO LONG.
UH-OH. I'M REGISTERING ANOTHER LARGE GROUP OF SUNTROOPERS HEADED STRAIGHT HERE.
THEY'RE TRACKING ME TO FIND G-MAN.
KID THUNDER! OPEN THE THUNDERDOME AND TAKE SOLAZZO UP TO THE ROOF, THEN WAIT FOR ME THERE!
HURRY!
THIS WAY, SOLAZZ!

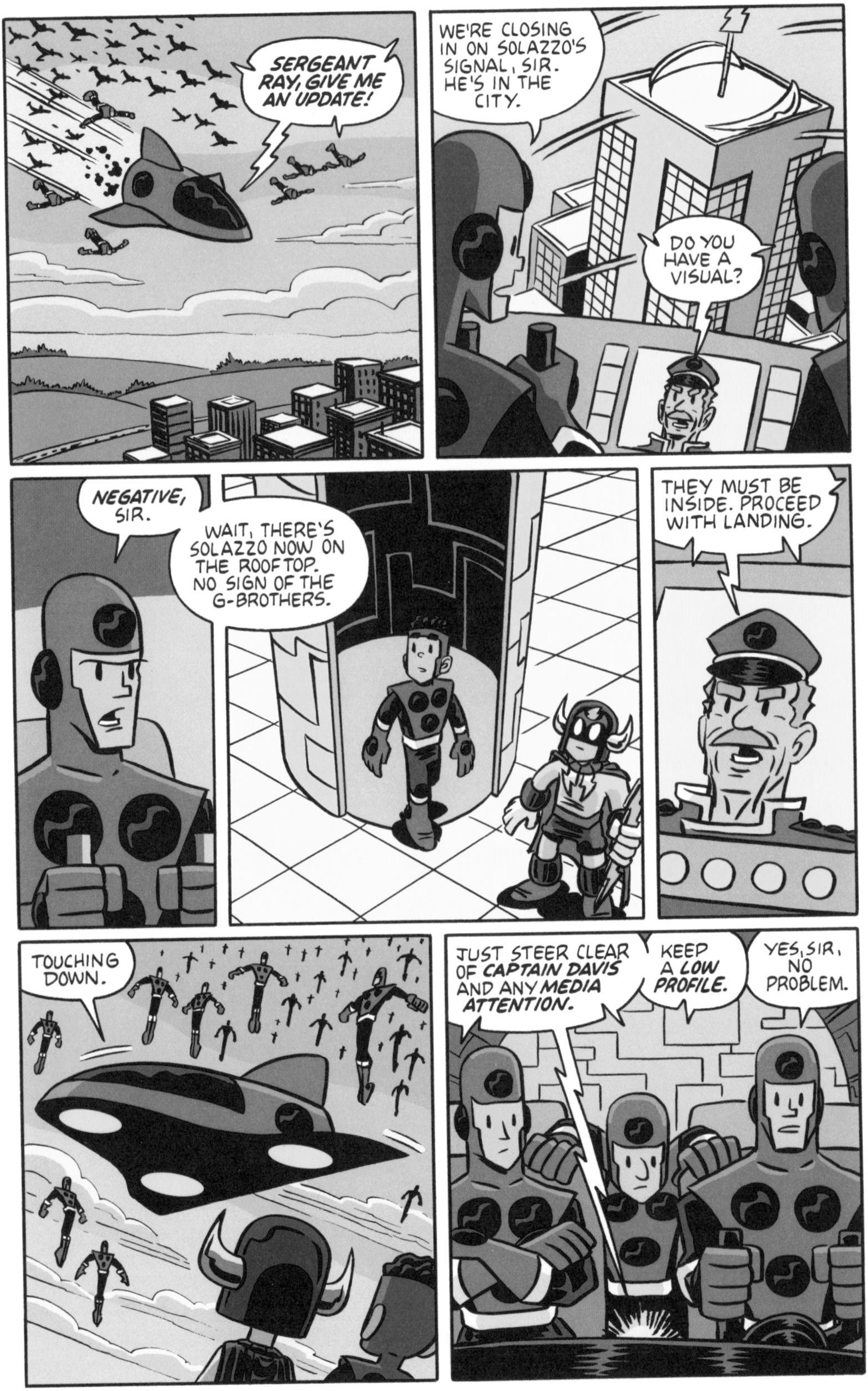
SERGEANT RAY, GIVE ME AN UPDATE!
WE'RE CLOSING IN ON SOLAZZO'S SIGNAL, SIR. HE'S IN THE CITY.
DO YOU HAVE A VISUAL?
NEGATIVE, SIR.
WAIT, THERE'S SOLAZZO NOW ON THE ROOFTOP. NO SIGN OF THE G-BROTHERS.
THEY MUST BE INSIDE. PROCEED WITH LANDING.
TOUCHING DOWN.
JUST STEER CLEAR OF CAPTAIN DAVIS AND ANY MEDIA ATTENTION.
KEEP A LOW PROFILE.
YES, SIR, NO PROBLEM.

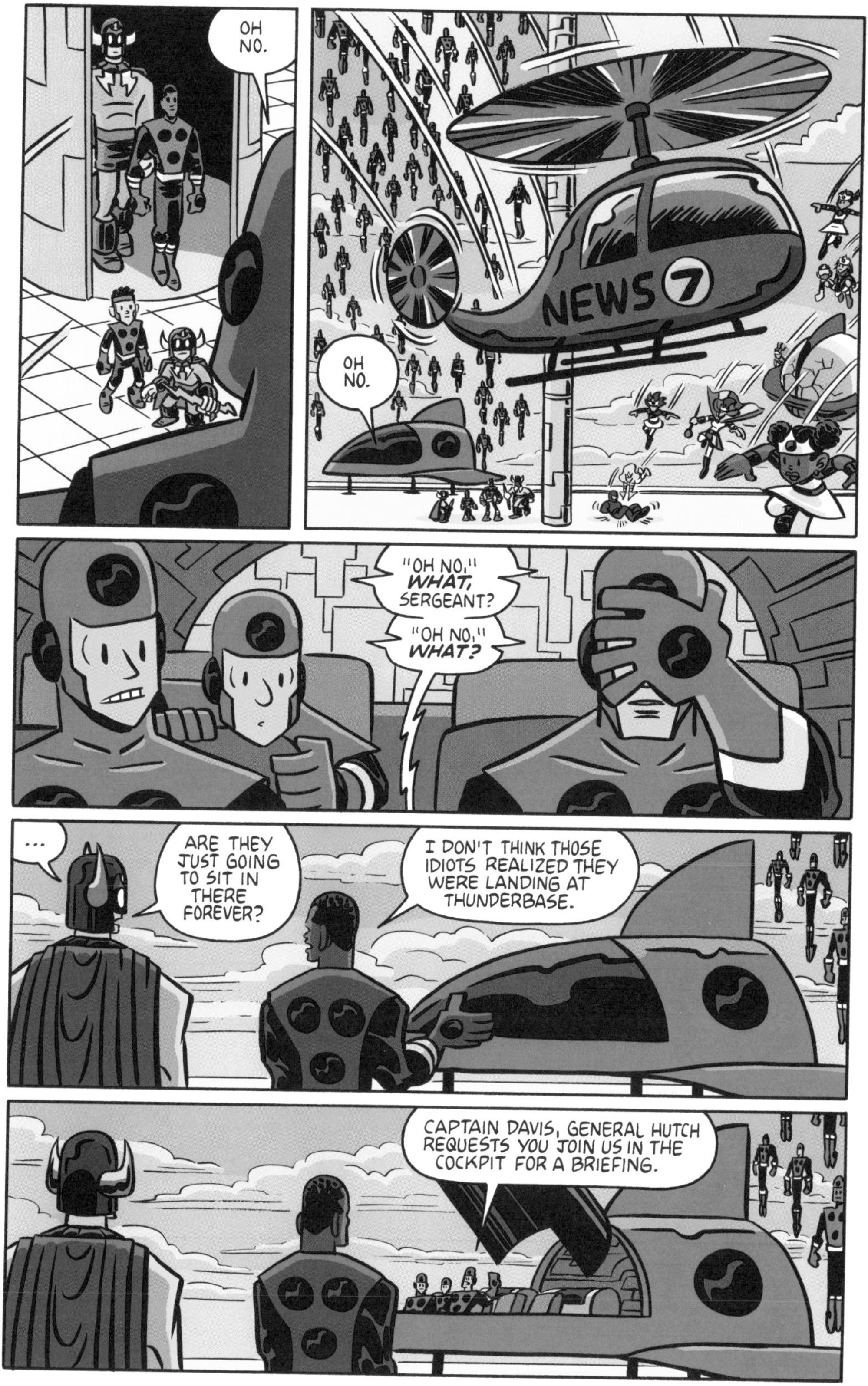
OH NO.
OH NO.
"OH NO," WHAT, SERGEANT?
"OH NO," WHAT?
...
ARE THEY JUST GOING TO SIT IN THERE FOREVER?
I DON'T THINK THOSE IDIOTS REALIZED THEY WERE LANDING AT THUNDERBASE.
CAPTAIN DAVIS, GENERAL HUTCH REQUESTS YOU JOIN US IN THE COCKPIT FOR A BRIEFING.
NEWS 7

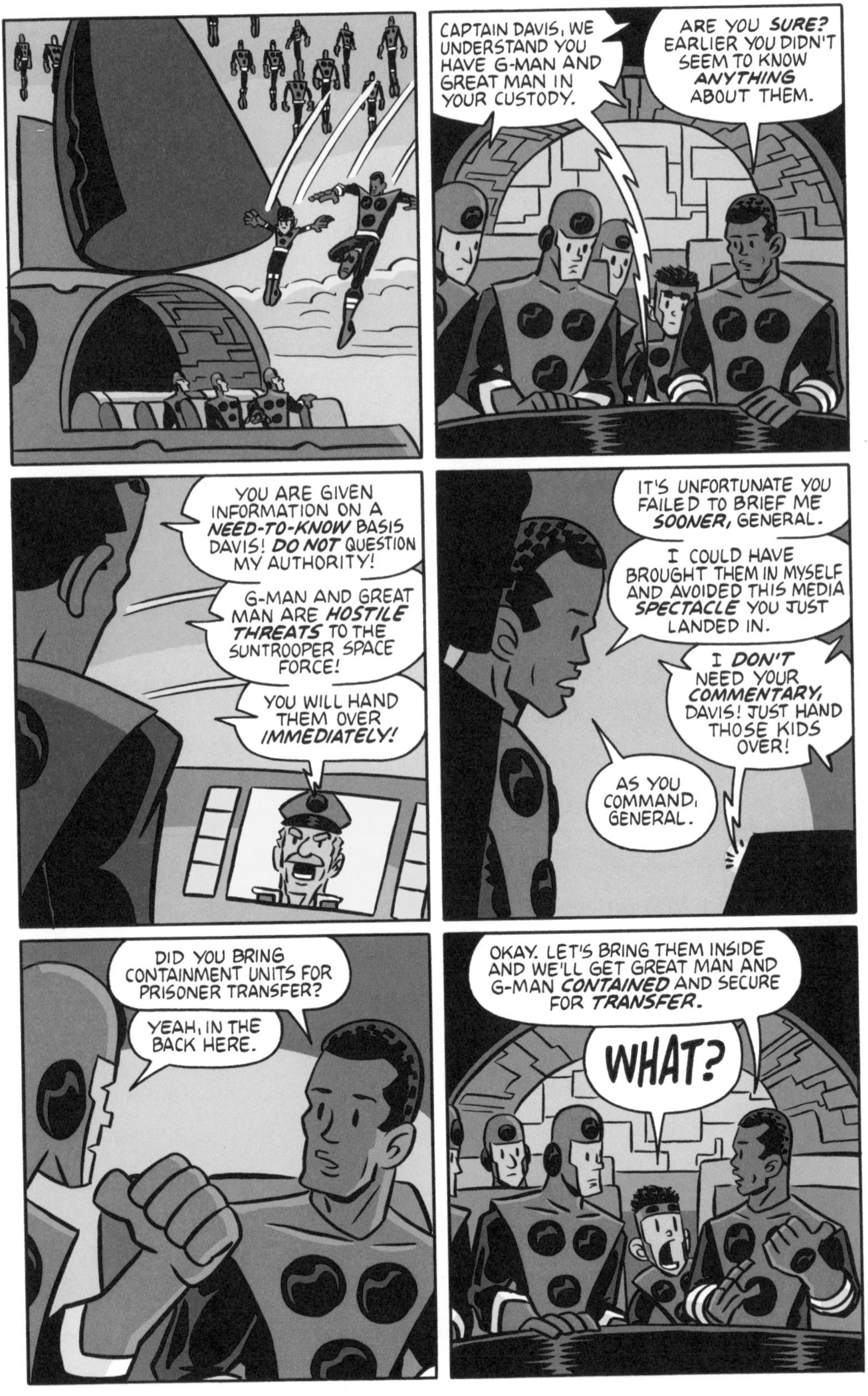
CAPTAIN DAVIS, WE UNDERSTAND YOU HAVE G-MAN AND GREAT MAN IN YOUR CUSTODY.
ARE YOU SURE? EARLIER YOU DIDN'T SEEM TO KNOW ANYTHING ABOUT THEM.
YOU ARE GIVEN INFORMATION ON A NEED-TO-KNOW BASIS DAVIS! DO NOT QUESTION MY AUTHORITY!
G-MAN AND GREAT MAN ARE HOSTILE THREATS TO THE SUNTROOPER SPACE FORCE!
YOU WILL HAND THEM OVER IMMEDIATELY!
IT'S UNFORTUNATE YOU FAILED TO BRIEF ME SOONER, GENERAL.
I COULD HAVE BROUGHT THEM IN MYSELF AND AVOIDED THIS MEDIA SPECTACLE YOU JUST LANDED IN.
I DON'T NEED YOUR COMMENTARY, DAVIS! JUST HAND THOSE KIDS OVER!
AS YOU COMMAND, GENERAL.
DID YOU BRING CONTAINMENT UNITS FOR PRISONER TRANSFER?
YEAH, IN THE BACK HERE.
OKAY. LET'S BRING THEM INSIDE AND WE'LL GET GREAT MAN AND G-MAN CONTAINED AND SECURE FOR TRANSFER.
WHAT?

WHAT?

CHAPTER
FOUR

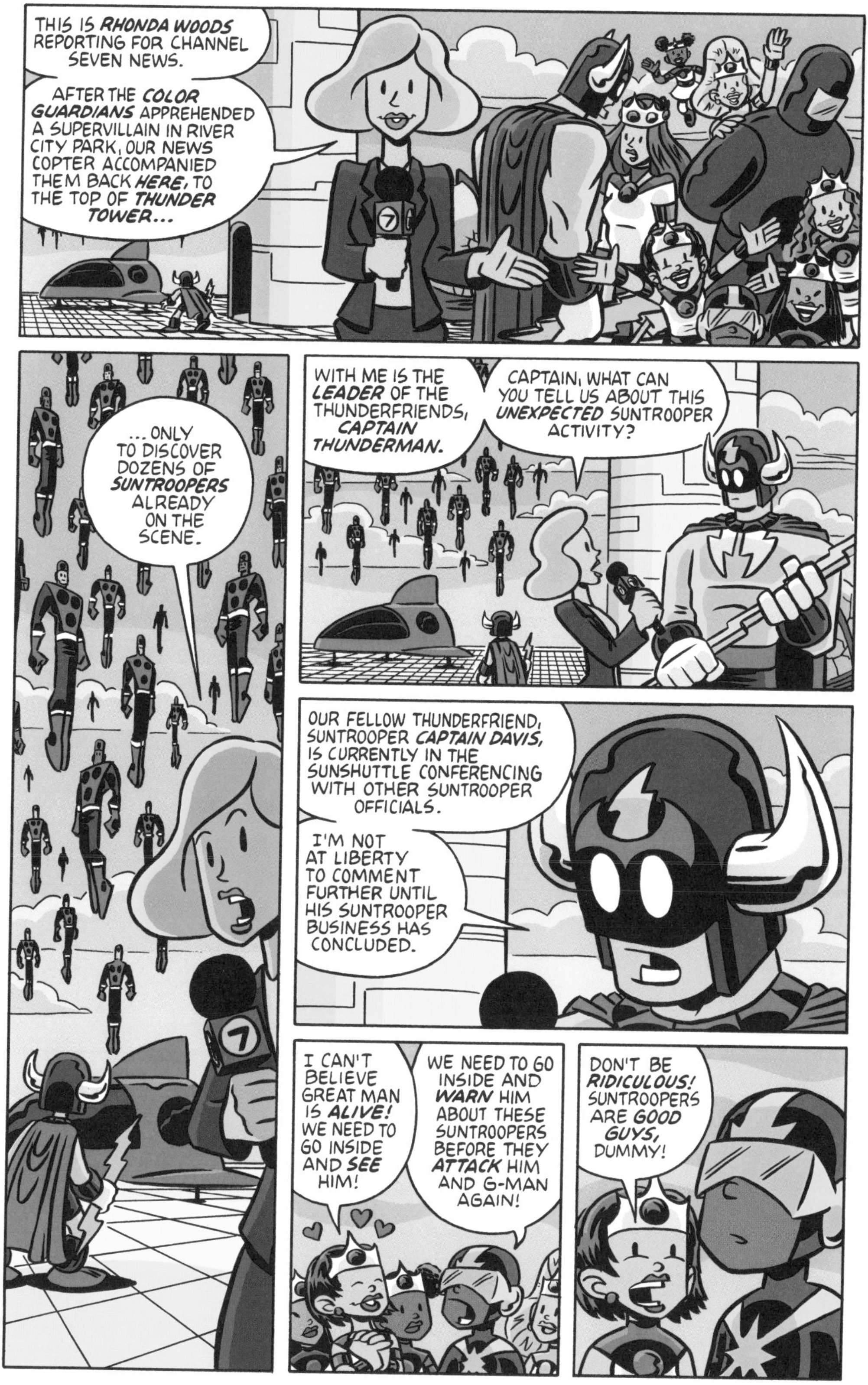
THIS IS RHONDA WOODS REPORTING FOR CHANNEL SEVEN NEWS.
AFTER THE COLOR GUARDIANS APPREHENDED A SUPERVILLAIN IN RIVER CITY PARK, OUR NEWS COPTER ACCOMPANIED THEM BACK HERE, TO THE TOP OF THUNDER TOWER...
...ONLY TO DISCOVER DOZENS OF SUNTROOPERS ALREADY ON THE SCENE.
WITH ME IS THE LEADER OF THE THUNDERFRIENDS, CAPTAIN THUNDERMAN.
CAPTAIN, WHAT CAN YOU TELL US ABOUT THIS UNEXPECTED SUNTROOPER ACTIVITY?
OUR FELLOW THUNDERFRIEND, SUNTROOPER CAPTAIN DAVIS, IS CURRENTLY IN THE SUNSHUTTLE CONFERENCING WITH OTHER SUNTROOPER OFFICIALS.
I'M NOT AT LIBERTY TO COMMENT FURTHER UNTIL HIS SUNTROOPER BUSINESS HAS CONCLUDED.
I CAN'T BELIEVE GREAT MAN IS ALIVE! WE NEED TO GO INSIDE AND SEE HIM!
WE NEED TO GO INSIDE AND WARN HIM ABOUT THESE SUNTROOPERS BEFORE THEY ATTACK HIM AND G-MAN AGAIN!
DON'T BE RIDICULOUS! SUNTROOPERS ARE GOOD GUYS, DUMMY!

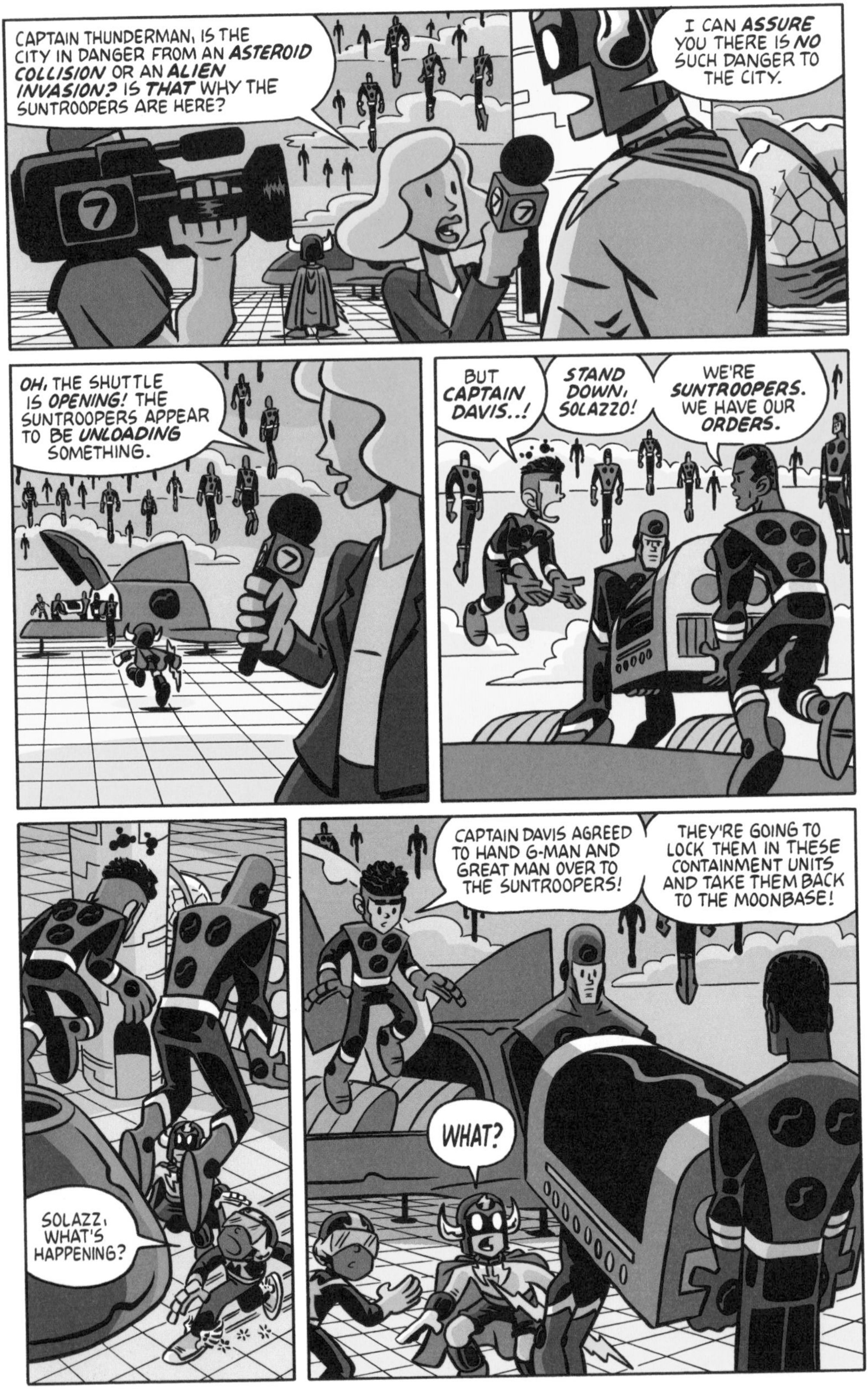
CAPTAIN THUNDERMAN, IS THE CITY IN DANGER FROM AN ASTEROID COLLISION OR AN ALIEN INVASION? IS THAT WHY THE SUNTROOPERS ARE HERE?
I CAN ASSURE YOU THERE IS NO SUCH DANGER TO THE CITY.
OH, THE SHUTTLE IS OPENING! THE SUNTROOPERS APPEAR TO BE UNLOADING SOMETHING.
BUT CAPTAIN DAVIS..!
STAND DOWN, SOLAZZO!
WE'RE SUNTROOPERS. WE HAVE OUR ORDERS.
SOLAZZ, WHAT'S HAPPENING?
CAPTAIN DAVIS AGREED TO HAND G-MAN AND GREAT MAN OVER TO THE SUNTROOPERS!
THEY'RE GOING TO LOCK THEM IN THESE CONTAINMENT UNITS AND TAKE THEM BACK TO THE MOONBASE!
WHAT?

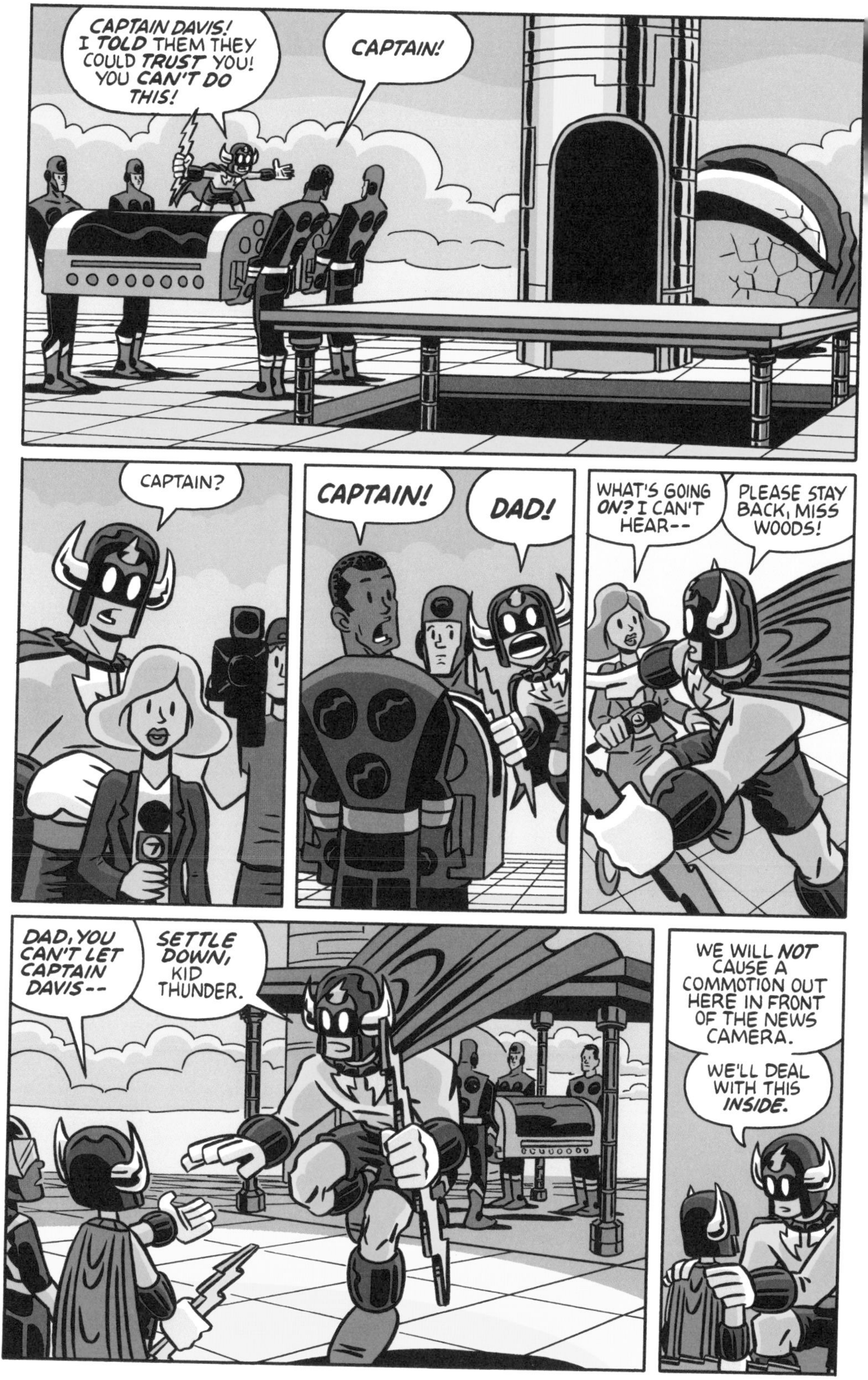
CAPTAIN DAVIS! I TOLD THEM THEY COULD TRUST YOU! YOU CAN'T DO THIS!
CAPTAIN!
CAPTAIN?
CAPTAIN!
DAD!
WHAT'S GOING ON? I CAN'T HEAR--
PLEASE STAY BACK, MISS WOODS!
DAD, YOU CAN'T LET CAPTAIN DAVIS--
SETTLE DOWN, KID THUNDER.
WE WILL NOT CAUSE A COMMOTION OUT HERE IN FRONT OF THE NEWS CAMERA.
WE'LL DEAL WITH THIS INSIDE.

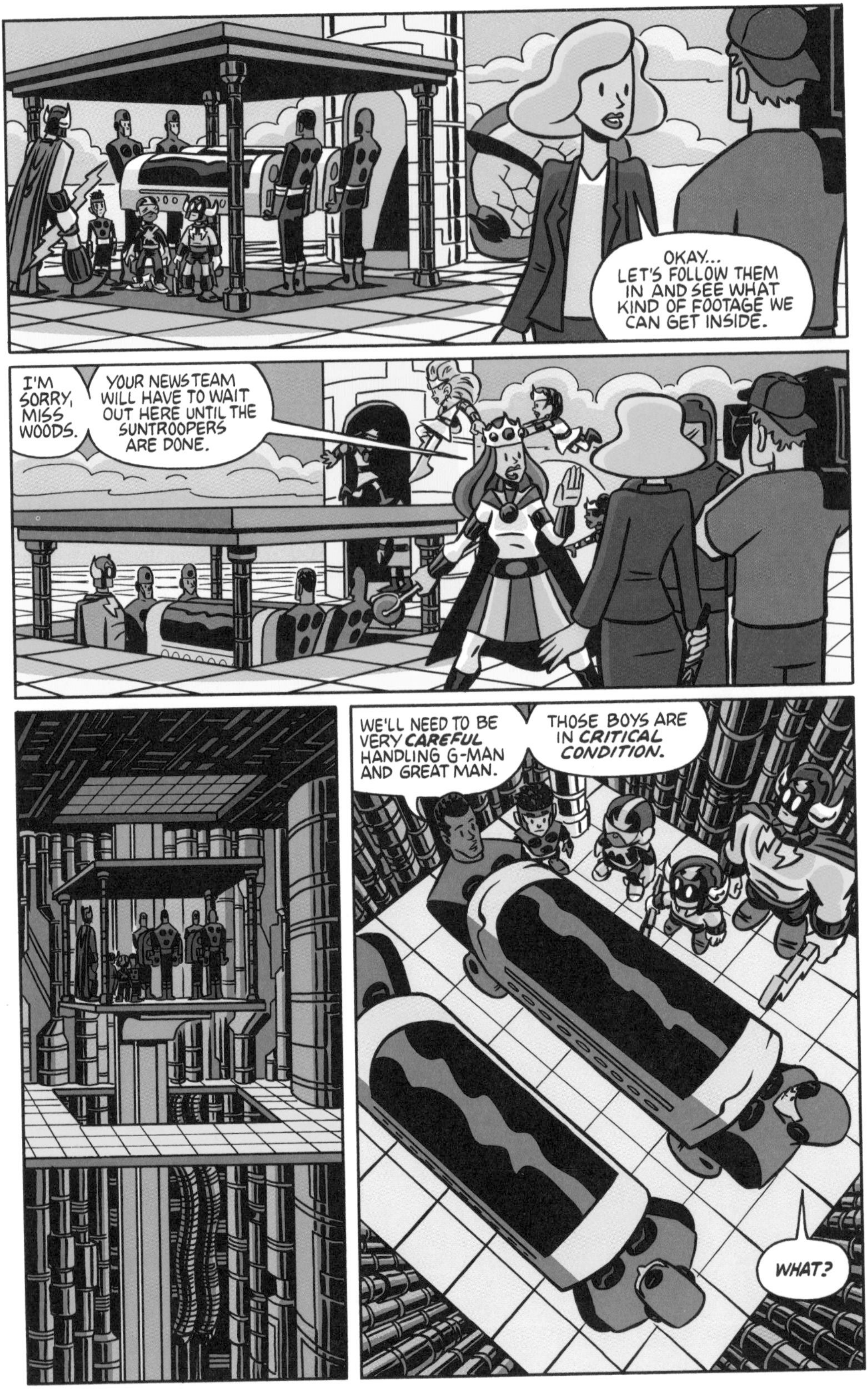
OKAY... LET'S FOLLOW THEM IN AND SEE WHAT KIND OF FOOTAGE WE CAN GET INSIDE.
I'M SORRY, MISS WOODS.
YOUR NEWSTEAM WILL HAVE TO WAIT OUT HERE UNTIL THE SUNTROOPERS ARE DONE.
WE'LL NEED TO BE VERY CAREFUL HANDLING G-MAN AND GREAT MAN.
THOSE BOYS ARE IN CRITICAL CONDITION.
WHAT?

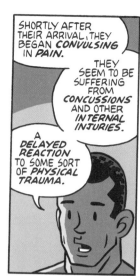

SHORTLY AFTER THEIR ARRIVAL, THEY BEGAN *CONVULSING* IN *PAIN.*

THEY SEEM TO BE SUFFERING FROM *CONCUSSIONS* AND OTHER *INTERNAL INJURIES.*

A *DELAYED REACTION* TO SOME SORT OF *PHYSICAL TRAUMA.*

FROM THE *FIGHT!*

CAPTAIN DAVIS, *THESE SUNTROOPERS* WERE *BLASTING* G-MAN AND GREAT MAN!

FULL FORCE FOR *NO REASON!*

THEY WERE *UNCONSCIOUS* WHEN I LEFT THEM.

IT SHOULDN'T BE A STRUGGLE TO SECURE THEM IN THESE *CONTAINMENT UNITS.*

DAD!

QUIET.

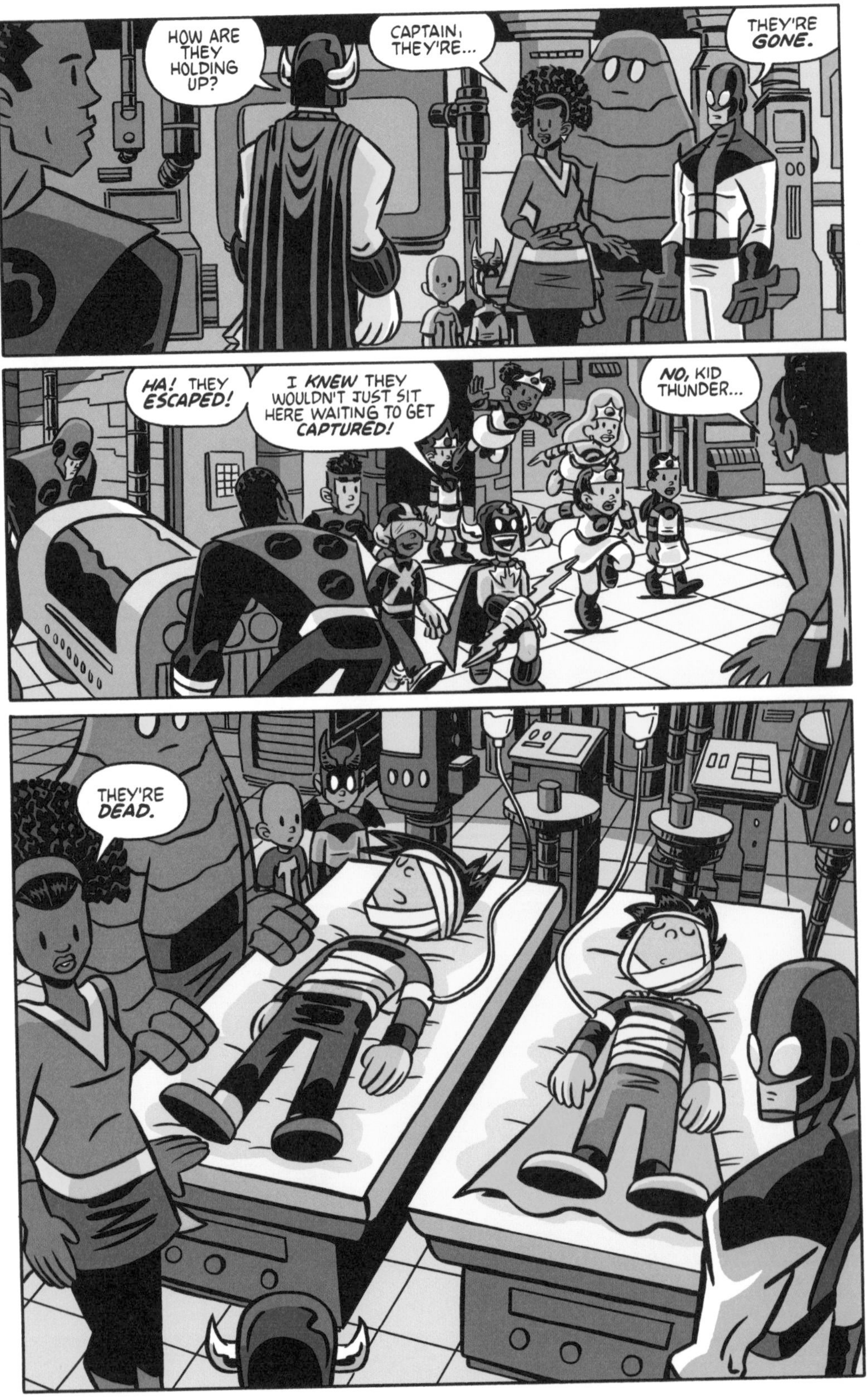
HOW ARE THEY HOLDING UP?
CAPTAIN, THEY'RE...
THEY'RE GONE.
HA! THEY ESCAPED!
I KNEW THEY WOULDN'T JUST SIT HERE WAITING TO GET CAPTURED!
NO, KID THUNDER...
THEY'RE DEAD.

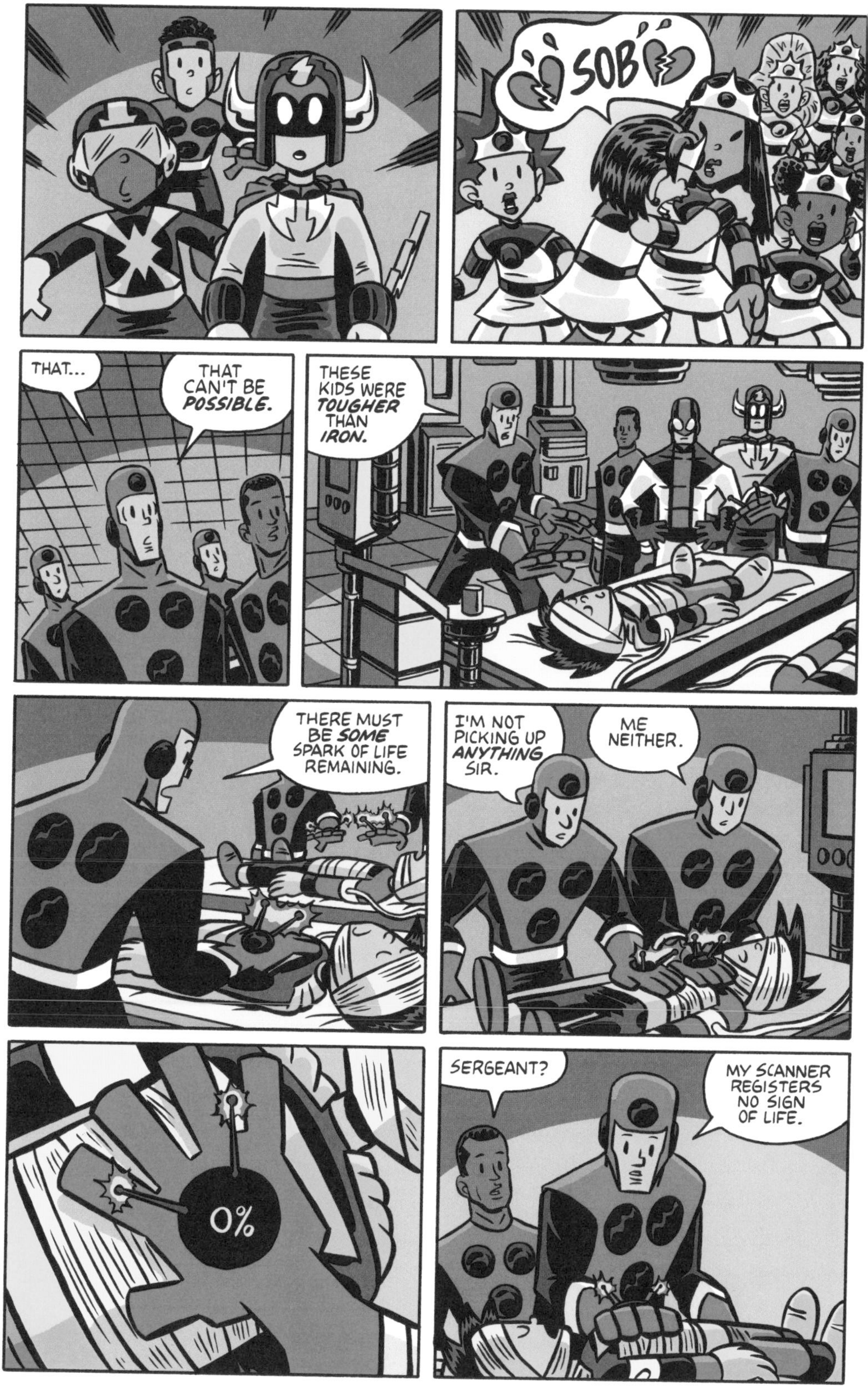
SOB
THAT...
THAT CAN'T BE POSSIBLE.
THESE KIDS WERE TOUGHER THAN IRON.
THERE MUST BE SOME SPARK OF LIFE REMAINING.
I'M NOT PICKING UP ANYTHING SIR.
ME NEITHER.
0%
SERGEANT?
MY SCANNER REGISTERS NO SIGN OF LIFE.

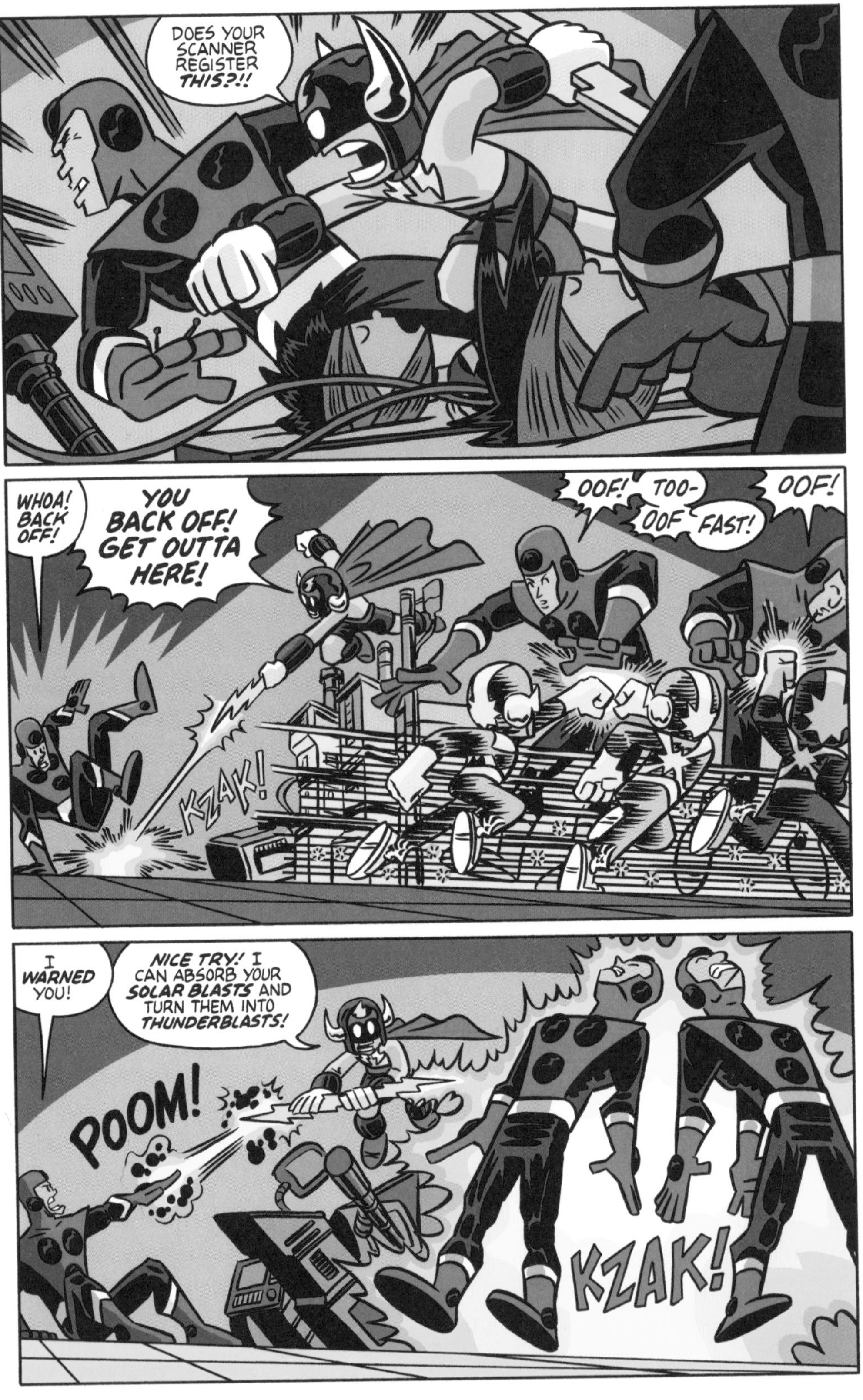
DOES YOUR SCANNER REGISTER THIS?!!
WHOA! BACK OFF!
YOU BACK OFF! GET OUTTA HERE!
OOF!
TOO- FAST!
OOF
OOF!
KZAK!
I WARNED YOU!
NICE TRY! I CAN ABSORB YOUR SOLAR BLASTS AND TURN THEM INTO THUNDERBLASTS!
POOM!
KZAK!

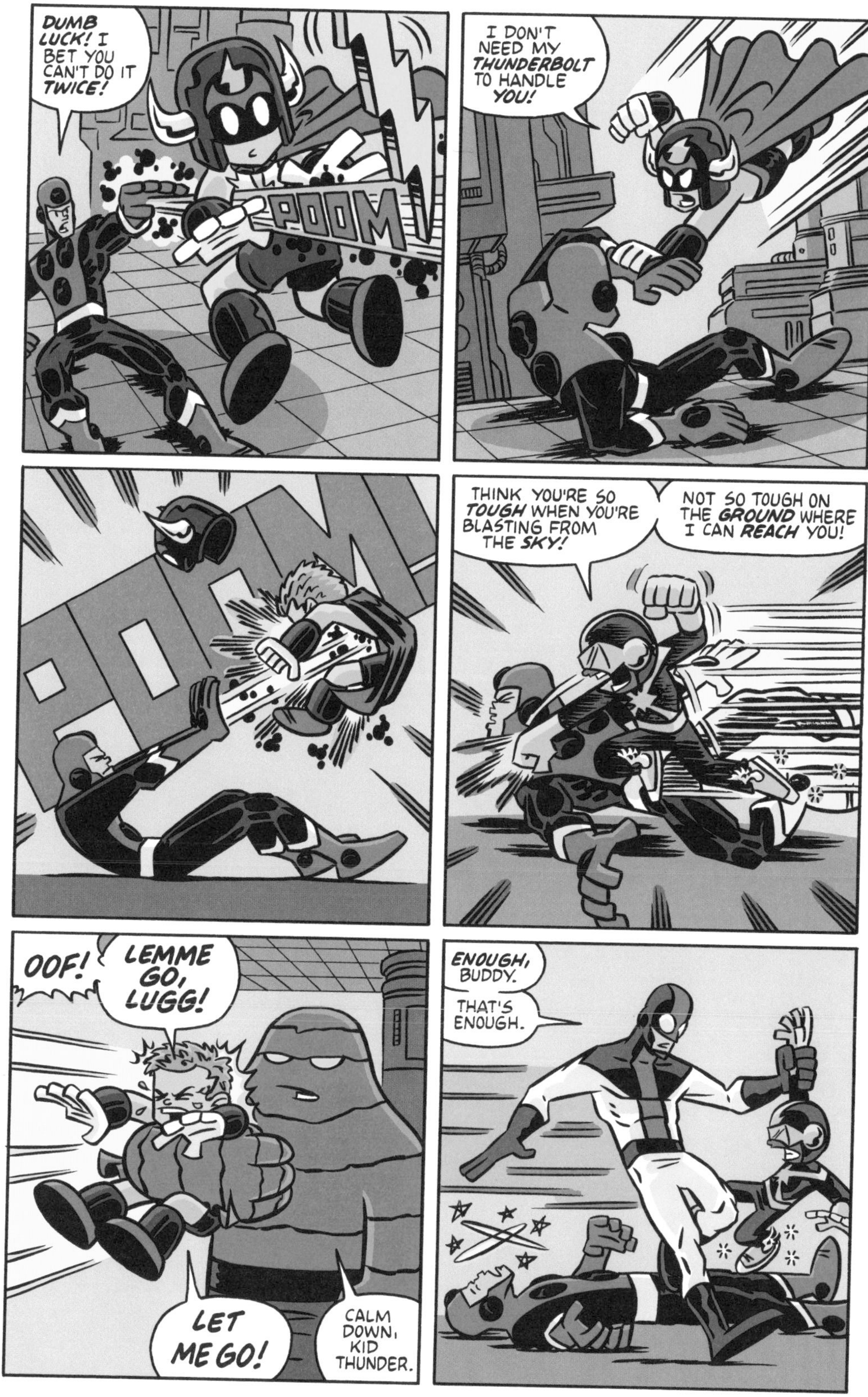
DUMB LUCK! I BET YOU CAN'T DO IT TWICE!
POOM
I DON'T NEED MY THUNDERBOLT TO HANDLE YOU!
THINK YOU'RE SO TOUGH WHEN YOU'RE BLASTING FROM THE SKY!
NOT SO TOUGH ON THE GROUND WHERE I CAN REACH YOU!
OOF!
LEMME GO, LUGG!
LET ME GO!
CALM DOWN, KID THUNDER.
ENOUGH, BUDDY.
THAT'S ENOUGH.

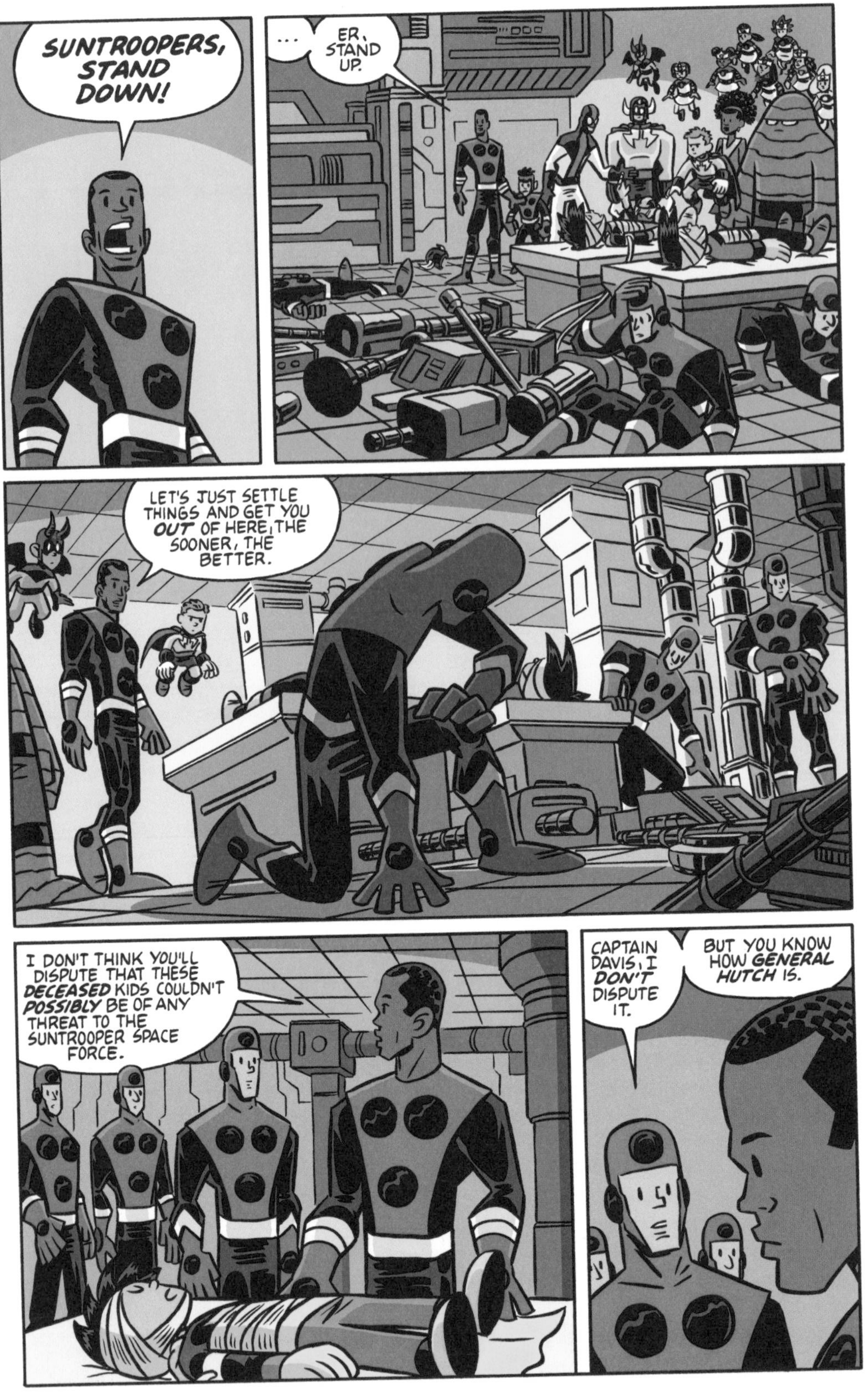
SUNTROOPERS, STAND DOWN!
...
ER, STAND UP.
LET'S JUST SETTLE THINGS AND GET YOU OUT OF HERE. THE SOONER, THE BETTER.
I DON'T THINK YOU'LL DISPUTE THAT THESE DECEASED KIDS COULDN'T POSSIBLY BE OF ANY THREAT TO THE SUNTROOPER SPACE FORCE.
CAPTAIN DAVIS, I DON'T DISPUTE IT.
BUT YOU KNOW HOW GENERAL HUTCH IS.

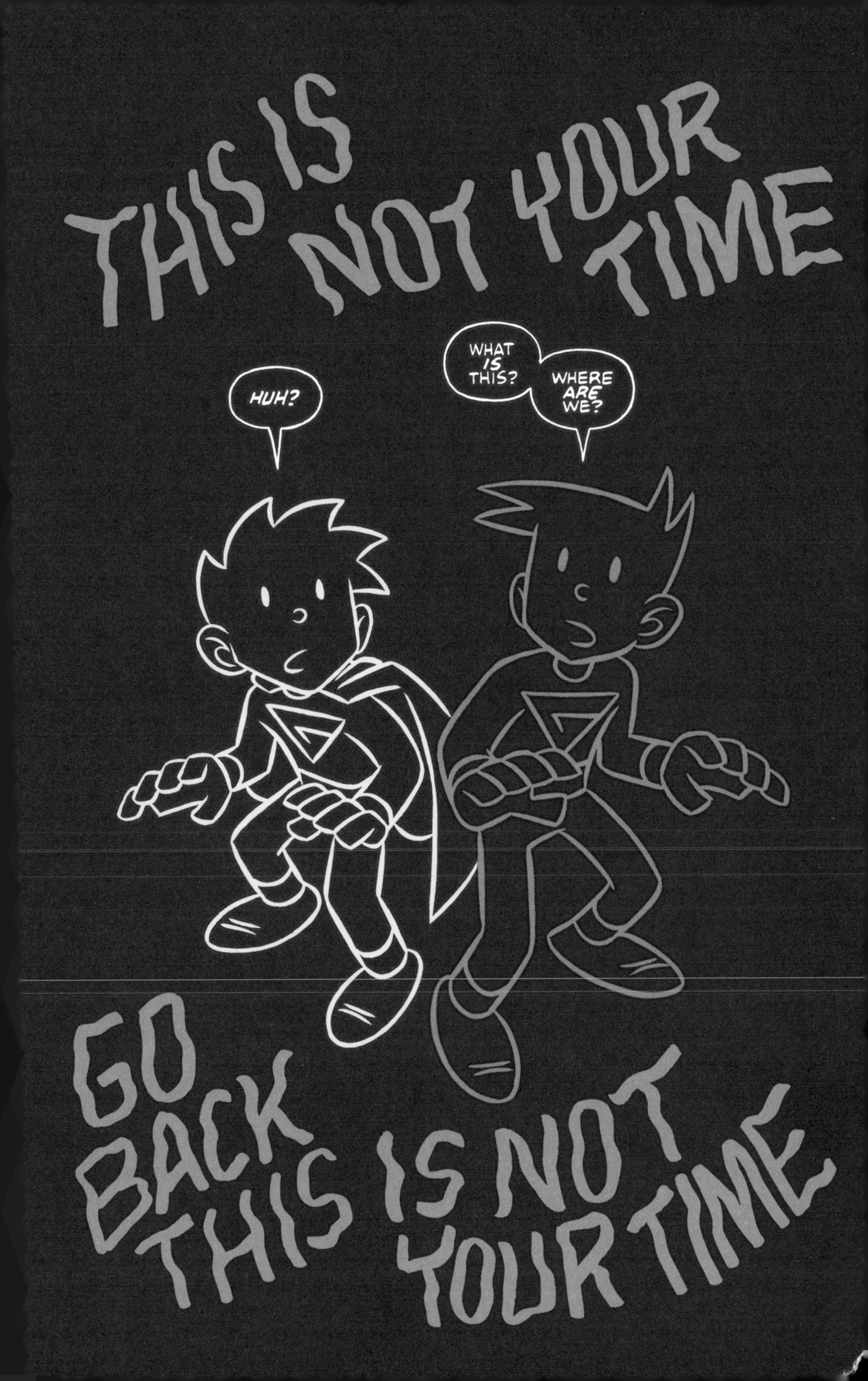
THIS IS NOT YOUR TIME
HUH?
WHAT IS THIS?
WHERE ARE WE?
GO BACK THIS IS NOT YOUR TIME

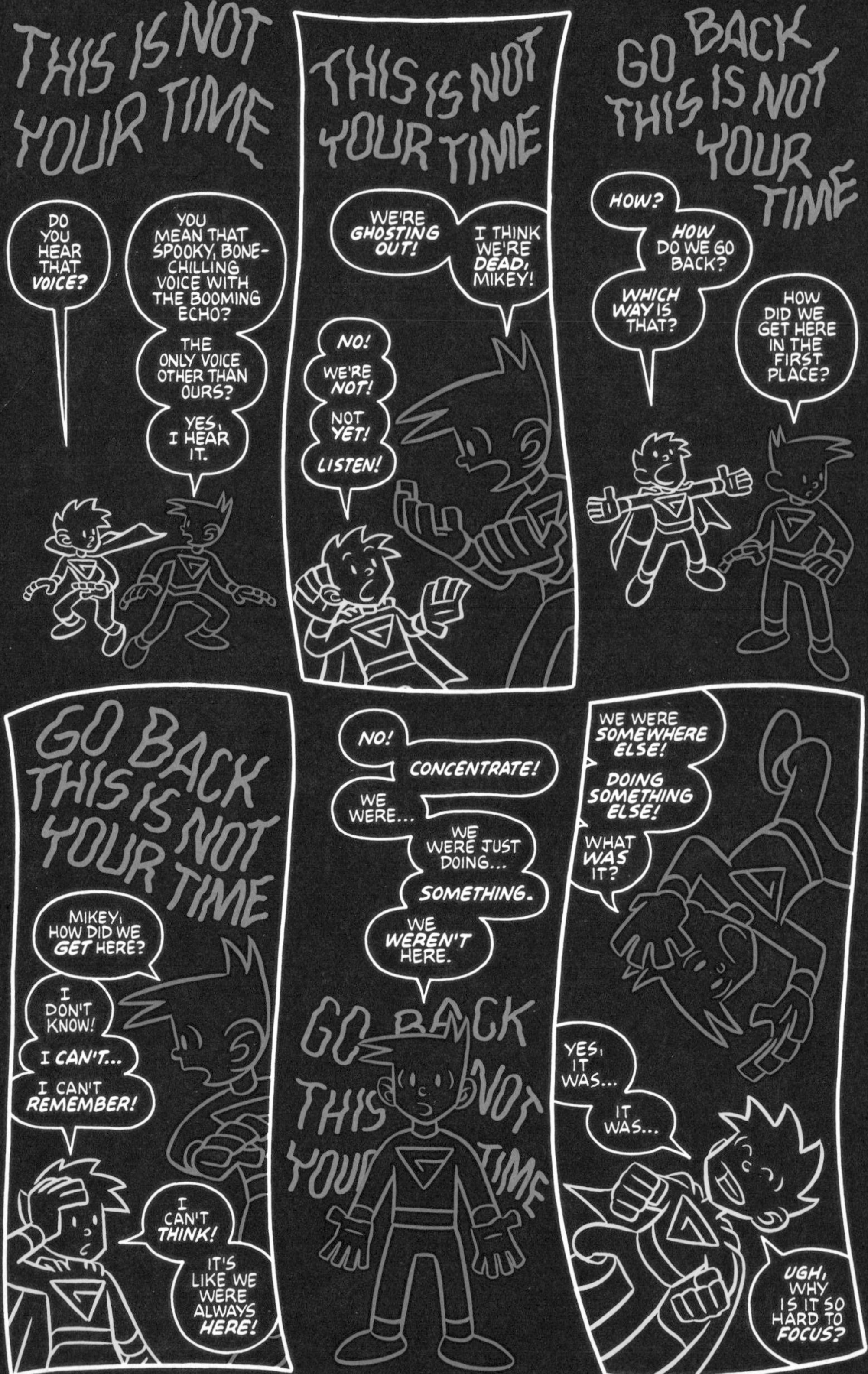
THIS IS NOT YOUR TIME
DO YOU HEAR THAT VOICE?
YOU MEAN THAT SPOOKY, BONE-CHILLING VOICE WITH THE BOOMING ECHO?
THE ONLY VOICE OTHER THAN OURS?
YES, I HEAR IT.
THIS IS NOT YOUR TIME
WE'RE GHOSTING OUT!
I THINK WE'RE DEAD, MIKEY!
NO!
WE'RE NOT!
NOT YET!
LISTEN!
GO BACK THIS IS NOT YOUR TIME
HOW?
HOW DO WE GO BACK?
WHICH WAY IS THAT?
HOW DID WE GET HERE IN THE FIRST PLACE?
GO BACK THIS IS NOT YOUR TIME
MIKEY, HOW DID WE GET HERE?
I DON'T KNOW!
I CAN'T...
I CAN'T REMEMBER!
I CAN'T THINK!
IT'S LIKE WE WERE ALWAYS HERE!
NO!
CONCENTRATE!
WE WERE...
WE WERE JUST DOING...
SOMETHING.
WE WEREN'T HERE.
GO BACK THIS NOT YOUR TIME
WE WERE SOMEWHERE ELSE!
DOING SOMETHING ELSE!
WHAT WAS IT?
YES, IT WAS...
IT WAS...
UGH, WHY IS IT SO HARD TO FOCUS?

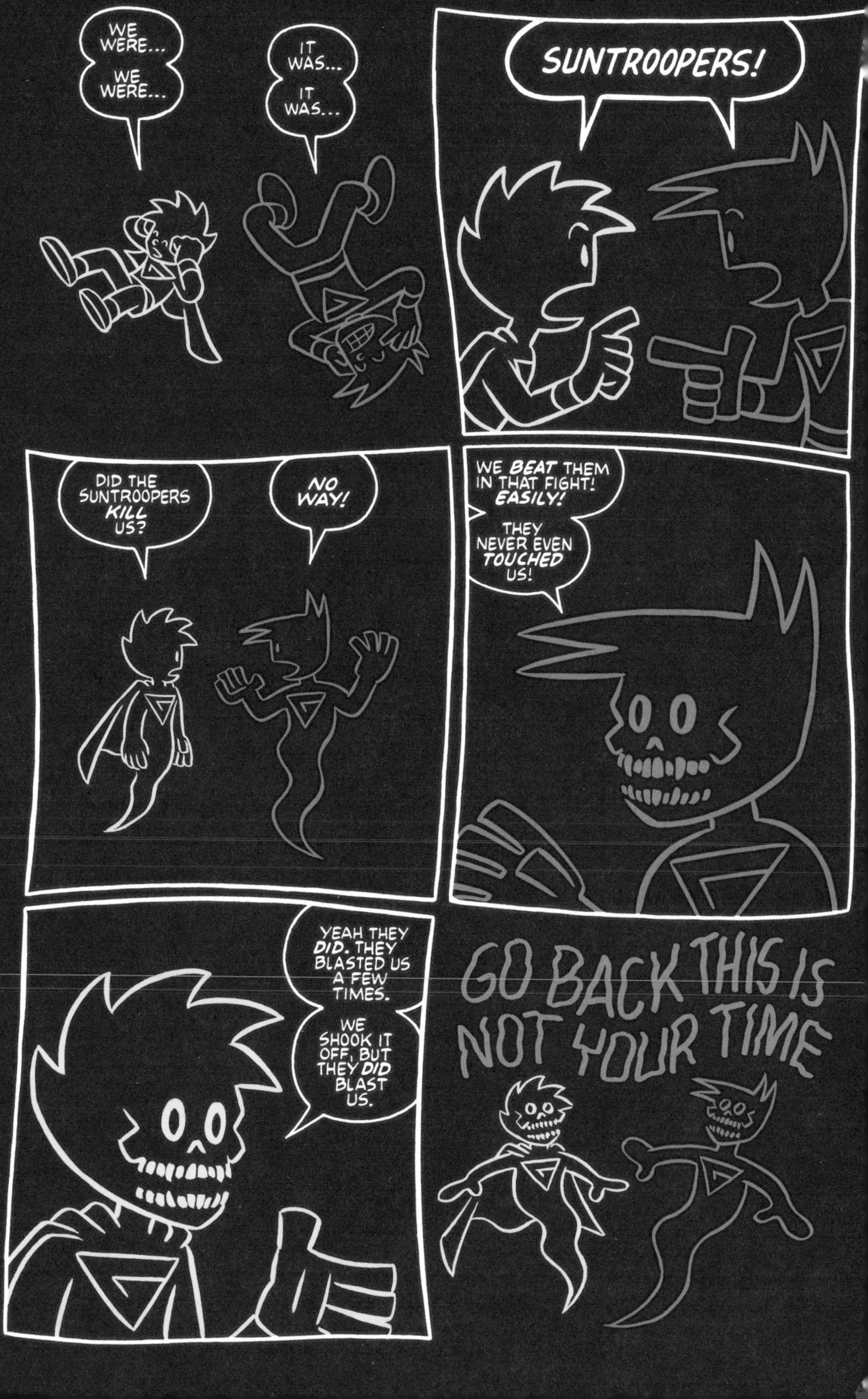
WE WERE... WE WERE...
IT WAS... IT WAS...
SUNTROOPERS!
DID THE SUNTROOPERS KILL US?
NO WAY!
WE BEAT THEM IN THAT FIGHT! EASILY!
THEY NEVER EVEN TOUCHED US!
YEAH THEY DID. THEY BLASTED US A FEW TIMES.
WE SHOOK IT OFF, BUT THEY DID BLAST US.
GO BACK THIS IS NOT YOUR TIME

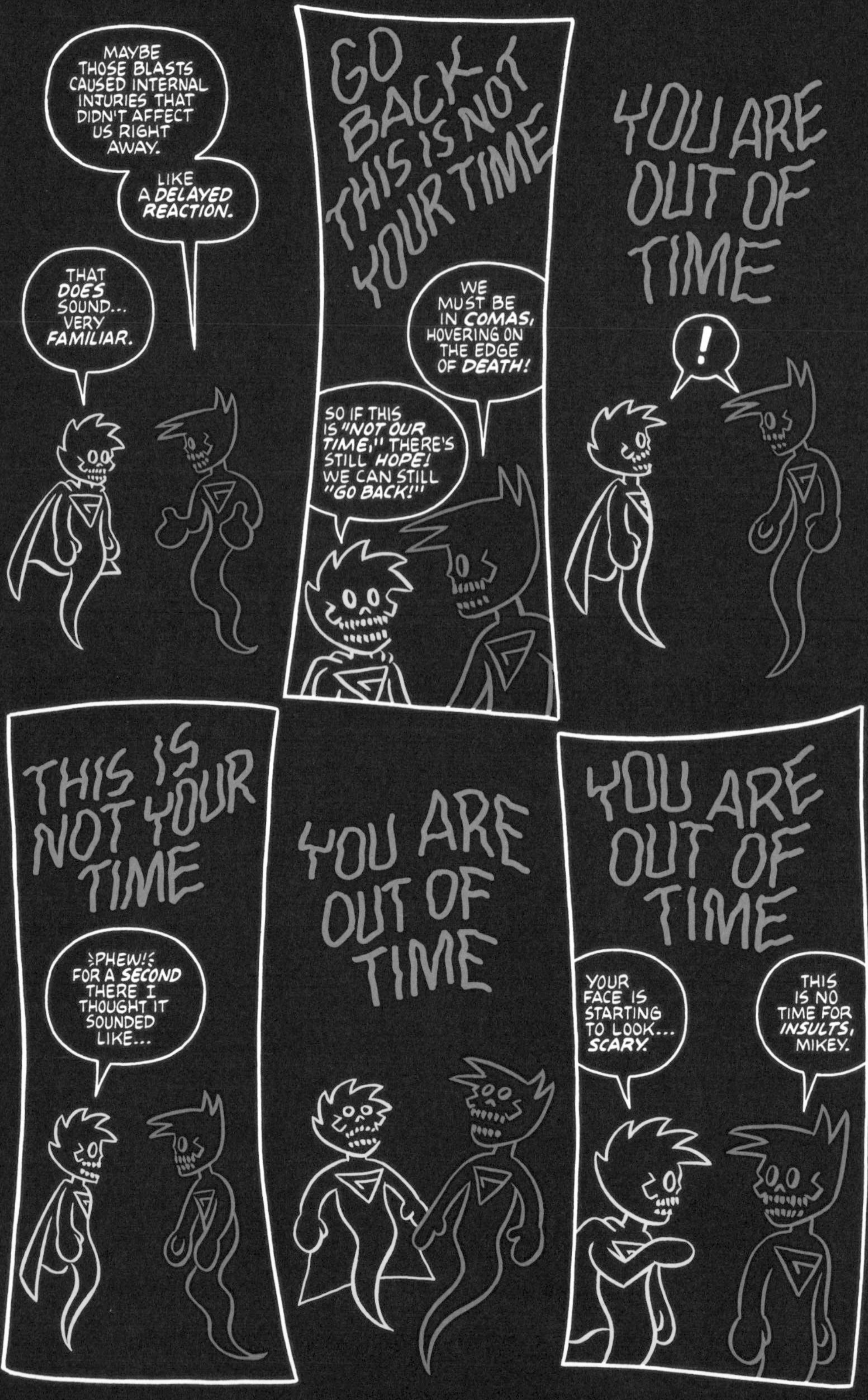
MAYBE THOSE BLASTS CAUSED INTERNAL INJURIES THAT DIDN'T AFFECT US RIGHT AWAY.
LIKE A DELAYED REACTION.
THAT DOES SOUND... VERY FAMILIAR.
GO BACK THIS IS NOT YOUR TIME
WE MUST BE IN COMAS, HOVERING ON THE EDGE OF DEATH!
SO IF THIS IS "NOT OUR TIME," THERE'S STILL HOPE! WE CAN STILL "GO BACK!"
YOU ARE OUT OF TIME
!
THIS IS NOT YOUR TIME
PHEW! FOR A SECOND THERE I THOUGHT IT SOUNDED LIKE...
YOU ARE OUT OF TIME
YOU ARE OUT OF TIME
YOUR FACE IS STARTING TO LOOK... SCARY.
THIS IS NO TIME FOR INSULTS, MIKEY.

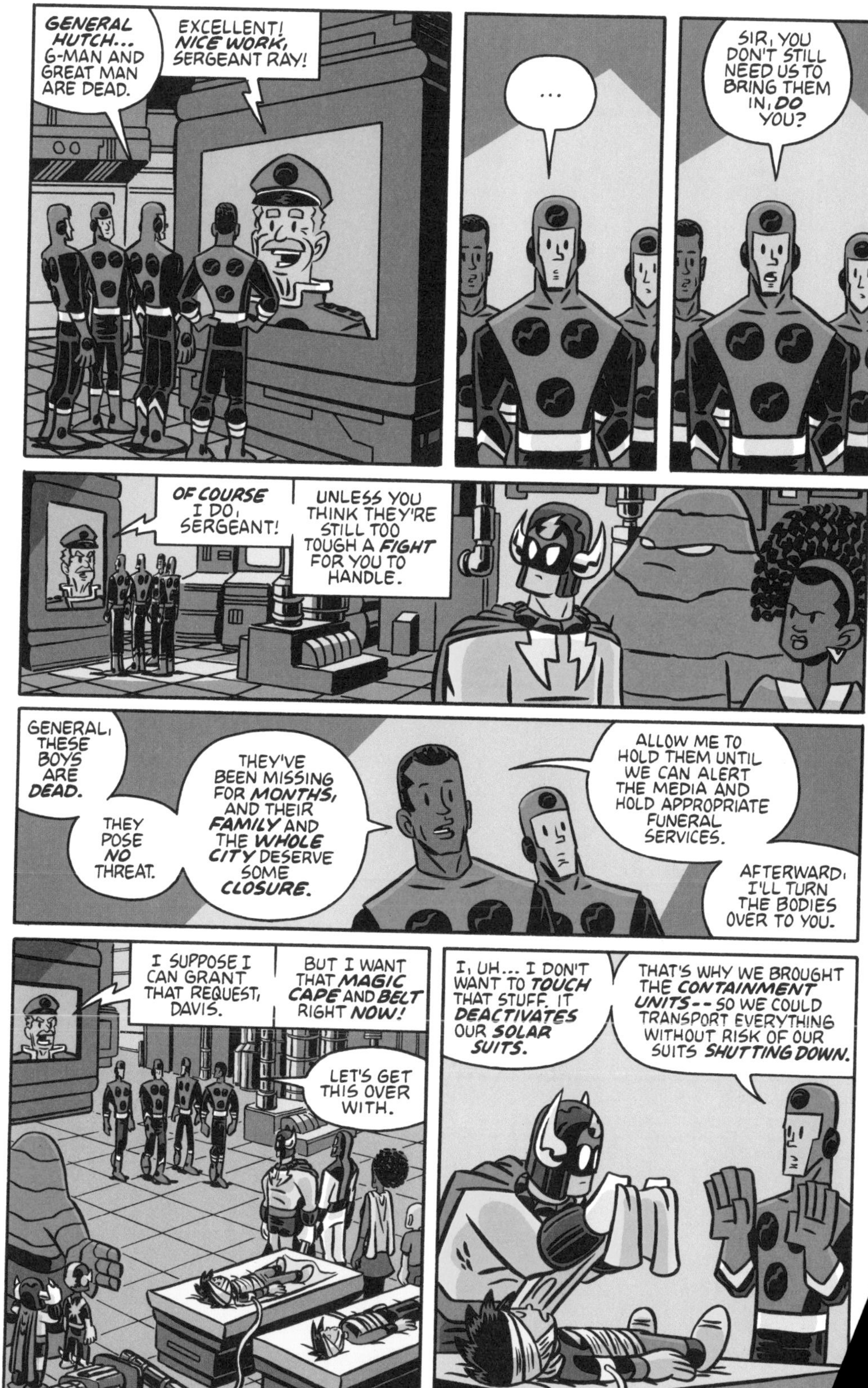
GENERAL HUTCH... G-MAN AND GREAT MAN ARE DEAD.
EXCELLENT! NICE WORK, SERGEANT RAY!
...
SIR, YOU DON'T STILL NEED US TO BRING THEM IN, DO YOU?
OF COURSE I DO, SERGEANT!
UNLESS YOU THINK THEY'RE STILL TOO TOUGH A FIGHT FOR YOU TO HANDLE.
GENERAL, THESE BOYS ARE DEAD.
THEY POSE NO THREAT.
THEY'VE BEEN MISSING FOR MONTHS, AND THEIR FAMILY AND THE WHOLE CITY DESERVE SOME CLOSURE.
ALLOW ME TO HOLD THEM UNTIL WE CAN ALERT THE MEDIA AND HOLD APPROPRIATE FUNERAL SERVICES.
AFTERWARD, I'LL TURN THE BODIES OVER TO YOU.
I SUPPOSE I CAN GRANT THAT REQUEST, DAVIS.
BUT I WANT THAT MAGIC CAPE AND BELT RIGHT NOW!
LET'S GET THIS OVER WITH.
I, UH... I DON'T WANT TO TOUCH THAT STUFF. IT DEACTIVATES OUR SOLAR SUITS.
THAT'S WHY WE BROUGHT THE CONTAINMENT UNITS-- SO WE COULD TRANSPORT EVERYTHING WITHOUT RISK OF OUR SUITS SHUTTING DOWN.

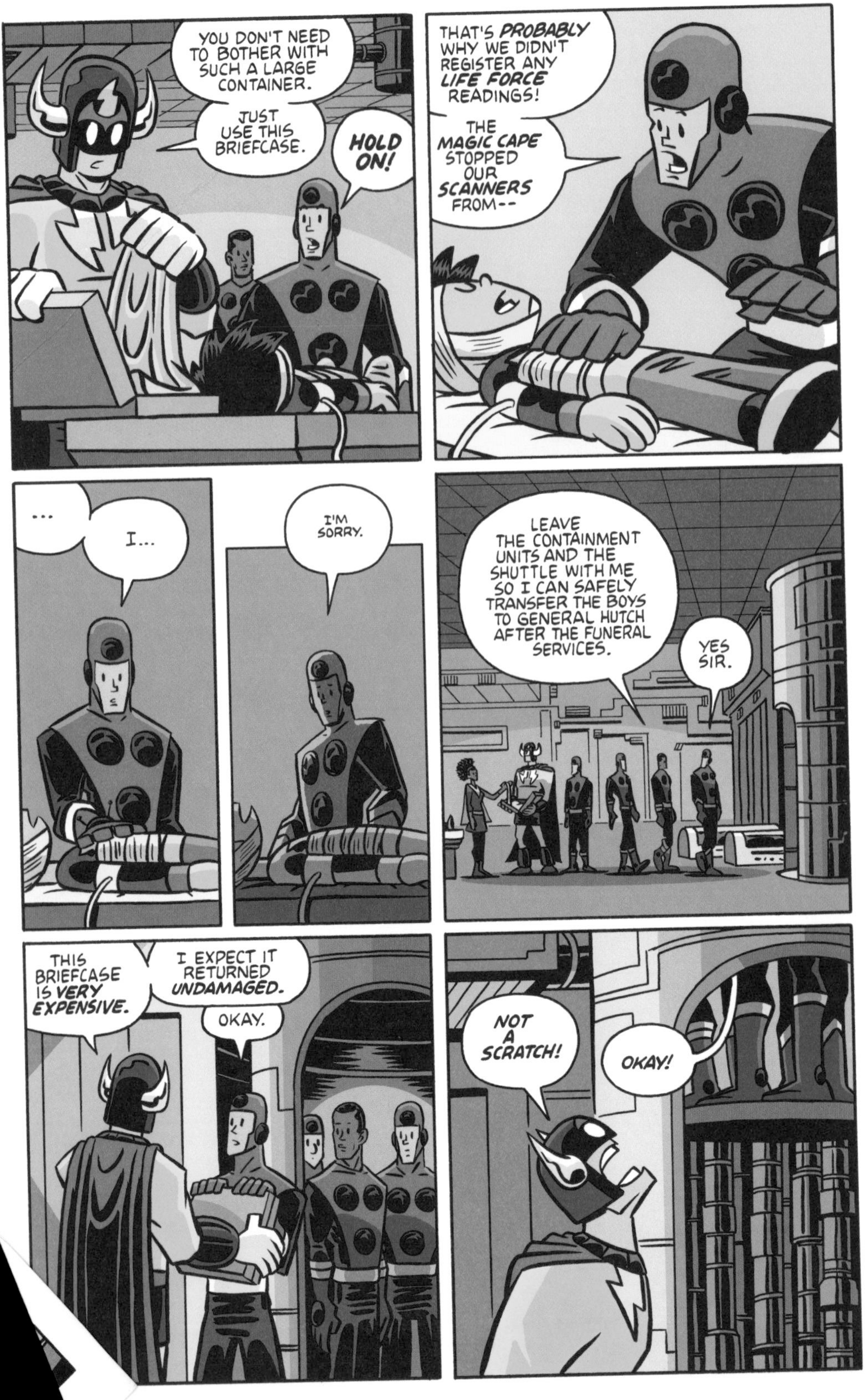
YOU DON'T NEED TO BOTHER WITH SUCH A LARGE CONTAINER.
JUST USE THIS BRIEFCASE.
HOLD ON!
THAT'S PROBABLY WHY WE DIDN'T REGISTER ANY LIFE FORCE READINGS!
THE MAGIC CAPE STOPPED OUR SCANNERS FROM--
...
I...
I'M SORRY.
LEAVE THE CONTAINMENT UNITS AND THE SHUTTLE WITH ME SO I CAN SAFELY TRANSFER THE BOYS TO GENERAL HUTCH AFTER THE FUNERAL SERVICES.
YES SIR.
THIS BRIEFCASE IS VERY EXPENSIVE.
I EXPECT IT RETURNED UNDAMAGED.
OKAY.
NOT A SCRATCH!
OKAY!

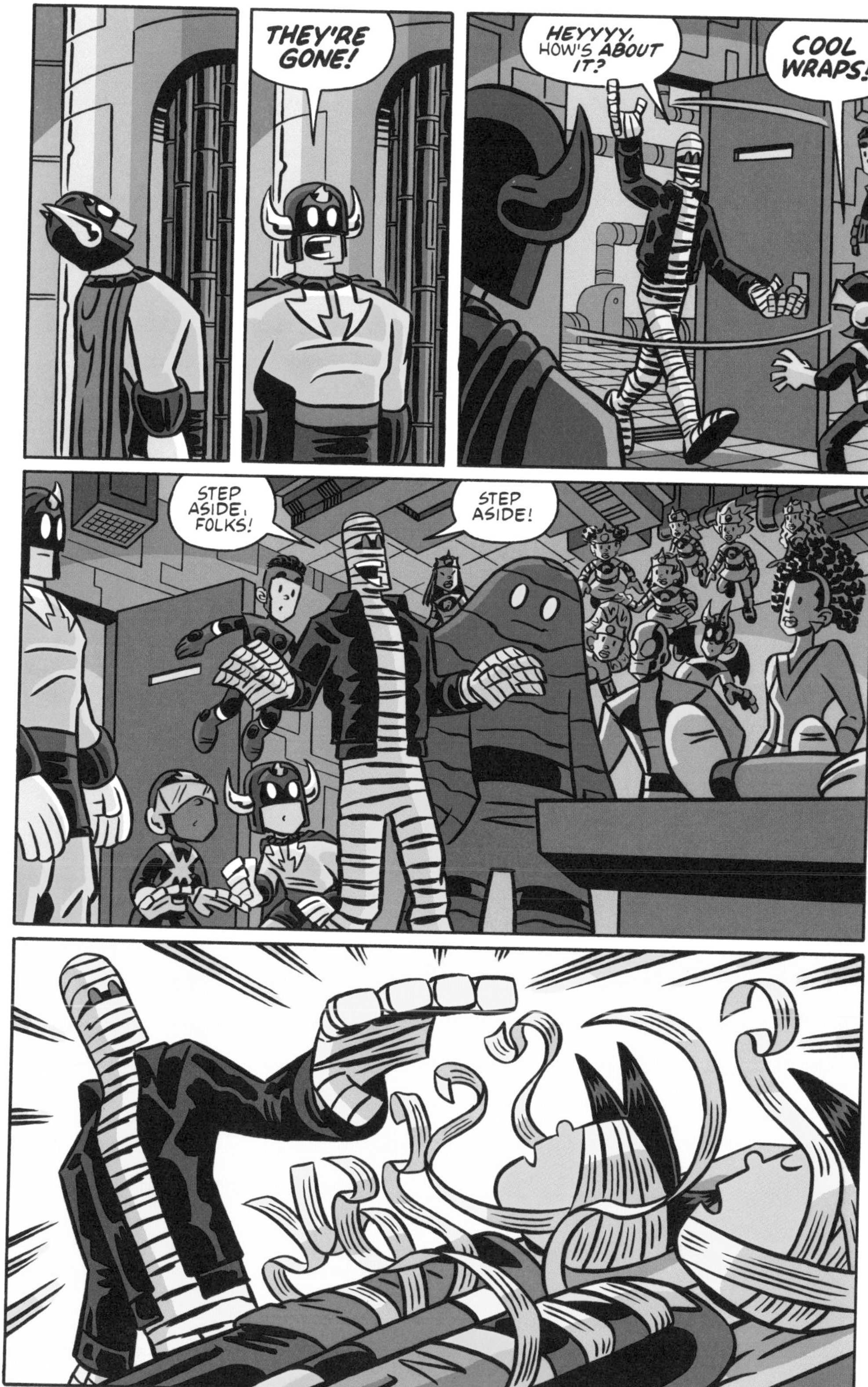
THEY'RE GONE!
HEYYYY, HOW'S ABOUT IT?
COOL WRAPS!
STEP ASIDE, FOLKS!
STEP ASIDE!

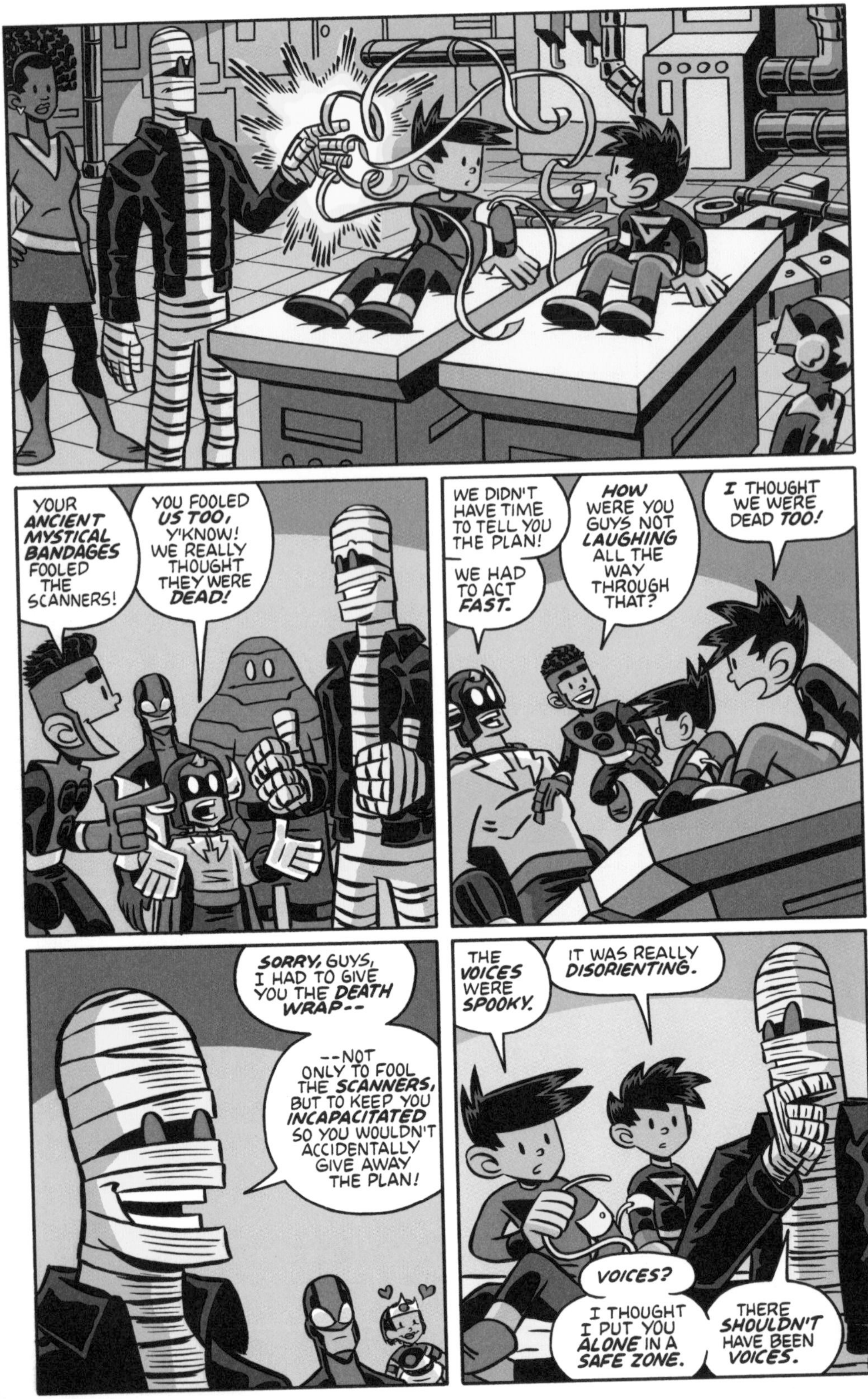
YOUR ANCIENT MYSTICAL BANDAGES FOOLED THE SCANNERS!
YOU FOOLED US TOO, Y'KNOW! WE REALLY THOUGHT THEY WERE DEAD!
WE DIDN'T HAVE TIME TO TELL YOU THE PLAN!
WE HAD TO ACT FAST.
HOW WERE YOU GUYS NOT LAUGHING ALL THE WAY THROUGH THAT?
I THOUGHT WE WERE DEAD TOO!
SORRY, GUYS, I HAD TO GIVE YOU THE DEATH WRAP--
--NOT ONLY TO FOOL THE SCANNERS, BUT TO KEEP YOU INCAPACITATED SO YOU WOULDN'T ACCIDENTALLY GIVE AWAY THE PLAN!
THE VOICES WERE SPOOKY.
IT WAS REALLY DISORIENTING.
VOICES?
I THOUGHT I PUT YOU ALONE IN A SAFE ZONE.
THERE SHOULDN'T HAVE BEEN VOICES.

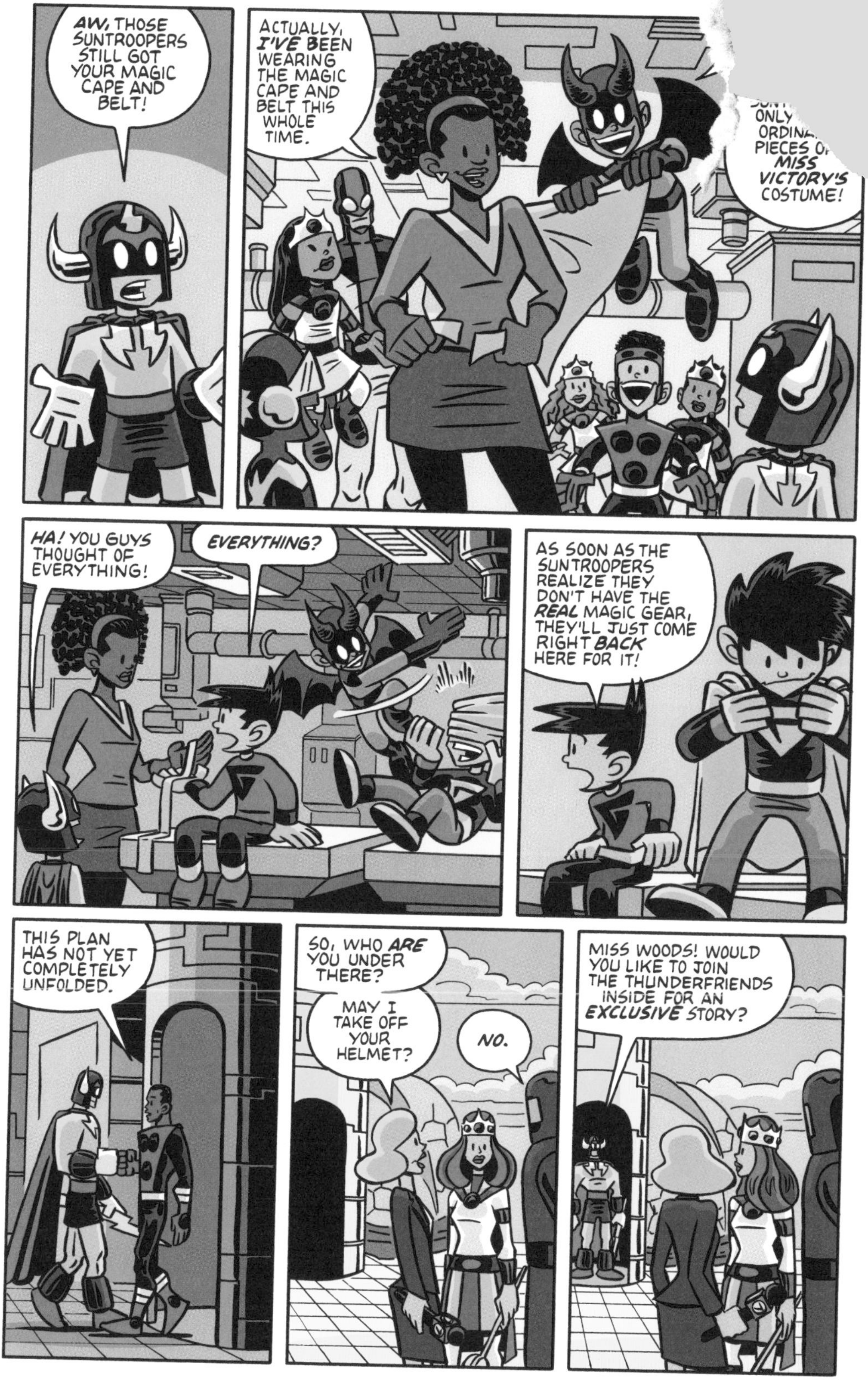
AW, THOSE SUNTROOPERS STILL GOT YOUR MAGIC CAPE AND BELT!
ACTUALLY, I'VE BEEN WEARING THE MAGIC CAPE AND BELT THIS WHOLE TIME.
ONLY
PIECES
MISS VICTORY'S COSTUME!
HA! YOU GUYS THOUGHT OF EVERYTHING!
EVERYTHING?
AS SOON AS THE SUNTROOPERS REALIZE THEY DON'T HAVE THE REAL MAGIC GEAR, THEY'LL JUST COME RIGHT BACK HERE FOR IT!
THIS PLAN HAS NOT YET COMPLETELY UNFOLDED.
SO, WHO ARE YOU UNDER THERE?
MAY I TAKE OFF YOUR HELMET?
NO.
MISS WOODS! WOULD YOU LIKE TO JOIN THE THUNDERFRIENDS INSIDE FOR AN EXCLUSIVE STORY?

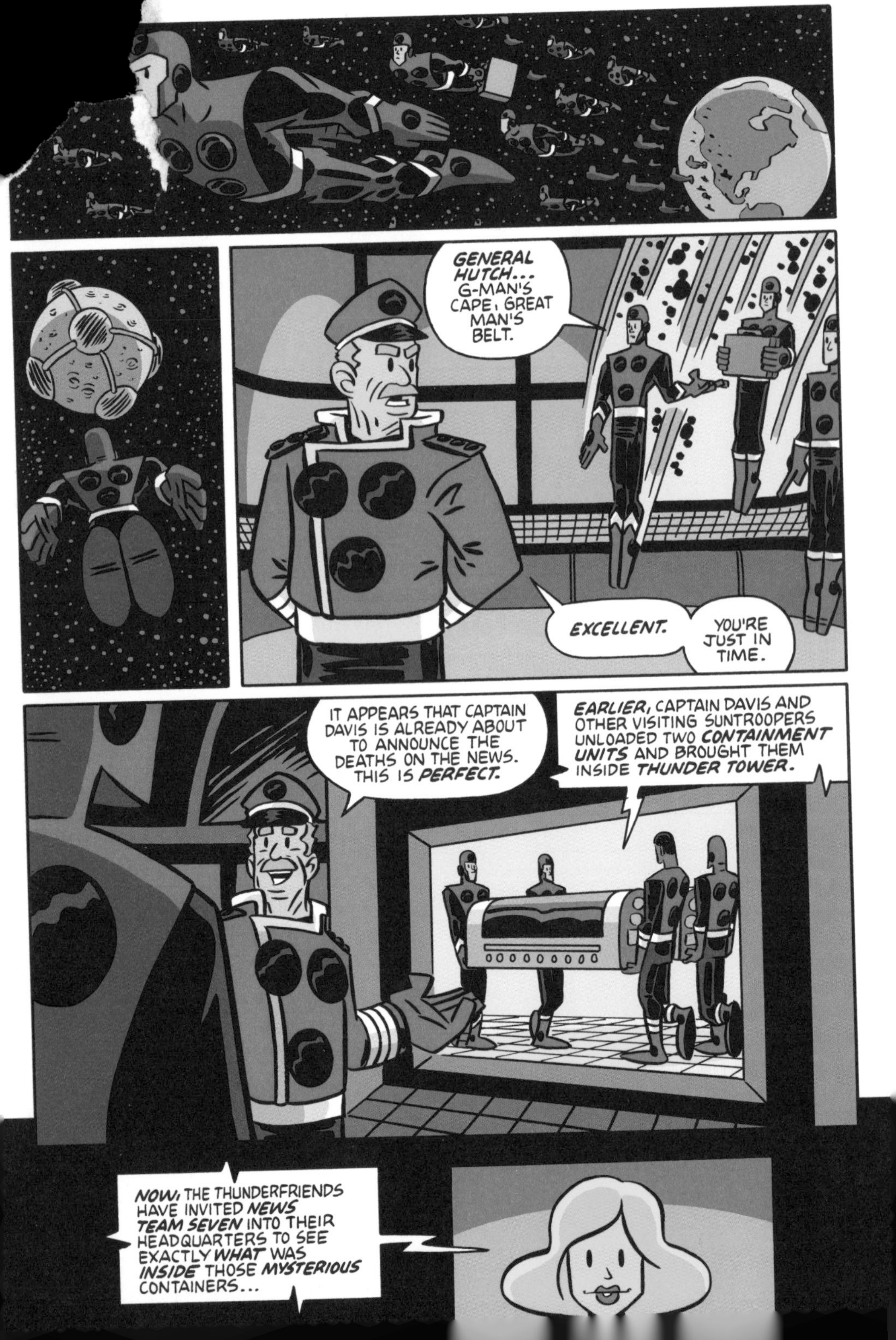
GENERAL HUTCH... G-MAN'S CAPE, GREAT MAN'S BELT.
EXCELLENT.
YOU'RE JUST IN TIME.
IT APPEARS THAT CAPTAIN DAVIS IS ALREADY ABOUT TO ANNOUNCE THE DEATHS ON THE NEWS. THIS IS PERFECT.
EARLIER, CAPTAIN DAVIS AND OTHER VISITING SUNTROOPERS UNLOADED TWO CONTAINMENT UNITS AND BROUGHT THEM INSIDE THUNDER TOWER.
NOW, THE THUNDERFRIENDS HAVE INVITED NEWS TEAM SEVEN INTO THEIR HEADQUARTERS TO SEE EXACTLY WHAT WAS INSIDE THOSE MYSTERIOUS CONTAINERS...

IN **FACT,** THE CONTAINMENT UNITS ARE HOLDING **EXACTLY** WHAT THE CITY HAS BEEN **HOPING** FOR ALL SUMMER LONG--

-- **GREAT MAN,** THE YOUNG HERO WHO ABSORBED A **NUCLEAR EXPLOSION** TO SAVE OUR CITY, RETURNED **ALIVE!**

AND ALSO HIS MISSING BROTHER, G-MAN.

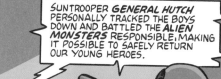

CAPTAIN DAVIS, CAN YOU TELL US HOW YOU CAME TO RECOVER THE BOYS?

ACTING ON LEADS INDICATING THE BOYS WERE ABDUCTED BY **SPACE ALIENS,** I MADE USE OF ALL SUNTROOPER SPACE FORCE RESOURCES TO SEARCH FOR THE BOYS THROUGHOUT THE UNIVERSE.

TODAY, THAT PLAN HAS FINALLY **PAID OFF.**

SUNTROOPER **GENERAL HUTCH** PERSONALLY TRACKED THE BOYS DOWN AND BATTLED THE **ALIEN MONSTERS** RESPONSIBLE, MAKING IT POSSIBLE TO SAFELY RETURN OUR YOUNG HEROES.

WHAT ARE **YOU** SMILING ABOUT?

NOTHING.

DAVIS JUST PLAYED US ALL FOR **FOOLS,** SERGEANT!

NOW I **ORDER** YOU TO **ANSWER** MY **QUESTION!**

WHAT ARE YOU **SMILING** ABOUT?

I'M GLAD WE DIDN'T **KILL** THEM, SIR.

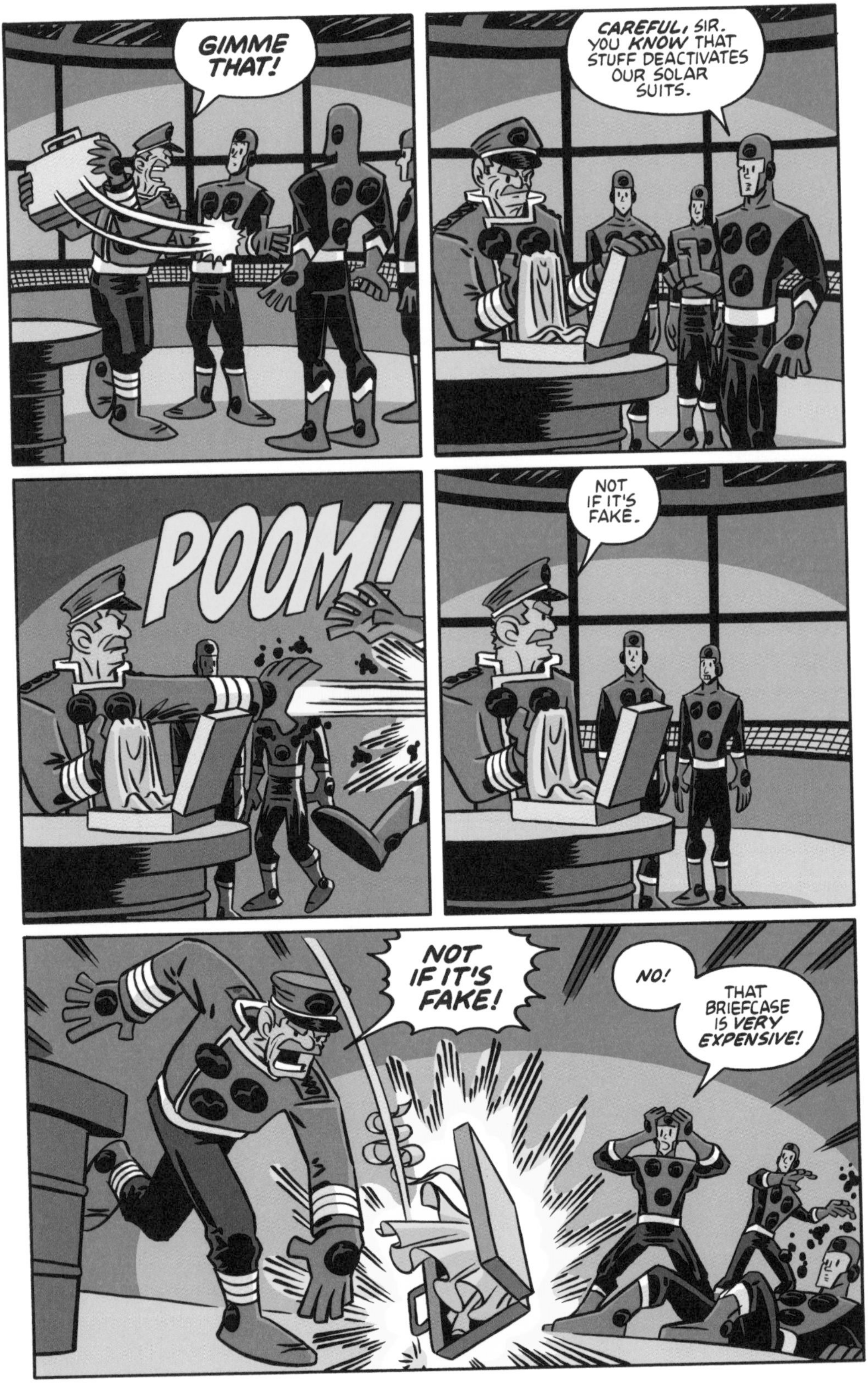
GIMME THAT!
CAREFUL, SIR. YOU KNOW THAT STUFF DEACTIVATES OUR SOLAR SUITS.
POOM!
NOT IF IT'S FAKE.
NOT IF IT'S FAKE!
NO!
THAT BRIEFCASE IS VERY EXPENSIVE!

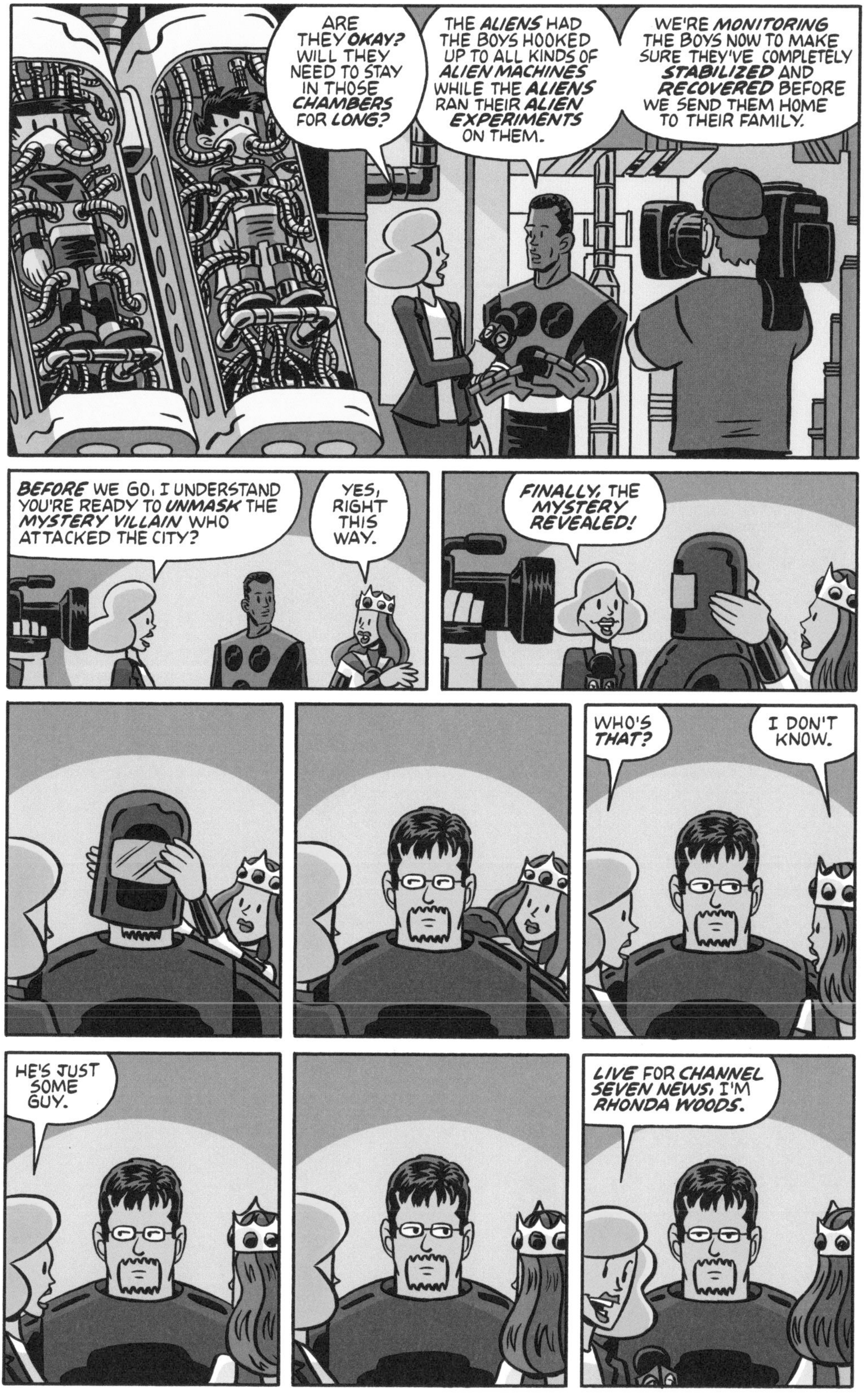
ARE THEY OKAY? WILL THEY NEED TO STAY IN THOSE CHAMBERS FOR LONG?
THE ALIENS HAD THE BOYS HOOKED UP TO ALL KINDS OF ALIEN MACHINES WHILE THE ALIENS RAN THEIR ALIEN EXPERIMENTS ON THEM.
WE'RE MONITORING THE BOYS NOW TO MAKE SURE THEY'VE COMPLETELY STABILIZED AND RECOVERED BEFORE WE SEND THEM HOME TO THEIR FAMILY.
BEFORE WE GO, I UNDERSTAND YOU'RE READY TO UNMASK THE MYSTERY VILLAIN WHO ATTACKED THE CITY?
YES, RIGHT THIS WAY.
FINALLY, THE MYSTERY REVEALED!
WHO'S THAT?
I DON'T KNOW.
HE'S JUST SOME GUY.
LIVE FOR CHANNEL SEVEN NEWS, I'M RHONDA WOODS.

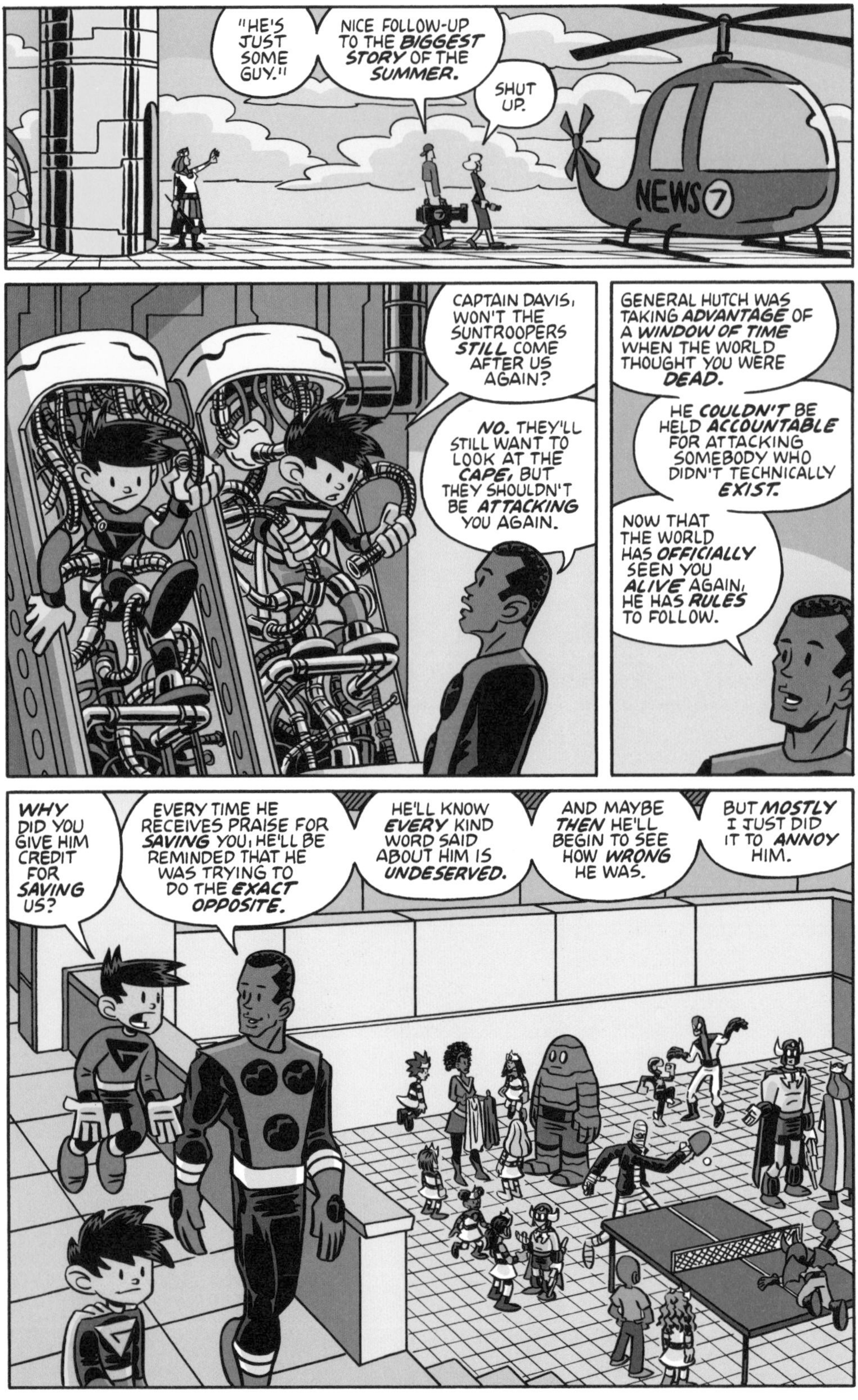
"HE'S JUST SOME GUY."
NICE FOLLOW-UP TO THE BIGGEST STORY OF THE SUMMER.
SHUT UP.
NEWS 7
CAPTAIN DAVIS, WON'T THE SUNTROOPERS STILL COME AFTER US AGAIN?
NO. THEY'LL STILL WANT TO LOOK AT THE CAPE, BUT THEY SHOULDN'T BE ATTACKING YOU AGAIN.
GENERAL HUTCH WAS TAKING ADVANTAGE OF A WINDOW OF TIME WHEN THE WORLD THOUGHT YOU WERE DEAD.
HE COULDN'T BE HELD ACCOUNTABLE FOR ATTACKING SOMEBODY WHO DIDN'T TECHNICALLY EXIST.
NOW THAT THE WORLD HAS OFFICIALLY SEEN YOU ALIVE AGAIN, HE HAS RULES TO FOLLOW.
WHY DID YOU GIVE HIM CREDIT FOR SAVING US?
EVERY TIME HE RECEIVES PRAISE FOR SAVING YOU, HE'LL BE REMINDED THAT HE WAS TRYING TO DO THE EXACT OPPOSITE.
HE'LL KNOW EVERY KIND WORD SAID ABOUT HIM IS UNDESERVED.
AND MAYBE THEN HE'LL BEGIN TO SEE HOW WRONG HE WAS.
BUT MOSTLY I JUST DID IT TO ANNOY HIM.

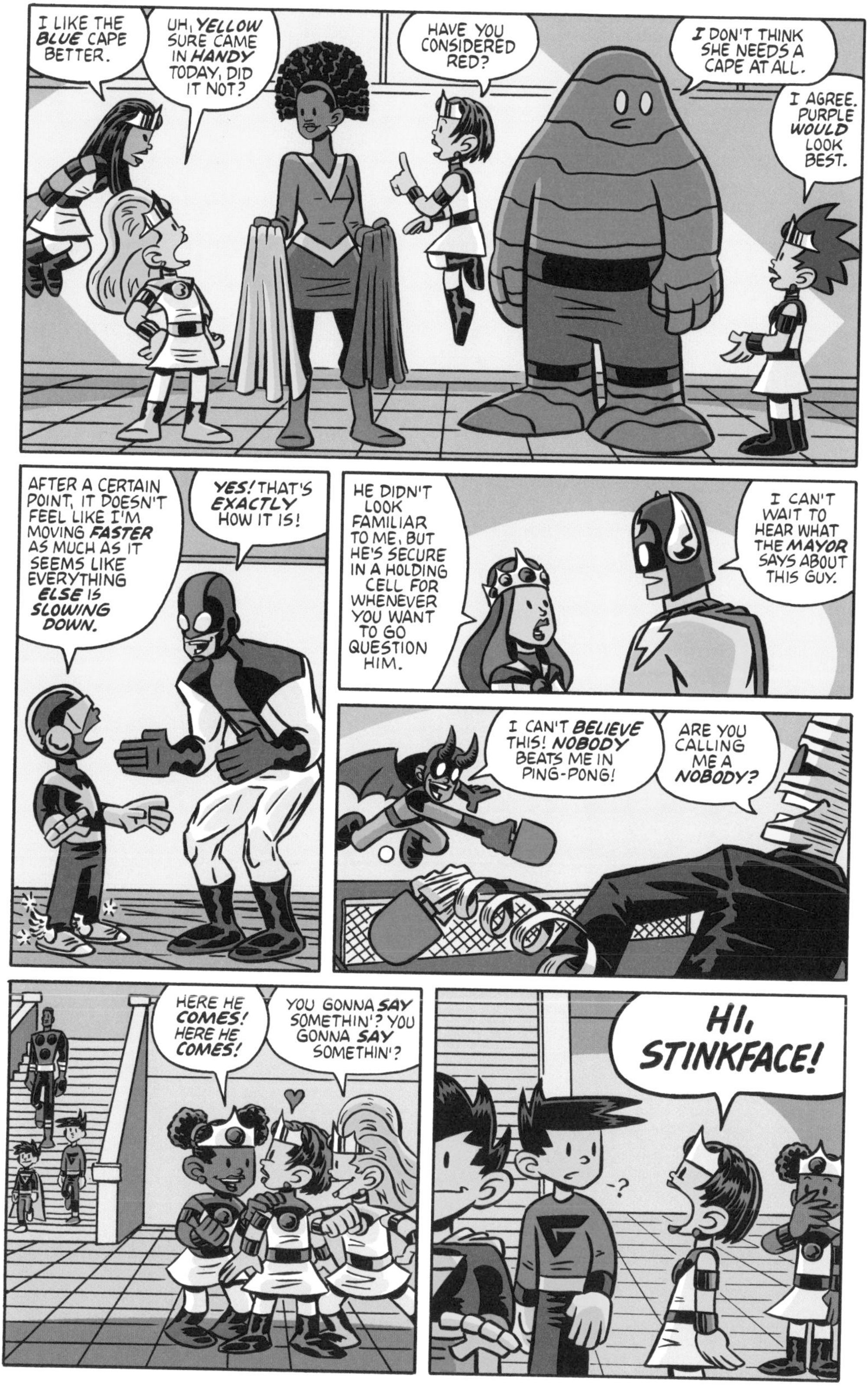
I LIKE THE BLUE CAPE BETTER.
UH, YELLOW SURE CAME IN HANDY TODAY, DID IT NOT?
HAVE YOU CONSIDERED RED?
I DON'T THINK SHE NEEDS A CAPE AT ALL.
I AGREE. PURPLE WOULD LOOK BEST.
AFTER A CERTAIN POINT, IT DOESN'T FEEL LIKE I'M MOVING FASTER AS MUCH AS IT SEEMS LIKE EVERYTHING ELSE IS SLOWING DOWN.
YES! THAT'S EXACTLY HOW IT IS!
HE DIDN'T LOOK FAMILIAR TO ME, BUT HE'S SECURE IN A HOLDING CELL FOR WHENEVER YOU WANT TO GO QUESTION HIM.
I CAN'T WAIT TO HEAR WHAT THE MAYOR SAYS ABOUT THIS GUY.
I CAN'T BELIEVE THIS! NOBODY BEATS ME IN PING-PONG!
ARE YOU CALLING ME A NOBODY?
HERE HE COMES! HERE HE COMES!
YOU GONNA SAY SOMETHIN'? YOU GONNA SAY SOMETHIN'?
-?
HI, STINKFACE!

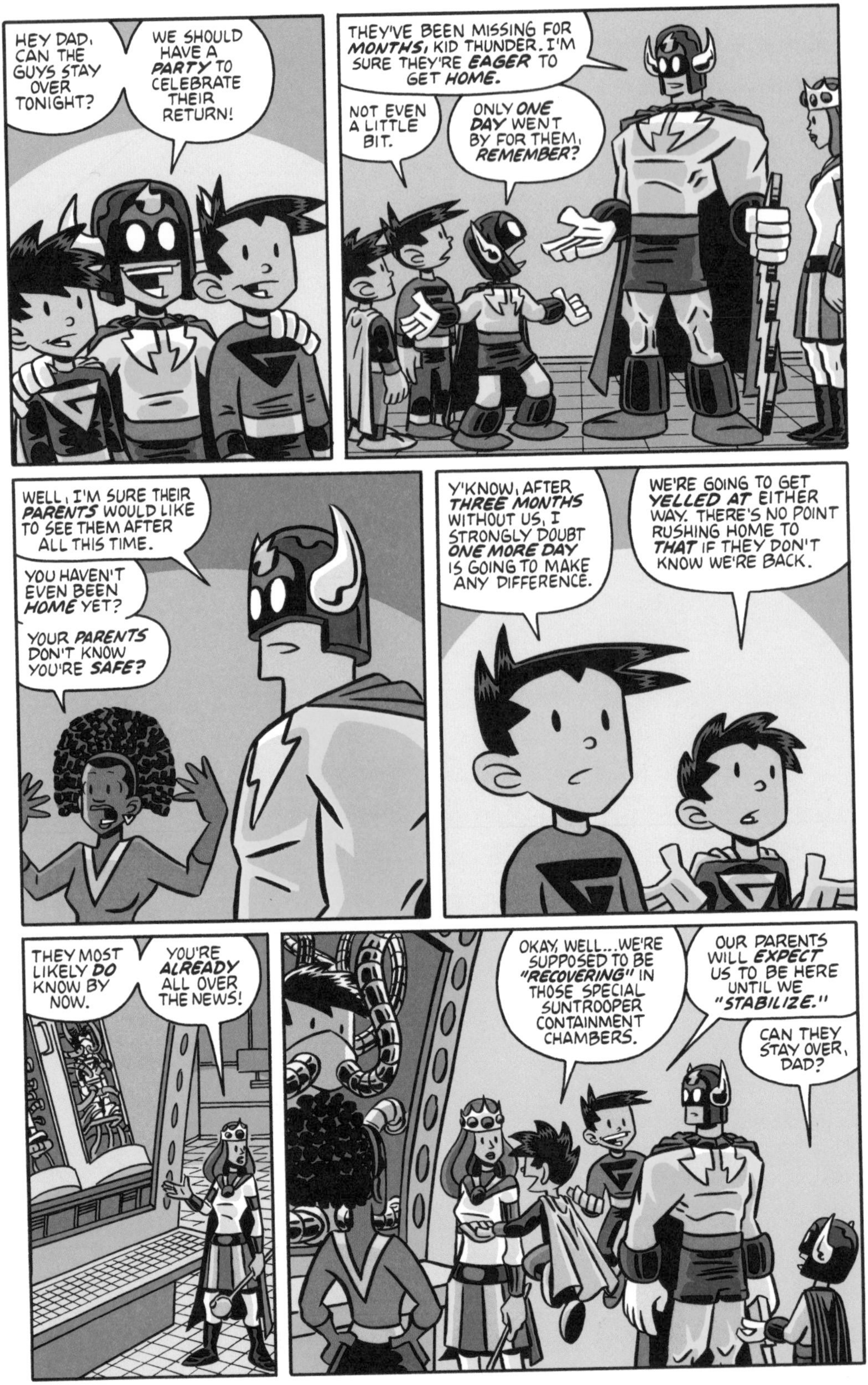

HEY DAD, CAN THE GUYS STAY OVER TONIGHT?
WE SHOULD HAVE A PARTY TO CELEBRATE THEIR RETURN!
THEY'VE BEEN MISSING FOR MONTHS, KID THUNDER. I'M SURE THEY'RE EAGER TO GET HOME.
NOT EVEN A LITTLE BIT.
ONLY ONE DAY WENT BY FOR THEM, REMEMBER?
WELL, I'M SURE THEIR PARENTS WOULD LIKE TO SEE THEM AFTER ALL THIS TIME.
YOU HAVEN'T EVEN BEEN HOME YET?
YOUR PARENTS DON'T KNOW YOU'RE SAFE?
Y'KNOW, AFTER THREE MONTHS WITHOUT US, I STRONGLY DOUBT ONE MORE DAY IS GOING TO MAKE ANY DIFFERENCE.
WE'RE GOING TO GET YELLED AT EITHER WAY. THERE'S NO POINT RUSHING HOME TO THAT IF THEY DON'T KNOW WE'RE BACK.
THEY MOST LIKELY DO KNOW BY NOW.
YOU'RE ALREADY ALL OVER THE NEWS!
OKAY, WELL...WE'RE SUPPOSED TO BE "RECOVERING" IN THOSE SPECIAL SUNTROOPER CONTAINMENT CHAMBERS.
OUR PARENTS WILL EXPECT US TO BE HERE UNTIL WE "STABILIZE."
CAN THEY STAY OVER, DAD?

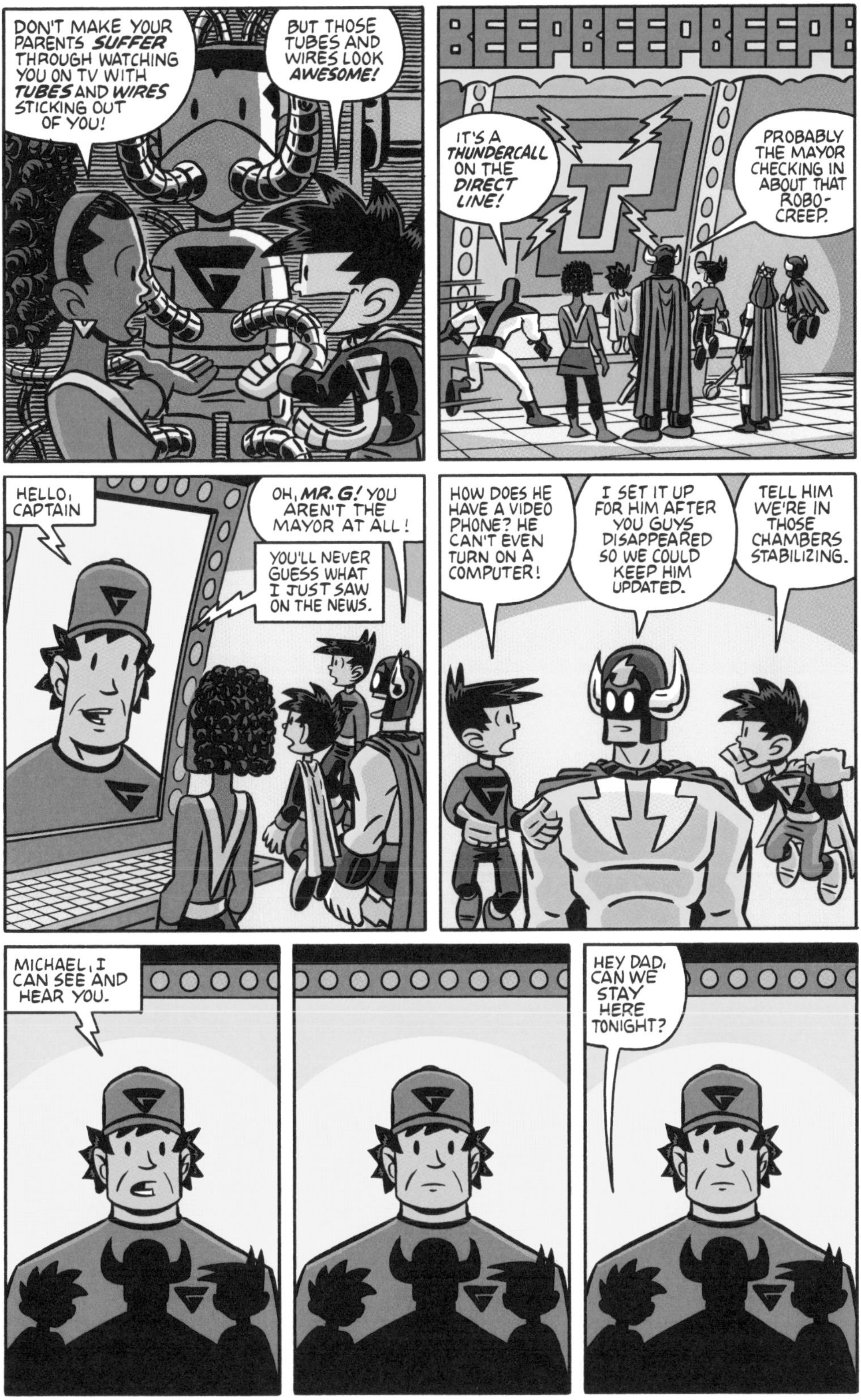
DON'T MAKE YOUR PARENTS SUFFER THROUGH WATCHING YOU ON TV WITH TUBES AND WIRES STICKING OUT OF YOU!
BUT THOSE TUBES AND WIRES LOOK AWESOME!
BEEPBEEPBEEPBEEPB
IT'S A THUNDERCALL ON THE DIRECT LINE!
PROBABLY THE MAYOR CHECKING IN ABOUT THAT ROBO-CREEP.
HELLO, CAPTAIN
OH, MR. G! YOU AREN'T THE MAYOR AT ALL!
YOU'LL NEVER GUESS WHAT I JUST SAW ON THE NEWS.
HOW DOES HE HAVE A VIDEO PHONE? HE CAN'T EVEN TURN ON A COMPUTER!
I SET IT UP FOR HIM AFTER YOU GUYS DISAPPEARED SO WE COULD KEEP HIM UPDATED.
TELL HIM WE'RE IN THOSE CHAMBERS STABILIZING.
MICHAEL, I CAN SEE AND HEAR YOU.
HEY DAD, CAN WE STAY HERE TONIGHT?

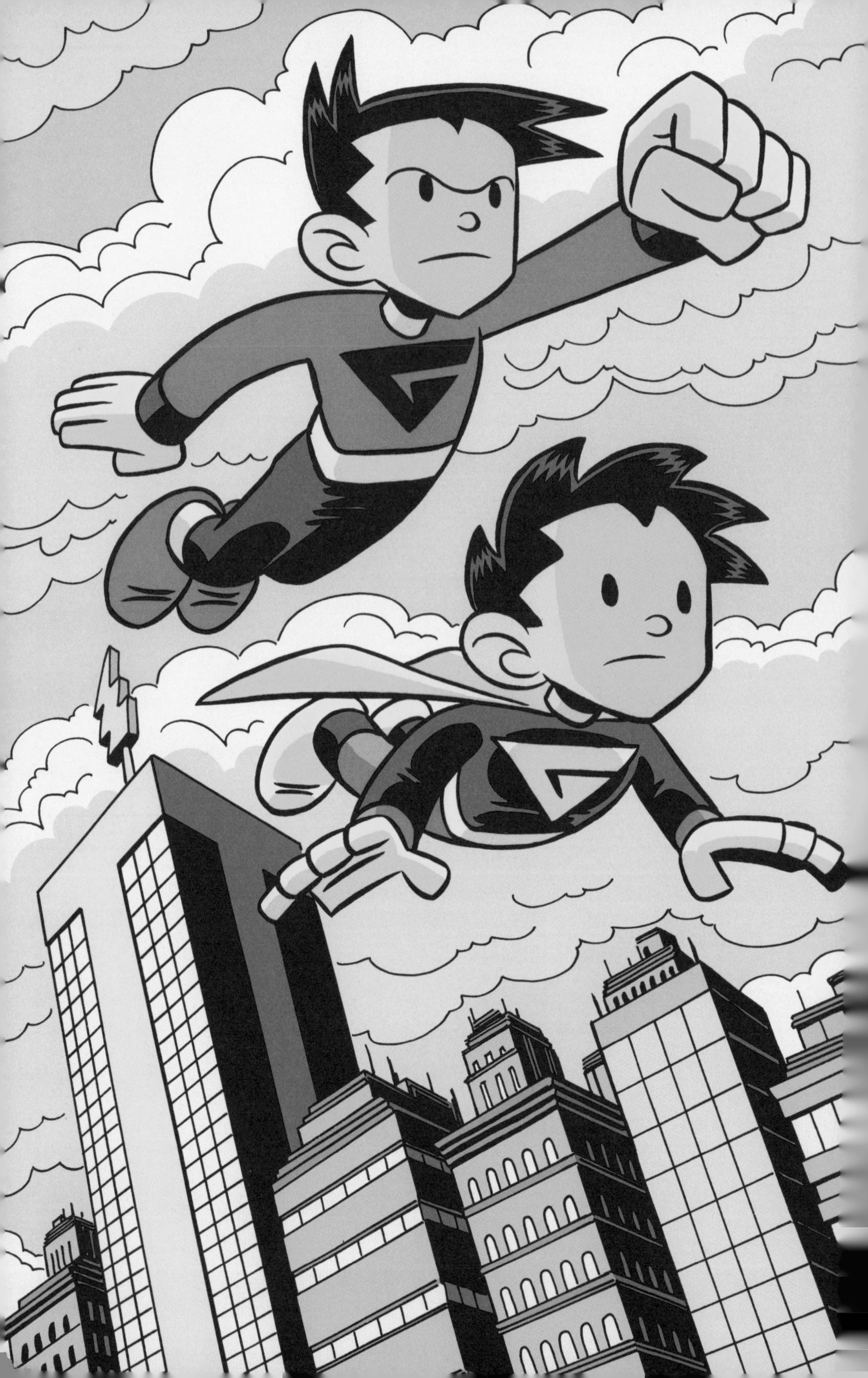

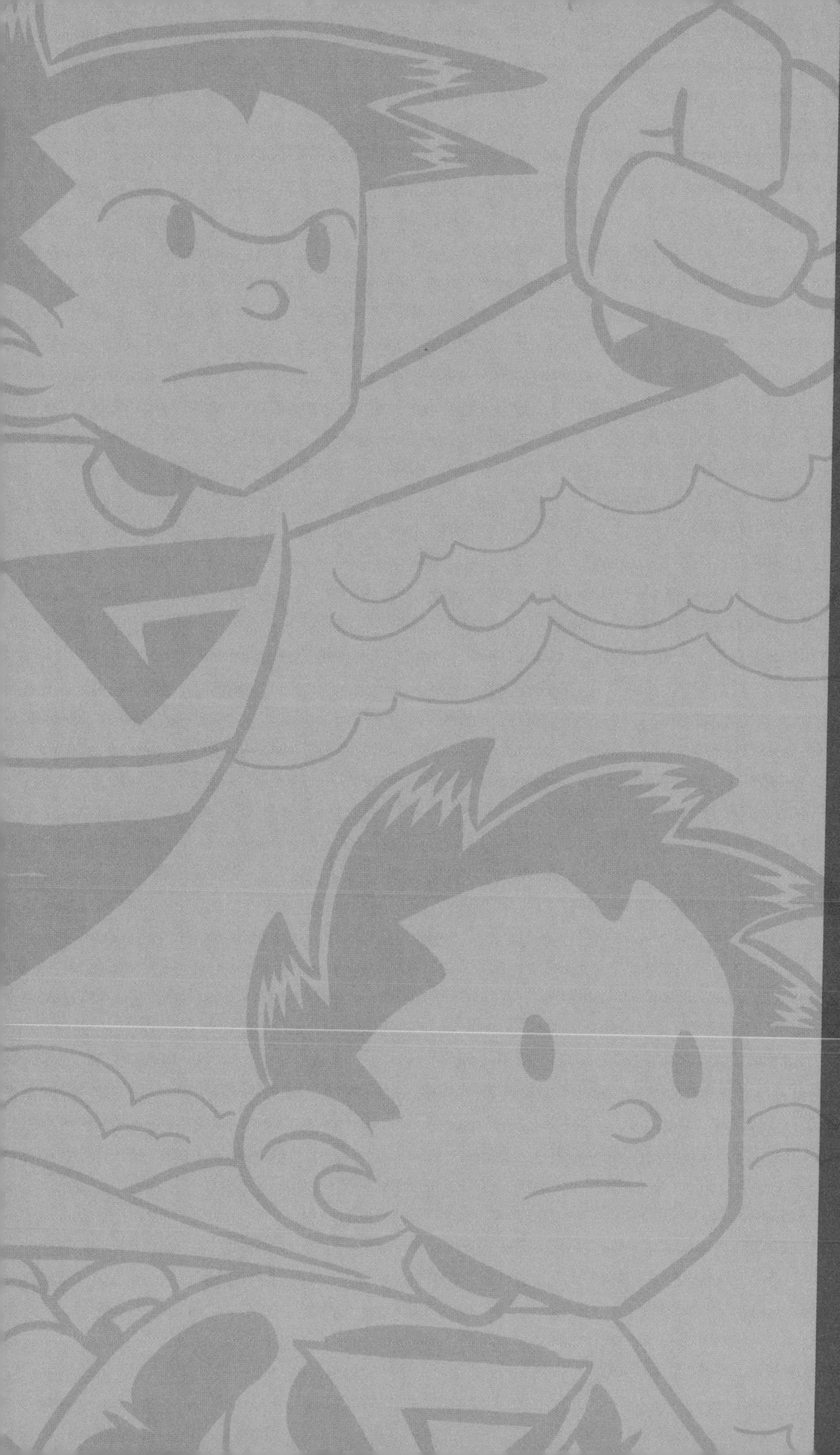

5

CHAPTER FIVE

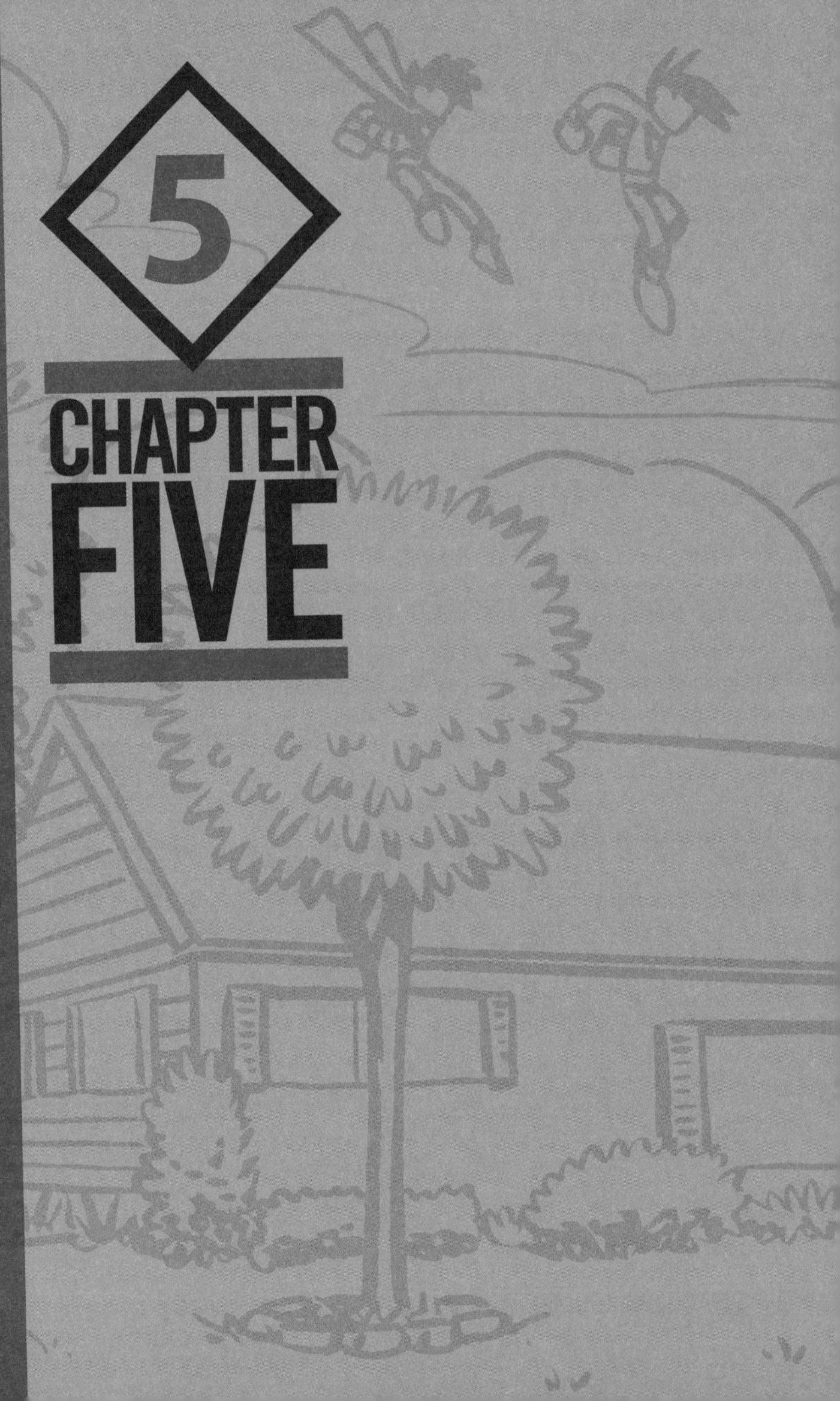

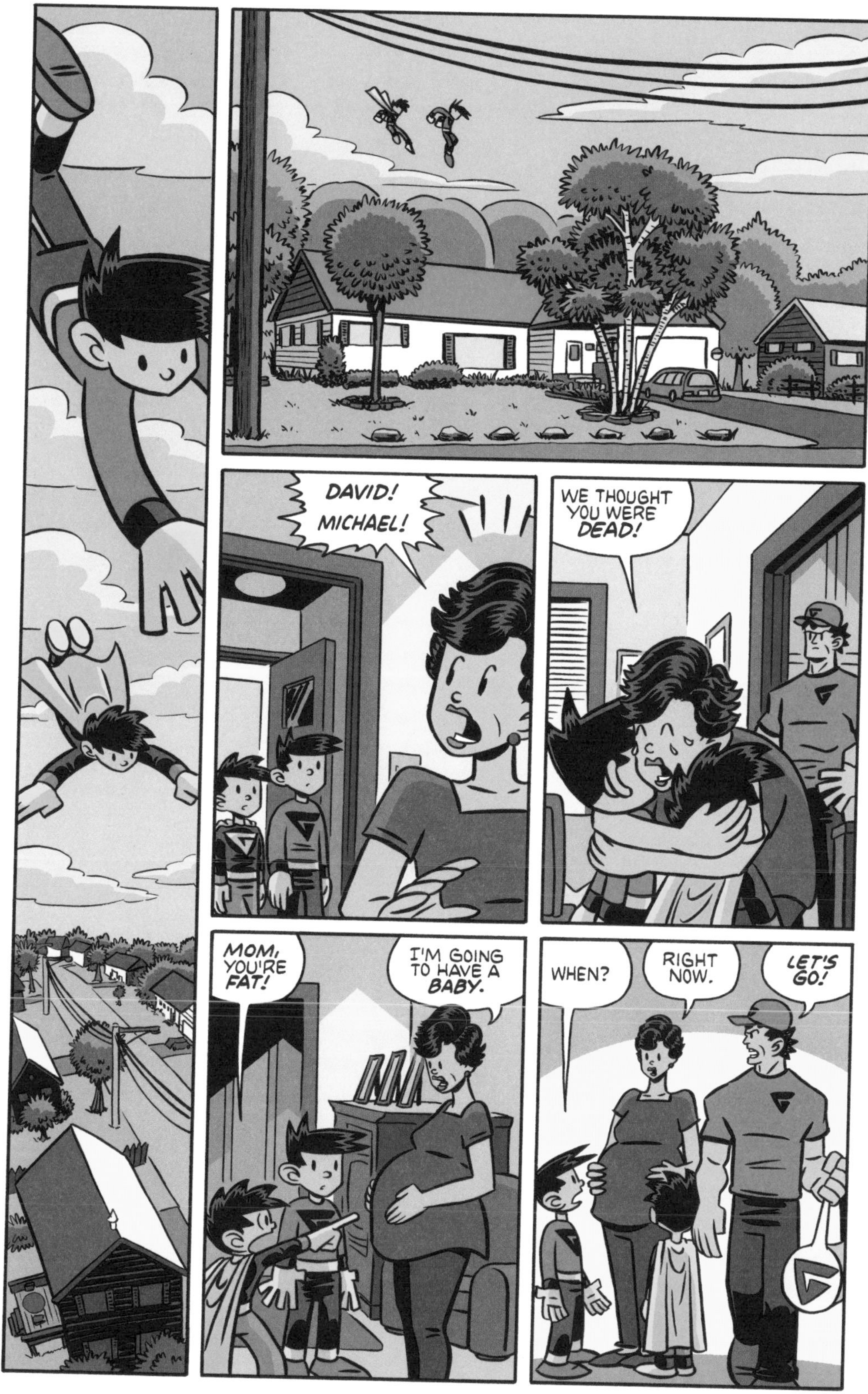
DAVID!
MICHAEL!
WE THOUGHT YOU WERE DEAD!
MOM, YOU'RE FAT!
I'M GOING TO HAVE A BABY.
WHEN?
RIGHT NOW.
LET'S GO!

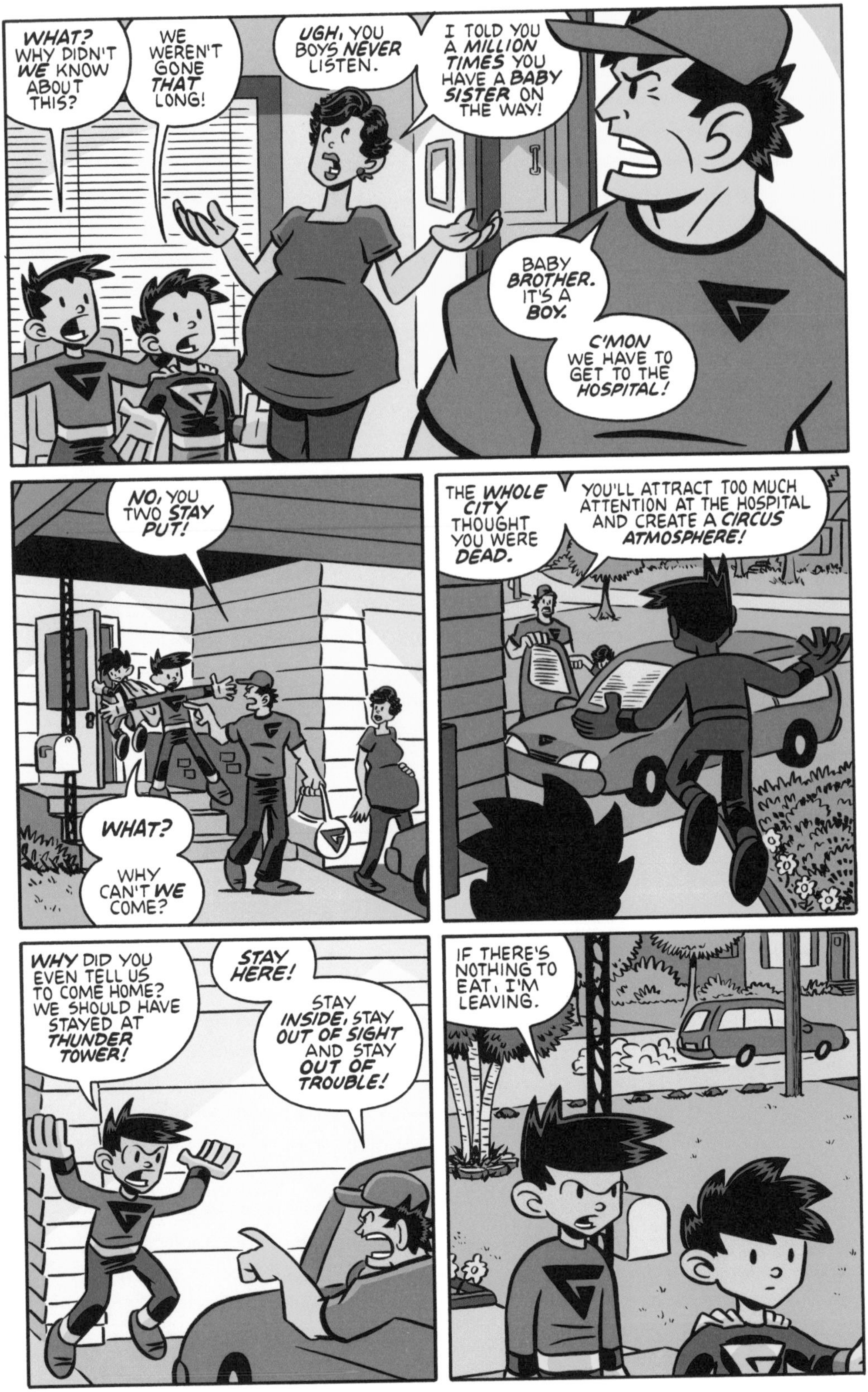
WHAT? WHY DIDN'T WE KNOW ABOUT THIS?
WE WEREN'T GONE THAT LONG!
UGH, YOU BOYS NEVER LISTEN.
I TOLD YOU A MILLION TIMES YOU HAVE A BABY SISTER ON THE WAY!
BABY BROTHER. IT'S A BOY.
C'MON WE HAVE TO GET TO THE HOSPITAL!
NO, YOU TWO STAY PUT!
WHAT?
WHY CAN'T WE COME?
THE WHOLE CITY THOUGHT YOU WERE DEAD.
YOU'LL ATTRACT TOO MUCH ATTENTION AT THE HOSPITAL AND CREATE A CIRCUS ATMOSPHERE!
WHY DID YOU EVEN TELL US TO COME HOME? WE SHOULD HAVE STAYED AT THUNDER TOWER!
STAY HERE!
STAY INSIDE, STAY OUT OF SIGHT AND STAY OUT OF TROUBLE!
IF THERE'S NOTHING TO EAT, I'M LEAVING.

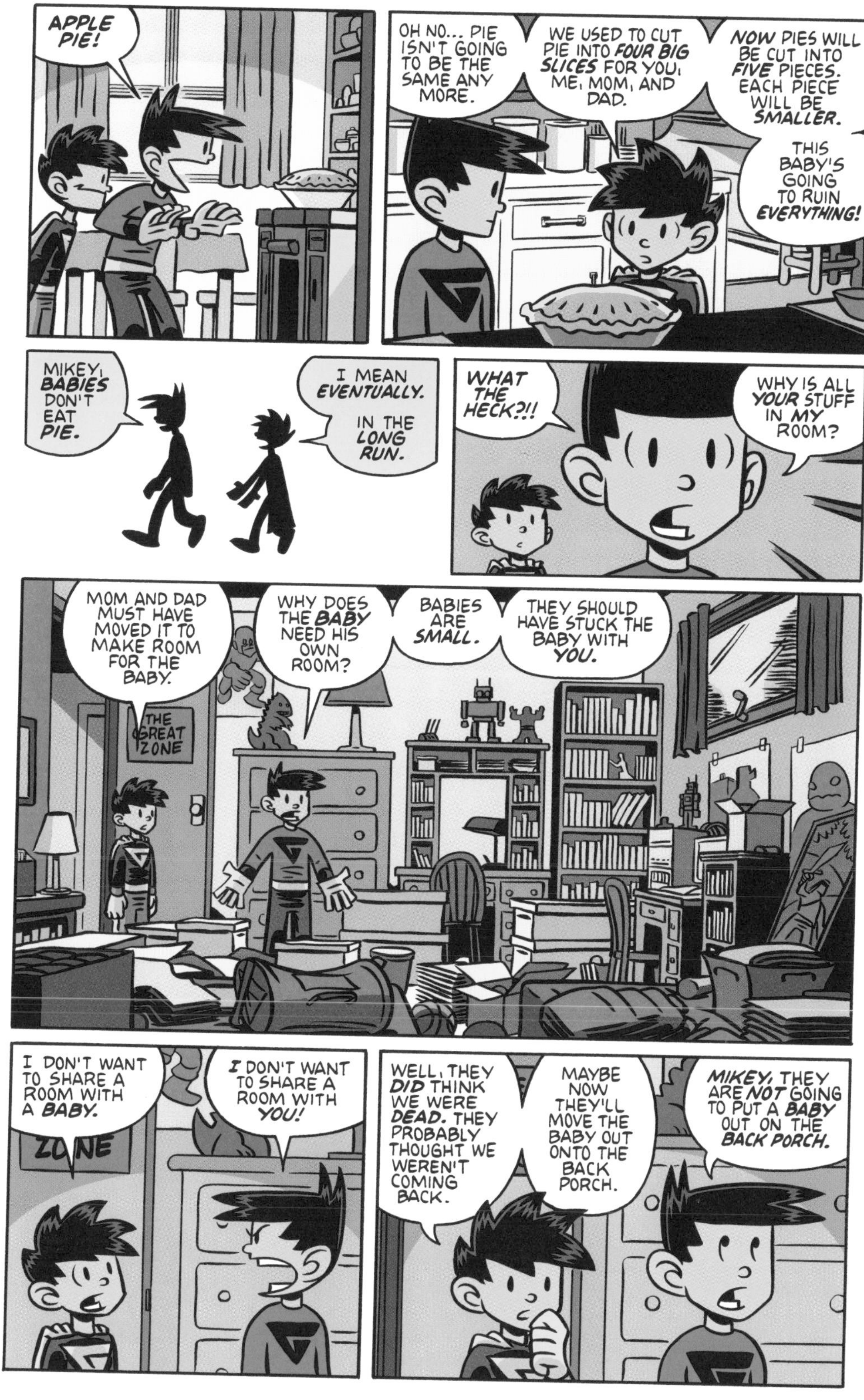
APPLE PIE!
OH NO... PIE ISN'T GOING TO BE THE SAME ANY MORE.
WE USED TO CUT PIE INTO FOUR BIG SLICES FOR YOU, ME, MOM, AND DAD.
NOW PIES WILL BE CUT INTO FIVE PIECES. EACH PIECE WILL BE SMALLER.
THIS BABY'S GOING TO RUIN EVERYTHING!
MIKEY, BABIES DON'T EAT PIE.
I MEAN EVENTUALLY.
IN THE LONG RUN.
WHAT THE HECK?!!
WHY IS ALL YOUR STUFF IN MY ROOM?
MOM AND DAD MUST HAVE MOVED IT TO MAKE ROOM FOR THE BABY.
WHY DOES THE BABY NEED HIS OWN ROOM?
BABIES ARE SMALL.
THEY SHOULD HAVE STUCK THE BABY WITH YOU.
THE GREAT ZONE
I DON'T WANT TO SHARE A ROOM WITH A BABY.
I DON'T WANT TO SHARE A ROOM WITH YOU!
WELL, THEY DID THINK WE WERE DEAD. THEY PROBABLY THOUGHT WE WEREN'T COMING BACK.
MAYBE NOW THEY'LL MOVE THE BABY OUT ONTO THE BACK PORCH.
MIKEY, THEY ARE NOT GOING TO PUT A BABY OUT ON THE BACK PORCH.

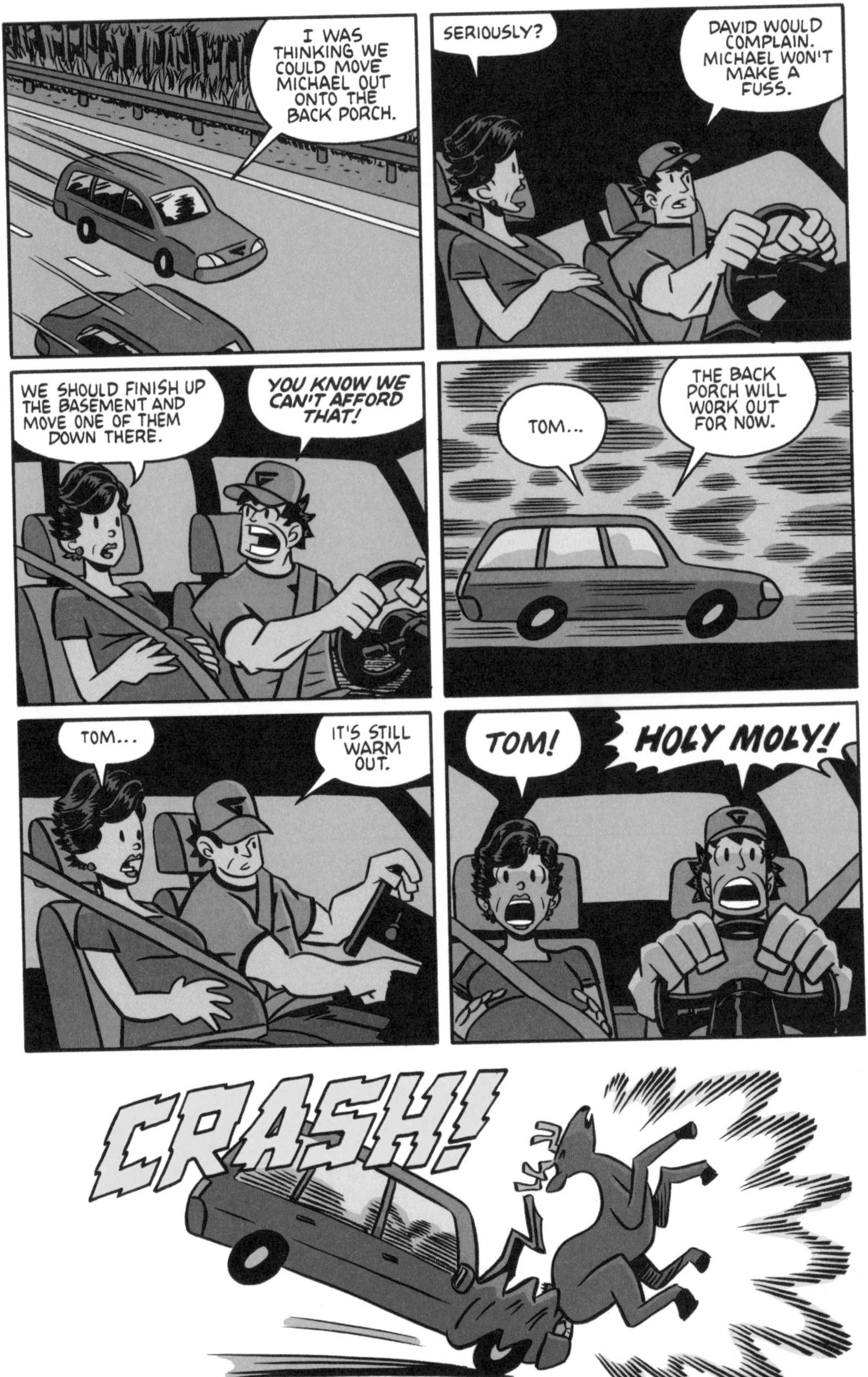
I WAS THINKING WE COULD MOVE MICHAEL OUT ONTO THE BACK PORCH.
SERIOUSLY?
DAVID WOULD COMPLAIN. MICHAEL WON'T MAKE A FUSS.
WE SHOULD FINISH UP THE BASEMENT AND MOVE ONE OF THEM DOWN THERE.
YOU KNOW WE CAN'T AFFORD THAT!
TOM...
THE BACK PORCH WILL WORK OUT FOR NOW.
TOM...
IT'S STILL WARM OUT.
TOM!
HOLY MOLY!
CRASH!

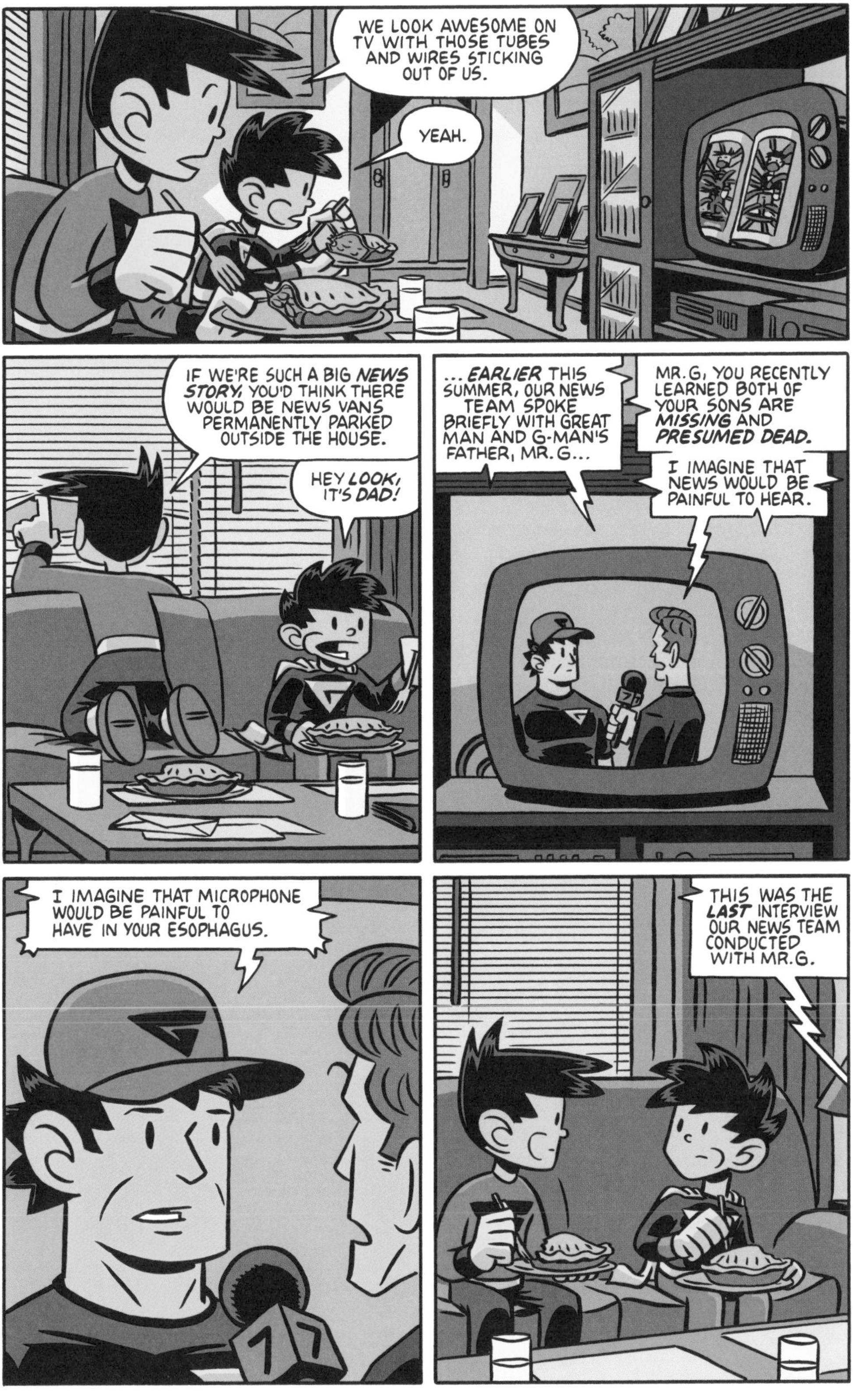
WE LOOK AWESOME ON TV WITH THOSE TUBES AND WIRES STICKING OUT OF US.
YEAH.
IF WE'RE SUCH A BIG NEWS STORY, YOU'D THINK THERE WOULD BE NEWS VANS PERMANENTLY PARKED OUTSIDE THE HOUSE.
HEY LOOK, IT'S DAD!
...EARLIER THIS SUMMER, OUR NEWS TEAM SPOKE BRIEFLY WITH GREAT MAN AND G-MAN'S FATHER, MR. G...
MR. G, YOU RECENTLY LEARNED BOTH OF YOUR SONS ARE MISSING AND PRESUMED DEAD.
I IMAGINE THAT NEWS WOULD BE PAINFUL TO HEAR.
I IMAGINE THAT MICROPHONE WOULD BE PAINFUL TO HAVE IN YOUR ESOPHAGUS.
THIS WAS THE LAST INTERVIEW OUR NEWS TEAM CONDUCTED WITH MR. G.

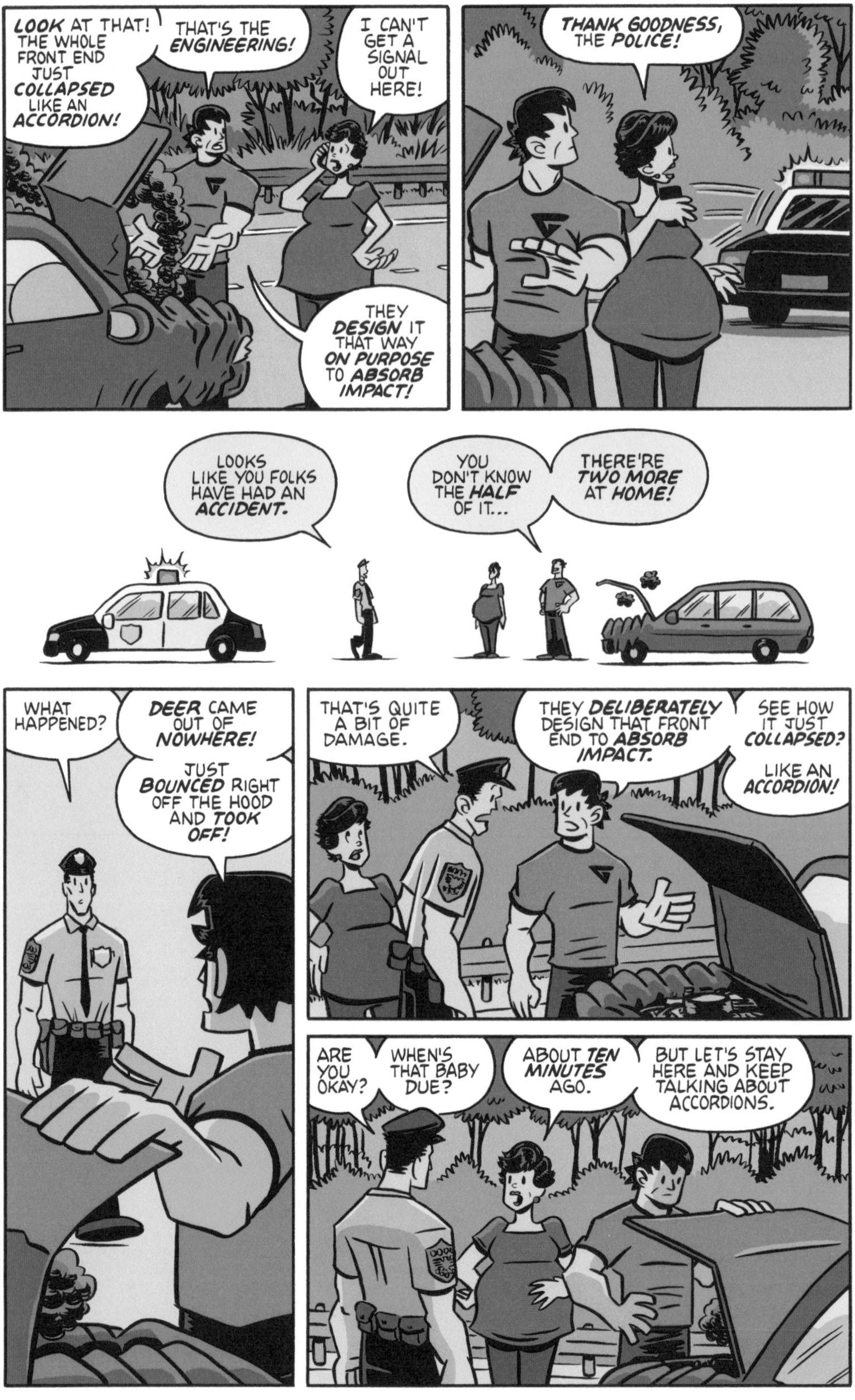

LOOK AT THAT! THE WHOLE FRONT END JUST COLLAPSED LIKE AN ACCORDION!
THAT'S THE ENGINEERING!
I CAN'T GET A SIGNAL OUT HERE!
THEY DESIGN IT THAT WAY ON PURPOSE TO ABSORB IMPACT!
THANK GOODNESS, THE POLICE!
LOOKS LIKE YOU FOLKS HAVE HAD AN ACCIDENT.
YOU DON'T KNOW THE HALF OF IT...
THERE'RE TWO MORE AT HOME!
WHAT HAPPENED?
DEER CAME OUT OF NOWHERE!
JUST BOUNCED RIGHT OFF THE HOOD AND TOOK OFF!
THAT'S QUITE A BIT OF DAMAGE.
THEY DELIBERATELY DESIGN THAT FRONT END TO ABSORB IMPACT.
SEE HOW IT JUST COLLAPSED?
LIKE AN ACCORDION!
ARE YOU OKAY?
WHEN'S THAT BABY DUE?
ABOUT TEN MINUTES AGO.
BUT LET'S STAY HERE AND KEEP TALKING ABOUT ACCORDIONS.

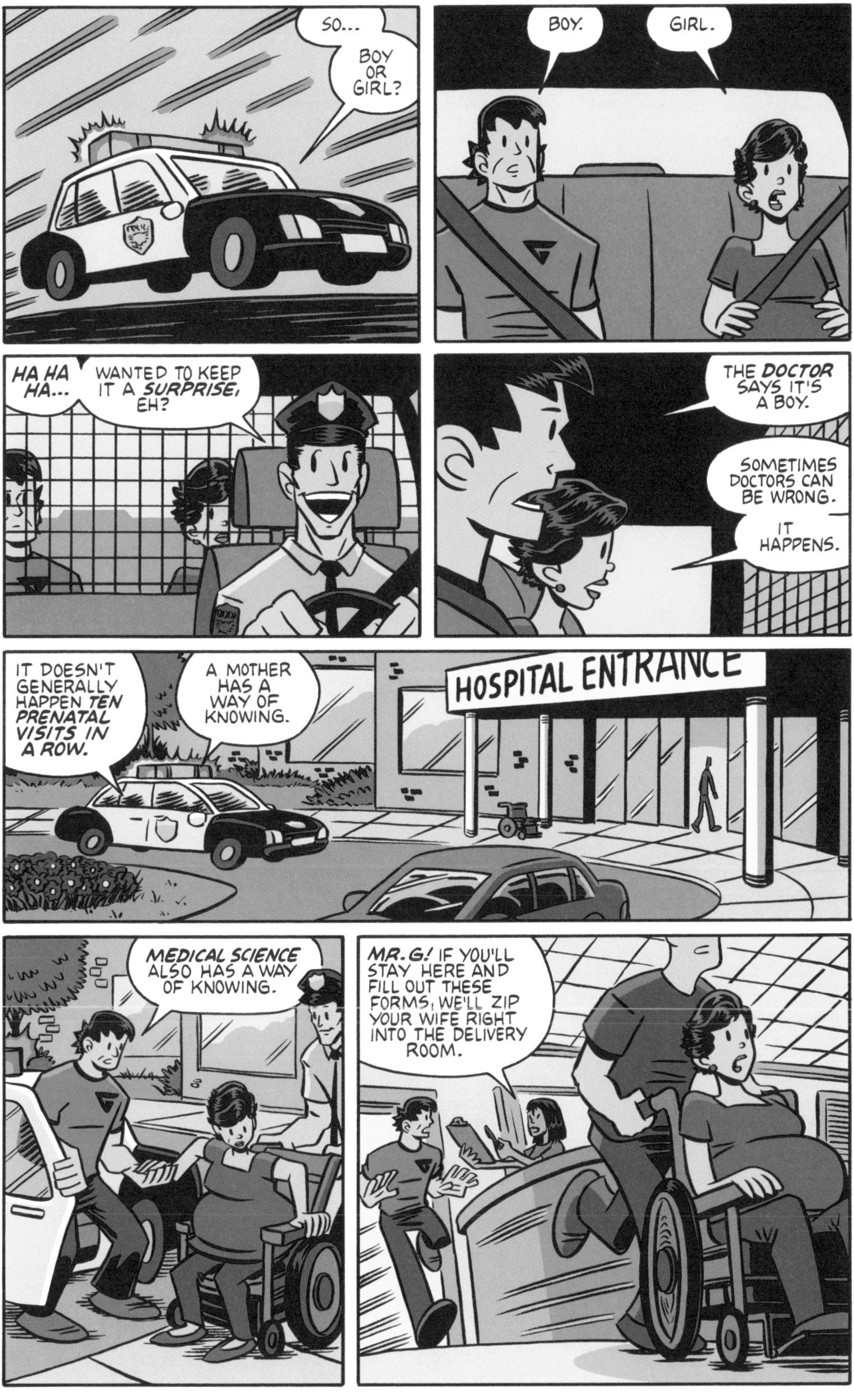
SO...
BOY OR GIRL?
BOY.
GIRL.
HA HA HA...
WANTED TO KEEP IT A SURPRISE, EH?
THE DOCTOR SAYS IT'S A BOY.
SOMETIMES DOCTORS CAN BE WRONG.
IT HAPPENS.
HOSPITAL ENTRANCE
IT DOESN'T GENERALLY HAPPEN TEN PRENATAL VISITS IN A ROW.
A MOTHER HAS A WAY OF KNOWING.
MEDICAL SCIENCE ALSO HAS A WAY OF KNOWING.
MR. G! IF YOU'LL STAY HERE AND FILL OUT THESE FORMS, WE'LL ZIP YOUR WIFE RIGHT INTO THE DELIVERY ROOM.

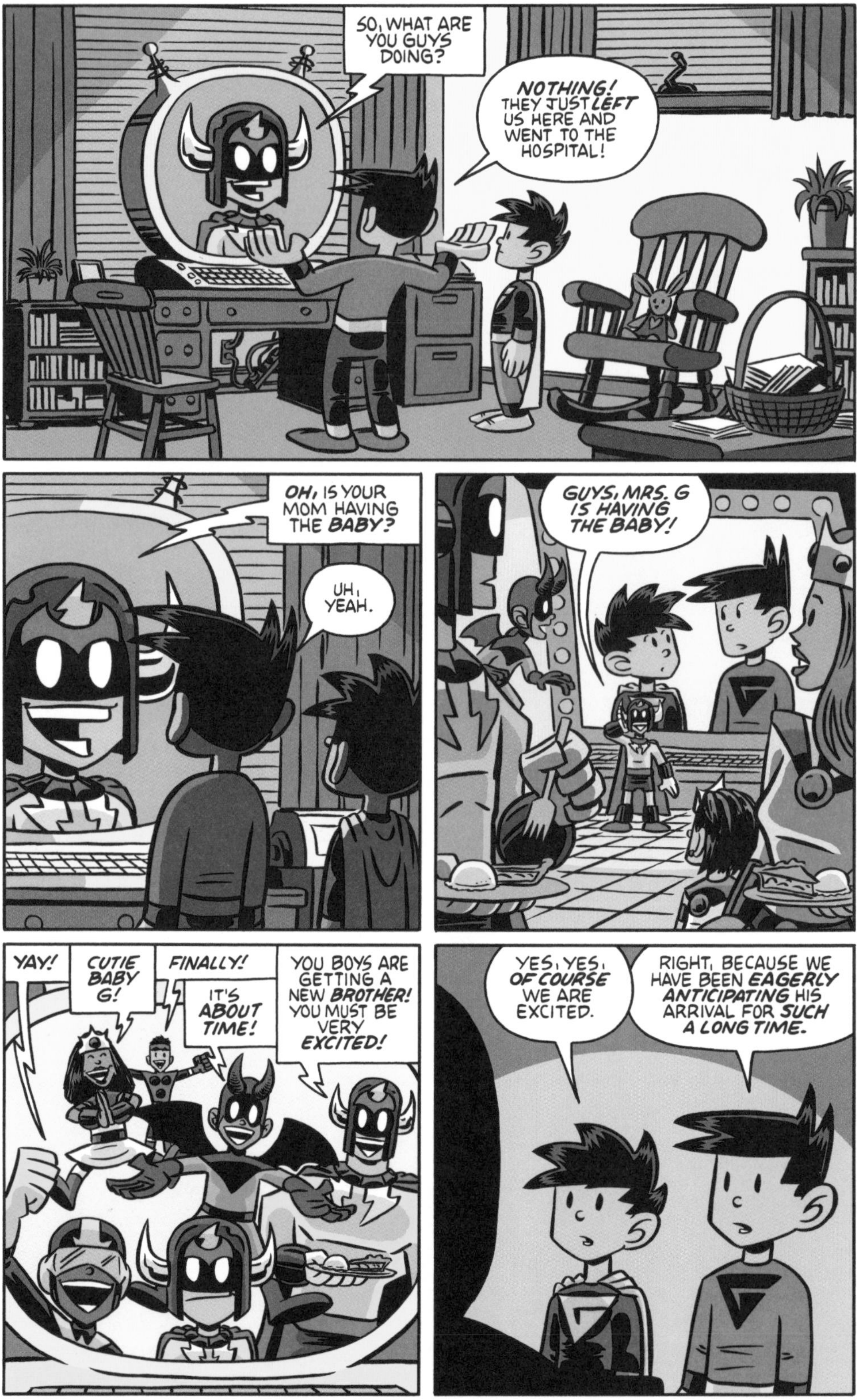

SO, WHAT ARE YOU GUYS DOING?
NOTHING! THEY JUST LEFT US HERE AND WENT TO THE HOSPITAL!
OH, IS YOUR MOM HAVING THE BABY?
UH, YEAH.
GUYS, MRS. G IS HAVING THE BABY!
YAY!
CUTIE BABY G!
FINALLY!
IT'S ABOUT TIME!
YOU BOYS ARE GETTING A NEW BROTHER! YOU MUST BE VERY EXCITED!
YES, YES, OF COURSE WE ARE EXCITED.
RIGHT, BECAUSE WE HAVE BEEN EAGERLY ANTICIPATING HIS ARRIVAL FOR SUCH A LONG TIME.

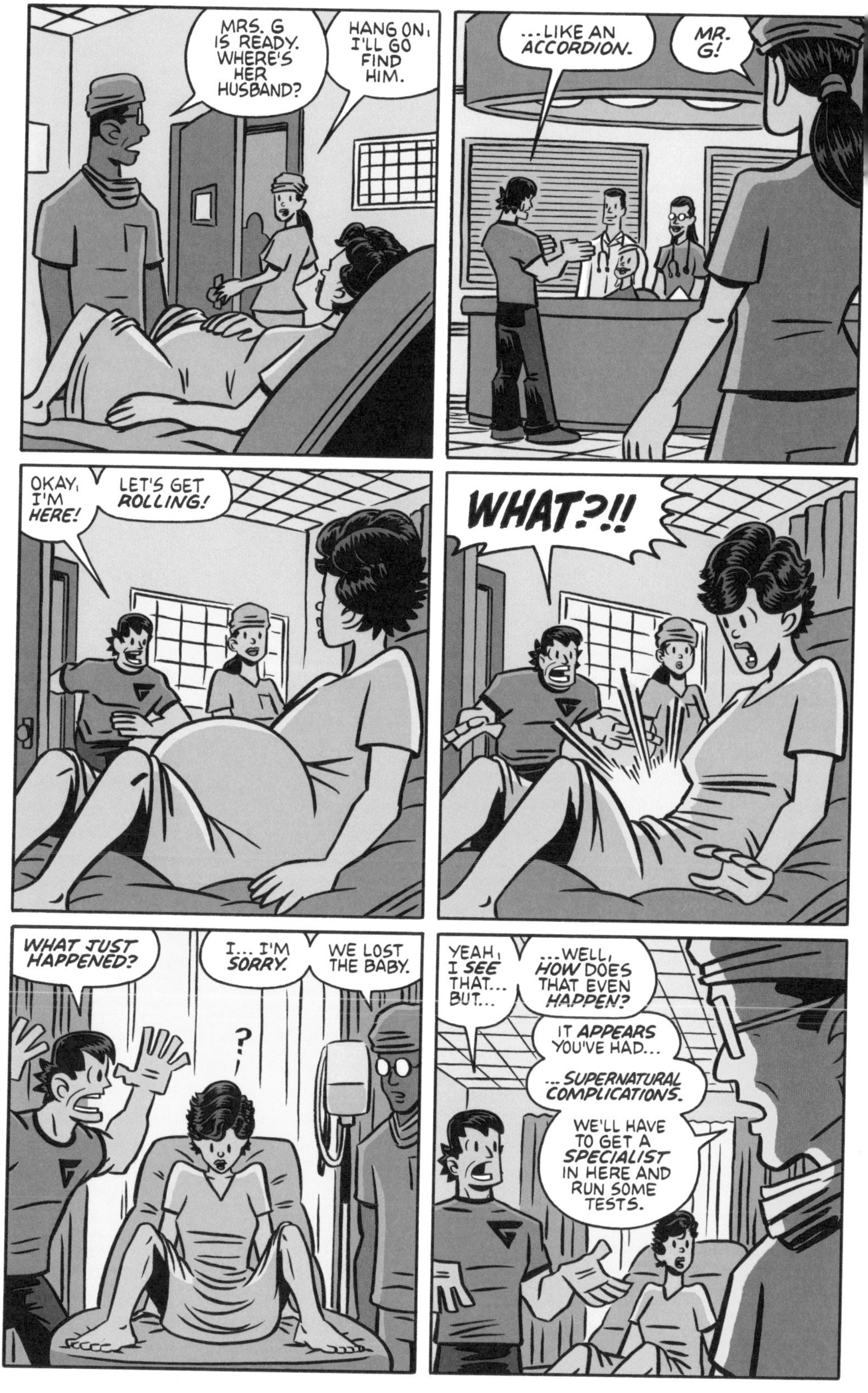
MRS. G IS READY. WHERE'S HER HUSBAND?
HANG ON, I'LL GO FIND HIM.
...LIKE AN ACCORDION.
MR. G!
OKAY, I'M HERE!
LET'S GET ROLLING!
WHAT?!!
WHAT JUST HAPPENED?
I... I'M SORRY.
WE LOST THE BABY.
?
YEAH, I SEE THAT... BUT...
...WELL, HOW DOES THAT EVEN HAPPEN?
IT APPEARS YOU'VE HAD...
...SUPERNATURAL COMPLICATIONS.
WE'LL HAVE TO GET A SPECIALIST IN HERE AND RUN SOME TESTS.

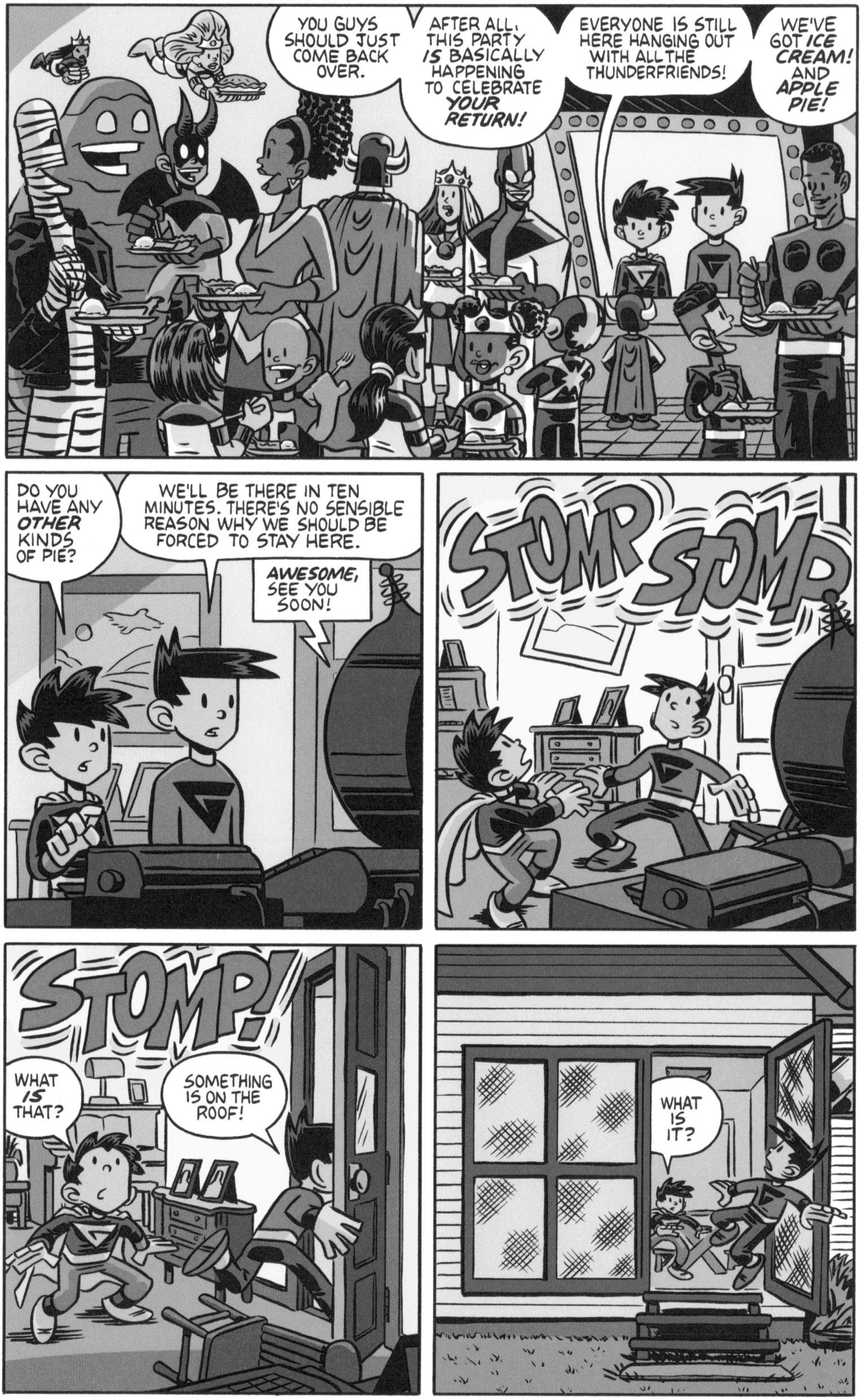
YOU GUYS SHOULD JUST COME BACK OVER.
AFTER ALL, THIS PARTY *IS* BASICALLY HAPPENING TO CELEBRATE *YOUR RETURN!*
EVERYONE IS STILL HERE HANGING OUT WITH ALL THE THUNDERFRIENDS!
WE'VE GOT *ICE CREAM!* AND *APPLE PIE!*
DO YOU HAVE ANY *OTHER* KINDS OF PIE?
WE'LL BE THERE IN TEN MINUTES. THERE'S NO SENSIBLE REASON WHY WE SHOULD BE FORCED TO STAY HERE.
AWESOME, SEE YOU SOON!
STOMP STOMP
STOMP!
WHAT *IS* THAT?
SOMETHING IS ON THE ROOF!
WHAT IS IT?

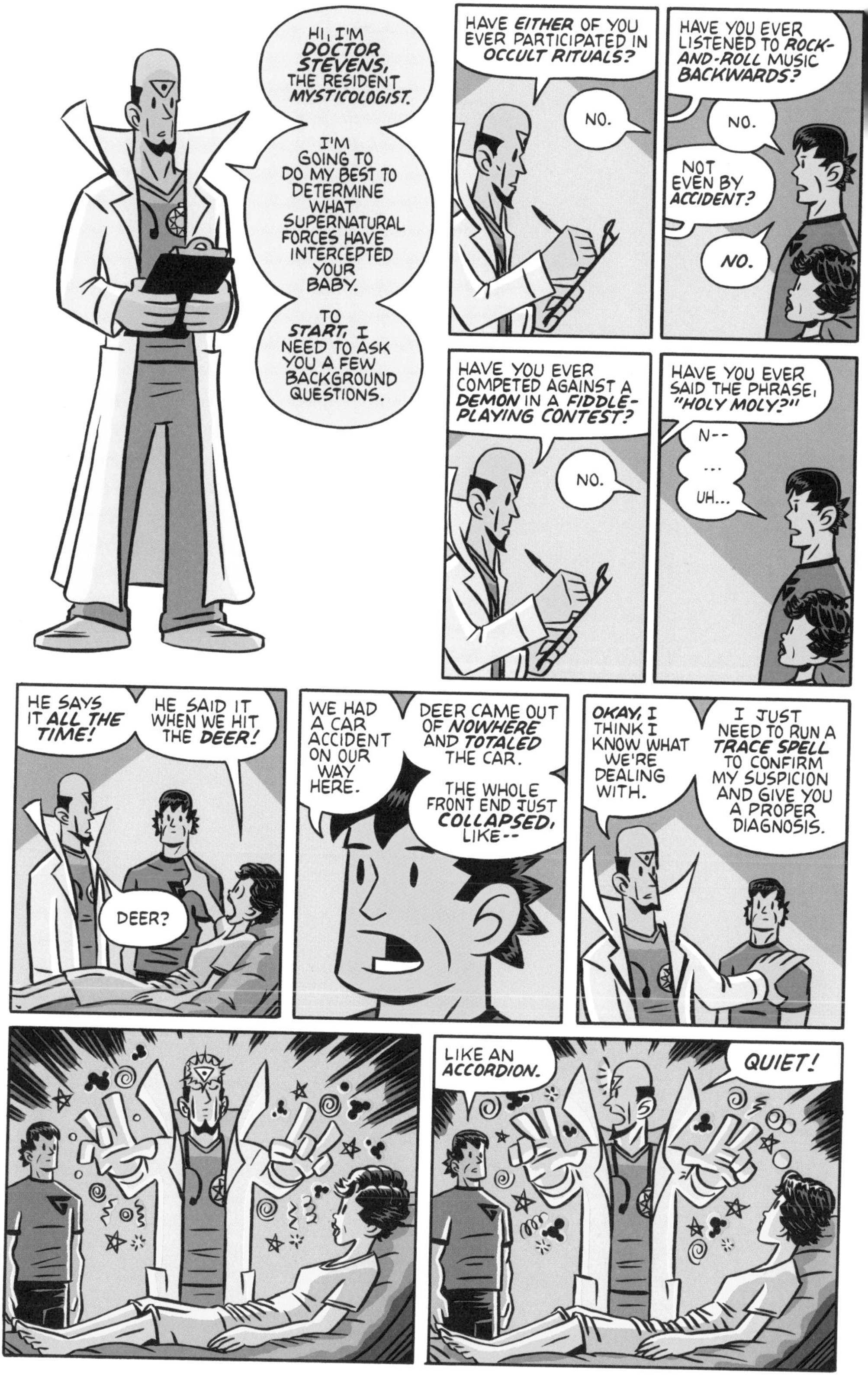
HI, I'M DOCTOR STEVENS, THE RESIDENT MYSTICOLOGIST.
I'M GOING TO DO MY BEST TO DETERMINE WHAT SUPERNATURAL FORCES HAVE INTERCEPTED YOUR BABY.
TO START, I NEED TO ASK YOU A FEW BACKGROUND QUESTIONS.
HAVE EITHER OF YOU EVER PARTICIPATED IN OCCULT RITUALS?
NO.
HAVE YOU EVER LISTENED TO ROCK-AND-ROLL MUSIC BACKWARDS?
NO.
NOT EVEN BY ACCIDENT?
NO.
HAVE YOU EVER COMPETED AGAINST A DEMON IN A FIDDLE-PLAYING CONTEST?
NO.
HAVE YOU EVER SAID THE PHRASE, "HOLY MOLY?"
N--
...
UH...
HE SAYS IT ALL THE TIME!
HE SAID IT WHEN WE HIT THE DEER!
DEER?
WE HAD A CAR ACCIDENT ON OUR WAY HERE.
DEER CAME OUT OF NOWHERE AND TOTALED THE CAR.
THE WHOLE FRONT END JUST COLLAPSED, LIKE--
OKAY, I THINK I KNOW WHAT WE'RE DEALING WITH.
I JUST NEED TO RUN A TRACE SPELL TO CONFIRM MY SUSPICION AND GIVE YOU A PROPER DIAGNOSIS.
LIKE AN ACCORDION.
QUIET!

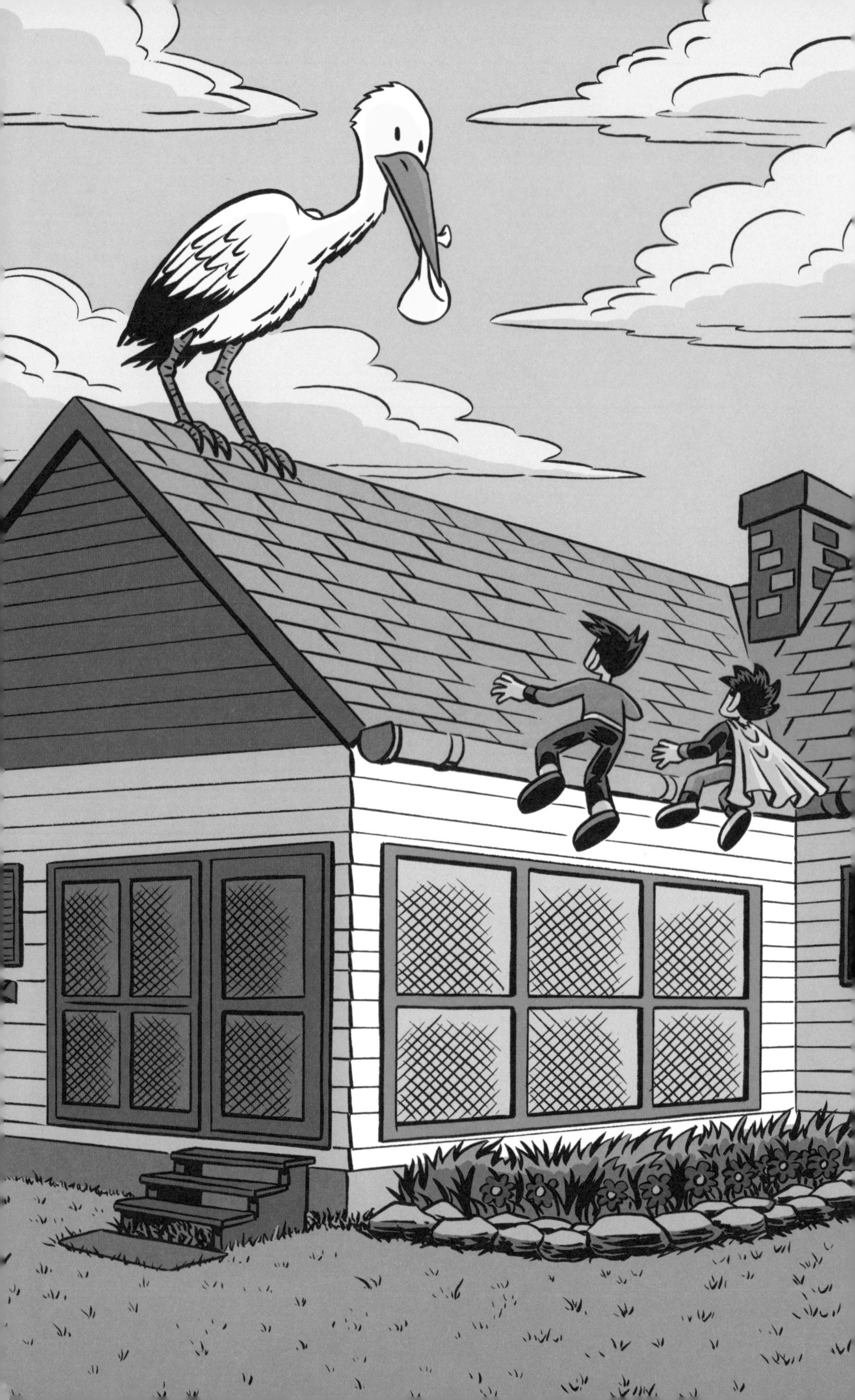

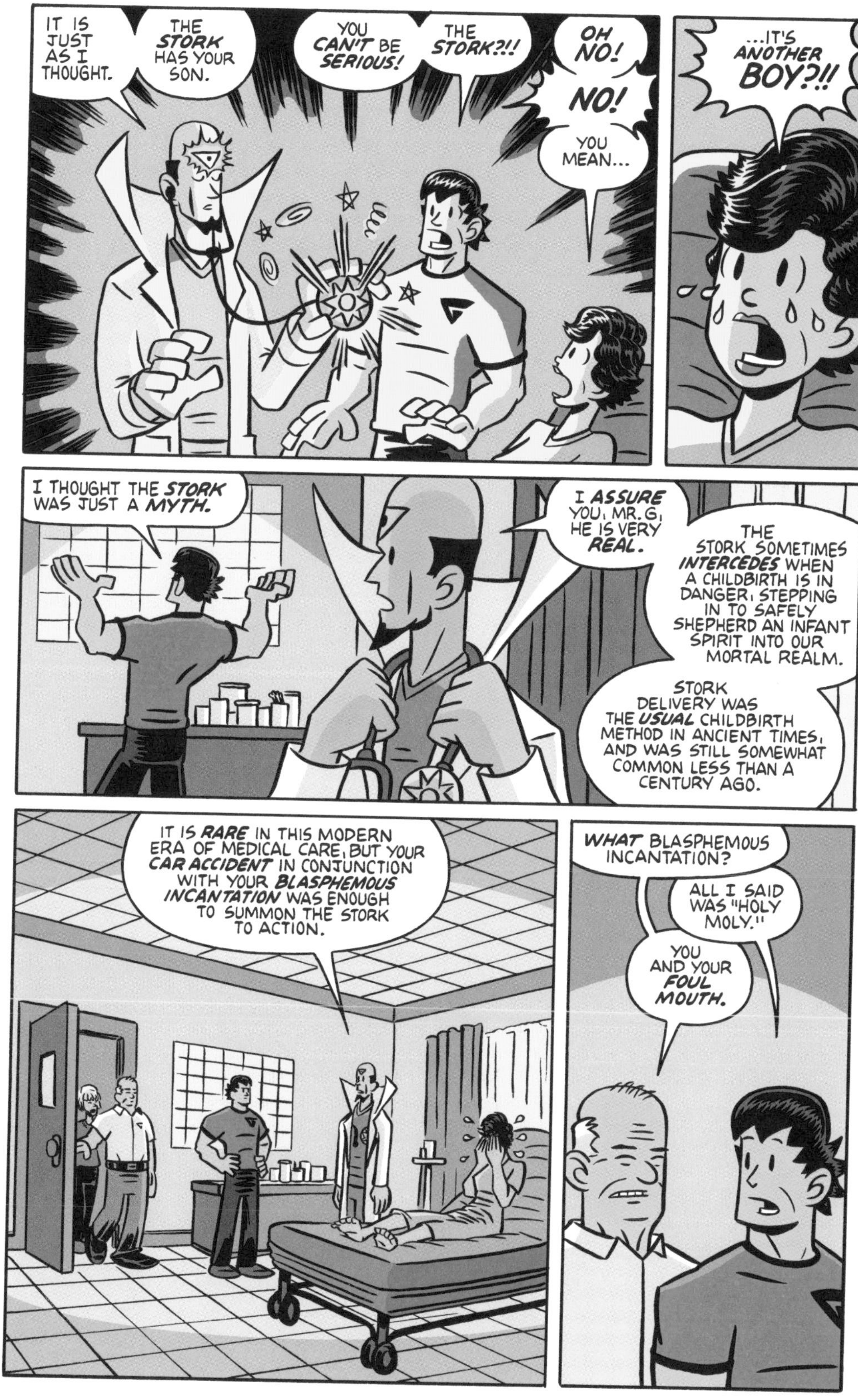
IT IS JUST AS I THOUGHT.
THE STORK HAS YOUR SON.
YOU CAN'T BE SERIOUS!
THE STORK?!!
OH NO!
NO!
YOU MEAN...
...IT'S ANOTHER BOY?!!
I THOUGHT THE STORK WAS JUST A MYTH.
I ASSURE YOU, MR. G, HE IS VERY REAL.
THE STORK SOMETIMES INTERCEDES WHEN A CHILDBIRTH IS IN DANGER, STEPPING IN TO SAFELY SHEPHERD AN INFANT SPIRIT INTO OUR MORTAL REALM.
STORK DELIVERY WAS THE USUAL CHILDBIRTH METHOD IN ANCIENT TIMES, AND WAS STILL SOMEWHAT COMMON LESS THAN A CENTURY AGO.
IT IS RARE IN THIS MODERN ERA OF MEDICAL CARE, BUT YOUR CAR ACCIDENT IN CONJUNCTION WITH YOUR BLASPHEMOUS INCANTATION WAS ENOUGH TO SUMMON THE STORK TO ACTION.
WHAT BLASPHEMOUS INCANTATION?
ALL I SAID WAS "HOLY MOLY."
YOU AND YOUR FOUL MOUTH.

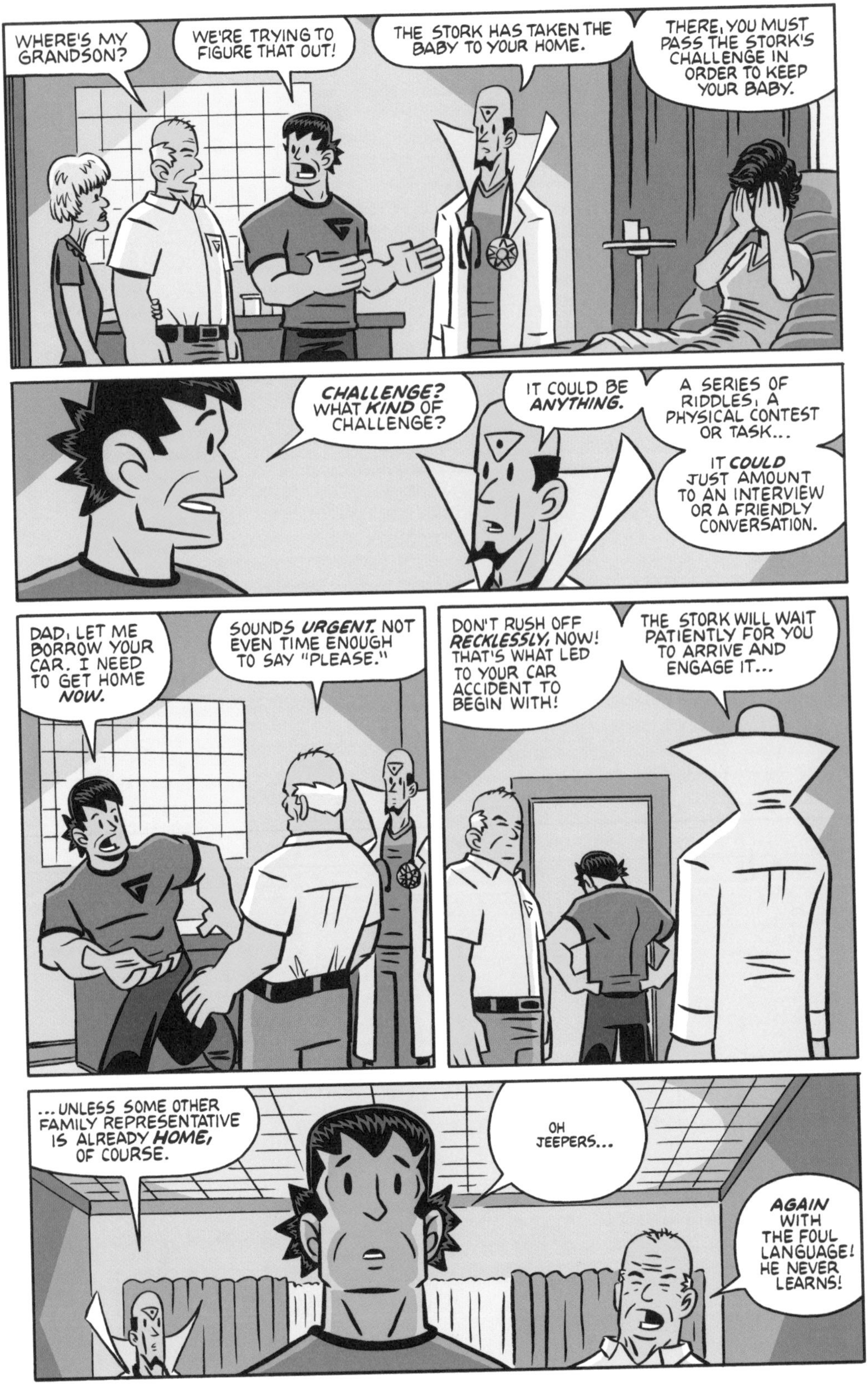
WHERE'S MY GRANDSON?
WE'RE TRYING TO FIGURE THAT OUT!
THE STORK HAS TAKEN THE BABY TO YOUR HOME.
THERE, YOU MUST PASS THE STORK'S CHALLENGE IN ORDER TO KEEP YOUR BABY.
CHALLENGE? WHAT KIND OF CHALLENGE?
IT COULD BE ANYTHING.
A SERIES OF RIDDLES, A PHYSICAL CONTEST OR TASK...
IT COULD JUST AMOUNT TO AN INTERVIEW OR A FRIENDLY CONVERSATION.
DAD, LET ME BORROW YOUR CAR. I NEED TO GET HOME NOW.
SOUNDS URGENT. NOT EVEN TIME ENOUGH TO SAY "PLEASE."
DON'T RUSH OFF RECKLESSLY, NOW! THAT'S WHAT LED TO YOUR CAR ACCIDENT TO BEGIN WITH!
THE STORK WILL WAIT PATIENTLY FOR YOU TO ARRIVE AND ENGAGE IT...
...UNLESS SOME OTHER FAMILY REPRESENTATIVE IS ALREADY HOME, OF COURSE.
OH JEEPERS...
AGAIN WITH THE FOUL LANGUAGE! HE NEVER LEARNS!

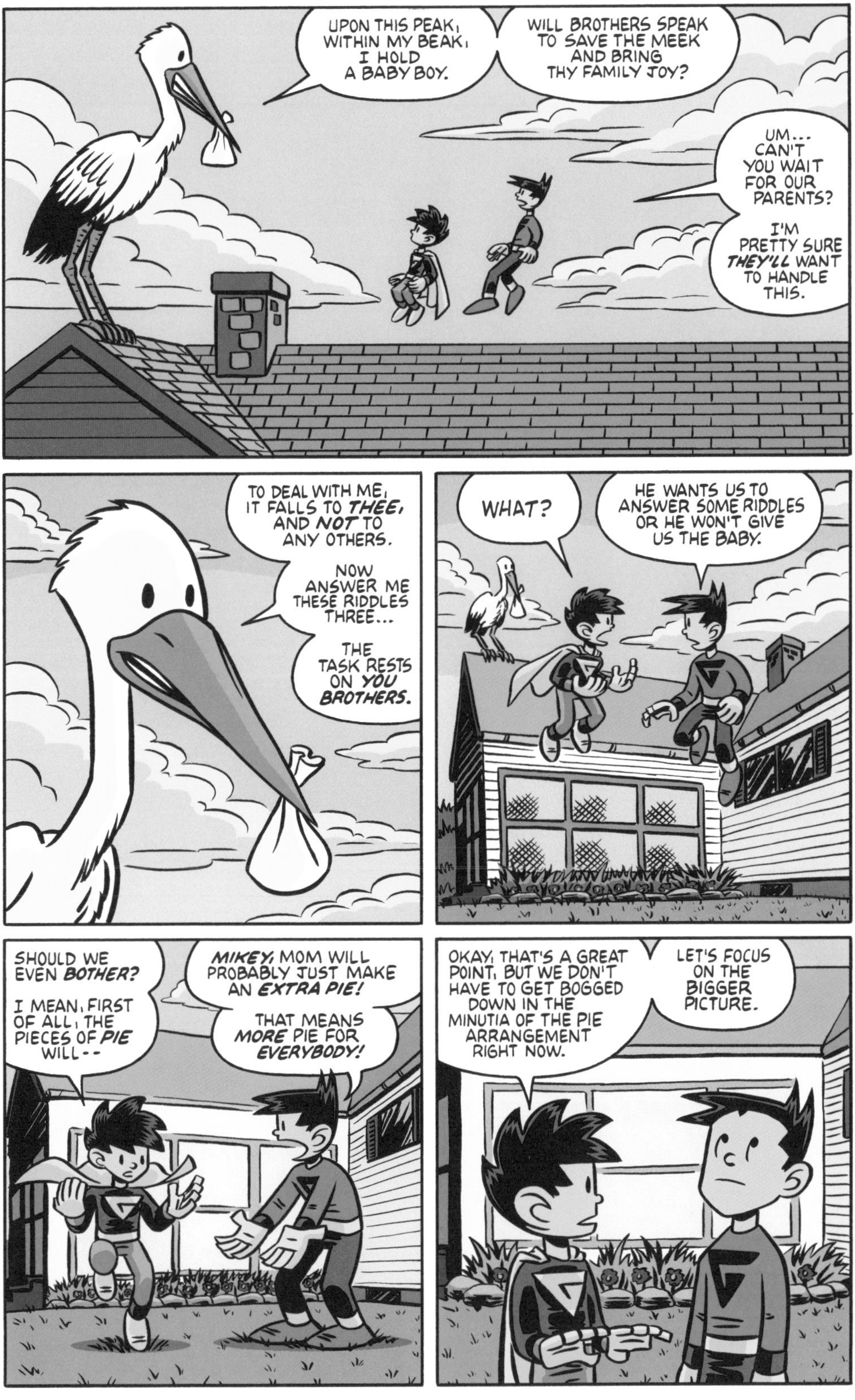
UPON THIS PEAK, WITHIN MY BEAK, I HOLD A BABY BOY.
WILL BROTHERS SPEAK TO SAVE THE MEEK AND BRING THY FAMILY JOY?
UM... CAN'T YOU WAIT FOR OUR PARENTS?
I'M PRETTY SURE THEY'LL WANT TO HANDLE THIS.
TO DEAL WITH ME, IT FALLS TO THEE, AND NOT TO ANY OTHERS.
NOW ANSWER ME THESE RIDDLES THREE...
THE TASK RESTS ON YOU BROTHERS.
WHAT?
HE WANTS US TO ANSWER SOME RIDDLES OR HE WON'T GIVE US THE BABY.
SHOULD WE EVEN BOTHER?
I MEAN, FIRST OF ALL, THE PIECES OF PIE WILL--
MIKEY, MOM WILL PROBABLY JUST MAKE AN EXTRA PIE!
THAT MEANS MORE PIE FOR EVERYBODY!
OKAY, THAT'S A GREAT POINT, BUT WE DON'T HAVE TO GET BOGGED DOWN IN THE MINUTIA OF THE PIE ARRANGEMENT RIGHT NOW.
LET'S FOCUS ON THE BIGGER PICTURE.

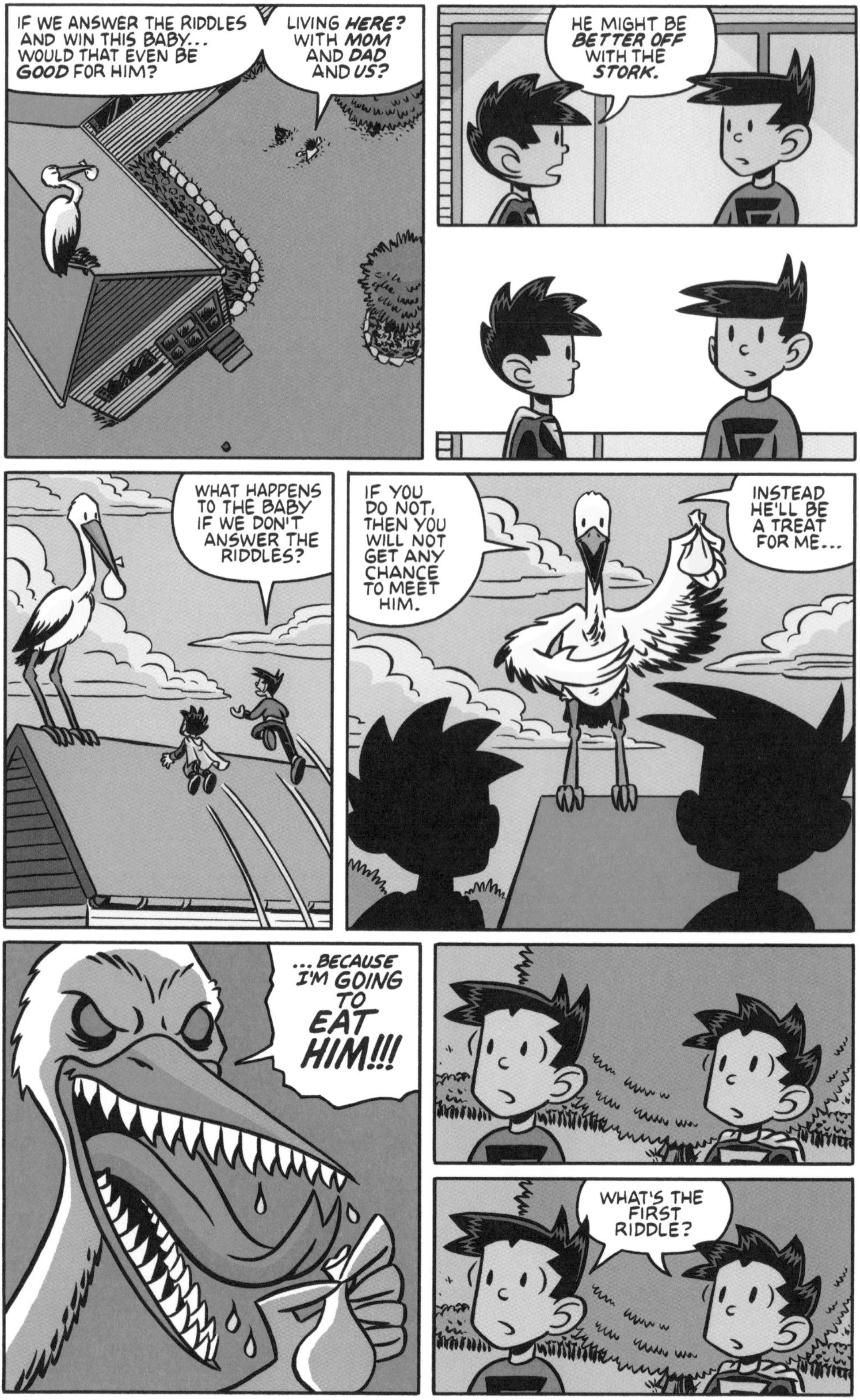
IF WE ANSWER THE RIDDLES AND WIN THIS BABY... WOULD THAT EVEN BE GOOD FOR HIM?
LIVING HERE? WITH MOM AND DAD AND US?
HE MIGHT BE BETTER OFF WITH THE STORK.
WHAT HAPPENS TO THE BABY IF WE DON'T ANSWER THE RIDDLES?
IF YOU DO NOT, THEN YOU WILL NOT GET ANY CHANCE TO MEET HIM.
INSTEAD HE'LL BE A TREAT FOR ME...
...BECAUSE I'M GOING TO EAT HIM!!!
WHAT'S THE FIRST RIDDLE?

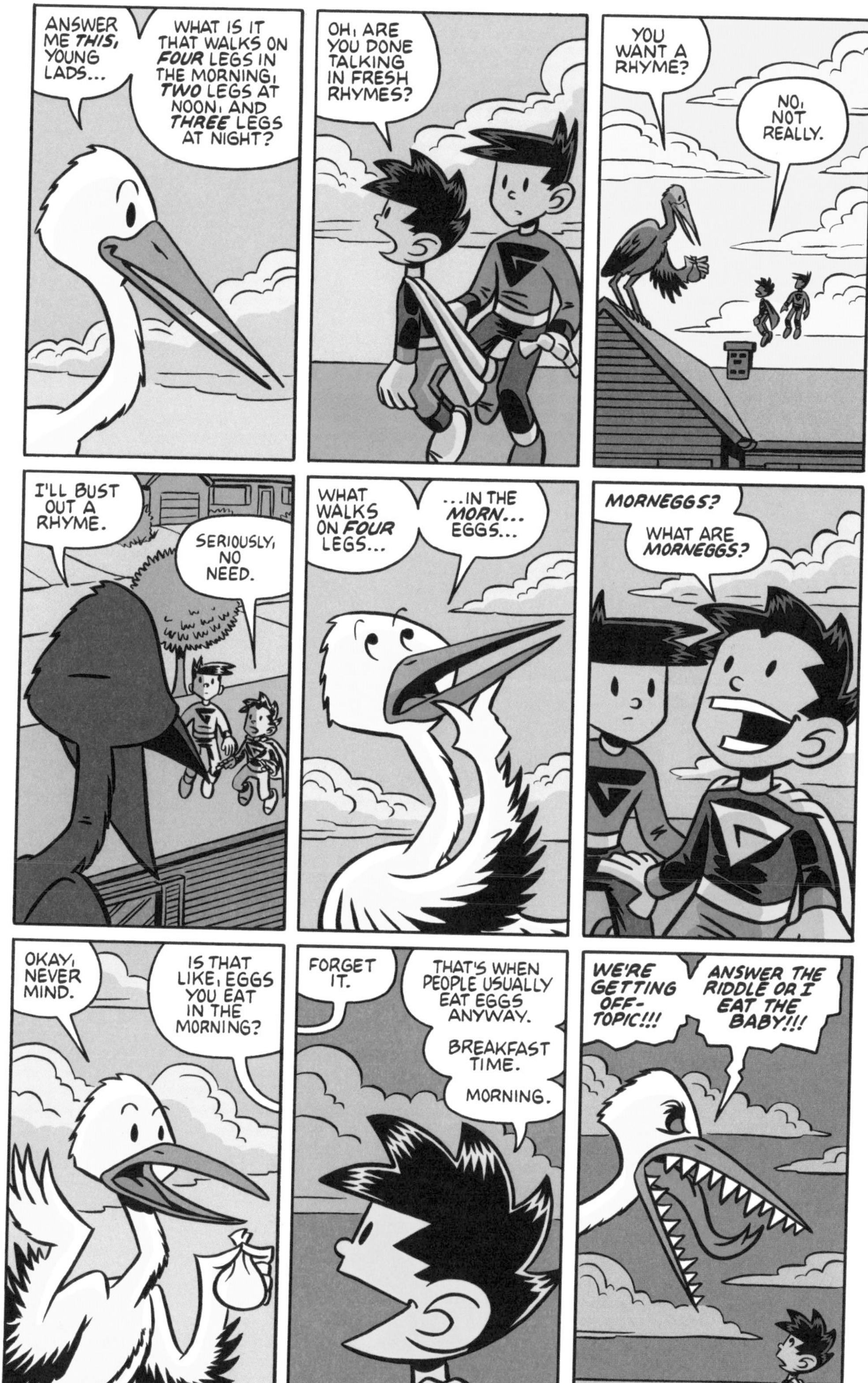

ANSWER ME *THIS,* YOUNG LADS...
WHAT IS IT THAT WALKS ON *FOUR* LEGS IN THE MORNING, *TWO* LEGS AT NOON, AND *THREE* LEGS AT NIGHT?
OH, ARE YOU DONE TALKING IN FRESH RHYMES?
YOU WANT A RHYME?
NO, NOT REALLY.
I'LL BUST OUT A RHYME.
SERIOUSLY, NO NEED.
WHAT WALKS ON *FOUR* LEGS...
...IN THE *MORN...* EGGS...
MORNEGGS?
WHAT ARE *MORNEGGS?*
OKAY, NEVER MIND.
IS THAT LIKE, EGGS YOU EAT IN THE MORNING?
FORGET IT.
THAT'S WHEN PEOPLE USUALLY EAT EGGS ANYWAY.
BREAKFAST TIME.
MORNING.
WE'RE GETTING OFF-TOPIC!!!
ANSWER THE RIDDLE OR I EAT THE BABY!!!

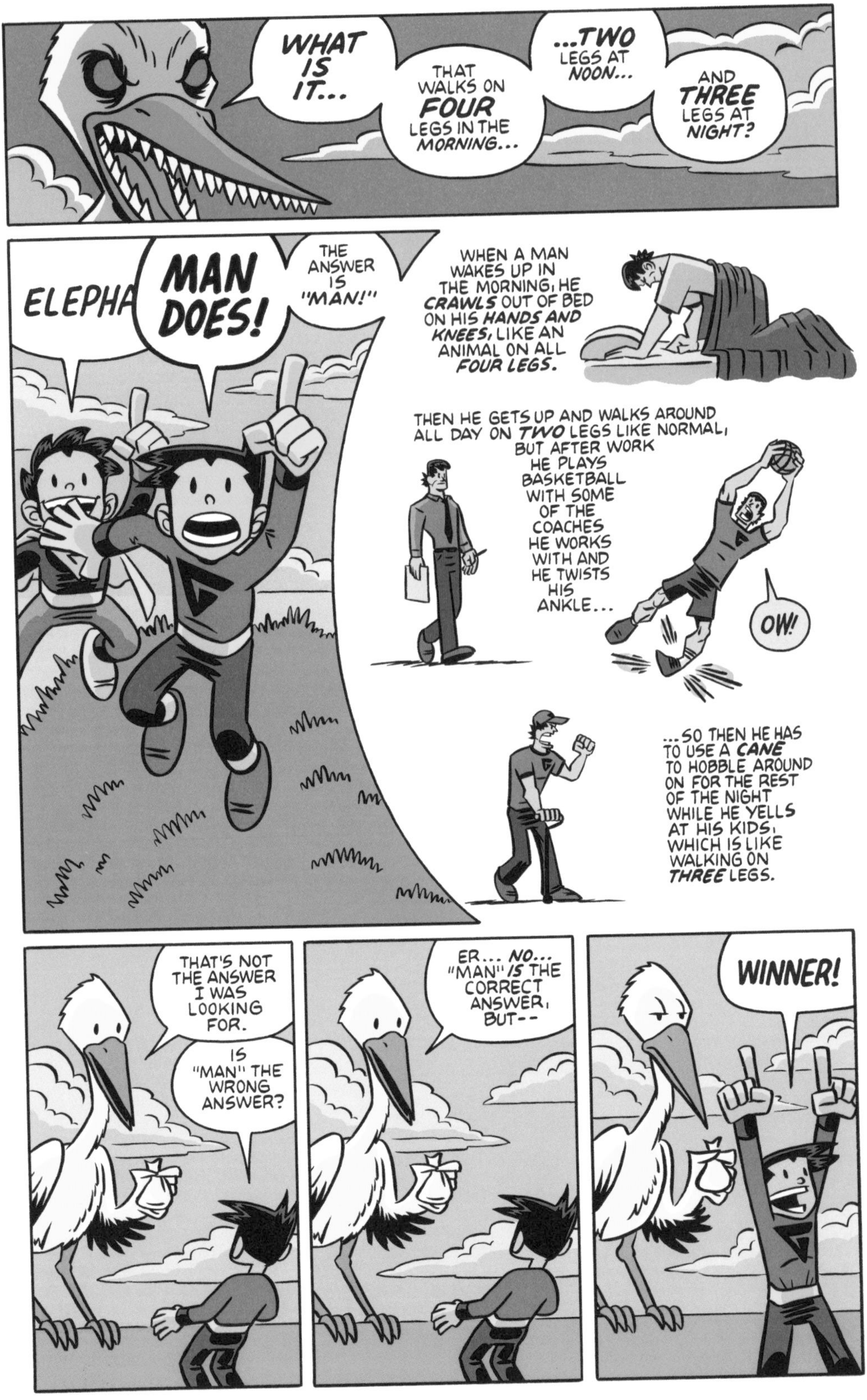
WHAT IS IT...
THAT WALKS ON FOUR LEGS IN THE MORNING...
...TWO LEGS AT NOON...
AND THREE LEGS AT NIGHT?
ELEPHA
MAN DOES!
THE ANSWER IS "MAN!"
WHEN A MAN WAKES UP IN THE MORNING, HE CRAWLS OUT OF BED ON HIS HANDS AND KNEES, LIKE AN ANIMAL ON ALL FOUR LEGS.
THEN HE GETS UP AND WALKS AROUND ALL DAY ON TWO LEGS LIKE NORMAL, BUT AFTER WORK HE PLAYS BASKETBALL WITH SOME OF THE COACHES HE WORKS WITH AND HE TWISTS HIS ANKLE...
OW!
...SO THEN HE HAS TO USE A CANE TO HOBBLE AROUND ON FOR THE REST OF THE NIGHT WHILE HE YELLS AT HIS KIDS, WHICH IS LIKE WALKING ON THREE LEGS.
THAT'S NOT THE ANSWER I WAS LOOKING FOR.
IS "MAN" THE WRONG ANSWER?
ER... NO... "MAN" IS THE CORRECT ANSWER, BUT--
WINNER!

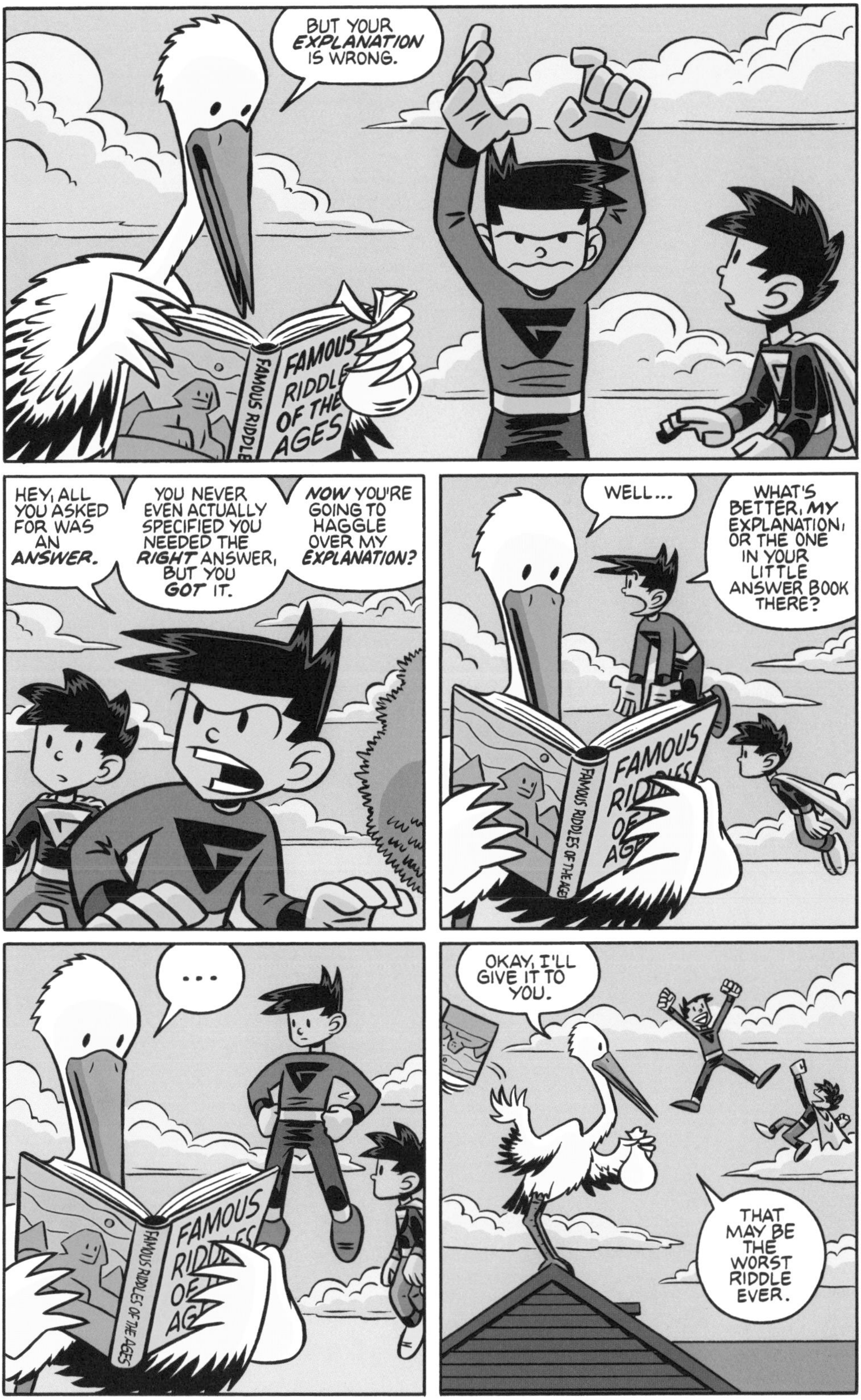
BUT YOUR *EXPLANATION* IS WRONG.
FAMOUS RIDDLES OF THE AGES
HEY, ALL YOU ASKED FOR WAS AN *ANSWER.*
YOU NEVER EVEN ACTUALLY SPECIFIED YOU NEEDED THE *RIGHT* ANSWER, BUT YOU *GOT* IT.
NOW YOU'RE GOING TO HAGGLE OVER MY *EXPLANATION?*
WELL...
WHAT'S BETTER, *MY* EXPLANATION, OR THE ONE IN YOUR LITTLE ANSWER BOOK THERE?
FAMOUS RIDDLES OF THE AGES
...
FAMOUS RIDDLES OF THE AGES
OKAY, I'LL GIVE IT TO YOU.
THAT MAY BE THE WORST RIDDLE EVER.

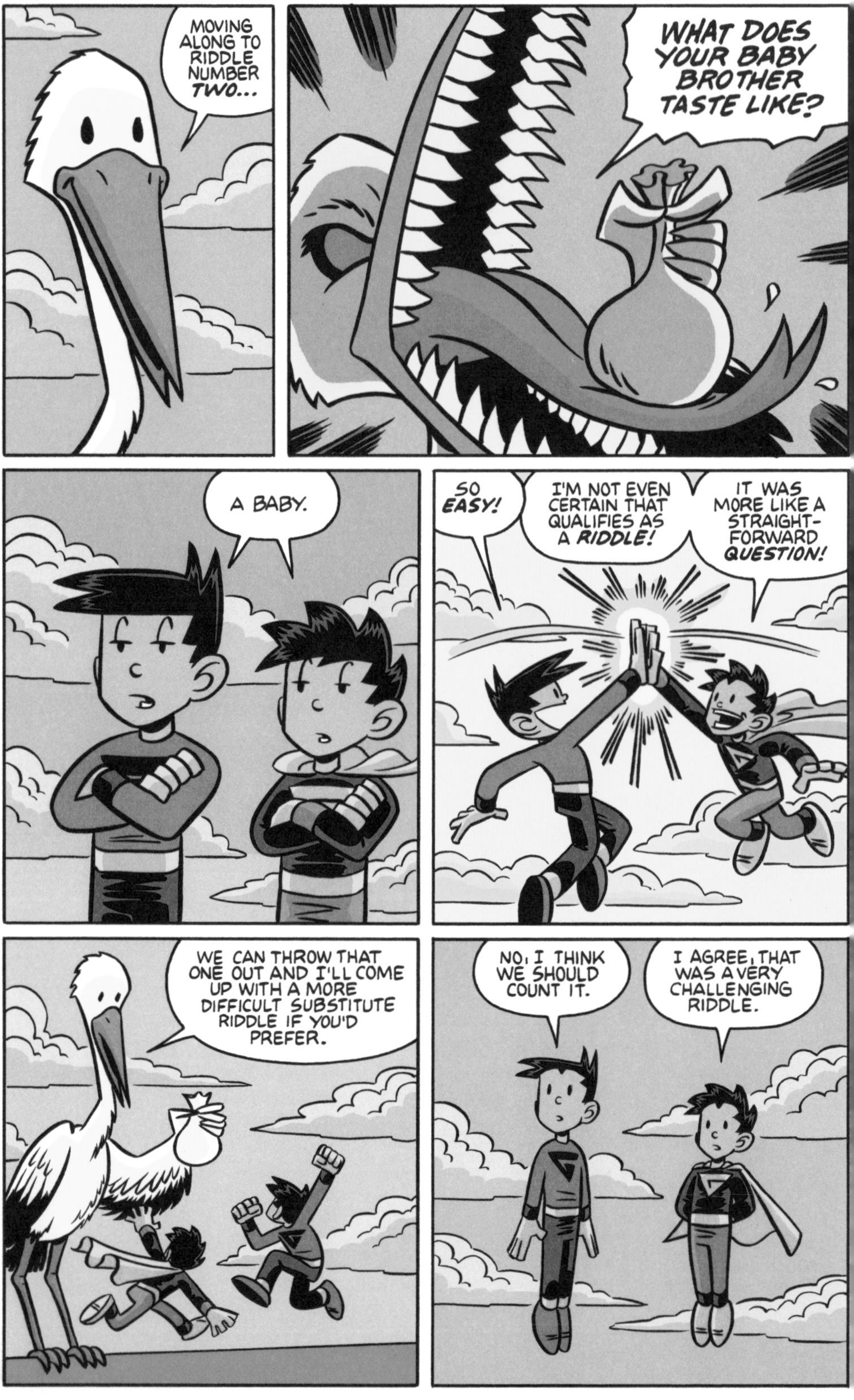
MOVING ALONG TO RIDDLE NUMBER TWO...
WHAT DOES YOUR BABY BROTHER TASTE LIKE?
A BABY.
SO EASY!
I'M NOT EVEN CERTAIN THAT QUALIFIES AS A RIDDLE!
IT WAS MORE LIKE A STRAIGHT-FORWARD QUESTION!
WE CAN THROW THAT ONE OUT AND I'LL COME UP WITH A MORE DIFFICULT SUBSTITUTE RIDDLE IF YOU'D PREFER.
NO, I THINK WE SHOULD COUNT IT.
I AGREE, THAT WAS A VERY CHALLENGING RIDDLE.

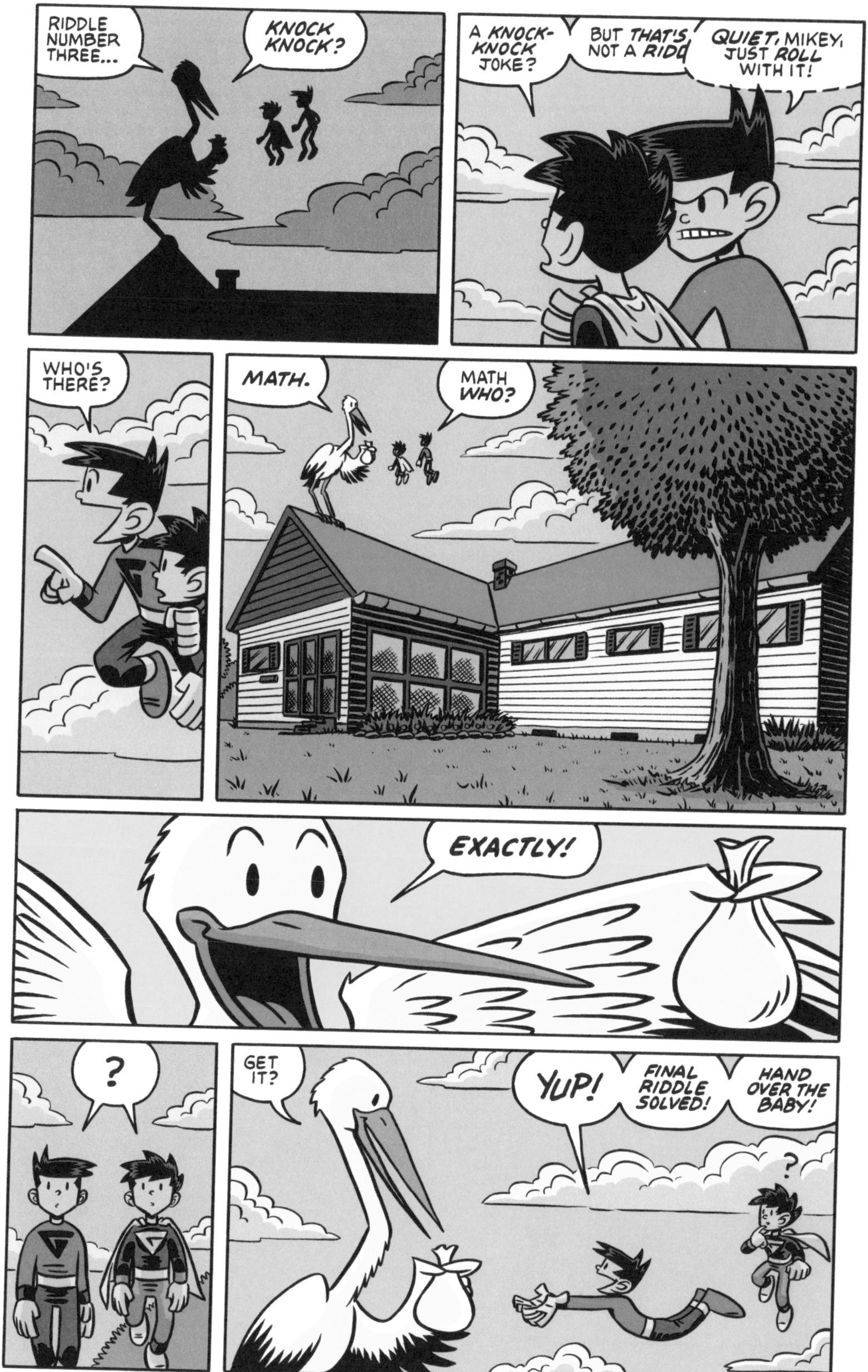
RIDDLE NUMBER THREE...
KNOCK KNOCK?
A KNOCK-KNOCK JOKE?
BUT THAT'S NOT A RIDD
QUIET, MIKEY, JUST ROLL WITH IT!
WHO'S THERE?
MATH.
MATH WHO?
EXACTLY!
?
GET IT?
YUP!
FINAL RIDDLE SOLVED!
HAND OVER THE BABY!
?

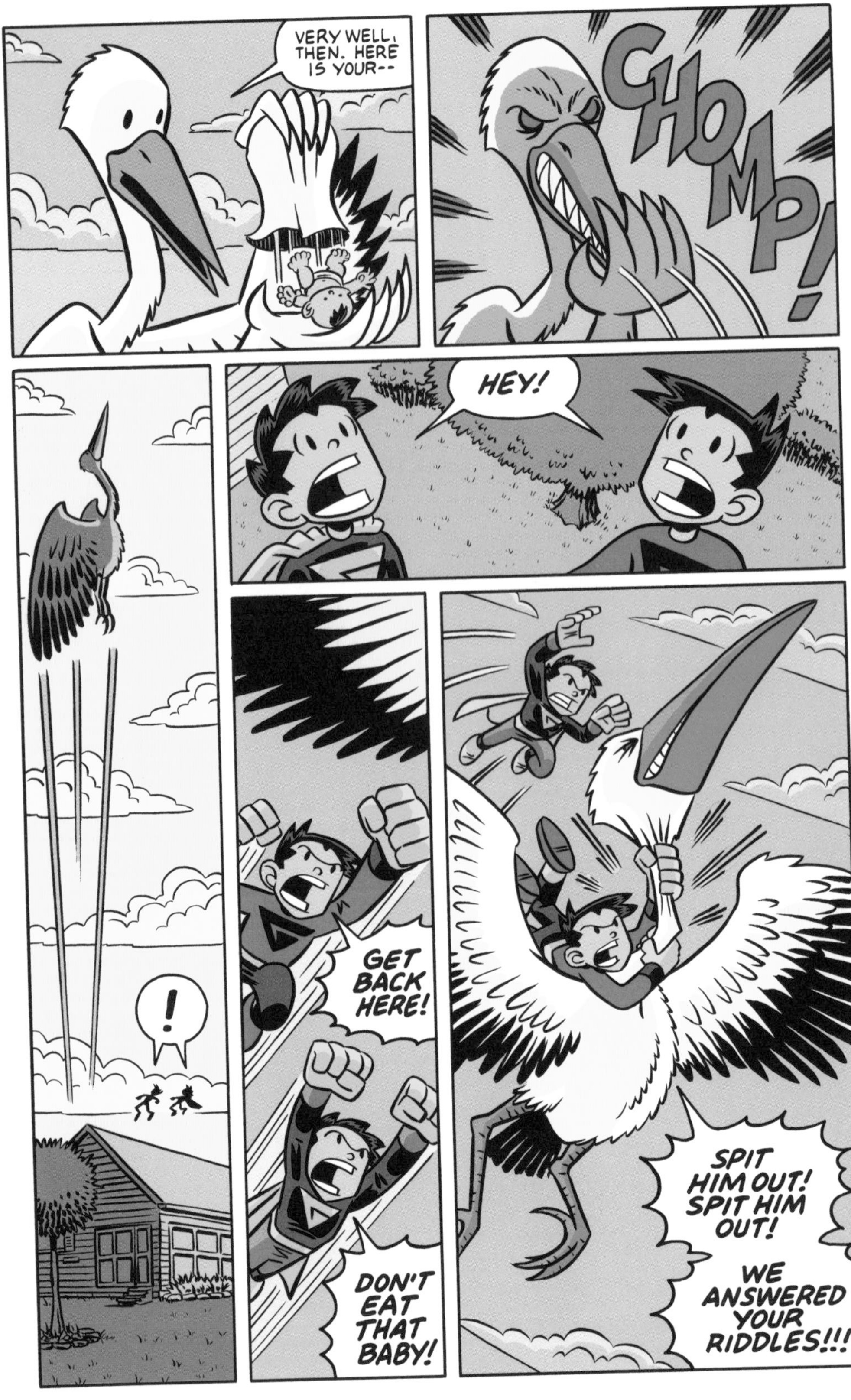

VERY WELL, THEN. HERE IS YOUR--
CHOMP!
HEY!
!
GET BACK HERE!
DON'T EAT THAT BABY!
SPIT HIM OUT! SPIT HIM OUT!
WE ANSWERED YOUR RIDDLES!!!

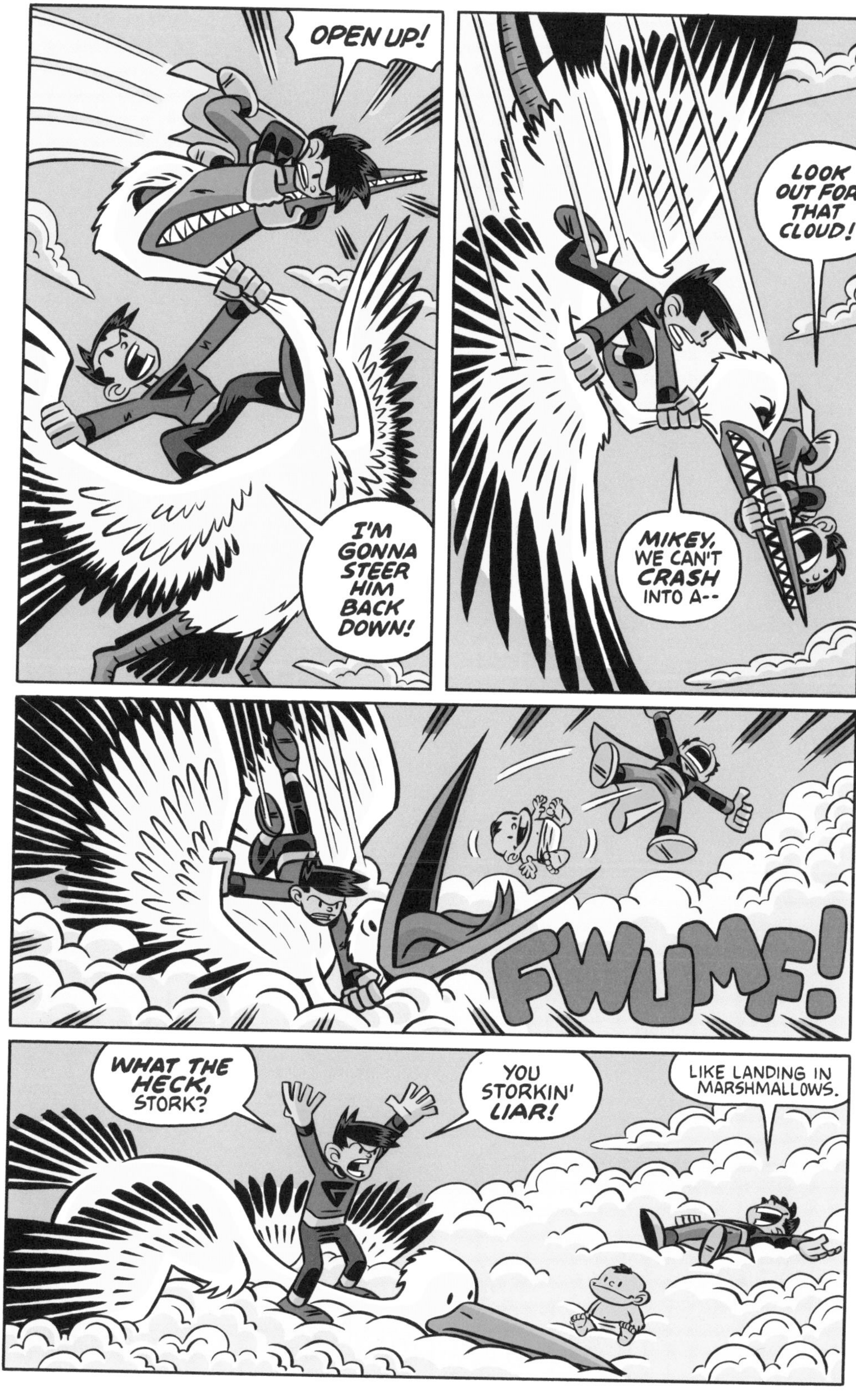
OPEN UP!
I'M GONNA STEER HIM BACK DOWN!
LOOK OUT FOR THAT CLOUD!
MIKEY, WE CAN'T CRASH INTO A--
FWUMF!
WHAT THE HECK, STORK?
YOU STORKIN' LIAR!
LIKE LANDING IN MARSHMALLOWS.

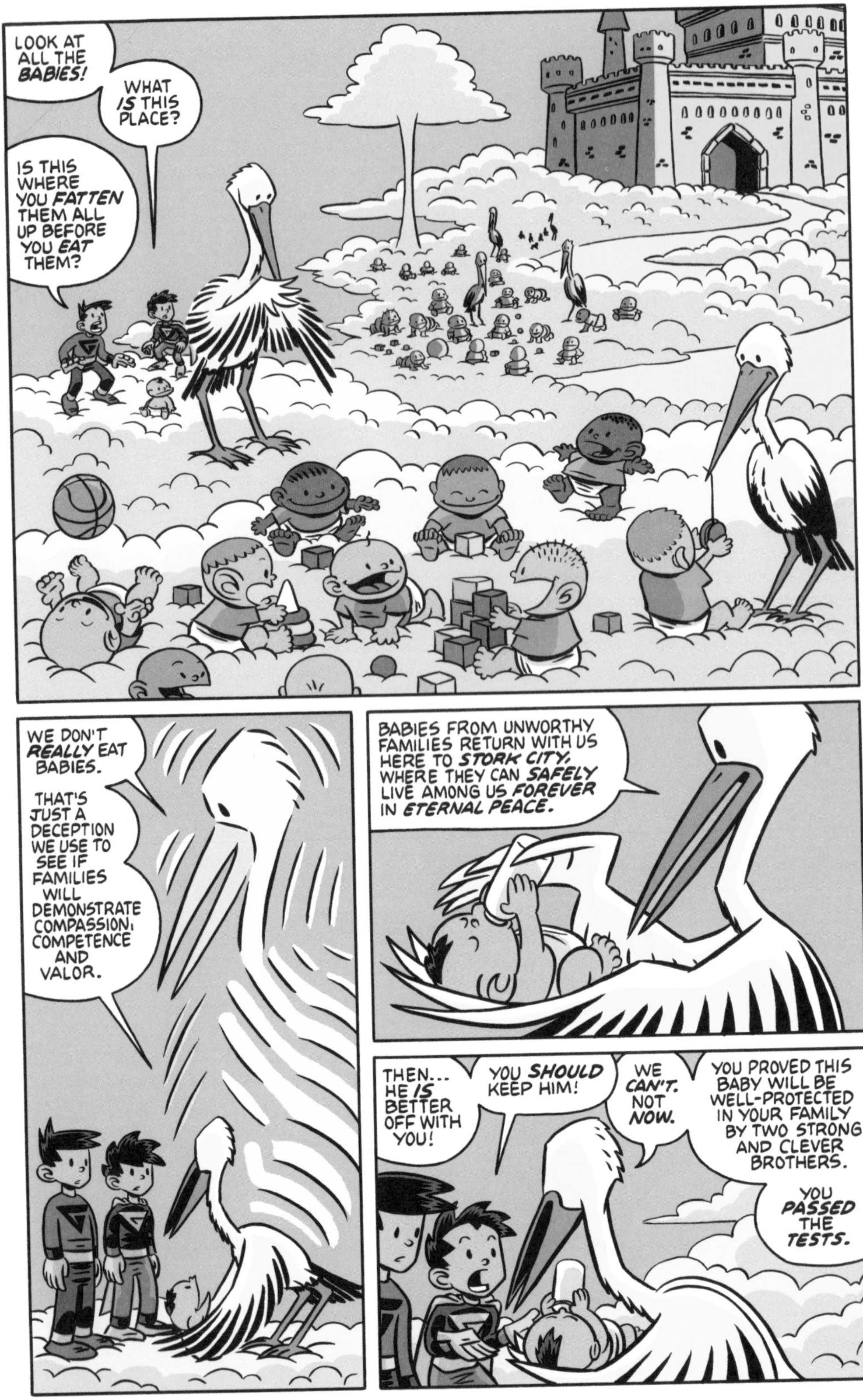
LOOK AT ALL THE BABIES!
WHAT IS THIS PLACE?
IS THIS WHERE YOU FATTEN THEM ALL UP BEFORE YOU EAT THEM?
WE DON'T REALLY EAT BABIES.
THAT'S JUST A DECEPTION WE USE TO SEE IF FAMILIES WILL DEMONSTRATE COMPASSION, COMPETENCE AND VALOR.
BABIES FROM UNWORTHY FAMILIES RETURN WITH US HERE TO STORK CITY, WHERE THEY CAN SAFELY LIVE AMONG US FOREVER IN ETERNAL PEACE.
THEN... HE IS BETTER OFF WITH YOU!
YOU SHOULD KEEP HIM!
WE CAN'T. NOT NOW.
YOU PROVED THIS BABY WILL BE WELL-PROTECTED IN YOUR FAMILY BY TWO STRONG AND CLEVER BROTHERS.
YOU PASSED THE TESTS.

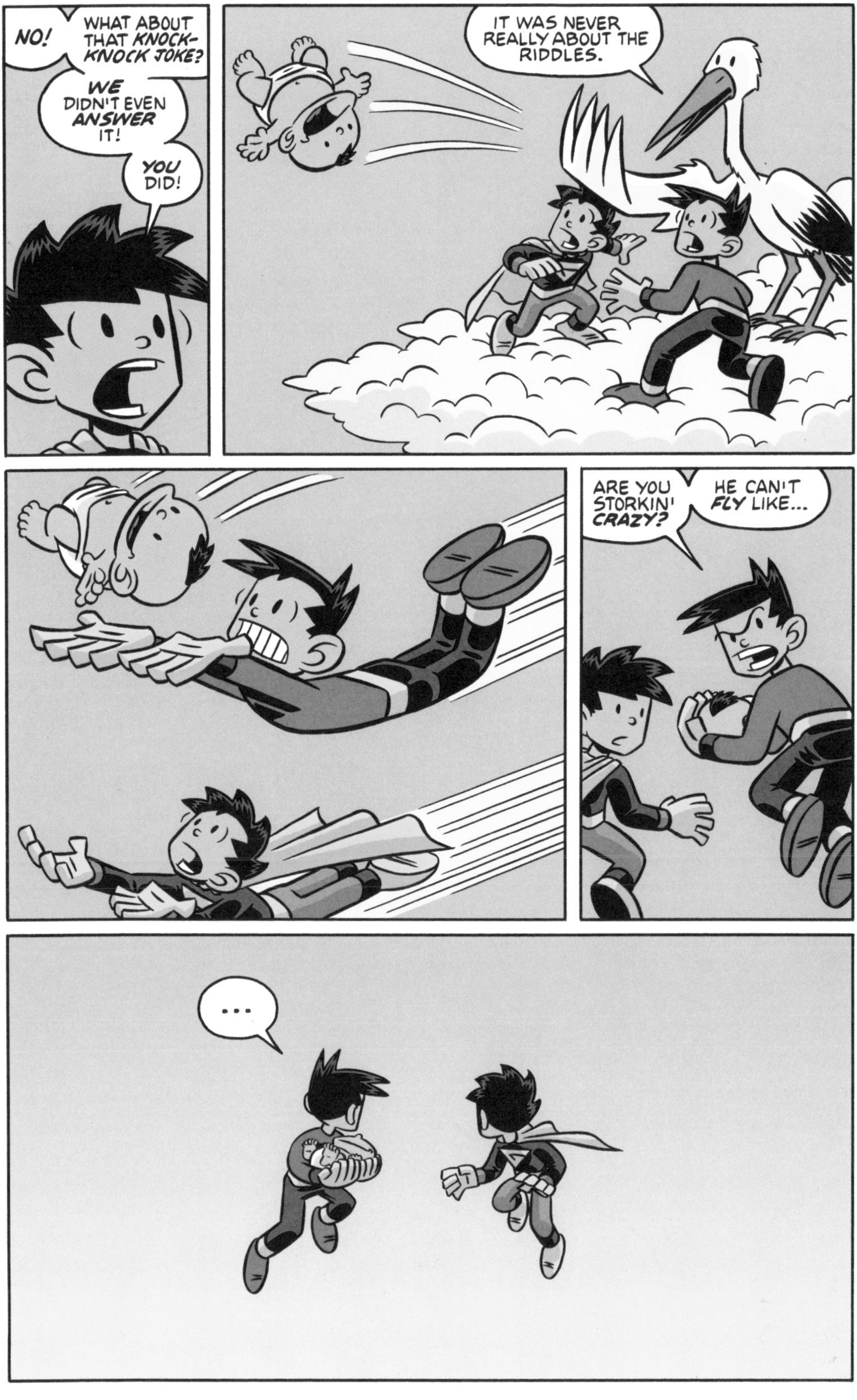
NO!
WHAT ABOUT THAT KNOCK-KNOCK JOKE?
WE DIDN'T EVEN ANSWER IT!
YOU DID!
IT WAS NEVER REALLY ABOUT THE RIDDLES.
ARE YOU STORKIN' CRAZY?
HE CAN'T FLY LIKE...
...

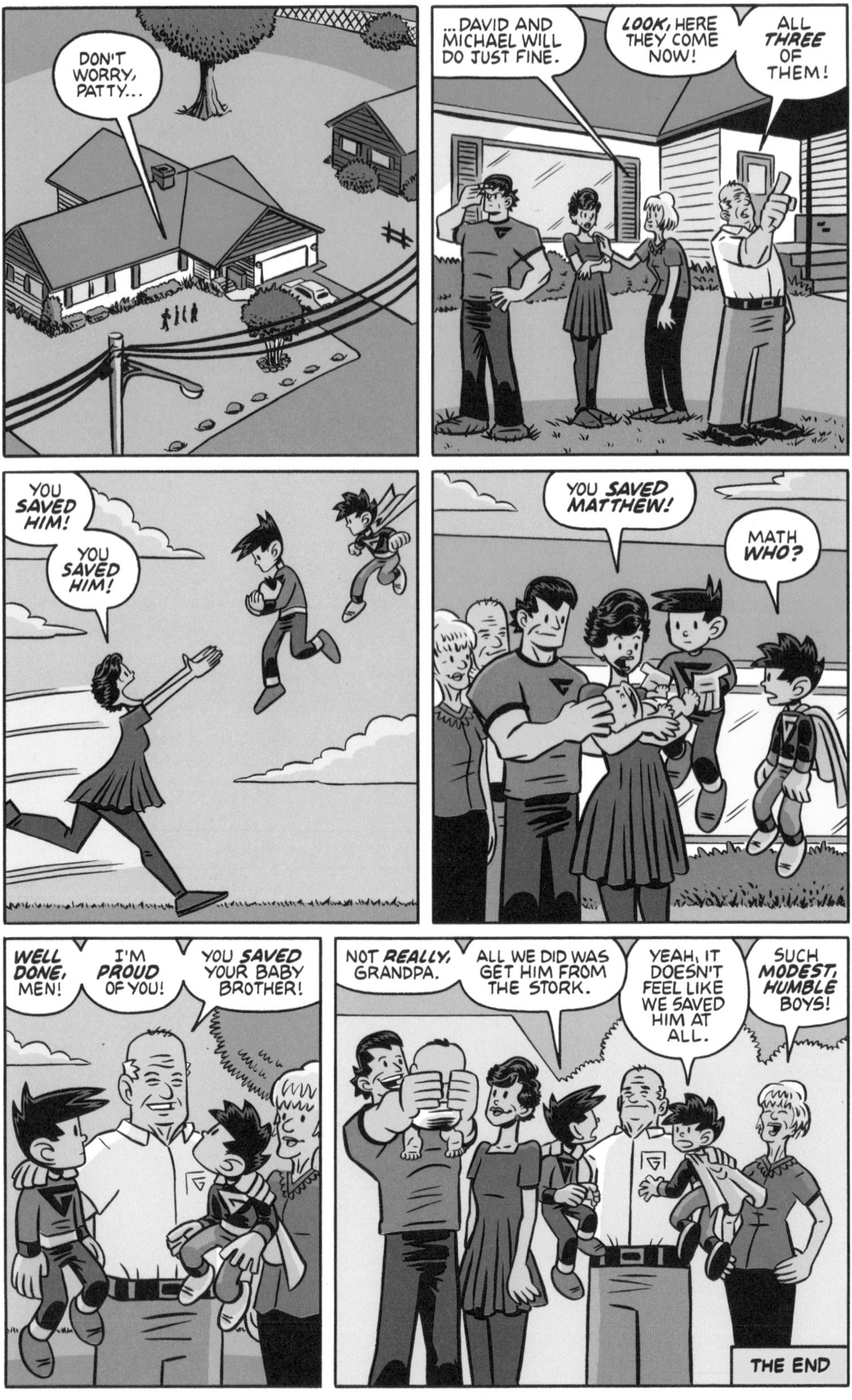
DON'T WORRY, PATTY...
...DAVID AND MICHAEL WILL DO JUST FINE.
LOOK, HERE THEY COME NOW!
ALL THREE OF THEM!
YOU SAVED HIM!
YOU SAVED HIM!
YOU SAVED MATTHEW!
MATH WHO?
WELL DONE, MEN!
I'M PROUD OF YOU!
YOU SAVED YOUR BABY BROTHER!
NOT REALLY, GRANDPA.
ALL WE DID WAS GET HIM FROM THE STORK.
YEAH, IT DOESN'T FEEL LIKE WE SAVED HIM AT ALL.
SUCH MODEST, HUMBLE BOYS!
THE END